Golden Gate

Erin Jennifer Mar

ISBN 0-9716812-6-0
Third Printing 2004
First Printing 2002
Cover photo by Limitless
Cover design by Anne M Clarkson

Published by:
Dare 2 Dream Publishing
A Division of Limitless Corporation
Lexington, South Carolina 29073
Find us on the World Wide Web
.http://www.limitlessd2d.net.

Printed in the United States and internationally by

Lightning Source, Inc.

Dedication

In my life, I have been fortunate enough to have several guardian angels. Though some of them are no longer with me, I know they still watch over me. This book is dedicated to them and to everyone else who has given inspiration, encouragement and support during this writing process.

Zuke, thanks for all the technical help and for setting me straight (so to speak) on the Bay Area Facts of Life.

Leslie, thank you for pushing me to follow my dream. Even when everyone else said I was nuts.

And most of all, thank you Isabelle. Thank you for being my guiding light, my heart, my soul and my constant source of inspiration. Without you, I could not have made it this far.

Chapter One

The fog rolled in from the bay and hung heavy and low over the city, obscuring the skyline and making visibility difficult for the driver of a black Toyota Corolla. Maggie McKinnon leaned forward over the steering wheel and peered through the thick blanket of greyish-white mist. No matter how long she lived in San Francisco, she swore she would never get used to this. An old Depeche Mode song blared through the speakers of her car stereo, and Maggie reached over to turn the volume down, as if that would somehow help her see better. The soft blue light of the digital clock told her that it was 1:13 a.m. She cursed under her breath as she strained to make out the numbers on the fog-enshrouded piers.

Lights glowed ahead, and the mist turned a ruddy orange. Maggie slowed her car to a crawl as she passed a row of emergency vehicles, red and blue lights strobing rhythmically. A uniformed policeman stepped in front of her car, holding his hands up to block her path. She hit the brakes and rolled down her window, putting on her most friendly midwestern smile as he approached. He leaned down, all business.

"Sorry, ma'am. This area is off limits," he said, sounding bored.

Maggie grabbed her plastic ID card off the dash and held it up. "I'm with the Chronicle."

The young officer groaned and rolled his eyes. He had been wondering how long it would take for the media vultures to show up. The call had come in twenty minutes before about a warehouse fire on the pier. It was the third suspicious fire in as many weeks, and the local media had been running all sorts of lurid stories about a serial arsonist. So far, Maggie was the first member of the press to come sniffing around this scene.

"Great," the officer muttered. "Ok, you can go through. Just stay out of the way."

1

He waved her forward, and Maggie slowly pulled her car up next to a row of unmarked police vehicles. She got out, shivering at the damp, chilly air and berated herself for forgetting her jacket at her desk. Ahead, flames shot out of the roof of an empty warehouse, lighting up the night sky, while dozens of firefighters grimly fought the blaze. She edged closer to a pair of official-looking men who appeared to be arguing with each other.

"I don't care. I want this son of a bitch caught," A tall, handsome man with silver-streaked brown hair was waving his finger in the face of a shorter, heavier man.

"Look, we're working on it. This guy doesn't give us much to go on," the other man said defensively.

Maggie dug her slim, well-used reporter's notebook out of the back pocket of her jeans and flipped it open to an empty page. Taking a deep breath, she started towards the two men. She nearly jumped out of her skin when a hand grabbed her elbow. Biting back a yelp, she turned to face the tall, dark-haired woman that had restrained her.

"I wouldn't do that, if I were you. They don't like reporters." the woman said.

She had a low, rich voice that rumbled pleasantly in Maggie's ears. A pair of startlingly blue eyes stared out of a face framed by perfect, high cheekbones, and dark hair fell past her shoulders, pulled back in a loose ponytail.

"Really? And who are you?" Maggie asked, pen poised above her notepad.

The woman chuckled, tickling the young reporter's senses. "Nobody you're gonna want to write down." She held her hand out. "Julia Cassinelli."

Switching her pen to her other hand, Maggie took the offered hand and found it warm and incredibly strong. A flutter of excitement raced through her stomach, but she shook it off, determined to keep her mind on business.

"Nice to meet you, Ms. Cassinelli. I'm Maggie McKinnon and I work for the Chronicle," she introduced herself. "Do you mind if I ask you a few questions?"

Julia cocked her head to one side and observed the determined, professional young woman in front of her. The reporter was a good six inches shorter than Julia's own 5'9" stature, but she seemed strong and athletic. The taller woman eyed the nicely toned arms that protruded from Maggie's short-sleeved, white linen shirt. Sun-bleached blonde hair stopped an inch above her collar and covered the tips of her ears, and green eyes that matched the color of the Bay on a sunny day stared at her expectantly.

Julia's lips curled into a faint grin, and she folded her arms across her chest. "Fire away."

"Um, okay. What can you tell me about this fire?"

"That warehouse over there," Julia pointed at the blazing structure. "It's burning."

Maggie stared at her, slightly flustered. Why did Californians have such weird senses of humor? She had only been living on the West Coast for a short time, but she had already noticed that the people there seemed far more amused by their own wit than anyone in the small midwestern town where she had grown up.

"Right. I can pretty much see that for myself," Maggie returned dryly. I meant, "Do you have any idea how the fire started."

"Nope," Julia replied.

"Well, then why are you here?" Maggie asked, exasperated by the tall woman's infuriating, faintly smug attitude.

Julia shrugged casually. "My office is near here. I heard the sirens and came over to see what was going on. The warehouse was pretty much gutted when I got here."

Maggie sighed, obviously she was wasting her time with this woman. She capped her pen and glanced around, looking for someone else to talk to. The two men she had been heading towards earlier had disappeared, but there were plenty of cops and firemen milling about. Other media people were arriving on the scene too, including the television news crews, and Maggie knew she ought to start interviewing real witnesses before someone else beat her to them. Somehow, though, she just couldn't seem to tear herself away from Julia Cassinelli.

A silver Mercedes zoomed in, forcing several policemen to nimbly leap out of its way, and they glared at the tall, thin redhead who emerged from the driver's seat. Maggie's eyes widened and she ducked behind Julia's taller frame, eliciting a puzzled grin from the woman.

"Problem?" Julia asked, eyebrows quirking.

"That's Catherine Richards. She, uh, she works for the Chronicle too."

"Let me guess. You're stepping on her beat?" Julia grinned.

Green eyes peered at her abashedly and Maggie's face reddened. "Something like that. I heard the call on the police scanner, and. . . .I've got to get out of here before she sees me."

Catherine Richards was a star at the newspaper, but not because she was a good reporter. Frankly, Maggie thought the vain redhead sucked, although she was too polite to admit that out loud. But

3

Catherine was the grandniece of the publisher, so the editors treated her like a goddess. Maggie shook her head in disgust as she watched Catherine work, oozing her seductive charm as she questioned an overweight cop who was clearly attracted to her.

"God, look at the way she's coming on to that guy!" Maggie said, obviously annoyed. "That's not how a good reporter gets a story."

She darted a quick glance at the hypnotic blue eyes that were gazing at her placidly. The tall, dark-haired woman seemed vaguely amused by her outburst, and Maggie wasn't sure what to make of her. She frowned slightly; she was usually so good at reading people, but Julia was a complete mystery.

"Ok, well . . .I guess I'm gonna go," she looked past the silent woman in front of her. "Looks like the fire's almost out, anyway."

Sidestepping Julia's tall, lean body, she started towards her car. Impulsively, she stopped and turned back, eyeing the dark-haired woman with a mixture of apprehension and veiled interest. It was a risk, but she was feeling unusually bold. Maybe it was that last cup of coffee, she mused.

"Is your car here?" Maggie asked, pausing for a breath when Julia shook her head. "It's awfully late. Can I give you a ride somewhere?"

Julia looked at her with that maddeningly cool gaze, and one dark eyebrow lifted a fraction of an inch. Idly, she wondered if Maggie McKinnon, cub reporter, was trying to pick her up. *Nah*, she told herself, *she's probably just one of those sickeningly nice people. The kid's definitely not from around here.* Julia shrugged; it wouldn't hurt and she really didn't feel like walking back to her office in the fog.

"Sure, why not?" she answered, following Maggie to her black Corolla.

Julia trailed a few steps behind the smaller blonde, and her gaze traveled slowly down the young woman's body, admiring the fit of her faded blue jeans. Then again, it might not hurt to see where this led, either. Noiselessly, she slid into the passenger seat. In a low voice, she gave Maggie an address, and the blonde nodded. The engine roared to life, and the Corolla cautiously eased out into the dark street and disappeared into the fog.

"Take a left at the light up here," Julia directed, her voice sounding unnaturally loud in the quiet. "It's the second building on the left."

Maggie made the turn smoothly, and since there was no other traffic on the street, she made a hasty u-turn and pulled up alongside the curb in front of the building Julia had indicated. It was a one-story, crumbling stone structure. The blinds were closed in the single window facing the empty street, but she could see the pale blue glow of a computer monitor shining through the slats. In the dark, she couldn't read the name on the sturdy wooden door. For the first time, it occurred to her to wonder what Julia Cassinelli did for a living.

The passenger door opened, letting in a chilly blast of night air, and Maggie made a face. Even in early October, San Francisco was freezing once the sun went down. She glanced at Julia as she exited, noting that, unlike her, the tall woman was dressed for the cool weather. She looked positively toasty in her khakis, black v-necked pullover and black leather jacket.

Julia knew that Maggie was looking her up and down, but she attributed it to a reporter's penchant for observation. Still, she couldn't deny that there was a crackling current of energy running between them, and she wondered if she should take a chance.

What's the worst thing that could happen? The kid says she's not interested and you never see her again, she reasoned with herself.

"I was gonna put on some coffee," Julia began, not quite believing she was doing this. "Why don't you come in for a cup?"

Maggie blinked at her, surprised and slightly uncomfortable. It wasn't every day that a woman she had just met invited her in for coffee at, she checked the time on the digital display, 1:55 in the morning. Julia saw the uncertainty on the young woman's face, and she mentally slapped herself in the head. She was about to rescind the offer when Maggie spoke up.

"Sure, I'd love some coffee."

Alarm bells went off in Maggie's head as she removed her key from the ignition and opened her door. What was she doing? She didn't know anything about this woman. Julia Cassinelli could be a serial killer, for all she knew. Except that the tall, striking woman looked more like a J. Crew model than a murderer. *Megan Elaine McKinnon, stop that right now*, Maggie chastised herself. Just before leaving Ohio six months earlier, she had come to terms with the realization that she was attracted to women. It was one of the reasons she had applied at the Chronicle, figuring the climate would be a lot more accepting than her small, conservative hometown. But she hadn't actually acted on that attraction. Yet. Sitting there with her car keys in her hand, Maggie gradually became aware that Julia was watching her with a bemused expression. She blushed furiously.

"Sorry, I got lost for a second there," she mumbled.

Julia's lips quirked into a lopsided half-grin. "Obviously."

Embarrassed, Maggie got out of the car and slammed the door a little harder than she had intended. She winced at the loud bang, but either Julia hadn't noticed it, or she was doing her best to pretend that she hadn't. A soft beep told her that the alarm was on, and Maggie shoved her keys into her hip pocket as she followed Julia to the door. Curiously, she read the plate out loud.

"JT Cassinelli Investigations. You're a p.i?"

Julia glanced over her shoulder as she unlocked the door and ushered the blonde woman inside her cluttered office.

"Yeah. Does that surprise you?"

"A little," Maggie admitted as she surveyed the small office. "So where are the rest of the Angels?"

Julia stared at her blankly and Maggie laughed nervously. "Oh, come on. Charlie's Angels? It was a bad joke, forget it." She missed seeing the tiny smile that flickered across the taller woman's lips.

As decrepit as the exterior of the building was, Maggie hadn't been expecting much and she was surprised by the interior.   Dark wood floors gleamed where they could be seen under a scattering of papers and file folders. A polished, expensive-looking cherry desk sat against most of one wall, and plush leather chairs waited on either side of it. Two black file cabinets rested along another wall, drawers were open with papers spilling out haphazardly.

"Sorry about the mess," Julia shrugged apologetically. "I was looking for something earlier."

"Don't worry about it," Maggie replied easily. "You should see my bedroom." She regretted the words the instant they left her mouth. *Oh my god. You should see my bedroom? That must have sounded like the world's lamest pick-up line.*

A half-open door led to a tiny bathroom, and Julia grabbed the coffee pot off her desk and headed for it. After a moment, Maggie heard the sound of running water. She continued her exploration.

The desk, she noticed was the only thing in the small office that was relatively neat. A recent-model PC hummed faintly as tropical fish floated by on the monitor. Other than that, all that sat on the desk was a coffee pot, a Hard Rock Café mug, and a multi-line telephone. Maggie's gaze fell on a large, framed poster hanging on the wall behind the desk. She had always liked that image of James Dean, brooding and moody, strolling down a lonely, rainy street. A smaller frame caught her eye, and she moved around the desk to examine it more closely. She looked up as Julia returned with the water.

"You graduated from Stanford?"

Julia shrugged as she carefully measured the coffee grounds. "Yeah."

"In what?" Maggie asked curiously.

"Political Science."

Maggie blinked at her, waiting for an explanation that evidently wasn't coming. She glanced at the diploma again. Most Stanford graduates with degrees in political science didn't wind up as private investigators. She reexamined the expensive furniture and technology that didn't seem to mesh with the crumbling building. For a split second, an odd image formed in her mind, and she pictured Julia as some kind of undercover secret agent. She struggled to keep a straight face. *Okay, Maggie, you've been watching too many Bond movies on cable.*

"Something funny?" Julia asked, watching her curiously.

"No, it's just that. . . your office is not what I expected." Suddenly, her brain made a connection. Cassinelli. "You're not related to Joseph Cassinelli, are you?"

Julia's angular face turned to stone, and Maggie realized that she had hit a nerve. Joseph Cassinelli was the city's most prominent criminal defense attorney. Though she didn't know exactly how much he was worth, Maggie knew that he was a millionaire who lived on a vineyard in the Napa Valley. Last year, he had represented a pro football player accused of a series of sexual assaults, and thanks to his legal wizardry, the guy had been found not guilty. After that case, a columnist for the Chronicle had called Joseph Cassinelli a cancer on the American justice system.

"He's my father," Julia said flatly.

An awkward silence fell over them as Maggie tried to think of something to say. *Gee, sorry my paper compared your dad to a disease*, just didn't seem to cut it. Thankfully, Julia spoke first.

"Let's not talk about him, okay?" She sat down in the big leather chair behind the desk and gestured for Maggie to sit in the other chair. Opening a drawer, she produced a second coffee mug and slid it across the polished surface to her guest. Carefully, Julia poured the hot, pungent liquid into both mugs.

"Cream or sugar?" Julia asked.

Maggie shook her head. She liked her coffee as black as possible without it turning to goo, and as she tasted the beverage in her mug, she noticed that Julia seemed to like it the same way. She smiled and examined the bright red Rocky Horror lips on the side of her mug.

"So, do you always invite strange women to your office in the middle of the night?" Maggie asked, surprised at her own directness. This wasn't at all like her small town, midwestern upbringing.

Julia seemed a bit taken aback, as well, and she bought herself some time by taking a long sip from her mug. The super-hot liquid scalded her tongue, and she cursed softly. She leaned back in her chair and regarded the woman sitting across from her, an amused glint shining in her eyes.

"Not usually," she replied. "Do you always offer rides to strange women in the middle of the night?"

Maggie snorted, nearly spilling her coffee. "Hardly."

She gazed across the desk at blue eyes that were burning into her with vivid intensity, and her stomach fluttered as she recognized the undisguised interest in the other woman's expression. Maggie's throat went dry and her breathing quickened as she realized that she was dancing dangerously close to a line that she wasn't sure she was ready to cross.

A thin, high-pitched ringing disturbed the electric silence between them, and Maggie jumped slightly in her chair. With a sheepish grin, she dug her pager out of her pocket and stared at the display, slightly annoyed by the interruption. She sucked in a sharp breath. It was her home number on the screen. *Who on earth is paging me from my apartment?* Her father was supposed to be the only person who had a spare key to her apartment, and he was in Ohio. She glanced up at the curiously watching dark-haired woman.

"Do you mind if I use your phone? It's a local call."

Wordlessly, Julia nudged the phone towards the blonde and swiveled around to gaze at the window, giving Maggie a bit of privacy. Barely aware that she was holding her breath, Maggie punched her own number into the receiver. She was caught off guard when a familiar, male voice answered on the first ring.

"Patrick? What are you doing in my apartment?" Maggie paused, listening to the voice on the other end. "Okay, calm down. I'm on my way."

Sighing, she replaced the receiver in its cradle and glanced at Julia, who was gamely pretending not to be listening. She smiled ruefully at the tall woman, regret clearly stamped on her features.

"I have to go," she said, setting her mug on the desk and rising from the comfortable leather chair.

Julia stood also. "It's okay. It's getting awfully late, anyway."

Who the hell was Patrick? A boyfriend maybe? Julia frowned slightly. She thought she'd been getting fairly strong signals from the blonde reporter. She could be wrong, she admitted to herself reluctantly. She'd been out of the game for quite some time now.

Maggie moved towards the door with Julia following her quietly. The fog had thickened considerably in the early morning gloom, and

Julia scowled at it darkly. She loved the city, but sometimes she could live without the damned fog. She escorted the blonde reporter to her car and waited while Maggie buckled herself in. Leaning against the open driver's side door, she bestowed one of her most charming grins on the young woman.

"Thanks for the ride."

Maggie smiled back, feeling a pang of disappointment at the fact that their evening, or early morning actually, had been cut short.

"Sure, no problem. Thanks for the coffee."

Julia inclined her head slightly. "Anytime. Drive carefully, Ms. McKinnon."

She shut the car door and stepped back as the Corolla pulled away from the curb. Standing on the sidewalk, she watched until the fog swallowed the glowing taillights, then she turned and went back to her office. A moment later, she reemerged, her briefcase slung over her shoulder. Moving purposefully, she got into a dark green Jeep Cherokee and drove away into the pre-dawn darkness. With one finger, she punched the power button on the stereo and filled the vehicle with the raw guitars of the Smashing Pumpkins. Julia listened as Billy Corgan sang about his rage, then her thoughts drifted back to Maggie McKinnon. Deep in her gut, she had a feeling that their paths would cross again.

Maggie drummed her fingers nervously against the steering wheel as she drove west across the city, towards her Richmond apartment. The fog was still very thick, and she navigated mostly by instinct. There were very few other cars on the street, so she pushed the speed limit as far as she dared. Her stomach was tied into knots. Why was Patrick here? Why wasn't back home in Ohio? She zoomed past the Presidio, slowing dramatically when she spotted the flashing lights of a patrol car half a block ahead. Luckily, the officer inside seemed to have better things to do than chase every speeding car that came along.

Several minutes later, Maggie pulled into the driveway of her small apartment complex. She parked her car in her assigned space and hopped out. The light was on in her living room, and as she came up the walkway, the front door flew open and a tall, thin man bounded out and grabbed her in a bear hug.

"Hey, Maggie! I thought you'd never get here," he greeted her enthusiastically.

"Shhh! You'll wake up my neighbors," Maggie shushed him and pushed him back towards her open door.

She eyed him critically in the light from her entryway. Patrick had lost weight since she'd seen him last. He was pale, and he looked tired. Dark shadows had taken up residence beneath his light brown eyes. His spiky blond hair was uncombed and his clothes were rumpled, as if he'd been sleeping in them. Maggie shook her head at him and pointed to the couch. He complied obediently as she detoured into the small kitchen and grabbed a bottle of water from the refrigerator. She took a long swallow, putting off the inevitable conversation for a few more seconds.

"What are you doing here, Patrick? Does anyone know that you're here?" Maggie turned to face the disheveled man on her couch.

Patrick blinked at her, slightly hurt by her attitude. "Jeez, sis. Is that any way to treat your baby brother? I thought you'd be glad to see me."

Maggie sighed and sat down on the couch next to her younger brother. "I am glad to see you. But you should have called to tell me you were coming. Now, what's this about you getting mugged?"

Patrick shifted uncomfortably and tugged at the scraggly goatee that covered his chin. Brown eyes glanced at her and then nervously darted away, and Maggie knew instantly that he was lying.

"Well, see, I got into the city yesterday afternoon, but it took me awhile to find your place. So I just sort of wandered around." He hesitated, working out the details of the story in his head. "Anyway, I was crossing through that big park when two guys jumped out of the bushes and took all my money. Honestly, Mags, I thought they were gonna kill me."

Maggie shut her eyes and rubbed the back of her extremely stiff neck. It had been a very long, unproductive day, and now she had to deal with her troubled brother on top of it all. At 22, he was her junior by four years, the youngest of the six McKinnon siblings. As a teenager, Patrick had developed a drug problem, and it had steadily escalated since his girlfriend had left him two years before. Maggie's parents had somehow scraped together the money to send him to a clinic after he nearly overdosed on a cocktail of speed and alcohol eight months previously. The family had hoped that he would straighten out, but Maggie took one look at his slightly glassy stare and knew that he was getting high again.

Patrick fidgeted, unable to keep himself still for very long, and he tapped the end of a pencil relentlessly against a small end table. The sound was getting on her nerves, and Maggie clenched her teeth, forcing herself to stay calm. He sniffed the air and made a face.

"You smell like smoke, sis," he commented.

Maggie lifted the collar of her shirt to her nose and inhaled. She did, indeed, reek of smoke. She sighed as she stood and headed for her bedroom.

"I was at a fire," she explained. "I'm gonna take a quick shower, and then we'll talk some more, if you want."

She poked her head back out of the doorway. Patrick had risen and he was roaming restlessly around her living room, examining various knick-knacks. He took a ceramic figurine of one of the dancing crocodiles from *Fantasia* off her bookshelf and tossed it casually into the air.

"Don't break anything," she warned him. "And call Mom and Dad. They're probably worried sick about you by now."

She ducked back into her bedroom and grabbed her pajama pants and a faded Ohio State t-shirt from her unmade bed. Kicking off her shoes, she headed for the bathroom and turned the shower on, examining her reflection in the mirror while she waited for the water to heat. She looked almost as tired as she felt. Her eyes were bloodshot, probably from the smoke, she mused, shaking her head as steam began to fog the surface of the mirror.

Maggie tossed her clothes into a pile on the floor and stepped into the shower. She closed her eyes and simply stood under the spray for several long moments, letting the stream massage some of the tension from her shoulders. Unbidden, an image of Julia Cassinelli smiling at her rose to her mind, and she felt that flutter of excitement run through her stomach again. She opened her eyes, blinking rapidly as water hit her eyelashes, and she seized the bar of soap from its dish and began scrubbing her arms vigorously. *God, Maggie, get a hold of yourself. You're acting like a schoolgirl with an adolescent crush.*

When she emerged ten minutes later, Patrick was sitting on the floor, flipping through cable channels on her television. He stopped on an infomercial and watched intently as a man enthusiastically demonstrated the power of a particular cleaning product. He looked up and grinned at his sister as she approached.

"Hey, have you ever wondered how you can use the same thing to scrub your barbecue grill as you can to wash your clothes?" Patrick pointed at the screen.

Maggie didn't respond. She was too tired to deal with him, especially since he was still clearly wired on whatever he had taken before showing up at her apartment.

"Did you call Mom and Dad?" She felt more like his babysitter than his sister.

His face fell, and he shook his head. "Naw. It's still too early there. I don't want to wake them up. I'll call later, I promise."

Maggie glanced at the clock. It was just after 3:00, which meant that it was 6:00 in Ohio, and her father would definitely be up and preparing for another day of teaching history at Warren G. Harding High School. She sighed and decided not to press the issue.

"Okay. I need to grab a couple hours of sleep before I have to go back to work," she said. "Will you be alright on the couch?"

Patrick nodded excitedly. "Yeah. I'm good with the couch."

Briefly, Maggie showed him where the extra blankets were in the hall closet. She retreated to the solitude of her own bedroom, leaving her brother engrossed in a bad science fiction movie starring Drew Barrymore in a dual role. Maggie checked to make sure that her alarm was set, and then she crawled gratefully beneath her cool cotton sheets. Within minutes, she was fast asleep.

****

Chapter Two

The electronic braying of an alarm clock shattered the pre-dawn stillness, and a single green eye opened, peering resentfully at the device. Maggie reached out and slapped the off button, groaning as she rolled over and kicked the covers off her bed. She sat up, shivering in the crisp morning air. Her head ached dully, her punishment for too many nights with far too little sleep.

"I really don't want to go to work today," she muttered hoarsely as she headed for the bathroom.

The tile warmed beneath her bare feet, and she wiggled her toes against it as she washed her face. Maggie stared at herself in the mirror, dismayed by the worst case of bed head she'd ever seen. It looked like a blonde porcupine had died on her head. She retrieved her brush from a drawer and tried to restore some semblance of order to her unruly locks.

Still brushing her teeth, Maggie wandered back into her bedroom, kicking the previous night's discarded clothes out of the way as she headed for her closet. She surveyed her wardrobe, finally deciding on a pair of neatly ironed khaki pants and a button-down, royal blue shirt. The best thing about being a newspaper reporter was the casual dress code. Unless a reporter was covering the political scene, pretty much anything went. Well, not anything. Maggie choked down a mouthful of minty toothpaste as she remembered her editor screaming at one of her colleagues over the summer. Mark had arrived at work in a pair of worn cut-offs and a threadbare t-shirt from a long ago concert. Her editor had roared at the sartorially challenged music critic in front of the entire newsroom. She chuckled at the memory and carried her outfit back into the bathroom. Pausing to spit into the sink, she hung her clothes on the shower rod before thoroughly rinsing her mouth out. She ran her tongue over her teeth, enjoying the clean, slick feel.

Maggie dressed quickly and moved out into the hall. Patrick was asleep on the couch, his long legs hanging over the end. The television, though muted, was still on, and Maggie sighed as she hunted for the remote. Giving up the search, she walked over and hit the power button, making the screen go dark. She checked her watch. Almost 6:30. Quietly, she slipped out the door, grabbing her keys and her shoulder bag as she left.

Twenty minutes later, Maggie was walking into the newsroom, juggling a tall cup of coffee in one hand and a chocolate croissant in the other. It was still relatively quiet; things wouldn't really start picking up for another half hour, but Maggie liked to be there early, before the craziness started. She sat down at her small desk and hit the space bar on her computer to clear the monitor of her screensaver.

Taking a long swallow of coffee, she checked her e-mail. Nothing interesting, other than a response to a query she had sent out the day before. She had the unenviable assignment of the annual "Things to do for Halloween" story. A brain-dead monkey could write that story, she thought bitterly, since it was basically just a listing of local haunted houses and pumpkin patches>

Someone mumbled a sleepy greeting in her direction, and Maggie looked up. Chris Garcia, one of the sportswriters waved to her as he entered the glass double doors leading into the newsroom. He was a nice-looking guy, tall and tanned, with thick, wavy black hair and perfect white teeth. Chris had asked her out twice, but she had politely declined both times. Maggie returned her attention to her monitor. Impulsively, she connected to the paper's massive archives and typed in a search request for information about Julia Cassinelli.

"Hmm. Daughter of Joseph Cassinelli. Okay, I knew that already. Mother committed suicide when she was three. Wow, that's pretty awful. Father remarried two years later, divorced three years after that. She has a half-brother." Maggie read the bio with interest and she scrolled down further.

She blinked, surprised, and she traced the headline on the screen with her finger. The year before, Julia had helped the SFPD crack a drug-smuggling ring operating from one of the piers. According to a police spokesman, Ms. Cassinelli had provided vital information and had even participated in the raid. Maggie's eyebrows rose as she continued to scan the article and found references to four other instances where Julia had helped the police. Twice, she had turned over information on the Asian youth gangs that were exploding throughout the city. Once, she had snapped photos of a local politician taking bribes from a well-known developer. And then, just three weeks

14

earlier, Julia had chased and apprehended a purse-snatcher who had been preying on elderly women walking through Washington Square. According to the story, Julia pursued the man for two blocks before catching him and holding him for the police, breaking the guy's nose in the process.

"Okay, so she's not James Bond, but she just might be Batman."

"Who might be Batman?" A voice over her shoulder made Maggie jump.

A pair of dark eyes regarded her curiously. Jessica Sato was one of the junior copy editors, and one of Maggie's few friends in the city. Jessica was tiny, even shorter than Maggie, and she had a round face framed by wire-rimmed glasses that were constantly slipping down her pug nose. Shoulder-length black hair was pulled into a neat French braid.

"Morning, Jess. You scared the crap out of me just now." Maggie greeted her friend cheerfully.

"Sorry. Didn't realize you were so absorbed in this," Jessica leaned closer, peering at the monitor as she pushed up her glasses with one finger. "Hey, is that Joe Cassinelli's daughter?"

Maggie flushed slightly, wondering how she was going to explain this. "Uh, yeah. I met her last night, and I was just curious, I guess. I don't know a whole lot about the Cassinelli's."

Jessica's cherubic face split into a wide grin and she tapped the file photo on the screen with the end of her pencil. The picture showed Julia, arriving alone at the city's famous Black and White Ball in 1998. She was dressed in a simple, but elegant, sleeveless black evening dress. A teardrop-shaped sapphire necklace rested just above her cleavage, and matching earrings dangled from her ears.

"She's kinda hot." Jessica was one of the few people that Maggie had confided in about her emerging sexuality. "No, actually, she's really hot."

Maggie made a face and slapped her friend's hand playfully. "It's not like that! We met and I just wanted to know more about her. End of story."

Jessica laughed and ducked to avoid another swat. She backed away, still giggling.

"If you say so, Maggie. I gotta get back to work. Barrett just sent his story over." Jessica and Maggie exchanged a knowing glance. Mark Barrett covered the local music scene, and his stories were notorious for their spelling and grammatical errors. All the copy editors wondered why he couldn't seem to find the spell-check function in his word processing program.

"Come find me around lunch time, if you're free."

Jessica disappeared. The newsroom was filling up as more people started to trickle in, all of them appearing harried and highly caffeinated. The clacking of keys and the shuffling of papers created a familiar hum that buzzed through the large room. Two desks behind her, Maggie heard one of the city reporters pleading with a source that was refusing to go on the record. She shook her head sympathetically. *Been there, done that, buddy.*

The glass double doors flew open with an attention-getting bang. Heads came up and turned toward the noise as Catherine Richards swept into the room, obviously enjoying the fact that all eyes were on her. She pinned Maggie with a cold stare and grinned mercilessly just before she stormed, unannounced, into her editor's office.

Maggie flushed and slid down in her chair as everyone's eyes turned to her. She knew they were all wondering what she had done to piss off the Hellcat, as Catherine was unaffectionately called behind her back. *Great. She must have seen me last night, after all. And now she can't wait to tell on me.*

Maggie exited out of the newspaper's archives and glanced at the row of clocks on the wall. Each clock was set to a different time zone. Chicago, New York, London, Paris, Moscow, Tokyo, etc. She focused on the one in the center that was actually displaying San Francisco time. Surprisingly, it was almost 8:30 already. She wondered if she should call to check on Patrick. Nah. He was probably still sleeping it off on her couch. She cast a surreptitious glance at the closed door to her editor's office. Sighing, she started to work on her assigned story, compiling her list of Halloween attractions in the Bay Area. *Hmm....a vampire tour. That actually sounds kinda interesting.*

Two hours later, the mahogany door to Sam Vogelsang's office swung open and Catherine emerged, a look of smug triumph on her face. Without looking at anyone, the red-haired reporter marched to her desk and sat down. Sam, a tall, stocky man with the build of an aging football player, leaned in the doorway for a moment. He scratched his balding, gray head and loosened his dark blue tie.

"McKinnon. Get in here." Maggie winced at the irritation in his voice. She scooted her chair back and stood, smoothing the wrinkles from her pants. Taking a deep breath to steel herself, she eased past her bulky editor and waited as he shut the door behind her.

"Have a seat, McKinnon." Sam nodded at an empty chair, rubbing his jowly chin as he stared at her with watery blue eyes.

Gingerly, Maggie sat down, waiting for the hammer to fall. It

16

didn't take long. Sam was famous for his quick temper, but in the six months that Maggie had been with the paper, she had learned not to take him too seriously. His short fuse was matched by his equally short memory.

Sam perched on the edge of his paper-strewn desk and stared at her, exasperated.

"I'm betting you already know why I called you in here." Sam paused, but Maggie kept her eyes firmly fixed on her hands. He grunted.

"Damn it, Maggie! How many times do I have to tell you to work the stories you're given? I don't care what you did back in your little farm town! You're in the big leagues now and you sure as hell better do what you're told! If you can't handle that, then I'll buy you a one-way bus ticket back to Smallsville, or wherever the hell you're from, and you can go back to covering bake sales and quilting bees!" He stopped to take a breath.

Serious green eyes lifted to meet his. "It wasn't a farm town." Maggie told him quietly.

"What?" Sam blinked at her. This wasn't exactly the reaction he'd been expecting. He was used to people quivering in fear when he blustered at them.

"My hometown. There weren't really that many farms in the area. Just because I'm from a small town in the Midwest doesn't mean that I learned to milk a cow before I could walk," Maggie said. "Just like I'll bet that not all Californians know how to surf."

Sam shook his head slowly. He liked this one. Out of all the reporters under his supervision, Maggie was just about the only one who would stand up to him. She had good instincts, too, he mused, recalling the portfolio she had sent with her resume. And she really was wasting her talents on that stupid Halloween story. Still, it was unwritten policy at the paper that newcomers had to work their way up the pecking order, unless they came from another established, metropolitan newspaper. He looked at Maggie thoughtfully, noting the resolve in those deep green eyes, and he found himself wanting to give her a chance. *Aw, what the hell.*

"Okay, McKinnon. First, you are going to stay out of Catherine's way. No more warehouse fires for you, or I swear I will personally eat your liver for lunch. Second, you are going to finish that goddamn Halloween piece-of-crap story, and it had better be the best one I've ever seen. You got that?" Sam leaned forward until he was almost in her face, but her gaze never wavered. Inwardly he grinned, impressed. *Damn, this kid might have a bigger pair than I do.*

17

He went on, lowering his voice to a deep growl. "And third, a little dot com over on Van Ness got broken into early this morning." Sam handed her a scrap of paper with an address on it. "Go see what you can find out." He straightened up and moved around his desk, collapsing in his chair.

Maggie sat there in frozen silence, stunned. Had she heard right? Had Sam just given her a real story? Something other than holiday fun and home and garden shows? A burglary at a small business wasn't exactly earth-shattering news, but it was better than anything she'd been assigned so far. Blinking, she stared at the piece of paper in her hand. *Netsports 1801 Van Ness.* She vaguely recalled hearing Chris mention the company once. It was a local business that sold sporting equipment and memorabilia over the Internet. Daniel Webber, a former Bay Area college sports star owned and operated it.

Sam looked up from the stack of papers he was sifting through. "McKinnon," he barked. "Get the hell out of my office!"

Maggie grinned at him gratefully as she rushed back out to the now bustling newsroom. As the heavy door swung shut behind her, she was fairly certain that she was still grinning like an idiot. Running her fingers through her short blonde hair in amazement, she headed for her desk to grab her keys and her ID.

"Hey, girlfriend. Where are you heading? I thought Sam was gonna have you for breakfast." One of the photographers, a small, wiry Latino named Rudy stopped by her desk.

"Yeah, me too. I sort of screwed up last night. But then he did the most incredible thing. He gave me an actual news story," Maggie said, loud enough for Catherine to hear. Out of the corner of her eye, she saw the look of disgust on the redhead's face, and she fought down the urge to burst out laughing. "Gotta go."

As an afterthought, she grabbed her jacket from the back of her chair, even though the forecast promised a nice, sunny day. She wasn't about to get caught out in the cold again. Hurrying down to the parking garage, she fumbled in her bag for her cell phone, locating it as she reached her car. She drove with one hand and dialed with the other, waiting as the line connected with a barely audible click.

"Hi, Chris, it's Maggie. Listen I need to know everything you can tell me about Netsports.com in the next fifteen minutes."

She fought her way up and down the narrow, hilly streets. It still made her nervous every time she had to stop at a light on one of the steep inclines. She had nightmares about her brakes failing and her car rolling helplessly into heavy traffic. It took her slightly more than fifteen minutes to reach the Netsports offices. Maggie parked across the street and darted across the busy lanes of traffic, ignoring the angry shouts as drivers slowed to avoid her. As usual, a uniformed police officer tried to stop her, but Maggie flashed her credentials at the severe-looking woman and ducked under her outstretched arm. She skidded to a halt at the door.

The glass door had been completely shattered, and shards of glass littered the sidewalk and the entryway. Inside, furniture was overturned, and receipts and invoices fluttered on the floor, stirred by the light breeze. Off to one side, police inspectors were questioning a young man and woman, both of them clearly shaken. Probably employees, Maggie noted, intending to talk to them later. She started to slide under the yellow police tape when a short, well-muscled Asian man with a close crew cut stopped her.

"Where do you think you're going?" He glared at her, only an inch or two taller than the small reporter. Maggie caught sight of the badge attached to his belt.

"It's okay, Henry. She's a friend of mine." A low, warm voice vibrated to Maggie's left.

Julia Cassinelli picked her way through the crowd of police investigators and curious bystanders. She grinned and winked at the young blonde, sending an unexpected wave of giddiness surging through the reporter. Julia shook the hand of the Asian cop and exchanged a pleasant greeting with him. She turned to Maggie.

"Inspector Henry Chow, this is Maggie McKinnon. She's a reporter." Julia made the formal introduction.

"A reporter?" The inspector eyed the dark-haired woman in surprise. "I thought you didn't talk to reporters, Jules."

Julia shrugged, humor glinting in her brilliant blue eyes. "It's not a rule, or anything. Usually all they want to talk about is my father. You're not here to ask me about Daddy, are you Ms. McKinnon?"

Maggie stuttered a negative reply. She was uncharacteristically tongue-tied by the presence of the enigmatic woman. It was weird, running into Julia twice at crime scenes like this. It was almost like . . .fate. With a disgusted snort, she shook the thought from her mind. This was not the time for silly romantic fantasies.

A white news truck from one of the local television stations double-parked next to the two police cars in front of the building. Maggie saw them out of the corner of her eye, and she sidled towards the two distraught Netsports workers, wanting to get to them before the TV crew did.

"Alright, Ms. McKinnon. Come with me," Inspector Chow beckoned to her with an impatient finger.

Maggie glanced at the Netsports' employees and then back to the waiting inspector. Julia's towering presence stood just behind the policeman's right shoulder and she tilted her head slightly, inviting the reporter over. Maggie sighed and walked towards them, irritation building in her.

"Look, the press has every right to be here . . ." she began indignantly.

Inspector Chow held his hands up. "Whoa, hey. I didn't say you didn't! Actually, I was going to say that if you'll follow me, I'll fill you in on what we know so far."

He and Julia ducked under the yellow crime scene tape and waited for her to follow. Very aware of the flush heating her face and neck, and of Julia's faintly amused expression, Maggie joined them inside the ransacked office.

"No one else comes through here," the inspector told the uniformed officer at the door.

He led the two women to a door at the rear of the office that opened onto a smaller room. This door had been forced open, as well, and judging by the splintered dents below the doorknob, Maggie guessed that it had been kicked. She walked into the private office and recorded everything in her notebook. Like the outer room, all the desk drawers had been emptied and overturned.

"At this time, we believe that this was a simple burglary," Inspector Chow said in an official voice. "The method of entry was pretty unsophisticated. Whoever did this used a blunt instrument to get through the outer door. Probably a bat, or something like that. Then, as you can see, the inner door appears to have been kicked open."

Maggie scribbled furiously, her fair head bent over her notebook in concentration. "Do you have any suspects? Was anything valuable taken?" She asked the standard questions.

Julia walked slowly around the perimeter of the room, sharp blue eyes examining everything. Absently, she listened while the inspector told Maggie that he thought the break-in was the work of kids, or an addict looking for money to get high. In her peripheral vision, Julia thought she saw Maggie flinch slightly at the mention of an addict. It wasn't much. Just a tiny twitch below her right eye, but Julia found it interesting. There was a lot about the reporter that she found interesting, though she was still reluctant to admit it to herself. Turning away, Julia filed Maggie's reaction away for later study.

"We're still doing an inventory, so I can't tell you for sure if anything valuable was removed from the scene." The inspector answered Maggie's queries.

Julia paused in the corner of the room and cocked her head thoughtfully. She knelt, running her fingers across four deep indentations on the light gray carpet. The square patch in the middle of the marks was a lighter shade than the rest of the wall-to-wall carpet, indicating that something had been removed from that spot.

"Henry, what was here?" She glanced up at her friend, one finger tracing the marks on the floor.

He jammed his hands in the pockets of his slacks and cleared his throat. "Uh, a small safe."

Maggie moved over to stand next to Julia, and she peered interestedly at the markings. She looked questioningly at the inspector.

"Do you know what was in the safe?"

Henry Chow rubbed at his bristling crew cut and shifted his weight uncomfortably. He hated talking to reporters. His discomfort grew as Julia slowly rose to her full height and intense blue eyes seemed to bore right through him. He coughed into his fist.

"Um, well, we're still waiting for confirmation on that."

Julia's eyebrows rose. She pulled a tiny phone from the inner pocket of her jacket and flipped it open with a snap of her wrist. She dialed from memory and waited as the phone rang four times before a man's voice answered.

"Hi, Danny, it's me. The safe is missing. I need to know what was in it and who knew the combination to the lock."

Julia listened intently, nodding occasionally. Danny Webber was the owner and president of Netsports. Finished with the brief conversation, Julia hung up and deposited the phone back in her pocket. Something about the missing safe bothered her, but she couldn't quite put her finger on the source of her uneasiness.

"The safe contained a hard copy of all their credit card transactions for the current quarter, $5, 000 in petty cash, and a .45 caliber handgun registered to Daniel C. Webber." Julia informed them smugly, taking a perverse delight in the thoroughly disgusted look Henry was giving her. She glanced over at Maggie and found that she liked the awestruck expression on the blonde woman's face even better.

"Jesus, Jules. Is there anyone in this whole city that you don't know?" Inspector Chow shook his head.

Julia shrugged modestly. "Oh, also, besides Danny, only one person knew the combo to the safe. His VP, Allison Davis. She's supposedly vacationing in Seattle at the moment."

She waited while both Henry and Maggie scribbled the information down in their notebooks. A very young, fresh out of the academy, officer poked his head through the doorway.

"Inspector, the TV crews out here are starting to get a little antsy," he said.

Henry Chow rolled his eyes and grimaced. He glanced at the two women. "You know, the only thing I hate worse than talking to print reporters, is talking to TV reporters," he commented dryly. He nodded at the waiting officer. "Tell them I'll be right there."

"Thanks for the tour, Henry." Julia clasped the man's hand warmly. "We'll get out of your way. I'm sure Ms. McKinnon wants to talk to the witnesses, anyway."

Julia led the way out of the ransacked office and through the front door as Maggie trailed after her hesitantly. An over-anxious cameraman jumped in front of the dark-haired woman, but she merely waved him aside and kept moving. A moment later, the inspector emerged, and the eager crowd fell on him. On the sidewalk, Julia nodded toward the two, slightly calmer, witnesses.

"You should get to work," she told the reporter.

Maggie tugged at her earlobe nervously. "Yeah, I should. Are you leaving?"

Julia grinned and leaned back against a squad car, folding her arms across her chest. She gestured at the shouting mob of reporters accosting her friend. "Nah. I'm gonna watch the circus for a while. I like watching Henry sweat."

Maggie traced an invisible circle on the sidewalk with the toe of her loafer. She looked up at the taller woman shyly. "Give me a few minutes with those two, and then maybe we can talk more?"

Julia arched a single dark eyebrow and let her lips curl into a lazy half-grin. Maybe she hadn't been wrong about the reporter's interest in her after all. "Sure. I'll be here."

****

Chapter Three

Forty-five minutes later, Julia was sitting at a small table in a mostly empty Italian restaurant in North Beach. Long fingers fiddled absently with the silverware, rearranging the utensils into a variety of patterns while blue eyes stared out the window, watching the endless hordes of people passing by on the busy sidewalks. Even in the middle of the week, the city was packed with tourists. Julia checked her watch again.

It had taken Maggie half an hour to conduct brief interviews with the two Netsports employees. Julia had enjoyed watching her work. Within minutes, the witnesses were smiling and talking freely with Maggie. The reporter exuded a compassion and warmth that quickly put her subjects at ease. Julia suspected it was a quality that could be very valuable to someone in her profession. *Or to a p.i.*, she mused wryly. *Maybe I should try that approach once in a while.* After Maggie had finished her interviews, she and Julia had agreed to have lunch together, which surprised the tall private investigator. Julia rarely dated anymore and even when she did, it wasn't usually someone that she had just met the night before. Of course, she still wasn't entirely sure if this meeting could be considered a date or not.

Julia took a sip from her water glass as she continued to scan the crowds outside. The sea of humanity parted briefly, and a small blonde emerged from its midst, peering at the names of the restaurants and cafés that lined the street. Unexpectedly, Julia felt a broad smile spread across her lips at the sight of the young reporter. She waved through the window and a warm, happy sensation rolled through her gut as Maggie's face lit up with a sunny grin.

Slightly out of breath, Maggie slipped through the door, squeaking past a pair of German tourists who were examining the menu in the entryway. She waved the hostess off and slid into a chair across the table from Julia.

"Sorry. Took me forever to find a parking place." Maggie took off her brown corduroy jacket and draped it over the back of her chair.

"Don't worry about it. Parking's a real bitch around here," Julia replied easily, handing Maggie a menu.

An awkward silence settled over them. Maggie looked around the interior of the restaurant, which featured tall potted plants in the corners and reproductions of famous Renaissance paintings on the walls. Besides the hostess, a single waiter and busboy appeared to be the only people working. Luckily, it wasn't crowded. Only two other tables in the long, narrow room had occupants. She decided she liked the intimate setting. It would give her a better opportunity to get to know the enigmatic woman across the table from her.

"So, this is North Beach, huh? I've never actually made it over here before," Maggie commented. She glanced up and smiled at the pale, sullen busboy as he placed a glass of water in front of her. "Thanks." The busboy was unmoved by her polite friendliness, and he slunk back to the bar to resume dusting the bottles of wine behind the counter.

Julia rolled her eyes in disgust. "He's always like that." She nodded towards the surly young man. "I usually come here in the evenings. After his shift." She smiled as Maggie suppressed a laugh. "You've really never been out here? How long have you been in the city?"

Maggie looked up from the menu she'd been studying. "Six months. I know, it's pathetic, but I haven't really seen much of the city yet. I have been to Golden Gate Park.... I liked the tea gardens. Oh, and Pier 39. That's about it, though. I've been.... busy." She didn't feel comfortable admitting that she really didn't have anyone to see the sights with.

Leaning back in her chair, Julia folded her hands on the table and regarded the blonde soberly. A reproachful frown tugged at the corners of her mouth and the beginning of an idea took form in her mind. She turned the concept over in her head, examining it from all angles. Julia knew she wanted to ask the reporter out on a real date. The trick was doing it without putting too much pressure on her.

"Six months is too long to be in this city without actually seeing it."

Maggie sighed and rested her chin in her hand. "I know."

They were interrupted by the appearance of their waiter, a gangly young man with bushy brown hair that stuck out from his head in odd angles. He set a basket of warm bread in front of them, along with a plate of seasoned olive oil and asked for their orders. Julia

24

ordered the pizza quattro formaggi and the waiter scribbled her request on his pad before turning to Maggie expectantly.

The blonde woman glanced at her menu again. "Um…. I'll have the prosciutto sandwich, please. And an iced tea."

Their waiter nodded and signaled to the decidedly unfriendly busboy behind the bar. He disappeared toward the kitchen with their lunch order, leaving his cohort to wordlessly deposit a glass of iced tea in front of the blonde.

Idly, Maggie touched a fingertip to a dewy drop of condensation rolling down the outside of the glass. Julia watched her as she tore a chunk of bread off and dipped it into the oil. She was fascinated by the way the reporter alternated between flirtation and shy uncertainty. It was…. cute. *Cute?* Inwardly, Julia made a face. *Jesus, what is wrong with me?* She tilted her dark head to one side, noticing that the sunlight streaming through the window was falling on the blonde's face, surrounding her with a warm glow. A lock of golden hair fell across Maggie's eyes, and Julia struggled against the urge to reach out and brush it away. *Get a grip, Jules. You've been single too long, or something.*

Maggie looked up quizzically, and their eyes locked. Both women swore they heard a faintly audible click, as if the last two pieces of a puzzle were fitting together. As a child, fairy tales and notions like love at first sight had entranced Maggie, but she had never dreamed that she would ever experience either one. An excited shiver raced down her spine. Looking at Julia was like looking at the other half of herself. It felt familiar, safe and inviting, and the feeling both thrilled and terrified the young woman. Suddenly, Maggie dropped her gaze and plucked at the tablecloth, feeling the heat on her skin as blood rushed to her face. She cleared her throat nervously.

"So, uh, what were you doing out at Netsports, anyway?" Maggie steered herself back towards neutral territory. She grabbed a piece of bread and dunked in the oil. "Oh, wow, this is really good." She chewed thoughtfully, recognizing garlic and a hint of rosemary.

"Mmm. Yeah," Julia agreed. "Anyway, to answer your question, Danny Webber is an old college buddy and he asked me to go check things out. One of the perks of knowing a p.i., I guess." She shrugged.

"That makes sense, I suppose."

Maggie kept her gaze firmly fixed on the window, anywhere except on the woman across the table from her. One more look into those captivating blue eyes and there would be no turning back. A middle-aged Chinese couple stopped on the sidewalk to argue with each other, and Maggie watched them gesticulate wildly as the rest of the passing pedestrians swerved around them. She was so wrapped up in watching them that she didn't even notice the small, bemused smile on Julia's face as she observed the oblivious reporter.

The restaurant was starting to fill up with the lunch crowd, and voices buzzed around them, conversing in a multitude of languages. Julia swirled her water glass in her hand, listening to the soft clinking of the ice cubes against the glass. Blue eyes quietly regarded the blonde, who was still refusing to meet her gaze. She let out a small sigh; obviously she was going to have to take the lead now, and Julia searched her brain for something intelligent to say. She wasn't used to this feeling. No one had ever left her completely tongue-tied before.

"Hey, I just remembered, there's a parade through Chinatown this weekend. On Saturday, I think." Julia offered, cautiously testing the waters.

Maggie perked up and tore her attention away from the window. "Really? That sounds like fun."

Julia nodded vigorously. "Yeah. They're usually pretty fun." Actually, she wasn't that fond of the noisy parades that clogged the streets with even more people than usual. Somehow, though, she found herself surprisingly willing to endure a minor annoyance if it meant seeing Maggie again.

"Maybe I'll check it out," Maggie said, hoping that Julia would offer to accompany her. She frowned slightly, her brow wrinkling as she remembered her brother. "Unless Patrick is still here this weekend." Maggie reminded herself to call her parents and let them know where her wayward brother was.

Julia blinked. Patrick, again. It felt like someone had just doused her with a pitcher of cold water. "Is he your boyfriend?" Julia tried her best to sound casual. Her eyes widened, startled, as Maggie burst out laughing.

"Oh god, no," Maggie giggled helplessly. "He's my little brother. I don't even know what he's doing here. He just sort of showed up at my apartment last night."

"Ah," Julia managed, an embarrassed flush creeping up the back of her neck.

She was saved by the reappearance of their waiter, bearing their lunch orders. He set their plates in front of them and gestured towards the surly busboy, pointing at Julia's half-empty water glass.

"Let me know if there's anything else I can get for you," he mumbled before hurrying off to the next table.

Maggie was busy examining Julia's four-cheese pizza. "The

crust is different. It looks like a cracker."

"It is like a cracker. Here. Try a piece." Julia transferred a generous slice, dripping with warm, gooey cheese, to Maggie's plate.

They chatted amiably over lunch, mostly discussing more sights that Maggie needed to see. Julia discovered that Maggie was originally from Marion, Ohio, a small town near Columbus. She let out a low whistle at the mention of the reporter's five siblings.

"I can't even imagine having a big family like that. It was pretty much just me and my father, when I was growing up," Julia admitted. "Actually, it was more like just me."

Maggie swallowed a bite of her sandwich. "I thought you had a brother."

Julia stiffened, her eyes narrowing, and Maggie sensed that she had crossed a line. "You did your homework." Julia's voice dropped to a cold snarl.

Julia's jaw tightened and her shoulders tensed. The reporter wasn't interested in her at all, she thought bitterly. At least, not on a personal level. She was just digging for a story, looking to advance her career using the Cassinelli name and money, just like all the others. It wasn't the first time that an eager young reporter had used her to get the dirt on her family. *Damn.* Julia swore to herself heatedly. *I thought this one was different.*

Maggie could feel the waves of anger radiating from the dark-haired woman. Julia's eyes had turned into a pair of icy chips. Impulsively, Maggie reached across the table and laid her hand on the other woman's wrist, feeling the muscles jerk beneath the skin. Oddly enough, Julia didn't pull away.

"I'm sorry. I didn't mean to pry into your personal life. I was just curious about you," Maggie explained quietly.

Tense silence fell between them for several long breaths. Slowly, Maggie removed her hand and dropped it to her lap, her shoulders slumping in defeat. She swallowed hard against the lump in her throat, and her eyes burned as she fought back tears. *Way to go, Maggie. You really messed this one up. Now she'll never trust you. And there just might have been something there, too.*

"Why?" Julia's whispered question broke through her thoughts.

Maggie blinked, perplexed. "Um, why what?"

"Why were you curious about me?"

"Oh." Maggie took a deep breath, wondering how to respond. *Because even though we've only known each other for less than twelve hours, I think I might be falling in love with you. Yeah, tell her that and watch her run screaming into the street.*

"I thought you were interesting." Maggie answered, finally.

Julia tilted her head to one side, considering Maggie's response. "Interesting," she echoed thoughtfully. "Is that a good thing?"

Maggie shrugged, a hesitant grin tugging at the corners of her mouth. "I think so."

The waiter returned, setting the bill on the table between the two women. Julia reached for it automatically, but Maggie snatched it out from under her hand. She glanced at the check briefly, and then pulled a credit card out of her pocket.

"I've got this," she insisted, waving off Julia's protest. Maggie took another deep breath and decided to throw herself headfirst over the edge. "You can buy me dinner on Saturday. After the parade."

Julia smiled, the sparkle returning to her eyes. "Deal."

****

The phone was ringing. Prying open one groggy eye, the young man sprawled on the couch stared up at the ceiling, momentarily disoriented. He rubbed the sleep from his eyes with the heel of his hand as he remembered where he was. San Francisco. His sister's apartment. The shrill ringing of the telephone drilled into his aching head, and Patrick scowled irritably at it, wondering if he should answer it. Then the answering machine on the kitchen counter clicked on.

"Patrick? Are you there? If you're there, pick up the phone." Maggie's disembodied voice floated across the living room.

Patrick groaned and threw his arms across his face. If he answered her, he knew Maggie would just lecture him about going home. And Ohio was about the last place he wanted to be. He buried his head beneath a pillow and waited.

"Okay. Listen; if you get this message, I'm at work if you need me. That number and my cell number are in the address book by the phone," Maggie continued. "And just so you know, I'm calling Mom and Dad. I'll try to be home early. Bye."

When he was sure that Maggie had hung up, Patrick sat up on the couch and stared blankly at the opposite wall. The swirling colors in a framed print of Van Gogh's *Starry Night* made him dizzy, and he shut his eyes. The previous night's events were fuzzy and jumbled in his mind. He remembered being in the park, and forking over the last of his cash for some truly spectacular heroin. And he recalled telling Maggie that he had been mugged so that she wouldn't suspect that he was high. But from the look on her face when she had come home, he realized that his sister knew the truth. He supposed he should feel remorse, but he was too tired and strung out to bother.

Patrick's head throbbed painfully, and he squeezed his eyes more tightly shut, trying to block out the afternoon sunlight streaming through the window. The dealer from the night before had mentioned something about a party. Frowning, Patrick thrust his hand into the pocket of his rumpled jeans and dug out two quarters and a bus ticket stub. He turned the ticket over and read the hastily scribbled address on the back, the location of the party. According to the note, it was in SoMa. *Wherever that is*, Patrick mused sourly as he shoved the scrap back into his pocket.

He stood, rubbing at the back of his neck where a night on the couch had left a nagging soreness. Moving into the kitchen, Patrick opened the woefully under-stocked refrigerator and let the cold air blast over him, prodding him further towards alertness. Other than the coffee pot and the microwave, it didn't look like Maggie's kitchen had seen much use. Patrick laughed softly, shaking his spiky blond head. His sister had never been much of a cook. In fact, Maggie was the only person he knew who could consistently burn scrambled eggs. A bottle of aspirin sat next to the coffee pot, and Patrick grabbed it, shaking three of the white pills into his hand. He popped them into his mouth, grimacing at the bitter taste, and washed them down with a mouthful of orange juice straight from the carton. Patrick closed the refrigerator and rested his forehead against the door, letting the cool metal soothe his aching skull. A thought occurred to him.

"I wonder if Mags has any cash around here," he croaked, poking through the drawers in the kitchen.

He would need more money if he was going to get high again later that night. He continued to rummage through drawers and cabinets, finding nothing useful as he worked his way down the hall towards his sister's bedroom. A brief surge of guilt tugged at him as Patrick pushed open the door to Maggie's room, but he shook the feeling off and stepped across the threshold.

A few crumpled dollars and some loose change littered the top of the dresser, and he quickly swept the money into his pocket. It wasn't even enough for a cab ride. He needed more. Shame burned his cheeks, but the craving for his next fix was stronger, and he pawed hurriedly through the black lacquered jewelry box sitting on top of the dresser. He had given it to Maggie for Christmas several years before; he was surprised she had kept it. Patrick found what he was looking for nestled inside the box --- the diamond studs that had been a present from their parents when Maggie had graduated from Ohio State. With

29

shaking hands, he scooped them up from their red velvet cushion and stared at them, glittering brightly in his palm. He would pay her back as soon as he could, he promised himself. Clutching the earrings tightly in his fist, Patrick left the apartment and headed for the park.

****

Chapter Four

Sighing heavily, Maggie leaned back in her chair and stared at her monitor. She went over the rough draft of her story as she replayed the recent phone conversation in her mind. As she suspected, her parents had no idea that Patrick had gone to San Francisco. Her mother had been practically frantic with worry until Maggie had assured her that the youngest McKinnon sibling was safe and sound in her apartment. Then she had spent the next ten minutes listening to her mother bemoan the fact that her daughter was living amongst a bunch of immoral, liberal degenerates. In Eileen McKinnon's world, that pretty much covered the entire population of California. It had taken all the self-control Maggie could muster to keep from hanging up. Instead, she had simply tuned her mother out as usual and spent the time transforming the day's notes into a coherent story. Their one-sided conversation had ended with Maggie promising to look after her brother and to try to convince him to go home.

Maggie sensed a presence behind her, and a long shadow fell over her computer. She spun around in her chair and found Catherine Richards glaring at her. If looks really could kill, Maggie would have burst into flames on the spot, and she steeled herself for the inevitable confrontation.

The thin redhead moved closer, effectively pinning the back of Maggie's chair against her desk. Her face was set in a mask of icy anger.

"So, how did you get Sam to give you a story? Got rug burns on your knees yet?" Catherine's voice rose so that everyone around them could hear.

The words stung, and Maggie fought to keep the lid on her temper. Her fingers twitched on her armrests as she considered

31

slapping the arrogant smirk off the other woman's face. That wouldn't get her anywhere, she realized, so she plastered an innocent smile on her face instead.

"That's not really my style, Catherine," she replied calmly. "But if I ever need any pointers, I'll be sure to let you know."

Behind her, someone snorted with laughter. Catherine's eyes shot daggers past her shoulder, and the transgressor fell silent. She leaned closer, and Maggie nearly gagged on the redhead's cloying perfume.

"Don't screw with me, Mary-Ann. I can make life miserable for you here. When I'm through with you, you'll wish you were back on Daddy's farm." With that, Catherine whirled and stormed out of the newsroom, the doors banging shut behind her.

Maggie ran her fingers through her hair and let out a shaky breath. "For the last time, I have never, ever lived on a farm," she muttered.

"Don't let her get to you, Maggie. Everyone knows she's just a spoiled, rich bitch who couldn't write her way out of a paper bag." Jessica Sato appeared at Maggie's elbow, sticking her tongue out in the direction of Catherine's departure.

Maggie laughed, letting the tension seep out of her body. "Come on, Jess, she's not that bad." She tried to be diplomatic.

Jessica rolled her eyes and readjusted her thick glasses. "Please. I just proofed her arson piece. I had to fix so many errors that the story should have my by-line instead of hers."

The diminutive copy editor perched on the edge of Maggie's desk, grinning wickedly at her friend. She tapped the plain white business card left carelessly atop a stack of papers.

"JT Cassinelli, huh?" She read the name on the card, poking Maggie's arm playfully. "Where'd ya get that from?"

Maggie blushed in spite of herself and lowered her voice. "I sort of had lunch with her today."

Jessica squealed with excitement and scooted closer, ignoring Maggie's frantic shushing motions. "Ooh! I want details!"

"Would you keep it down?" Maggie laughed helplessly. "It just so happened that she was out at the Netsports thing. She helped get me an inside look at the crime scene and then we went to lunch. No big deal." Maggie told her eagerly listening friend. "Oh, and we're sort of going to some parade this weekend and having dinner."

Jessica's dark eyes widened in amazement. "No big deal, huh? You've got a date with Julia Cassinelli and you're telling me that it's 'no big deal'?"

32

Maggie frowned slightly. "It's not a date, exactly. I mean, I guess it is, sort of. Look, we're just two people having dinner together, okay? I don't even know for sure if she's…you know."

"Are you serious? Maggie, *everybody* knows that! She's always been pretty open about being gay. And her having dinner with you is a big deal. She was living with this model a few years back, and the break-up was really ugly. There were all kinds of accusations and a lawsuit. It was big local news. She dropped out of the spotlight after that."

Maggie's brow furrowed as she thought about what Jessica had just told her. When she had looked Julia up in the archives earlier that day, she hadn't seen anything about a lawsuit. Then again, Jessica had interrupted her before she had gone through everything. She would have to check again later. Suddenly, chubby fingers snapped in front of her nose.

"Hello? Earth to Maggie, anyone in there?" Jessica waved her hand in front of her friend's face.

"Sorry. I was thinking about something." Maggie saw the knowing look on Jessica's face and she slapped her friend's knee. "Nothing like that!"

"Okay, okay," Jessica laughed and changed the subject. "So, how's the story coming along? I heard Sam finally gave you a break."

Maggie grinned happily. "Yeah, it's not much, but it's better than what I've been doing so far. I'm trying to get a quote from Daniel Webber. His secretary said he would call me back, so I'm just waiting for that."

Jessica slid off the desk and straightened her clothes. "Okay, well, I'll be here pretty late tonight. So send the story to my inbox when you're done, and I'll take a look at it for you." She paused, shooting a meaningful look at Catherine's empty desk. "Not like you need much editing. Not like some people."

Maggie shook her head. "You're terrible," she scolded her friend. "I'll send the story over later. Thanks, Jess."

After Jessica left, Maggie returned her attention to her computer screen. She scrolled down, skimming through her work again. The Netsports story was basically ready, but she really wanted to get something more from Daniel Webber. She glanced at the phone, trying to will it to ring. Her gaze fell on Julia's business card, and she flipped it over, reading the neat, precise handwriting on the back --- Julia's home telephone number. The private investigator had said that she was Danny Webber's friend, and for a split second, Maggie considered calling and asking her to use her influence. Maggie shook her head and tucked the card into the pocket of her jacket. She didn't want to ask Julia to intervene on her behalf, didn't want to take advantage of their budding friendship.

Maggie started to delve into the newspaper's archives again, but she stopped herself just before hitting the submit button. Julia had reacted rather badly to her first innocent background check. She didn't think she wanted to risk that again, so it would probably be better to ask Julia about her past directly, she decided. Wrestling with her curiosity, she exited out of the paper's morgue and drummed her fingers impatiently on her desk. It was after 4:00, and she had promised Patrick that she would try to be home early. She chewed her lower lip thoughtfully and reached a decision. Maggie called the paper's central operator and requested to have her calls forwarded to her cell phone. It was just as easy to finish the story and send it from her laptop at home.

She pushed her chair back from her desk and stood, arching her back to stretch the stiff muscles. She shoved a few loose sheets of paper into her shoulder bag and left the newsroom, ignoring the surreptitious looks from her co-workers, who were still curious about the spat between her and Catherine.

The drive home seemed to take forever as she fought her way through the downtown traffic. At a particularly long red light, Maggie pulled her phone out of her bag and tried to call her brother again. Still no answer. Frustrated, she tossed the phone back on the seat, wondering where Patrick had disappeared to and how much trouble he was getting into.

The sky was just beginning to turn a warm orange as Maggie pulled into her parking space. The complex was quiet; most of her neighbors wouldn't be home for another hour or so. Her only witness as she walked up to her front door was a lazy gray cat sunning himself on the concrete walkway. He darted away into the bushes as she approached, and she smiled at him as he eyed her suspiciously.

"Relax, Oscar. I'm not gonna bother you."

The cat belonged to a couple that lived two doors down from her. Even though it had been six months since Maggie moved in, he still wasn't quite used to the reporter's presence. Maggie stopped abruptly, a wave of fear surging through her. The door to her apartment was ajar. Licking her lips nervously, she let her shoulder bag slide to the ground and she cautiously pushed the door open.

"Patrick?" Maggie called out. There was no answer.

She stepped inside, her eyes sweeping the living room for signs of an intruder. With her foot, she dragged her shoulder bag into the entryway and shut the door behind her, trying to make as much noise as

34

possible. Hopefully if there were someone in her apartment, he would hear her and jump out a window or something. She looked around again. Nothing appeared to be missing or out of place; the television and VCR were still in their normal positions and Patrick's duffel bag was still on the floor next to the couch. Maggie crossed to the kitchen and grabbed a frying pan out of a cabinet, hefting it in her hand, testing its weight. It wouldn't hurt to be safe, she thought, as she moved down the hall. She poked her head into the bathroom, but again, nothing seemed to be amiss, and she continued towards her bedroom. The door was open, even though she distinctly remembered closing it before she left for work. She slipped inside, tightening her grip on the frying pan as she checked the closet and her bathroom. Still nothing.

Maggie dripped her makeshift weapon on her bed and sank down on the mattress. Running both hands through her hair, she let out a shaky, relieved breath. The phone on her nightstand rang, and Maggie let out a startled yelp.

"Hello?" she barked into the receiver.

A brief pause. "Maggie?" It was Julia on the other end of the line. "Is everything okay?"

Maggie emitted a sound somewhere between a laugh and a sob. "Julia. Hi. I'm fine, the phone just scared the hell out of me."

Through the phone, Maggie heard the soft creak of leather and she pictured Julia in her office, tilting back in her chair, her feet crossed at the ankles and propped up on her desk. She was surprised by how easily the image popped into her mind.

"Are you sure nothing is missing? No sign of a break-in?" Julia asked after Maggie finished her story.

"Yeah, I'm sure. I. . ." Maggie broke off as her gaze fell on the open jewelry box on her dresser. "Son of a . . .. damn you, Patrick!"

"Maggie? What is it?" Julia's voice was strained with concern.

Maggie examined the contents of her jewelry box. The diamond earrings from her parents were gone. She thought she recalled leaving a few dollars on her dresser, but that was gone too. It wasn't hard to guess that Patrick had taken the money and the earrings.

"Sorry, Julia. It looks like my brother took something from my room. A pair of diamond studs that my parents gave me after I graduated from college."

Julia stayed silent. Maggie berated herself mentally for dumping her family problems on her new friend. She doubted that Julia wanted to hear about her troublesome brother, but Maggie couldn't stop herself. She felt comfortable talking to Julia, as if they had known each other forever.

"He's an addict," Maggie blurted out. She surprised herself; she had never told anyone about Patrick's drug problem. Not even her friends back in Ohio, even though most of them had known anyway.

She heard Julia exhale softly. "I'm sorry." Julia said quietly. "Is there anything I can do?"

Maggie sighed bitterly. Was there anything that Julia could do? Not really. Then why was she tempted to ask the dark-haired woman to come over? Maggie shook her head. This wasn't the time.

"No, thanks for asking, though. I guess I'm just gonna hang out here and wait for him to come back."

"What does your brother look like? I'll make a few calls, and maybe we can find him before he gets himself into too much trouble."

There was a light, rhythmic tapping, like fingernails or a pen clacking against the desk. Maggie hesitated. She didn't want to drag Julia into her problems, but the private investigator sounded like she genuinely wanted to help. Maggie let out and inaudible sigh. It wouldn't hurt to see what Julia could come up with.

"That would be really great. Thank you."

Maggie was suddenly very tired. She lay back on her bed and closed her eyes, trying to picture her brother in her head. Patrick was just over six feet and rail-thin, though she didn't know exactly how much he weighed. He had blond hair, a little darker than her own, and muddy brown eyes. She related this information to Julia, along with a description of what Patrick had been wearing the night before.

"What's his thing? His drug, I mean. It might give me an idea of where to look for him." Julia asked, all business.

Maggie could hear the scratch of a pen against paper as Julia jotted all of the information down. She toyed with the business card in her hand, twirling it between her thumb and forefinger. She examined Julia's handwriting. The strong block letters were an indication of her strength and determination. What am I doing? Maggie wondered, aghast. Patrick is missing and I'm busy analyzing Julia's handwriting? She was so distracted that she nearly missed the next question.

"Is your brother straight?" Julia asked bluntly. For a long moment, the only response was shocked silence.

"Yes. He's straight," Maggie answered finally.

Julia let out a long breath. "Okay. Look, I didn't mean to offend you or anything. It's just . . .if he's straight, then he's probably not in the Castro."

"No, probably not," Maggie agreed. "And you didn't offend me. You just caught me off-guard."

"Oh. Good. Okay, well, I guess I'll make some calls then. I'll let you know if I find him." Julia paused. "Are you sure you're alright?"

"I'm fine. Thank you . . .for everything."

They said their good-byes and Maggie punched the off button on her phone. She curled up on her side and pressed her face into her pillow, choking back tears. She was worried about her brother, sure, but she was also furious with him for mixing her up in his problems. In the living room, her cell phone rang, and Maggie groaned and launched herself off the bed. She dashed down the hallway and grabbed the phone out of her bag. It was Daniel Webber, the president of Netsports. Hastily, Maggie scrambled for a pencil and a piece of paper, using the few seconds to compose herself as she deliberately put her brother out of her mind and concentrated on the interview at hand. She glanced at the clock on the VCR. There was plenty of time before her 7:00 deadline.

After hanging up with Maggie, Julia called one of her contacts at the S.F.P.D. and asked him to have the night shift keep an eye out for someone fitting Patrick McKinnon's description. The officer owed her a favor, and he agreed to have someone call her if they picked up Patrick. Restlessly, Julia roamed around her office, trying to bring some order to a long-neglected stack of old case files. Her thoughts kept drifting back to Maggie, and she wondered again if the young woman was all right. It was ridiculous, she told herself; they'd known each other for less than 24 hours. She couldn't possibly be this attached to the reporter yet. Muttering to herself, Julia shoved a handful of folders into her overflowing file cabinet. She regarded it with disgust.

"I've really got to clean this thing out one of these days," she announced to no one in particular.

Behind her, she heard a soft whoosh of air as the door opened. Footsteps clacked against the wood floor as someone stepped into her office, not saying a word. The door swung shut again.

"Can I help you?" Julia started to turn around, but rough, gloved hands seized her shoulders and shoved her up against the file cabinet.

A drawer handle dug painfully into one of her ribs. Anger building in her, Julia tried to twist free, but her attacker tightened his grip and slammed her into the file cabinet again. She winced and sucked in a sharp breath. It was definitely a man; she vaguely recognized the scent of his expensive aftershave. A deep, sandpapery voice whispered into her ear, and she could feel his hot breath on her skin.

"Stay out of things that don't concern you. If you don't, it could be bad for your health."

Julia almost laughed out loud at the threat, and she bit her tongue just in time. This guy had been watching too many bad gangster movies, or something. Several sarcastic retorts rolled through her mind, but she wisely decided to stay silent, since there was no sense in antagonizing the guy. He seemed a bit surprised by her complacency, like he had been expecting her to fight back. He squeezed her upper arms, and she grimaced in pain, realizing that he was going to leave bruises.

"Did you hear what I said? Keep your nose out of other people's business."

"I heard you! I don't know what you're talking about!" Julia snapped back.

She managed to turn her head slightly, and almost caught a glimpse of her attacker's face before a hard elbow caught her across her temple. She closed her eyes as stars exploded in her head, and she fought to stay conscious. She didn't want to give him the satisfaction of seeing her pass out. Her mind whirled as she tried to figure out what he was warning her away from. It had to be the Netsports thing. The only other open case she had was a basic cheating-husband thing.

His lips unpleasantly close to her ear, her assailant laughed, a low, raspy chuckle that turned her blood to ice. Julia's breathing quickened, and a rush of adrenaline swept through her body. She was getting a very bad feeling about this. Propping her foot against the bottom of the file cabinet for leverage, Julia struggled to break free. His hand slipped from her shoulder, just long enough for her to spin around, swinging at him wildly. Pain jolted all the way up her arm as her fist connected with his shoulder, and he cursed loudly. She got the briefest look at his face. Square jaw, dark hair and eyes. Then his fist was coming towards her, much too fast for her to duck. Fireworks lit up the inside of her skull, and then everything went dark.

"Bitch," he spat at her unconscious form. He kicked her once in the ribs as he stepped over her prone body and slipped out the door.

Whistling casually, he sauntered down the street, waiting until he was a block away before he pulled a small phone out of the pocket of his neat wool slacks. He selected one of the preset numbers.

"Message delivered," he growled.

Cocking his head to one side, he listened to the voice on the other end, nodding occasionally.

"I'll take care of it," he said.

Scowling darkly, he jammed his fists into the pockets of his slacks and continued down the street. A bus pulled up to the curb next to him, and he hopped on it, glancing up at the marquee and noting that

38

it was heading in the right direction. That was good. He slumped into a seat and stared out the window. His shoulder throbbed where that Cassinelli bitch had hit him, but he had gotten her back good. He grinned and flexed his right hand, feeling the black leather glove tighten against his sore knuckles. His good mood was returning and he started to whistle again as the bus pulled away from the curb and headed down the street.

****

Chapter Five

Julia's eyelids felt like they had been glued shut, and she struggled to pry them apart. Her vision blurred and dimmed around the edges as the stark fluorescent light sent bolts of pain shooting through her head. With a hiss, she sucked in a sharp breath, her nose wrinkling in distaste at the antiseptic smell of the room. She was aware of a presence to her right, and she tried to lift her head. Gentle hands pressed her back into the pillows.

Julia reacted instinctively, her body remembering the attack in her office. The muscles in her arms and shoulders went rigid, and she fought to break free from someone's firm grip. A low growl ripped its way loose from her throat.

"Whoa. Take it easy. You're safe. It's just me." Maggie's soft voice murmured in her ear.

Slowly, Julia's vision cleared and she looked up into a pair of worried green eyes. Still dazed, she blinked twice, making sure that she wasn't seeing things. Maggie smiled at her tentatively, the deep furrow in her brow giving away her concern.

"Where?" Julia rasped, her throat horribly dry.

Maggie poured water into a plastic cup and handed it to Julia, putting a hand on her elbow to steady her as she sipped gratefully.

"You're in the hospital," Maggie informed her. "The doctor said you have a concussion and a couple of bruised ribs, but you're going to be just fine."

Julia shut her eyes, trying to block out the nauseating throbbing in her head as she took all of this in. She remembered being in her office. Her back had been turned when a man had come through the door and grabbed her, throwing her against her file cabinet. He had given her a warning, and then everything had gone black. She thought

41

she had seen his face, but her memory wasn't cooperating and she couldn't quite recall what he looked like. Scowling in frustration, Julia shook her head, grimacing as the movement sent another wave of pain crashing against her skull.

"Hey, stop that!" Maggie's voice jolted her back to the present. "I'm pretty sure you're not supposed to move your head around like that."

Julia's dark eyebrows bunched together and a questioning look flickered across her face. She had almost forgotten that Maggie was in the room.

"What are you doing here?" she asked.

The blonde woman squirmed slightly in her hard, standard-issue hospital chair. Not quite able to meet Julia's eyes, she examined her fingernails nervously. A deep pink blush spread over her cheeks and the tips of her ears.

"I, um, sort of found you," Maggie confessed. "I tried calling you, but there was no answer at any of the numbers you gave me. And, I don't know.... I just had this awful feeling that something was wrong. So I went to your office." She paused.

"You were on the floor. And there was blood," she whispered.

From the stark, haunted look in her eyes, Julia could tell that the reporter was reliving every moment. She tried to interrupt, but Maggie insisted upon relating the rest of the story. Julia fell silent and listened.

Restless and tired of waiting by the phone for her missing brother to contact her, Maggie had decided to call her new friend and find out if the private investigator had heard anything. She had tried Julia's office first but had just gotten voice mail. Calls to Julia's home number and her cell phone had met with the same results, and Maggie had grown increasingly worried. She couldn't explain the uneasy feeling gnawing at her stomach. Finally, she had decided to take a drive past Julia's office.

Julia's dark green jeep had been parked across the street, and the light was burning in her office when Maggie arrived. She had opened the door to find Julia crumpled unconscious on the floor. Dark red blood had dried on the side of her face. An ugly gash marred her temple and a lurid purple bruise covered her left cheek. Frantic with worry, Maggie had called for an ambulance and she had been at Julia's side since.

"Anyway, I followed you to the hospital. And I figured I'd hang around until you woke up, at least." Maggie finished. She hesitated. "Do you.... remember what happened?"

Julia considered the question and made a face. "Vaguely. A guy came into my office and told me to stay out of other people's business, or something like that. I took a swing at him and he hit me. I can't quite seem to remember what he looked like, though."

Without thinking, Maggie laid a comforting hand on the other woman's forearm, absently stroking the soft skin with her thumb. Surprised, Julia inhaled sharply, but said nothing.

"It doesn't matter. All that matters is that you're okay," Maggie declared.

Suddenly, Maggie seemed to realize what she was doing, and green eyes widened in shock as she stared at her hand. Stuttering an incoherent apology, she started to pull away. Julia swiftly grabbed her hand and folded her fingers around Maggie's, waiting until the reporter looked at her, a mixture of confusion and wonder in her expression. Julia smiled at her reassuringly, the motion pulling against the swollen bruise on her cheek.

"It's okay, Maggie," she told her softly. "I'm…. glad you're here."

Julia's pulse raced and her heartbeat thundered in her ears as she waited anxiously for Maggie's response. It was all happening so fast. She'd never bonded with anyone so quickly and so completely. Not like this. Cursing herself silently, Julia swallowed hard and began to loosen her grip on the reporter's hand. She was pushing too hard. Her chin dropped towards her chest as she suddenly found something fascinating in the weave of her thin hospital blanket.

Gently, Maggie brushed the backs of her fingers across Julia's uninjured cheek. Her hands were trembling, and Julia could sense her nervousness. She tilted Julia's face up until she could see the faint misting of tears glittering in those brilliant blue eyes. Julia blinked at her uncertainly. A slow smile spread across Maggie's lips, crinkling the bridge of her nose and lighting up her eyes.

"You know what? Right now, there's no place else I would rather be."

A dark eyebrow twitched. "Really? So your ideal evening consists of sitting in a hospital room and watching me?"

Maggie noticed that Julia's hand was still in hers, and she squeezed it lightly. She winked mischievously. "Well, maybe I could do without the hospital part," she drawled.

In spite of Julia's objections, the doctor, a soft-spoken Pakistani man, insisted that she remain in the hospital overnight. It was for her own good, he'd said. Julia had grumbled and complained, but eventually she had relented, mostly because Maggie had offered to keep her company. That was an offer she couldn't turn down.

Eyeing the door anxiously, Julia chewed on the clear plastic straw sticking out of her water cup. By her estimation, fifteen minutes had passed since Maggie had excused herself in search of coffee. Julia hated hospitals, especially the sterile, antiseptic smell. Again, she wondered what was keeping Maggie. She scowled irritably at the closed door, and her eyebrows knit together, tugging at the stitches in her temple. She had hit her head when she fell, opening an inch-long gash above her left eye. Just before Maggie had stepped out, a severe, no-nonsense nurse had come in and forced Julia to swallow a painkiller the size of a horse tranquilizer.

The silence in the room was getting on her nerves, and she reached for the television remote on the small bedside table. She aimed it at the ceiling-mounted monitor and clicked a button. It was well after midnight, and her viewing options were slim, she noted sourly as she flipped through the channels. Nothing but infomercials and silly talk shows. Julia paused as a man and women screamed bleeped obscenities at each other as the host shook his head in mock concern.

"My husband cheated on me with my gay lover," she snorted, reading the caption out loud.

"Really? That must suck." Maggie was leaning casually in the doorway, a steaming Styrofoam cup in her hand.

"Took you long enough. What did you do, pick the beans yourself?" Julia grinned, nodding at the cup. Her spirits perked up immediately at the sight of the blonde reporter.

Maggie grinned back as she reclaimed her spot next to Julia's bed. "You're just jealous 'cause the doctor said you couldn't have any." She took a long sip, holding the hot liquid in her mouth for a moment before swallowing. "Actually, I smuggled this out of the staff lounge. I figured it had to be better than the stuff that comes out of those vending machines."

"Mmm. You're probably right about that," Julia agreed. She inhaled deeply, savoring the rich, pungent scent of the coffee. She was dying for a cup, but the doctor had temporarily forbidden her from anything caffeinated. She pinned him with an evil glare when he had suggested switching to decaf for the next couple of days. What was the point of coffee without caffeine? Sulking, she noisily slurped water through her straw.

Maggie was absorbed in the drama unfolding on the TV screen, and Julia used the moment to silently observe her new friend. She was watching the talk show intently, a faint crease wrinkling her forehead. Warm intelligence shone from those jade green eyes, and Julia had the feeling that the young reporter didn't miss much. Maggie took another

44

swallow of her coffee as she tucked a few strands of hair behind her right ear. She froze, feeling Julia's gaze on her, and she turned to the dark-haired woman, both fair eyebrows raised in question. Caught, Julia smiled sheepishly and shrugged.

"Any word from your brother?" Julia asked, smoothly shifting gears.

Maggie shook her head sadly. "Nothing yet. He'll turn up, though. He always does."

Julia heard the note of doubt in her voice and realized that Maggie was more concerned than she was letting on. She had the impression that Patrick McKinnon had pulled a stunt like this more than once. She wondered how often he had upset his sister in this manner, and Julia's dislike for the young man grew.

"Yeah. I'm sure he'll be fine." She tried to reassure the young woman.

Maggie shifted in her chair, turning s☐ that she was facing Julia directly. Those blue eyes drew her into their depths, and she had to shake herself to keep from getting lost in them.

"So, do you want to tell me why someone would want to hurt you?" she asked, slamming the door shut on the subject of her brother.

Julia bit her lower lip as she considered the question. She had a pretty good idea that the attack had been prompted by her inquiry into the Netsports burglary. The last thing she wanted to do was get Maggie mixed up in the situation. Not if it was going to turn dangerous. She hesitated, wondering where that surge of protectiveness had come from. Maggie was waiting for an answer, tapping her fingers on her armrest, a little impatiently. Julia sighed. Lying to her probably wouldn't be the best way to start off their relationship. If that was where they were heading, she amended quickly.

"I'm not entirely sure, but I think someone's trying to warn me away from that Netsports thing," Julia began. "That's the only explanation that makes sense to me. Most of my cases are pretty routine --- cheating spouses, background checks, that sort of thing."

Maggie's reporter instincts perked up. "Hmm. So what's so important about Netsports, then?"

Mentally, she reviewed what she knew about the earlier break-in. The police believed that it was a simple burglary. She recalled Inspector Chow's words . . .. kids or an addict looking for a fix, he had said. Briefly, her thoughts turned to Patrick, and she wondered if her brother would ever sink that low. Maybe he already had, she conceded reluctantly, thinking about her stolen earrings.

"Embezzlement?" Maggie threw out a suggestion.

Julia pursed her lips and tilted her head to one side. "Possibility," she replied thoughtfully. If someone was stealing from the company, that might give him a strong enough motive to have her roughed up a little. Still, something about that didn't feel right. She couldn't quite put her finger on it yet, but she had the distinct feeling that there was something more going on. Absently, she rubbed the back of her hand across her tired, burning eyes.

"Okay, I think that's enough private investigating for now," Maggie said lightly, noticing Julia's drooping eyelids. "You should get some rest."

Julia made a dismissive gesture with her hand. "I'm fine. It's the damn pills that sadistic nurse made me take," she retorted grumpily. "Besides, you're the one who brought the subject up."

"Yeah, well, now I'm closing the subject," Maggie replied calmly. She gave her friend a fond, amused look. "The nurse wasn't that bad. She was a little abrupt, but hardly sadistic."

Julia glared at her stubbornly, looking like a petulant child. She folded her arms across her chest. "Did you ever see 'One Flew over the Cuckoo's Nest'?"

Maggie burst out laughing. "She was not that bad!"

"Was too."

"Go to sleep, Julia. I'll protect you from Nurse Ratchet."

Grumbling, Julia settled back against her pillows and pulled the blanket up to her chin. The room was cool, and the thin hospital gown didn't provide much warmth. She was glad she didn't have to go to the bathroom or anything, since there was no way she was going to traipse across the room with her butt flapping in the breeze. Not until they knew each other better, anyway. She bit back a wicked grin as her eyes slid closed. She heard Maggie get up and amble over towards the window. Carefully, she cracked one eye open and peeked at the blonde.

Maggie had pried apart two of the blinds with her fingers, and she was staring outside, a sad, wistful expression on her face. As Julia watched, Maggie stifled a yawn and arched her back to stretch the stiff muscles.

"You don't have to stay, you know," Julia said, clearing her throat softly.

"I know. I want to." Maggie responded without turning around.

Unseen, Julia smiled up at the ceiling, savoring those simple, straightforward words. She couldn't remember anyone ever wanting to stay with her before, at least not without some ulterior motive. Even during the rare times she'd been sick as a child, her father had usually left her alone in her room, sending the housekeeper to check on her occasionally. She shut her eyes again as exhaustion pressed down on her.

"Thanks," she mumbled.

Maggie didn't reply. She turned, watching quietly as Julia's breathing became deep and even. Once she was sure that her friend was asleep, she resumed her seat by her bedside. She pulled her jacket tighter around her thin shoulders as she searched for a comfortable position in the hard, unyielding chair. Leaning forward, she brushed a lock of dark hair away from Julia's face, letting her fingertips linger on the soft skin a bit longer than necessary. Maggie took a deep breath as she studied her new friend's sleeping countenance. The high cheekbones. The smooth, tanned skin. The full, sensual lips. A familiar flutter of excitement raced through Maggie's stomach, and she shook her head. *'She's gorgeous. She's dated supermodels, for god's sake. What would someone like that want with someone as ordinary as me?'* Sighing, Maggie closed her eyes firmly. Stretching her legs out in front of her, she slumped down further in her chair and tried to sleep.

****

Julia's brow wrinkled as she tried to identify the unfamiliar sounds. Her eyes were still shut, but she knew she was lying on her back with her head propped up slightly more than usual. The pillows behind her were firmer than the soft feathers she was used to. On the edges of her hearing, muffled voices conversed, and she could make out the whisper of soft-soled shoes scuffing across the floor. Slowly, she opened one eye, her vision adjusting to the darkened room. The hospital. She opened the other eye and cautiously moved her head from side to side. It still hurt, but not with the intense pain of the night before. She took that as a good sign. A sift hiss escaped her as she propped herself up on her elbows. *'Bruised ribs, right. Forgot about that.'* Julia turned her head and smiled at the sight of Maggie, still fast asleep in the chair. The blonde was turned almost sideways in her seat, her legs tucked up beneath her and her cheek pressed against the back of the chair. Julia squinted, trying to make out the time on Maggie's silver wristwatch. It was almost 8 a.m. She hoped the reporter wasn't supposed to be at work.

The door swung open and the same dour nurse from the previous night bustled in. She grunted at Julia as she passed by the bed, barely glancing at the patient in it. With a sharp jerk of the cord, the nurse yanked the blinds open, letting in the weak morning light. Maggie stirred at the noise.

"The doctor will be in shortly," the nurse announced curtly. She checked Julia's temperature and blood pressure, scribbling notes on a clipboard. Without another word, she marched out of the room, leaving the two women staring after her.

Maggie started to giggle, covering a yawn with her hand. "Good morning to you, too, Nurse Ratchet," she called out after the nurse left. "I guess she missed class the day they gave the bedside manner lecture."

Julia chuckled. "I guess so. You know, most nurses are probably perfectly nice. How come I always get the grumpy one?"

"Must be your captivating charm." Maggie joked. "Thank God my editor said I can work from home today. I can't remember the last time I was this stiff."

She stood, groaning at her aching back. She twisted her upper body, wincing at the audible cracking as she worked the kinks out of her spine. She yawned again. Lacing her fingers together, she stretched her arms above her head. The movement pulled her long-sleeved t-shirt out of the waistband of her jeans, momentarily exposing her navel. Julia blinked twice and quickly found something else to look at.

"Think we'll get out of here before they serve breakfast?" Maggie asked.

Julia made a face. "I hope so. With my luck, it'll be oatmeal."

Maggie laughed and summoned up her best impression of her mother, shaking her finger at Julia. "There's nothing wrong with oatmeal, young lady. It's a fine, healthy way to start your morning, and there are children all over the world who would love to have just a little of what the good Lord has provided you."

"Let me guess, your mother?" Julia lifted both eyebrows.

Maggie nodded. "Yep. I don't think a single day started without some variation on that speech. With six kids, there was always something that one of us didn't like. My oldest brother, Steven, hated oatmeal. With me, it was raisin toast."

Julia's gaze went very distant, and an aching sadness shone from her eyes. "No one ever cared what I ate for breakfast. Or if I even ate breakfast at all," Julia revealed softly, not really aware that she was speaking out loud.

Maggie stared at her in dismay. "I'm sorry, I . . ." she trailed off.

Expressionless blue eyes met hers. "It's okay. My father was a busy man. He really didn't have the time to fix me breakfast every morning."

The doctor walked in before Maggie could respond. He checked

Julia over thoroughly, peering into her eyes to check the response of her pupils. He scratched the end of his neat moustache as he reviewed her chart.

"Well, Ms. Cassinelli, you seem to be recovering nicely. I believe I will send you home, but you must promise me that you will take it easy for a few days. No strenuous activities," he said sternly. "You may take over-the-counter ibuprofen for pain, if you wish. If you have any vision problems, dizziness, or shooting pain, you must call me at once."

"Yes, doctor. I understand completely." Julia nodded solemnly.

He scrawled his name across the bottom of her chart and carefully placed the silver-plated pen back in the pocket of his immaculate white coat. "Very well, then. Please make an appointment with your regular doctor to have those stitches removed in about ten days. I will have a nurse return with your discharge papers." He smiled kindly at her as he exited.

Maggie exhaled slowly as the door swung shut. In a few minutes, Julia would be released and they would probably go their separate ways. It was a disappointing thought since she was enjoying the other woman's company more and more. *'Oh well, it's just two more days until Saturday'.* Maggie rolled her eyes and slapped herself in the head. *'She's just getting out of the hospital, you idiot. She's probably not gonna want to have dinner with you.'*

A muffled groan caught her attention, and she spun towards the sound. Julia was sitting on the edge of the bed, her bare feet on the floor. One hand was pressed to her left side, and she was grimacing in obvious pain. Three quick steps, and Maggie was at her side, gently touching her shoulder.

"Julia? Are you okay? Should I call the doctor back in here?" Maggie asked, her voice tinged with concern.

Biting her lower lip, Julia shook her head. Rueful blue eyes glanced up. "No, no. I'm fine. Just a little sore." She managed a weak smile.

Maggie was acutely aware of the warm skin beneath her hand. Her eyes traveled downward, across the lean, powerful body that was mere inches from her own. The translucent hospital gown left little to the imagination, and the room was on the chilly side, and. . . .Maggie swallowed hard, her throat suddenly dry, as all the moisture in her body seemed to be flooding elsewhere.

"Uh, Maggie?" Julia's voice broke through her haze and Maggie looked up to find Julia regarding her curiously. "Do me a favor and hand me my clothes?"

A deep blush heated Maggie's face and neck as she hurriedly retrieved the requested items. She handed the neatly folded clothing to Julia and backed away hastily, unable to meet the other woman's gaze.

"I'll, um . . . I'll be outside. I need to make some phone calls, anyway," Maggie mumbled as she slipped out of the room.

She paused just outside the door and leaned back against the wall while she waited for her heartbeat to slow. She'd never had such an intense response to anyone before, and the experience had left her somewhat shaken. A nurse passed by, glancing at her curiously. Maggie ran her fingers through her disheveled hair as she pushed off from the wall and headed for the waiting area.

Julia stared after her departing friend speculatively. The reporter's reaction to her had been . . . interesting, and it helped confirm her suspicion that the attraction she felt for Maggie was mutual. A slow grin tugged at her lips as she began to get dressed.

Maggie put her cell phone away with a sigh. Patrick still hadn't returned, and there was no word from him on her answering machine either. He was in trouble again; that much was obvious. She closed her eyes and rubbed her temples. It was time to call the police, she decided. A loud, belligerent voice interrupted her thoughts and brought a tiny smile to her face. Patrick and the cops would have to wait a bit longer.

"I don't need to be trucked around like some goddamn invalid!" Julia's voice rose until the last two words were practically bellowed.

A tired-looking orderly in blue hospital scrubs sighed heavily. "I told you, Ms. Cassinelli, it's hospital policy. You have to sit in this wheelchair until I put you in a cab. You don't want me to lose my job, do you?"

Maggie stepped in, rescuing the orderly from Julia's sarcastic retort. "No, she doesn't want that. That's why she's going to be a good girl and let you do your job, Seth," she said, reading the young man's name off his ID badge. She gave him a sympathetic smile, which he returned gratefully.

Julia's dark eyebrows were hiked practically into her hairline. "A good girl? Me?" She snorted. "You really don't know me very well."

It was Maggie's turn to raise a blonde eyebrow. "Well, I guess we'll just have to work on that, won't we?" She turned to Seth without waiting for a response. "Follow me. I'll save the poor cabdriver the headache and drive her home myself."

Seth laughed. "Sounds like a plan." Ignoring Julia's protests, he expertly spun her around and followed the small blonde towards the

50

exit.

****

Chapter Six

With the heel of his hand, Patrick rubbed the crusty gunk out of the corners of his tired, red-rimmed eyes. He had been walking since dawn. With all of its hills, San Francisco wasn't an easy city to walk in, and Patrick's calves ached from the exertion. Sweat darkened the back of his threadbare gray t-shirt, in spite of the chilly morning air. He jammed his fists into the hip pockets of his faded, olive green pants. Nothing. Not even enough change for a phone call. He wondered if Maggie would accept a collect call from him. She was probably furious with him by now. He wiped his nose with the back of his hand and decided not to call her yet. He wasn't in the mood for her lecture.

His stomach rumbled insistently, reminding him that it had been a long time since he had eaten. In fact, Patrick couldn't even remember his last meal. Veering to his left, he approached an officious-looking man in a crisp, navy blue suit. The man eyed him suspiciously, disdain evident in his sneering gaze.

"Hey, man, do you think you can spare a couple bucks for some food?" Patrick mumbled, swallowing the last shreds of his dignity.

"Get a job, loser," the man spat, brushing by him without a second glance.

Patrick spun around, anger twisting his features. "Oh yeah? Well, fuck you too!"

He scrubbed his face with his hand again and resumed walking. Other people on the street gave him a wide berth, shooting fearful glances at him as they passed. Patrick ignored them all. He kept plodding forward mechanically, his eyes focused on his scuffed, dirty running shoes. His throat was dry and he swallowed around a tongue that felt far too thick for his mouth. The little plastic baggie inside his shoe beckoned to him, but he ignored that too. 'Not yet,' he told himself. Cars crawled past him, stuck in the morning commute, and

Patrick wondered if his sister was in any of them.

He turned a corner, bumping into a tall, imperious redhead in a tailored gray skirt and jacket. Coffee splashed to the sidewalk, and she cursed loudly at him. He didn't even hear her venomous insults as he stared up at the large building that loomed before him. Tilting his head back, he read the sign on the front. The San Francisco Chronicle. Patrick smiled in relief. Maggie would be here. He pushed the door open and stepped inside.

****

"I don't need any help." Julia swatted the offered hand away irritably as she emerged from the passenger seat of a black Corolla. A mild wave of dizziness forced her to grip the top of the doorframe until she was sure that her knees wouldn't buckle.

Maggie sighed and put a steadying hand on Julia's elbow. She held her other hand out, palm up. "Okay, give me your keys. Let's get you inside."

Deaf to Julia's protests, Maggie slid her arm around her friend's waist and supported her as they made their way towards the front door. She had half-expected Julia Cassinelli to live in one of the multi-million dollar mansions in the upper crust Nob Hill area. Instead, she was pleasantly surprised to discover that her new friend resided in a relatively modest two-story Victorian in Pacific Heights. Expensive, yes, but not as imposing as the mansion she'd been anticipating. Cautiously, they navigated the narrow steps leading up to the wooden porch, and Julia leaned against the rail as Maggie fumbled with the door.

"The lock sticks sometimes. Just jiggle the key a little," Julia advised.

Maggie did as she was instructed, grinning triumphantly as the door swung open. "Tricky. Just like its owner," she shot a sly glance at the taller woman.

Julia managed a wry grin in return. Her head was beginning to pound again, and all she wanted was a handful of painkillers and a nice, cool glass of water. Maggie seemed to sense her discomfort, and she gently took Julia's arm and led her inside.

All of the drapes were closed, casting the house into near total darkness. After taking a moment to let her eyes adjust, Maggie helped Julia into the living room and sat her down on the rich leather sofa. She reached for a lamp, but Julia shook her head.

"No. Leave it off, please."

Maggie nodded in understanding. "Okay, sure. Can I get you anything? Some aspirin, maybe?"

Slumping down on the sofa, Julia let her headrest against the cool leather. She closed her eyes, trying to will away the nausea that was accompanying her headache.

"Yeah, that would be great. There's a bottle of Advil on the kitchen counter, near the phone." Julia gestured towards the back of the house.

"Okay. I'll be right back." Maggie picked her way through the darkness, the heels of her loafers clacking against the hardwood floor.

She found the kitchen without much trouble. The blinds were open on the small window above the sink, and weak sunlight streamed through, throwing patterned shadows across the counters and floor. The Advil was right where Julia had said it would be, and Maggie popped the top of the bottle off with her thumb and shook two of the pills out into her palm. She replaced the bottle and started opening cabinets at random until she found one containing neatly ordered glasses. She stuck a glass under the dispenser in the refrigerator door and filled it with water. As an afterthought, she tore a chunk off the loaf of sourdough bread on the counter.

From the living room, Julia could hear Maggie rooting around in the kitchen. It was a strangely comforting sound. It had been such a long time since there had been anyone else in her house. Keeping her eyes closed, she listened as Maggie made her way back down the hall. The soft creak of leather told her that the blonde was sitting on the sofa's armrest, and she opened one blue eye. Sure enough, Maggie was perched next to her, studying her intently. A warm smile spread across the reporter's face as their eyes met.

"I thought you fell asleep," she said.

Julia rolled her head to the left. "Nope. Not quite."

Maggie held out the pills and the water, watching as Julia swallowed both. She handed the bread over, as well. "Eat a little of that, too. I don't think you're supposed to take ibuprofen on an empty stomach."

She waited until Julia had followed her instructions. "You should probably get some rest now."

"Mmm. Probably," Julia agreed. "Thanks for bringing me home, but you can go now. I'm sure you have better things to do."

Maggie's face fell and she fought to keep the disappointment out of her voice. "Oh, well, okay. If that's what you want."

'Damn.' Julia's dark eyebrows met as she scowled. 'Admit it, you want her to stay.' Julia sighed and ran both hands through her hair.

"Well, I mean, you're welcome to stay. If you want to, that is," she amended hastily.

Maggie's smile returned immediately. "I think I should. For a little while, anyway.... just to make sure you're really okay."

"Okay. I guess I'll just stretch out here, then," Julia said, indicating the sofa. "There's a computer and a TV in my office upstairs. First door on the right. Make yourself at home."

Julia reached down to unlace her boots. She grimaced as the motion caused her head to throb even worse. Maggie swiftly moved to help her, removing Julia's boots and setting them aside. She helped the injured woman lie back and covered her with the chenille blanket that was draped over the back of the sofa. Julia smiled at her gratefully and let her eyelids droop shut.

Not wanting to disturb the dozing woman, Maggie kicked off her loafers and placed them neatly by the front door. She climbed the stairs to the second floor and found the door to Julia's office open. A black leather loveseat, matching the sofa downstairs, sat against the wall, facing a large television with a built-in VCR. A video game system rested on the floor, the worn controller showing signs of frequent use. Maggie opened the tray and examined the game inside, one of those tournament-fighting games. She chuckled softly as she flopped down on the loveseat. The soft, supple leather warmed quickly to her body, a welcome change after a night spent in a hard plastic hospital chair. She shut her eyes. *'I should check in at work. I'll just rest my eyes for a second.'*

Thirty minutes later, a ringing phone awakened her. Dazed green eyes looked around blankly, trying to locate the source of the noise. It was her cell phone, she realized suddenly, extracting the small phone from the pocket of her jacket.

"Hello?"

"Is this Maggie McKinnon?" a woman asked pleasantly.

"Yes. Who is this?"

"Hi, Maggie. This is Carol at the Chronicle."

Maggie thought for a moment. Carol was the receptionist at the front desk, she recalled finally.

"Listen, Maggie. We have a situation. There's a guy in the lobby demanding to see you. He claims to be your brother." Carol lowered her voice to a whisper. "I think he's on something."

Maggie groaned inwardly. At least Patrick was safe. "Can you put him on the phone, please?" She could hear muffled voices in the background. A few seconds later, Patrick's voice boomed through the phone.

56

"Hey, Mags! Where the heck are you? I was hoping you could give me a ride back to your place."

Maggie ground her teeth, fighting to keep the lid on her temper. She counted to ten and exhaled slowly. "Stay there, Patrick. I'm on my way." She hung up the phone, cutting off his response. *'Damn him. I swear, one of these days, I'm just gonna strangle him.'*

Still muttering curses under her breath, Maggie made her way back downstairs. She detoured into the living room to check on Julia, who was still sleeping soundly. She didn't want to leave, torn between her loyalty to her younger brother and her growing interest in her new friend. She pulled the ever-present notepad out of her pocket and scribbled a hasty note to explain her departure. Grabbing Julia's house keys, she picked up her shoes and quietly slipped out the front door, making sure it was tightly locked behind her.

Maggie pulled into the parking lot of the newspaper and slammed her car door. Anger was evident in the tense set of her shoulders and the uncharacteristic scowl on her face. She stormed through the doors to the lobby. Patrick was sitting in a chair, nervously tapping his foot against the marble floor. He bounded to his feet at Maggie's entrance, his happy smile fading quickly as he noticed the fire blazing in her green eyes. Maggie studied her brother critically.

He looked terrible. His hair was greasy and unkempt; stubble dotted his cheeks. Bloodshot eyes stared at her. He was drawn and pale, and shaking from the drugs or the exhaustion. Probably a little of both, she acknowledged. His clothes were rumpled and stained with sweat and other stuff that she really didn't want to know about. She wasn't sure if she should shake him or hug him as he stared at her with those wounded puppy dog eyes.

"Damn it, Patrick," she whispered, stepping forward to pull her brother into a fierce hug. "Come on, let's get you out of here."

He followed her meekly to her car. Patrick knew his sister was extremely angry with him, and he wisely kept his mouth shut. He couldn't keep still on the drive to Maggie's apartment, and he fiddled with the radio, flipping through the preset stations. While they were stopped at a red light, he started playing with the automatic windows. Up. Down. Up. Down. Without saying a word, Maggie glared at him, and Patrick's hand fell away from the button.

"Sorry," he mumbled, drumming his fingers on his knee. She didn't respond.

They pulled into Maggie's apartment complex, and his face brightened. A shower and a hot meal sounded like a really good idea. He jumped out of the car, almost before it had stopped moving, oblivious to Maggie's startled warning.

"Hello, cat," he solemnly greeted the gray cat glaring at him through narrowed yellow eyes.

Maggie grabbed his upper arm and dragged him towards her apartment. She unlocked the door and roughly shoved him inside. She pushed him over to the couch.

"Where the hell have you been?"

The tone of her voice warned him that he was in deep trouble. His shoulders dropped. Staring at the floor, he shrugged.

"I dunno."

"You don't know where you've been?" Maggie asked skeptically.

Patrick shrugged again, defeated. He tried to press his body further back into the corner of the couch. His eyes, downcast, darted back and forth, and Maggie knew he was trying to come up with a story to tell her. She sighed and sat down next to him, putting her arm around his thin, trembling shoulders.

"Patrick, you know I love you, right?" She paused, but Patrick remained quiet. "Well, I do. But this can't go on. You've got to get your life together."

Patrick sniffled loudly and wiped his nose with the back of his hand. "I know. That's . . . partly why I came out here. To try and start over."

Maggie watched him carefully, trying to gauge his sincerity. As far as she could tell, he was telling her the truth. She stood and held out her hand. Patrick blinked at her uncertainly.

"Give them to me," she said quietly.

"What?"

Maggie sighed impatiently. "The rest of the drugs. If you're really serious about starting over, then give them to me."

Patrick hesitated. He put on his most innocent expression and gazed up at his sister.

"It's all gone, Mags. I did the last of it earlier this morning, I swear." He picked at a hangnail on his index finger. "I'm, uh, I'm really sorry about your earrings. I'll pay you back, I promise."

Maggie wasn't sure if he was lying to her about the drugs or not. She'd always been able to read him, but lately, she just didn't know how to reach him anymore. She didn't have the time or the energy to deal with Patrick's self-destruction. Instantly, Maggie felt guilty for not being the supporting, understanding sister that she thought she should be. She could hear her mother's voice echoing inside her head, and if she closed her eyes, she could actually picture the pleading look on her mother's face. *'Megan Elaine, what is the matter with you? Can't you see that your brother needs you? You've moved out to California and now you're too good for your family, is that it? Please, Maggie. You're the only one he listens to.'* It wasn't true, exactly. Patrick didn't listen to any of them and he never had. But he was closer to Maggie than he was to anyone else in the family.

"Go take a shower and get cleaned up. I'll fix us some breakfast, okay?" Maggie headed for the kitchen.

"But you can't cook," Patrick reminded her.

She shot him a dirty look over her shoulder. "I think I can manage eggs and toast," she replied dryly.

He gave her a weak grin and grabbed his duffel bag. Moments later, Maggie could hear the water running and her brother's warbling tenor as he sang along to her shower radio. She smiled, in spite of herself. Reaching into the refrigerator, she took out a carton of eggs and began to methodically crack them into a large glass bowl. Her thoughts drifted and she found herself wondering if Julia was still asleep.

****

Julia sat up groggily, rubbing the back of her neck. The house was silent and still, and disappointment crashed down on her as she realized that she was alone. Squinting, she looked at the clock on the fireplace mantle and discovered that she'd been asleep for nearly two hours. That was surprising, since she wasn't usually prone to naps. There was a piece of paper on the coffee table. Its stark whiteness stood out against the dark wood. Julia picked it up and reached over to turn on a lamp, wincing as the bright light stabbed at her aching head.

Julia,
I didn't want to wake you. I had to go take care of something.
I'll be back as soon as I can. Hopefully before you wake up.

Maggie

Julia snorted softly. *'Yeah, right. She probably just got sick of babysitting you.'* She swallowed the bitterness rising in her throat and pushed herself up from the couch. No dizziness this time, just the same dull ache. That was a good sign, she mused. *'I guess my brains didn't turn to Jell-O after all.'* She was still abnormally tired, and the idea of her bed upstairs suddenly seemed very inviting. Moving carefully across the slippery hardwood floor, she made her way to the foot of the stairs. Gripping the banister for support, she climbed the steps, stopping at the top to catch her breath.

"I must be even more wiped out than I thought," she muttered. Julia prided herself on being in excellent physical condition, and the trip up the stairs shouldn't have been enough to wind her.

The doorway at the end of the hall led to her bedroom. It was large and spacious, mostly due to the lack of furniture. A mahogany four-poster bed loomed against one wall, a matching night table next to it. A tall armoire was the only other piece of furniture in the room. In her socks, Julia glided across the floor and sat down on the edge of her bed. She unbuttoned her olive green shirt and slid it off her shoulders, leaving herself in just her jeans and a black cotton bra. Gingerly, she probed at her injured ribs with her fingers, grimacing a little at the tenderness. A wave of lethargy passed over her, and she lay back on top of her sheets, too tired to finish undressing. Almost instantly, she was asleep again.

****

Maggie looked up from the kitchen sink as Patrick approached. His hair was still wet from the shower, and he was dressed in a pair of baggy red sweatpants that hung from his gaunt frame. His nose twitched at the familiar smell of smoke, and he chuckled.

"I burned the eggs a little bit," Maggie informed him ruefully as he took a seat at the small table.

She set a plate of toast and well-done scrambled eggs in front of him. She took two mugs from their hooks above the counter and filled them with coffee, handing one to her brother. Nibbling on a piece of wheat toast, Maggie watched as Patrick ravenously wolfed down his breakfast.

"Just like when we were kids." He grinned at her around a mouthful of eggs.

"Patrick, can I trust you to stay here for the rest of the day?"

"Sure."

Maggie sat down across from him and stared at him intently. "I mean it. I need you to stay here and stay out of trouble. I'm supposed to be looking after a sick friend, and I need to get back there."

Patrick's eyebrows shot up and he folded his arms across his bare chest. "Oh yeah? And what's this 'friend's' name?"

Maggie gave him a withering look as she sipped her coffee. "None of your business."

He laughed. "So it's a guy friend, huh?"

Maggie rolled her eyes, choosing not to answer him. She stood.

"You have my cell number if you need anything." Surprising him, she leaned over and kissed his forehead. "Please try not to get into any more trouble."

****
*

It was late morning when she walked up to Julia's front door again. She considered knocking, but she didn't want to wake Julia if she was still asleep. Instead, she pulled her friend's keys out of her pocket and opened the door herself. The drapes were still shut, and she had to pause in the foyer to let her eyes adjust to the dim light. Julia wasn't on the sofa anymore. Maggie cocked her head to one side, listening. Lines of worry creased her brow as all sorts of wild scenarios raced through her mind. What if Julia had woken up and her head had gotten worse? She could be passed out in one of the rooms. Or even worse, what if the man who had attacked her had returned?

Maggie searched the bottom floor first, her shoes sounding abnormally loud on the floor. There was no sign of Julia. Fear grew in the pit of her stomach as she cautiously climbed the stairs. She poked her head into Julia's office first, finding it exactly as she had left it. The door at the end of the hall was open. It hadn't been open earlier, had it? Maggie frowned, trying to remember. She froze in the doorway.

In the middle of the bed, Julia was lying on her back. Shirtless. Maggie watched, fascinated, as her tanned, flat stomach rose and fell with her steady breathing. On unsteady feet, barely aware of what she was doing, Maggie moved towards the bed. Asleep, Julia looked peaceful and relaxed. The bruises on her face and side already appeared to be fading. Slowly, Maggie's gaze traveled down the woman's long body.

"Maggie?"

Green eyes widened in horror and blood rushed to her cheeks. She tore her gaze away from Julia's navel and met a pair of curious blue eyes. Taking a step backwards, Maggie stammered nervously.

"I...I'm sorry. I came back and you weren't downstairs and, and I got worried...."

Julia sat up, smiling. "It's okay, Maggie. I'm glad you came back." She frowned, noticing that the blonde's eyes were firmly focused on the floor. "Is something wrong?"

Maggie glanced up shyly, blushing an even deeper shade of pink. She swallowed hard.

"You're, uh, you're not wearing a shirt," she mumbled.

Julia blinked and looked down at herself. She was, indeed, sitting there in her bra. *'Good going, Julia. No wonder she's so freaked out. She probably thinks you're trying to seduce her.'*

"Sorry, I wasn't expecting you to come back," she reached down for her discarded shirt, hissing in pain as she pulled at her injured side.

Maggie lunged forward, grabbing the tall woman's arm. Through clenched teeth, Julia gave her a wry grin.

"I'm okay . . . just twisted the wrong way."

Maggie didn't answer. Slowly, she slid her fingers up to Julia's shoulder. Julia sucked in a breath as her skin tingled at the contact. Reaching out, she touched Maggie's face, tilting her chin up until their eyes met. She expected to find confusion, maybe even a hint of fear. Instead, Maggie's eyes shone with warmth and desire. The hand on Julia's shoulder moved up the side of her neck, making her shiver. Careful not to touch the fading bruises, Maggie took Julia's face between her hands and leaned closer as Julia's hands found her waist.

Their lips met, gently at first, barely making contact. Caught off-guard, Julia let Maggie take the lead as the blonde eased herself onto the bed beside her. Thoroughly enjoying herself as the kiss intensified, she accepted Maggie's tentatively exploring tongue, tasting it with her own. She shivered again as hands glided past her shoulders, brushing past the curves of her breasts. Reluctantly, Julia pulled back. She searched the green eyes, just inches from her own.

"Are you sure this is what you want?" Her question was met by a dazzling smile.

"I'm sure," Maggie replied confidently. "Are you sure you're up to it? The doctor said to avoid strenuous activities," she teased.

Julia's lips curled into a sultry, predatory grin and her blue eyes twinkled wickedly.

"Well, then, I guess we'll just have to take this really slow."

Strong, sure hands tugged Maggie's t-shirt loose from the waistband of her jeans, slipping beneath the cotton to caress the warm flesh. Her injuries temporarily forgotten, Julia kissed and nibbled her way down Maggie's neck, her tongue tracing a lazy path across the blonde's collarbone. A soft moan told her that her efforts were appreciated, and she smiled against the soft skin beneath her lips. Desire threatened to overwhelm her. She could feel her need growing as she captured Maggie's lips again, crushing against them with her own. At the same time, Julia slowly slid her hand up Maggie's spine, deftly unhooking her bra. The smaller woman's breathing caught as Julia eased her thumbs beneath the cups and lightly stroked the hardening nipples. Julia broke the kiss and pulled her head back, blue eyes questioning.

"Are you okay?" she asked.

In response, Maggie threw her arms around Julia's neck and gently nibbled on the nearest earlobe, getting an appreciative groan from its owner. Craving the contact, she pressed her body closer, and as her hips shifted, her jeans rubbed against her in interesting places. She shuddered.

"Oh god, yes," she breathed into Julia's ear.

Julia found the edge of Maggie's shirt and lifted, pulling the fabric over the blonde's head. The white cotton bra quickly joined the shirt on the floor. Gently, she eased Maggie onto her back and stretched out beside her, ignoring the slight twinge in her side. Ducking her dark head, she began to place slow, teasing kisses around one of the blonde's breasts.

Maggie's eyes slid shut, and a sound halfway between a squeak and a moan escaped her throat as lips closed over her nipple. The tender flesh hardened inside Julia's mouth, and she could feel herself losing control of her own desire. Capturing the younger woman's nipple lightly between her teeth, she began to flick it with her tongue, slowly at first, and then increasing in speed until Maggie was gasping for air. Maggie tangled her fingers in the long, dark hair, losing herself in the sensations coursing through her. Trembling hands fumbled with the clasp to Julia's bra.

"Here, let me help you with that." Julia pushed herself up to a sitting position and hastily stripped away the rest of her clothes.

Naked, she stretched out on her side again, pressing herself against Maggie's hip as trusting, desire-filled green eyes gazed at her. She smiled as Maggie's hands began to wander across her bare body, never lingering in one place for very long.

"You can touch me, you know. I promise I won't break," she encouraged.

"I.... I know. It's just; I've never done this before. Not this far, anyway." Maggie confessed. "I'm not sure I know what to do."

Julia had suspected as much. "Ah. I'll walk you through it, then" She winked, getting a grin from the blonde.

Unbuttoning Maggie's jeans, she slowly worked the zipper down. Slipping her fingers under the waistband, she peeled back the denim and cotton as Maggie raised her hips to help. Carefully, Julia lowered her body until they were nearly touching, groaning in unrestrained pleasure as curious fingers explored her breasts, squeezing and kneading the firm flesh. She planted a line of kisses down the center of the blonde's body, pausing to languidly circle her navel with her tongue, tasting the faint saltiness of her skin. Smiling reassuringly up at the reporter, Julia parted Maggie's thighs, her fingers sliding through the wetness coating the sensitive skin. She dipped her head lower and Maggie cried out, arching her back as her new lover found her target.

"Oh my god."

A strangled moan escaped her as the leisurely licking and stroking coaxed her towards heights she had never before experienced. Unabashedly, Maggie spread her legs wider, her hips rocking in an unconscious rhythm. A thin film of sweat covered her body, and her thighs began to tremble. One hand clutched at the sheets, the other entwined itself in Julia's hair as the sensations built within her. Julia recognized the signs, and she increased her attentions, focusing on Maggie's most sensitive areas. Without stopping her hungry nibbling, she slid two long fingers into the reporter's slick center, drawing Maggie towards her climax. Inexplicably, tears streamed down Maggie's cheeks and soon, she couldn't contain herself any longer. She cried out again, and again, until she was left spent and shaking, wrapped in Julia's strong embrace.

"Okay, I've got you. Breathe, Maggie." Julia stroked her hair, pressing her lips against the blonde's temple.

"Easy for you to say," Maggie panted as she snuggled closer, reveling in the skin on skin contact.

Julia chuckled deep in her throat, the vibration tickling Maggie's ear. The laugh quickly turned into a gasp as a teasing tongue snaked out and playfully flicked her nipple. She looked down to find a pair of green eyes gazing at her impishly.

"Now let's see if I can take your breath away." Maggie said with a smirk.

Much later, they slept, still entangled in each other's arms. Julia rested flat on her back; her long arms securely folded around the small blonde nestled against her uninjured side. Even in sleep, a satisfied smile was plastered on Maggie's lips, her head pillowed on Julia's chest.

It was nearly dark outside when Maggie finally woke. Without opening her eyes, she could tell that Julia was still asleep as she listened to her lover's deep, even breathing. Her lover. She savored the words, rolling them around inside her mouth. Sighing happily, she wriggled closer to the warm, naked body wrapped around her own, simply enjoying the closeness. Julia mumbled something unintelligible in her sleep and tightened her hold on the blonde woman, but she didn't wake up.

Maggie pulled the soft flannel sheet up to her chin, covering them both with its warmth. Turning her head a fraction, she placed a gentle kiss on the breast beneath her cheek, smiling at the crease that appeared on Julia's forehead as she stirred. Still, she didn't wake. It was probably for the best, Maggie realized. Julia needed the rest; especially after all the energy she'd expended that afternoon. Maggie licked her lips, tasting the faint evidence of their recent lovemaking. She laughed softly to herself. She had a lover. A gorgeous, intelligent, sexy-as-hell lover that she was absolutely crazy about. Maggie paused, frowning. *'Crazy about? Where did that come from? Don't get too attached yet, Maggie, you barely even know each other. This could be an everyday occurrence for her.'* She didn't think that was true. She couldn't quite put her finger on it, but something about the way Julia looked at her suggested that this was more than some random fling. There was a deep longing in those blue eyes, and a strange familiarity that made Maggie forget that they'd only known each other for...*'god, has it really only been two days?'*

"Has what only been two days?" A sleepy voice inquired.

Maggie raised her head and met a pair of drowsy blue eyes. She grinned, embarrassed. "Sorry. Did I say that out loud?"

Julia stretched, wiggling her toes. "Either that, or I read your mind."

Laughing, Maggie leaned forward and pecked her lover on the lips. "You're a very talented woman. I wouldn't be surprised if you did." She kissed her again, longer this time, though both of them were still pleasantly sated. "I was just realizing that we've only known each other for two days."

"Best two days of my life," Julia replied without thinking.

Maggie snorted, amused. "Yeah, right. I'll bet you say that to all the girls."

Her offhand comment had been meant as a joke, and she was surprised to feel Julia's arms and shoulders stiffen around her. Disentangling an arm, she reached up to gently stroke her lover's cheek as Julia stared sightlessly at the ceiling.

"Hey, I'm sorry. I didn't mean to upset you."

Julia exhaled slowly. She was being overly sensitive, she knew. There was no way Maggie could have known how long it had been since anyone had shared her bed. Three years. More than one thousand long, lonely nights spent shutting out the rest of the world, teaching herself not to care about anyone or anything. The alternative was far too complicated, and Julia had vowed never to let anyone hurt her ever again. But then Maggie McKinnon had walked out of the fog, and into her life, and she could feel even her last line of defense crumbling. It made no sense, Julia told herself. They'd known each other for two days....she couldn't possibly be falling in love. Could she?

"Julia?" Maggie's concerned voice pulled her back to reality.

The blonde was staring at her, looking deeply worried, tears threatening to spill down her cheeks. A sad ghost of a smile flitted across Julia's lips and she brushed her fingertips against Maggie's lower eyelashes, capturing the salty tears. She hugged the young woman closer, burying her nose in her fair hair, and she let the thick walls around her heart collapse, toppled by the magnetic pull that Maggie had over her.

"I don't say that to all the girls," she said quietly. "In fact, there hasn't been anyone else in a long time."

"Really?" Maggie whispered.

"Really. And I meant what I said. These past couple of days have been.... incredible."

"For me, too." Maggie concurred.

They both fell silent, savoring the moment. The spell was broken by a loud, gurgling growl that rose from somewhere beneath the flannel sheets. Maggie blushed, giggling helplessly.

"Was that your stomach?" Julia asked, struggling to keep a straight face.

"I'm hungry!" Maggie explained. "I had an unexpected workout this afternoon."

Julia sighed good-naturedly, reaching for the phone on the nightstand. Without looking, she hit a button on the speed dial.

"Hi, it's Julia Cassinelli. I need a medium combination pizza delivered," she paused, listening to the person on the other end. "No, the home address. Twenty minutes, great. Thanks."

She set the phone back on the mahogany nightstand, squawking as Maggie rolled halfway on top of her. Playful green eyes sparkled down at her.

"Twenty minutes, huh? Wonder what we can do to pass the time."

Julia groaned as Maggie nuzzled the base of her throat. "Oh, I'm sure we'll think of something."

****

Chapter Seven

Patrick was sprawled on the floor of Maggie's apartment, his chin propped up on an overstuffed couch cushion. On the television screen in front of him, an animated coyote was building a rocket, the latest in a series of dastardly plots to capture his arch-nemesis. As usual, the plan backfired and the cartoon roadrunner scooted away, unscathed. Patrick laughed, shoving a handful of microwave popcorn into his mouth. It was about the only edible thing he could find in his sister's kitchen, other than a fuzzy green block that might have been cheese at one time.

During a commercial break, he rolled over onto his back, trying not to think about the plastic baggie stuffed into the toe of one of his shoes. Dark blond eyebrows knit together and he chewed his lower lip anxiously. He'd promised Maggie that he would be good. Patrick scowled, his mood darkening. Who the hell did she think she was, anyway? He was tired of being treated like a naughty child. Or as an after-thought.

When Patrick was seven, his older brother Jack, in a fit of adolescent rage over a broken skateboard, had told him that he was an accident. That their parents hadn't planned on having any more children after Maggie. The rest of his siblings had laughed, but Maggie had jumped to his defense, pummeling Jack with her 11-year old fists, forcing him to take it back. Patrick had known that it was true, though, and he had never forgotten it.

A loud knock on the front door startled him. Frowning, he scrambled to his feet, wondering if he should answer it. Maggie hadn't mentioned any visitors. On bare feet, he padded noiselessly to the door and carefully placed his eye to the peephole. A short, tattooed man with bulging muscles was pacing in front of the door. His inky black hair was slicked back and he was wearing sunglasses, even though it was almost dark outside. Patrick tugged at his goatee thoughtfully. The guy looked vaguely familiar.

"Yo, Patrick! You in there, or what?"

At the sound of the street-tough voice, something clicked. This was the guy he'd scored off of the night before. Eddie something. Grinning, Patrick opened the door.

"Hey, what are you doing here, man?" Patrick nodded at him, shivering a bit as the crisp bay breeze touched his bare chest. With a jerk of his head, he invited the other man inside.

Eddie Machado sauntered through the door, fairly oozing oily charm. He removed his sunglasses and hung them from the front of his tight white t-shirt. A smile revealed a flash of white teeth, and Patrick noticed that one of the front ones was badly chipped.

"You gave me your address last night, remember? Said you might be interested in some more of that shit I hooked you up with. That was some gooood shit, right?"

Patrick thought furiously. His memories of the party were still fuzzy, but he thought he remembered music and dancing. It had been hot and crowded inside the darkened warehouse. He definitely recalled buying a baggie of some truly excellent stuff from Eddie. Then he had made out with some blonde chick on the dance floor, her hands sliding inside his pants. Patrick shook himself. Not the right time for that memory to surface. He regarded Eddie curiously and had the feeling that Eddie had introduced him to the blonde with the wandering hands. He didn't remember giving out Maggie's address, but it wouldn't have been the first time he did something like that when he was high.

Fingers snapped impatiently in front of his face. "Hey! You in there?"

Patrick blinked. "Yeah. Sorry about that. Yeah, that was some really good shit."

Eddie beamed at him, nodding. "Hell yeah, it was. Listen, I know this guy, DC. Lives down on Mission where all the yuppies are moving in. He can hook you up, if you're interested."

Patrick thought for a moment. He didn't have any money left, though he wasn't sure where it had all gone. He knew he hadn't spent $350 on drugs. Someone had probably stolen the rest from him at the party. It wouldn't have been the first time that had happened to him either. Eddie seemed to sense his indecision.

"Don't worry about the cash, man. DC's a fair guy. He'll work something out for you."

Patrick licked his cracked, dry lips, already thinking about his next hit. He nodded.

"Okay. Just lemme get dressed."

Leaving Eddie prowling around the living room, Patrick pulled a set of fresh clothes out of his bag and disappeared into Maggie's bedroom. It wouldn't hurt to meet with this DC guy, he reasoned. If he didn't like the terms, he could just say no. He emerged from the bedroom, dressed in a pair of worn khakis and an ancient Cleveland Browns sweatshirt. Eddie grinned at him as he put his sunglasses back on and led the way out the door.

****
****

"Hang on, I'm coming!" Julia yelled down the stairs as the doorbell chimed a second time.

"I thought you already did that. Twice, as a matter of fact." Maggie smirked at her unrepentantly, causing an unexpected flush on the dark-haired woman's cheeks.

Julia turned from where she was pulling a bathrobe out of her closet and gaped at the young blonde in amazement.

"Sshh. You're terrible." She grinned fondly at Maggie, who was looking her up and down with open admiration.

"Hmm. Well, you're gorgeous," Maggie breathed happily.

Julia was completely flustered and her blush deepened at the compliment. She shook her head, speechless, as she wrapped a thick bathrobe around herself and hurried downstairs. Her leather jacket was thrown casually over the banister at the foot of the stairs, and she fished in the inner pocket for a $20 bill.

"Hi, Hector. You're right on time, as usual," she greeted the gawky teenage pizza boy.

"Always," Hector agreed solemnly. "Did I wake you up, Ms. Cassinelli? You look like you just got out of bed."

Julia coughed into her fist. "Uh, yeah. Something like that." She took the hot cardboard box from the boy and handed him the money, waving him off as he started to dig in his pockets. "Keep the change."

Hector smiled. He loved delivering here. Unlike many of the people he delivered to regularly, Ms. Cassinelli was always nice to him, and more often than not, she let him keep the change.

"Thanks, Ms. Cassinelli," he called over his shoulder as he bounded down the front steps towards the scooter parked haphazardly at the curb.

"Have a good night, Hector. Drive safe," Julia called back.

Something caught her eye in the neatly kept flowerbed next to the steps. It was the morning newspaper, half-hidden beneath the lilies.

"Oh, hey. I bet Maggie's story is in there," she murmured as she descended the steps to retrieve the paper. She set it on top of the pizza box and headed back inside, pausing to pull two bills and another annoying credit card offer out of her mailbox. She stopped in the foyer, smiling up at Maggie, fully dressed, coming down the stairs.

"Pizza's here," she said, holding up the box.

Maggie eyes brightened. "Good. I'm starved."

"Heh. Can't imagine why," Julia returned, leading the way to living room.

She turned on the light, revealing more of the room than Maggie had been able to see earlier. As in the rest of the house, dark cherry floors gleamed at her. The long, black leather sofa took up most of one wall, facing a big screen TV. An antique rocking chair sat in the corner, next to a cozy fireplace. Maggie sat down in the chair, running her hands over the polished wood.

"Oooh. I bet this is comfortable in the winter. Get a nice fire going, curl up with a book."

Julia swept aside a scattering of magazines on the coffee table and set the pizza down.

"Yeah, it is. Only in my case, it's usually a case file instead of a book." She pushed an unruly lock of hair back from her face. "I'll get some plates and stuff. Is iced tea okay?"

"Sounds great."

While Julia was occupied in the kitchen, Maggie examined the contents of her bookshelves. Lots of heavy law books alongside a few worn paperbacks. Mysteries mostly, she noted. A vast CD collection containing selections from just about every musical genre filled two shelves. Each disc was categorized by genre and then alphabetized. A smaller DVD collection, dominated by science fiction and horror titles, took up another shelf.

Maggie wandered over to the other side of the room. The fireplace mantle was empty, except for a single, framed photograph. It was a picture of a woman, tall and striking with midnight hair swept back from her face and piercing blue eyes. She was smiling and happy, standing on the beach, the ocean behind her.

Julia watched from the doorway. "My mother," she supplied quietly.

Maggie spun around, startled. She hadn't heard Julia return. "You look like her." She walked over and took the two glasses of iced tea from her, setting them on the coffee table.

Julia handed her a plate. "She died when I was very young. That picture was taken the week before."

"I'm so sorry, Julia. That must have been really hard for you, growing up without a mother."

Julia shrugged noncommittally, seating herself on the sofa. She patted the space next to her.

"I never really thought about it," she lied blandly. "Come on and eat before the pizza gets cold."

Maggie joined her on the sofa as Julia turned on the TV and began flipping through channels until she found an entertainment news program. They each took two slices of the warm, gooey pizza, and Maggie was glad that Julia had thought to grab extra napkins. 'Although the alternatives are interesting too.' A blonde eyebrow rose thoughtfully as she noticed a spot of pizza sauce near the corner of Julia's mouth. Leaning over, she licked it clean.

"You had a little bit of sauce there," she explained, getting a bemused chuckle from the taller woman. "Hey, is that today's paper?" Maggie switched gears, noticing the rolled up newspaper on the table.

Julia pushed it over towards her. "Yep. Think there's anything interesting in it?"

Maggie grinned and seized the paper, opening it with as much excitement as a child on Christmas morning. Quickly, she thumbed through the pages until she reached the local news section. There it was on page two . . .her byline. The story had been pared down a bit to fit in the allotted space, but most of her words were still intact. She reminded herself to thank Jessica for the great editing job. '*Jessica. The paper.*'

"Oh shit!" Maggie smacked her forehead, her outburst nearly causing Julia to spill her drink. "I have to make a quick phone call. I haven't checked in at work all day."

"See, that's one of the advantages of being your own boss. You never have to check in with anybody," Julia laughed. "Use the phone in the kitchen."

"Okay, thanks. I'll be right back."

Maggie hurried down the hall towards the kitchen, her socks sliding precariously along the polished floor. She couldn't believe she had gone all day without bothering to check in at work. Picking up the cordless phone, she glanced at the clock on the microwave. Probably ought to check up on Patrick, too, she mused. Dialing from memory, she punched in Jessica's extension, waiting as the phone rang six times before a slightly breathless voice answered.

"Hello, Jessica Sato."

"Hi, Jess. It's Maggie."

The sound of crinkling papers came through the receiver, and Maggie could picture her friend, perched on the edge of her desk like usual. Jessica never seemed to use a chair if there was something else she could sit on.

"Maggie? It's about time! I was getting ready to send out a search party, or something."

Maggie laughed, hopping up onto one of the high barstools next to the counter. She swiveled back and forth while she talked.

"Yeah, I know. I got kind of tied up with something. Sam wasn't looking for me, was he? I told him I would be at home today if he needed me."

"Not really, although he was surprised you didn't at least call in to gloat about your big story. Congratulations, by the way. I did hear him bellowing something about that Halloween piece, though. He said it better be Pulitzer-worthy, for as long as you're taking on it."

Maggie rolled her eyes, used to her editor's blustering. "Tell him not to worry. It'll get done." She stopped spinning on the barstool and rested her elbows on the black tile counter. "By the way, thanks for the editing job. You made me look really good."

"Oh, as if," Jessica snorted. "You did that all by yourself, Maggie."

A strident voice cut through the background, and Maggie groaned out loud, recognizing Catherine's haughty tones. Jessica yelped, and then there was a muffled commotion, ending with Catherine wresting the phone out of the junior copy editor's hands.

"McKinnon, is that you?" Catherine's voice seethed with irritation. She didn't bother to wait for Maggie to respond. "I bumped into your drooling idiot of a brother outside the building and he spilled coffee all over me. Practically ruined my new shoes."

Maggie pressed her forehead against the cool counter, blocking out most of Catherine's tirade. Obviously, someone had told the arrogant redhead who Patrick was. She waited until Catherine was forced to take a breath.

"Look, I'm sorry about your shoes, okay? My brother wasn't feeling well and I'm sure he didn't mean to spill your coffee." Maggie attempted to mollify the angry woman. "Just give me the bill for whatever got damaged, and I'll take care of it."

"Hmph. Well, I guess that's the absolute least you can do." The phone slammed down on the desk, and Maggie could hear Catherine's heels as she stomped away.

Quickly, Jessica retrieved the phone. "She's such a bitch," she said disgustedly. "You're too nice to her. I would've told her exactly where she could stick those heels of hers." Jessica paused, listening to Maggie's laughter on the other end. "So, I take it that you aren't at home then?" she asked delicately.

"Um, not exactly. I'm sort of looking after a friend," Maggie replied, grinning broadly.

"Uh-huh. And would this friend be tall, dark hair, blue eyes to die for?"

"Maybe," Maggie drawled, playing along.

"That's what I thought. So, I bet she looks really good naked, huh?"

"Yeah," Maggie sighed dreamily. She bolted upright, sputtering indignantly as she realized she had been tricked. "Hey!"

Her outrage was met by peals of laughter, and she scowled grumpily. "That wasn't fair, Jess."

"Aw, c'mon, Maggie. I'm happy for you. I think you were the only woman in the city getting less than me. Now spill, I want details."

"Not a chance. Gotta go Jess, sorry. Bye." Maggie hung up on her friend, ignoring Jessica's protests.

Maggie set the phone down on the counter and rubbed at her burning cheeks. She couldn't believe Jessica had the nerve to ask her for details about her sex life. She'd never been comfortably talking about that sort of thing, though her college roommate had insisted on telling her about each and every encounter with her boyfriend, Maggie remembered wryly. Resting her chin on her hands, she replayed her afternoon with Julia in her mind. She certainly hadn't been shy then, she realized with a start, her lips twitching into a sultry grin. *Maggie McKinnon, where did you learn how to do those things?* Her smile broadened at the sound of footsteps in the hall, and she swiveled around, as Julia appeared a few feet away.

"Just getting some more iced tea," she said, holding up her empty glass as evidence. "Everything okay at work?"

"More or less. Although I'm gonna have to buy Catherine Richards a new pair of shoes. Apparently, my brother spilled coffee on her shoes this morning."

Julia cast a surprised look over her shoulder as she refilled her drink. "Your brother? He's okay, then?"

"More or less," Maggie repeated. "He turned up at the paper this morning. That's why I had to sneak out of here earlier. He's fine, I guess. He swears he's going to clean up, but I don't know. I've heard his promises before." She picked up the phone again. "I need to check up on him. God knows what kind of trouble he could be in by now."

"Oh, okay. I'll give you some privacy." Julia started to move away, stopping as Maggie grabbed her arm as she passed.

"Stay. Please," Maggie said softly, her fingers lightly encircling the other woman's wrist.

Julia hesitated for a moment, unsure if she should intrude on what was obviously a family matter, but the pleading look in those green eyes tugged at her heart. Maggie needed her to stay, and that was all that mattered. Silently, she took a seat on the other barstool and propped her elbow up on the counter. Her other hand rested on Maggie's thigh, and she squeezed encouragingly as her lover took a deep breath and dialed.

The phone rang. No answer. Maggie's eyes closed and her stomach dropped. Patrick wasn't there. '*Ok, wait, maybe he's asleep or in the shower. Give him a few more seconds,*' she told herself as the fifth ring sounded in her ear. Her answering machine clicked on, and she ground her teeth in frustration while she listened to the sound of her own scratchy, muffled voice on the outgoing message. Julia had inched closer, and recognizing Maggie's tension, she began rubbing the blonde's lower back. The answering machine beeped.

"Patrick, are you there? Pick up the phone, dammit!" Maggie felt her temper slipping away from her. Anger flashing in her eyes, she turned to Julia.

"He's not there," she said, disgusted.

Maggie hit the off button as the irritation built inside her. She had asked her brother to stay out of trouble for one day. Just one day. He had been in San Francisco for less than a week, and he was already turning her life upside-down. Just like he had before. She wasn't going to let him do it again, she vowed silently. Not when her future suddenly looked so bright.

Julia watched the mix of emotions play across her lover's face, darkening her usually cheerful countenance. Clearly, there was a history between Maggie and her brother that she knew nothing about. Julia reviewed her last thought with a wry grin. There was a lot about Maggie that she didn't know, given that they had only met a short time before. She promised herself that she would work on fixing that situation immediately.

"Son. Of. A. BITCH!" Maggie burst out suddenly, slamming the receiver down against the tile counter so hard that the plastic cracked.

Julia jerked backwards, nearly toppling off her barstool. Waves of fury radiated from the young blonde who was now pacing angrily around her dining room. Frozen in place, Julia watched as Maggie muttered to herself, her hands gesturing forcefully. She tried desperately to think of an appropriate response. People skills had never been one of her strong points. She slid down from her barstool and warily approached the fuming blonde.

"Um, Maggie?" She began slowly.

"Why did he come here? Why can't he just leave me alone?" Maggie asked, teetering on the edge of tears.

Julia stepped forward and pulled Maggie into a tight hug. At first, Maggie resisted the comforting embrace, but as Julia's lips tenderly brushed the top of her head, her anger began to melt away. The tears started then, increasing until she was sobbing like a heartbroken child. Through it all, Julia held her and rubbed her back gently until her sobs had slowed to faint hiccups. Maggie tucked her head beneath Julia's chin, resting her cheek against the taller woman's chest. She frowned, listening to her lover's pained, shallow breaths. Suddenly, she remembered Julia's bruised ribs.

"Oh God, Julia. I'm so sorry. Why didn't you tell me I was hurting you?" Maggie pulled away quickly, angry with herself for forgetting Julia's injuries.

Julia caught her hand and lifted it to her lips, kissing the backs of her knuckles. "Shhh. It's okay. You didn't hurt me."

Gently, she wrapped her arms around Maggie's shoulders again and wished she could take away her lover's pain. She hadn't met Patrick McKinnon yet, but Julia was beginning to like him less and less, and she silently vowed to protect Maggie from her brother. Maggie mumbled something against her chest.

"What was that?" Julia asked, tilting the blonde's chin up.

Maggie sniffled, scrubbing at her tear-stained cheeks with the back of her hand. "I'm sorry I broke your phone," she repeated mournfully, staring past Julia's shoulder.

Unable to help herself, Julia started to laugh. After a moment of confusion, Maggie joined in, leaning against the taller woman until they were both giggling helplessly. The tension around them dissolved, and with one arm draped across the blonde's shoulders, Julia led the way back to the living room.

"Don't worry about the phone. I can always get a new one," she said, guiding Maggie to the sofa. She was about to resume her seat in front of the television when Maggie stopped her.

"Wait." Maggie bit her lip as she searched frantically for the right words to describe what she was feeling. It was crazy. She made her living as a writer, but now, when it was important, her mind was a complete blank.

"Maggie? What is it?"

Fear tightened around Julia's chest, and, irrationally, she began to wonder if the reporter had changed her mind about their relationship. She swallowed hard, bracing herself for the blow. Inhaling deeply, Maggie took both of Julia's hands in her own.

"I just want to thank you for everything you've done for me," Maggie began. She shook her head, cutting off Julia's protests. "Wait, there's more. I know I shouldn't say this. I shouldn't even feel this. It's too soon." She paused, steeling herself. "I think.... no, I know.... that I'm falling in love with you."

Maggie watched as the color drained from Julia's face and blue eyes widened in astonishment. Julia swayed slightly, blinking rapidly, and Maggie feared that she was about to faint. Carefully, she helped Julia sit down on the sofa. As she seated herself on the edge of the coffee table, Julia opened her mouth to speak. At first, nothing but a faint squeak emerged. Maggie smiled as her friend stammered nervously.

"Maggie.... I..."

Leaning forward, she placed two fingers on Julia's lips, silencing her. "You don't have to say anything."

Gently, Julia took her hand and kissed the palm, sending a warm shiver through the blonde's body. Oblivious to her bruised and tender ribs, she pulled Maggie into her lap, wrapping her arms securely around the younger woman's waist. Her inner voice screamed inside her head, telling her to return the sentiment. Taking a deep breath to steady herself, Julia summoned every ounce of courage she could muster.

"I love you too," she whispered, scarcely believing that she was saying the words out loud.

It had been three years since Julia had opened her heart to anyone. Not since that awful day when she had come home early and found her lover, Kirsten, in bed with someone else. She had tried then, but it had been too late to save their relationship, and Kirsten had simply laughed at her awkward declaration of love. She still remembered the harsh words and the cruel, mocking tone. "*You love me? Don't make me laugh, Jules. You're great in bed, babe, but you're incapable of love. You have the emotional range of an ice cube. I'm sick of it and I'm sick of you. I can find plenty of other people who are just as great in bed. Hell, my vibrator gets the same results.*" With that, Kirsten had stormed out of the house, setting off a nasty chain of events that led Julia to swear off love for good. Until now. Julia shoved the bad memories of her time with Kirsten into a dusty corner of her mind and locked the door on them.

Maggie was staring at her, a look of utter disbelief on her face. "Did you just say what I think you said?"

"I don't know. What do you think I said?"

"Hey, don't play games with me, Cassinelli." Maggie punched her lightly in the shoulder. "What did you just say?"

Julia cleared her throat as a slightly embarrassed, lopsided smile spread across her face. "I love you, Maggie," she said firmly. The words had never sounded so right.

Maggie beamed in wonder as the words penetrated her brain. Julia loved her. It was a dizzying, exhilarating feeling --- like standing at the edge of a cliff. Only she knew that Julia would keep her safe and never let her fall.

"Oh," she murmured, gazing intently into those brilliant blue eyes.

"Oh!" A different tone this time, as insistent fingers wormed their way beneath her waistband. A small sigh escaped her and she scooted closer, eager for the touch.

"Aren't you tired yet?" She teased, tilting her head back as teeth nibbled at her throat.

Julia lifted her dark head and grinned at her devilishly, her eyes twinkling. "Nah. I work out."

"Hmm. Good to know. Whaddya say we test that stamina?" A blonde eyebrow arched suggestively and curious hands slipped inside the thick folds of Julia's bathrobe.

A low, sultry laugh was her only answer, and without realizing how, Maggie was lying on the sofa. Julia knelt above her, straddling her hips.

"The pizza's gonna get cold," Maggie pointed out reasonably.

Julia shrugged. "That's why God invented microwaves."

Maggie started to laugh, giddy with pure happiness. She put all other thoughts out of her mind, focusing her attention on the woman smiling down at her. *So this is what love feels like. I think I like it. Yeah, definitely.* Reaching out, she tugged on the belt to Julia's bathrobe.

"C'mere you."

Laughter filled the room and quickly turned to low, passionate moans --- followed by a scream or two. Julia winced inwardly for a moment and wondered what the neighbors were going to think. *'Oh, who the hell cares?'*

****

Erin Jennifer Mar

Chapter Eight

Patrick leaned back in the passenger seat of the red Camaro, one arm dangling out of the open window. The heavy bass in the music blaring from the stereo was making the whole car vibrate, and Patrick nodded along with it. He stole a sideways glance at Eddie Machado and wondered briefly how the muscular, tattooed man could drive at night with those dark sunglasses plastered to his head. Eddie took a long drag from his cigarette and flicked the glowing orange butt out the window. Both men laughed and hollered wildly as they sped through a red light and narrowly missed two cars.

The cool night air whipped past them as they careened through traffic, weaving in and out of the lanes. Honking horns and shouted curses drifted their way, but neither man cared. For a moment, Patrick thought about his sister. Maggie was going to be furious with him when she found out he had left again. He shrugged and took a swig from the beer bottle in his left hand. She would get over it. She always did. Idly, he opened the glove compartment. He jerked his hand back in surprise when Eddie reached over and slammed it shut. Eddie glowered at him menacingly. At least, Patrick thought he did; it was hard to read the other man's expression behind his sunglasses.

"Yo, dude, stay out of there," Eddie warned.

Patrick nodded agreeably, dangling his arm out the window again. He didn't want to upset his new friend, especially since Eddie was hooking him up with his dealer. The last thing Patrick wanted to do was blow his chance at some really good stuff. He decided to forget about the gun in Eddie's glove compartment.

After a lengthy drive, they pulled up at the wrought-iron gates of a sprawling mansion. Confused, Patrick tried to get his bearings. He had no idea where Eddie had taken him, though he suspected that they were no longer in the city.

In his little booth, the security guard nodded at Eddie and pressed a button. Slowly, the gates swung inward and Eddie drove up the long driveway, gravel crunching beneath his tires.

"C'mon, man," Eddie said, hopping out of the car and starting towards the imposing front doors.

"Where the hell are we?" Patrick asked. "I thought this guy lived in town."

"He does. This is his girlfriend's place," Eddie replied. He glanced at Patrick, who was gaping at the enormous estate, his eyes practically bulging out of his head.

"Look, just keep your mouth shut when we get in there, okay? Let me do the talking."

Patrick nodded, following Eddie up the steps. He wished he had dressed better for the occasion, but a glance at his companion told him that it probably didn't matter. Eddie rang the doorbell, and they waited for several long minutes while the sonorous tones reverberated throughout the house. Finally, they heard slow footsteps approaching and a hulking man in a neatly pressed suit opened the door. The man gave Eddie a contemptuous look and barely glanced in Patrick's direction.

"He's out back," the man grunted at them, standing aside so they could enter.

Patrick gawked openly at the expensive furniture and the artwork on the walls as he followed Eddie to the rear of the house. They exited through a set of double doors and found themselves standing on the terrace. A vast, plush green lawn spread out before them, and to the left, under a set of lights, a man was practicing on a putting green. He looked up as they drew near and rested his golf club on his shoulder. He was a few inches shorter than Patrick, but more athletic-looking. Pushing his tousled, sandy hair out of his friendly hazel eyes, he watched as they approached. He smiled at them and stepped forward to shake Eddie's hand warmly.

"Eddie, good to see you, man." His eyes flicked to Patrick curiously.

"This is Patrick, the guy I told you about last night." Eddie made the introductions. "Patrick, this is DC."

"Right. Patrick." DC held his hand out, and Patrick took it. He was mildly surprised by the man's crushing grip. "Have a seat, guys. I'll have Gloria bring some drinks." He indicated a table on the terrace and nodded to a middle-aged woman waiting near the doors.

"So, Patrick, Eddie tells me you might be interested in coming to work for me," DC said after they were seated. He settled back in his chair, casually resting one ankle across his knee.

Patrick looked at him, then at Eddie uncertainly. No one had mentioned anything to him about a job. He shifted nervously in his chair. Gloria returned with a tray of imported beers and the distraction gave him a few extra minutes to think.

"Um, I don't know. What kind of work?" Patrick asked.

DC and Eddie exchanged a look. "I operate several warehouses in the city. I'm always looking for reliable guys to help unload merchandise. That sort of thing."

"Oh. Yeah, I could do that." Patrick said, relieved. He had been worried that DC was going to ask him to deal or something. That was a line he had promised himself he would not cross.

"Good. That's very good, Patrick." DC smiled at him. "It's hard work, but I think you'll find the pay is worth it. Plus, there are a few perks."

DC produced a plastic baggie from his pocket and tossed it on the table in front of Patrick. He met Patrick's gaze and nodded once, indicating that he should take it. He smiled again, exposing two rows of perfectly straight, white teeth as Patrick pocketed the drugs.

"Excellent," DC grinned, sounding very pleased. With a wave of his hand, he beckoned Gloria over. "Gloria, this is Patrick. He's going to be working for me. Would you take him inside, please? Have Tom get him set up." He glanced at Patrick. "I believe you met Tom Becker on your way in. He's my right hand guy. He'll get you all taken care of."

"Oh, okay." Patrick stood. "Listen thanks Mr....." he trailed off uncertainly.

"Just call me DC," Patrick's new employer continued to grin at him like a Cheshire cat.

DC watched until Patrick disappeared into the house. He turned to Eddie, all traces of good humor gone from his face. His eyes, friendly and engaging just moments before, went flat and cold. Eddie took a long swallow of the dark German beer that his employer preferred. He jumped, spilling the amber liquid down the front of his shirt as DC swatted the sunglasses from his head. The false bravado slipped for a split second and fear shone in his eyes.

"Take those damn things off." DC demanded. "What do you know about this guy?"

Eddie shrugged, composing himself quickly. "He's a junkie, for starters. He was already wasted by the time I found him at that rave last night."

"Yeah, that much is pretty obvious. Did you see him light up when I tossed that shit in front of him? Thought he was gonna cream his shorts right here. Loser." DC spat, disgusted. "What about his background? Anyone gonna come looking for him?"

"Nah," Eddie said. "He's from some small town in Ohio. He has a sister out here, but from what he says, she's pretty busy. Probably won't even miss him. He's your guy, DC."

"He'd better be. For your sake," DC snarled, eyes glinting dangerously.

Gloria, DC's housekeeper, led Patrick down a long hallway. His dirty running shoes sank into the thick carpet, and he was acutely aware of his scruffy appearance. He swore internally at Eddie, wishing the man had told him where they were going. He would have dressed better. Everything in the house screamed of money.

Gloria stopped in front of a door, and Patrick nearly crashed into her back. He mumbled an apology, grinning sheepishly as a flush crept up his neck. The housekeeper regarded him impassively for a moment. Shaking her head sadly, she pointed at the door and walked away, leaving Patrick alone in the corridor. Patrick pushed up the sleeves on his faded sweatshirt and knocked on the door.

"Yeah." A gruff voice barked at him from within.

Patrick tentatively opened the door. The same hulking man he'd seen earlier was pouring himself a drink at a well-stocked bar. As Patrick stood quivering in the doorway, Tom Becker swirled the golden Scotch in his glass, listening as the ice cubes clinked together. He took an appreciative sip, letting the smooth alcohol slide down his throat and warm his stomach, while he eyed the other man speculatively. Tom wasn't especially tall, but what he lacked in height, he made up for in sheer bulk. The expensive suit he wore was stretched tight over his powerful frame, and his massive hands looked as if they could crush Patrick's throat with an effortless squeeze.

Patrick fought the urge to turn and run away. "Uh, DC said I should come see you."

The brawny man grunted. "You came in with that Machado punk, right?" He didn't wait for a response as he poured himself another drink. "I don't know why DC keeps taking in pathetic scum like you. Siddown."

Patrick did as he was told, taking a seat in front of a large desk. He waited nervously while Tom tossed back his second Scotch. Finally, the big man circled around him, like a jungle cat stalking its prey, and sat down behind the desk. He tore a sheet off a memo pad and scribbled something on it, pushing the paper over to Patrick.

"Show up at that address tomorrow. Seven a.m.. Don't be late."

Tom opened a drawer and took out a bundled stack of crisp one hundred dollar bills. Licking his thumb, he counted out ten and laid them on the desk. It was more cash than Patrick had ever had at one time, and he could smell the newness of the bills. Waving his hand, Tom indicated that Patrick should take them. Quickly, before Tom could change his mind, Patrick snatched the money and shoved it into his pocket.

"That's an advance on this week's salary." Tom advised him. "Where are you living?"

"My sister's place. It's in the Richmond district, I think," Patrick offered hesitantly.

Tom shook his head. "No good." He paused to think for a moment. "Okay, listen. You're gonna move into one of the guest rooms here. You call you sister and tell her you're fine, but don't tell her where you are. She wouldn't understand anyway, right?"

Patrick agreed readily. Maggie definitely wouldn't understand this. He didn't think he understood this either, exactly, but he certainly wasn't going to turn down $1,000 a week. Reaching for the phone that Tom was offering him, he paused, frowning.

"What's the problem?" Tom asked, his flinty eyes narrowing.

A cold sweat trickled down Patrick's back and under his arms. He was scared to death of Tom Becker. He swallowed hard.

"I…I don't remember her number."

Tom gave him a disgusted look and yanked the phone out of his hands. His thick fingers punched the numbers so hard that Patrick thought they would break.

"Yeah, I need a number in San Francisco for a." He looked at Patrick. "What's your sister's name?"

"Maggie. I mean, Megan. Megan McKinnon." Patrick wasn't sure which name his sister would be listed under.

"Maggie or Megan McKinnon," Tom repeated, waiting as the operator searched for the number. He nodded, carefully writing on another scrap of paper. "Thanks."

Tom dialed Maggie's phone number himself and thrust the receiver at Patrick. "Here."

Several cover stories rushed through Patrick's mind as he took the phone. Maggie was bound to ask a bunch of questions that he couldn't answer. He breathed a sigh of relief when the answering machine picked up.

"Hey, Mags. It's me. Look, I know you're pissed, but I just wanted to let you know that I'm okay. I found someplace else to stay so I won't cause you any more trouble, okay? Bye." He set the phone back on the desk and wiped his sweaty palms on his pants.

Tom Becker stared at him, a disdainful sneer on his face. Hoisting his bulky frame out of his chair, he loomed over Patrick, close enough to smell the sour sweat that was pouring off the nervous young man. Patrick was clearly terrified and the corner of Tom's mouth lifted in a satisfied smirk. Crooking a finger at Patrick, he started towards the door.

"Follow me."

Tom led him upstairs to a guest room at the back of the house. It was large and neat, with an adjoining bathroom containing fresh towels and a new toothbrush. There was a television and a clock radio, but no windows and no telephone. Still, the queen-sized bed looked soft and inviting, especially after the couch in Maggie's apartment.

"This is your room," Tom said brusquely. "Be ready to leave by 6:30 tomorrow morning. Someone will drive you to the warehouse."

Abruptly, Tom shut the door, leaving Patrick alone in his new surroundings. Patrick started toward the bed when a soft click sounded behind him. Whirling around, his stomach heading for his feet, he gripped the doorknob. It wouldn't turn. He had been locked in.

As panic began to set in, Patrick backed away until his knees hit the edge of the bed. He sat down with a thump, bouncing a little on the mattress. Scratching furiously at his goatee, he tried to force himself to calm down. There was probably a perfectly good reason why he had been locked in this room. He just couldn't think of any at the moment.

****

Maggie opened her eyes two minutes before the alarm was set to go off. Blinking to clear her sleep-blurred vision, she stretched an arm out and flipped the switch to the off position. The cool plastic cube felt strange under her fingertips, and she suddenly remembered that it was not her clock. She was not in her own bed, and she definitely was not alone. She lightly stroked the arm that circled her waist, smiling as Julia's fingers flexed in response. Work was the last place Maggie wanted to be this morning.

Sighing regretfully, she slid out from under Julia's arm. The weather was starting to turn, and Maggie wrapped her arms around herself, shivering, but happy. There was no good explanation for why she and Julia had clicked so completely. It defied all logic. They had just met, and yet, it was as if she had been looking for Julia all her life. Someone who made her feel wanted and safe. Someone who cared for her without asking anything in return. She smiled down at her sleeping lover as memories of the previous night surfaced --- Julia, slowly and tenderly making love to her, her hands and lips all over her body. Maggie's stomach fluttered as the rest of her body was instantly jolted awake.

"Ok, enough of that," she scolded herself. "Gotta go to work. Now where the heck are my clothes?"

She thought hard, her forehead wrinkling in concentration. Downstairs. Her clothes were downstairs on the living room floor where they had been so hastily abandoned. She headed for the bedroom door, stopping when a warm hand grabbed the back of her thigh. Turning, she found a pair of sleepy blue eyes gazing up at her.

"Hey, where ya going?" Julia mumbled petulantly, trying to draw the blonde back into bed.

Maggie leaned down and kissed the bridge of her nose. "Good morning to you, too. I have to go get dressed and go to work."

Julia pouted, poking her lower lip out comically. She shook her dark, disheveled head and tried to pull Maggie back to bed again. Maggie laughed, slapping her hands away playfully.

"Stop that! I have to go get dressed. It's cold out here." Goosebumps covered her body, and her teeth were starting to chatter.

Propping herself up on one elbow, Julia stretched her other hand out and traced a slow spiral around one of Maggie's breasts. The blonde gasped as the wandering fingers hit their mark.

"There are certain advantages to keeping it cold in here," Julia gave her a seductive grin. "Besides, it's nice and warm under the covers." She patted the bed invitingly.

Maggie backed out of reach. "Don't tempt me. I have to go to work today," she said firmly.

"Oh, all right, then," Julia said, letting out an exaggerated sigh as she threw the blankets back. She winced as the cold air hit her bare body. "Whoa, you weren't kidding. It's freezing out here."

She slid out of bed, dragging the flannel sheet with her. Pulling Maggie into her arms, she folded the sheet around them both and kissed the young woman soundly.

"Come on, let's go get you dressed." Still wrapped in the sheet, she tugged Maggie toward the door.

Laughing, Maggie stumbled along with her, trying to keep their feet from tangling together. "I can let myself out, you know. You don't have to get up."

"I want to. I have stuff to do today, anyway." They had reached the top of the stairs.

"If we fall down the stairs and you hurt yourself, it's gonna be your own fault," Maggie warned.

Julia grinned, hearing the challenge in Maggie's voice. "Guess we'd better not fall then."

They made it downstairs in one piece, and Maggie extricated herself from the sheet. She dressed hurriedly while Julia curled up on the sofa. Sitting on the edge of the coffee table, Maggie put on her socks and fished her shoes out from underneath the sofa.

"So what are you doing today?" she asked.

Julia yawned and stretched luxuriously. "I have a case to work on, remember?"

Maggie thought for a moment.... the Netsports burglary. She nodded. "Right. Well, take it easy, okay? You're not supposed to do too much."

Julia rolled her eyes. "Yes, mother. I'm just gonna make some calls. I want to talk to Danny again, see if he remembers anything else yet." She paused, grinning wickedly. "Besides, if I could survive the workout you put me through last night, I think I can handle just about anything."

Maggie blushed and fidgeted awkwardly. "Yeah. Last night was.... incredible. All of it."

"For me too," Julia assured her, following Maggie to the front door.

"I have to stop at home and grab a shower. Maybe Patrick turned up again." She shrugged, not wanting to go into it any further at the moment. She glanced up shyly. "I'll, uh, call you later?"

"You'd better."

Lowering her head, Julia kissed her. Totally oblivious to the fact that she was clad in nothing but a sheet, she stood on the porch and watched Maggie get into her car. The engine roared to life, and Maggie lifted a hand to wave before speeding away into the early morning gloom. Julia waved back, waiting until the car had disappeared from view before turning back to the house. There was surprisingly little fog, but a brisk wind was blowing inland and dark storm clouds loomed to the west. Rain was on the way, Julia noted sourly. She sighed, pulling the sheet tighter around her body.

"Oh well. It's better than the damn fog."

Chapter Nine

Drying her long hair with a towel as she moved, Julia hurried down the stairs. She had just stepped out of the shower when someone had started banging on her front door. Throwing the damp towel over her shoulder, she ran her fingers through her dark tangles and pressed her eye to the peephole in the door. A short, stocky Asian man stood on her front porch, his image distorted by the glass.

"What are you doing here, Henry?" Julia opened the door, greeting the police inspector.

Without being asked, Henry Chow edged past Julia into the entryway. With an exasperated sigh, Julia shut the door behind him and ushered Henry into the living room. He sank down on the sofa, stretching his arms across the back as he regarded her calmly.

"I hear you ran into some trouble recently," he said finally.

Crossing her arms, Julia leaned against the corner of the bookcase. "Nothing I couldn't handle," she replied, a hint of irritation in her voice.

"Yeah, you handled it so well that you ended up in the emergency room," Henry pointed out. "Now, do you want to tell me what's going on?"

"It was nothing, Henry." Julia lifted her damp hair away from the back of her neck. "Besides, you know I can't discuss my cases with you."

Frustrated, Henry slapped his open hand against the leather sofa with a loud thwack. "Last time I checked, you weren't a doctor, lawyer or priest. There is absolutely nothing that says you can't talk to me about your cases!"

He paused, shifting his approach. Years of experience had taught him that yelling at Julia wouldn't get him anywhere. The more someone shouted at her, the more quiet and obstinate she would become. Henry relaxed his demeanor and summoned up a friendly, concerned smile.

"How long have we known each other, Jules? Over ten years. As your friend, I just want to make sure you're okay. Maybe I can help you," he offered.

"I appreciate your concern, but I'm fine. Really." Julia assured him.

He looked at her skeptically. "You've got stitches in your head and a bruise the size of Alcatraz on the side of your face. That's not my definition of 'fine,' sweetheart." He broke off, peering at her more closely. "Hey, what's that on your neck? My god, Julia! Is that a hickey?

He looked around wildly, as if expecting the perpetrator to leap out of the couch cushions. Spotting a clue on the sofa armrest, Henry snatched up the incriminating evidence between two fingers. His eyebrows lifted into his bristling crew cut, and a giant grin spread across his face.

"Blonde, huh?" He held up a strand of hair. His eyes widened. "Not that reporter from a couple of days ago!"

It took every ounce of control she had, but Julia remained impassive. She stared at him calmly, refusing to answer. She'd known Henry Chow since high school, and he was one of the few friends she'd kept over the years.

"What was her name? Mc-something, wasn't it?" Henry continued, undaunted. "She was cute. I was thinking about asking her out myself. Figures you'd steal her away from me."

That finally got the reaction he was seeking. Julia started to laugh, her stony mask crumbling. It made her look more like the teenager he remembered and less like the quiet, isolated woman she had become, Henry noted thoughtfully.

"You're an idiot," Julia chuckled fondly.

"Yeah, well, we can't all be evil geniuses like you," Henry replied. "So, come on, tell me about the girl." He leaned forward eagerly.

"I thought you came here to ask about my case," Julia countered.

"Screw your case. I want to hear about the girl." He cocked his head, noticing the lopsided grin on her lips and the faint blush coloring her cheeks. "You really like this one, don't you?"

Julia shrugged casually, but Henry could read the emotions flickering just beneath the surface. He crossed the room and hugged her, startling her.

"I'm happy for you, Jules. It's about time."

"Thanks." Julia ducked out of his friendly embrace. "I really do like this one, Henry. It makes no goddamn sense."

She moved over to the window and opened the heavy curtains. A ghostly howl filled the air as the wind whipped through the branches in the trees outside. As Julia stood at the window, staring at the dark sky, the first heavy drops of rain spattered against the glass. This was going to be an ugly one. She turned back to Henry, who had resumed his seat on the sofa.

"Why doesn't it make sense?" Henry asked her gently. "With everything you've been through in the last few years, you deserve a little happiness. Besides, she was hot." He grinned at her.

Julia gave him a semi-disgusted look. "Quit talking with your zipper for once! This isn't just sex. She's...different."

Henry nodded, flipping through an imaginary notebook. "Mmhmm. 'Leaping to her defense.' Yep, just as I thought. It's a definite early warning sign. I'm afraid your white-knight syndrome is flaring up again." He sighed, shaking his head mournfully. "I'm sorry to inform you that there's no known cure."

Julia rolled her eyes and snapped her towel at him. "It's not like that, either. Well, not totally anyway." She paused. "Okay, she's got this brother who's causing her a lot of grief. And, yes, I offered to help her out with that. But there's something more. I can't really explain it."

"Jules, I've learned that it's best not to question these things too much. You'll just make yourself crazy. Well, crazier, in your case." Henry grinned at her, blithely ignoring the dirty look she shot him. "Just go with your heart."

With an exaggerated sigh, Julia flopped down beside him on the sofa and propped her bare feet up on the coffee table. She glanced sideways at her friend, arching a dark eyebrow thoughtfully.

"Henry, in all the time I've known you, I think that's the most intelligent thing I've ever heard you say."

"Thanks," Henry replied smugly. His self-satisfied smirk turned into a frown as he absorbed what she had said. "Hey! Wait a minute!"

Julia burst out laughing and the warm, vibrant sound filled the room. Henry glared at her irritably for a moment, but even he could not resist her charm, and soon, he joined her laughter. They sat in companionable silence as their chuckles subsided. Henry rubbed his bristling crew cut as his mood turned serious.

"Look, Julia, I think it's great that you've found someone," he started. "But I really did come here on slightly more official business."

Julia chewed her lower lip, trying to decide how much information to share with the police inspector. She'd learned the hard way that the cops tended to get in the way of her investigations. Even though she knew Henry meant well, she was reluctant to tell him too much. *'Still,'* she mused, *'it might not hurt to throw him a bone and see what he can dig up through official channels.'*

"I think there's more to the Netsports break-in," she said flatly, holding up a hand to cut off his question. "I don't have anything more solid than a gut feeling yet, but there's something about that whole situation that just doesn't feel right."

Henry waited, hoping for more, but apparently that was all she was willing to share with him. He fiddled absently with his shoelace while he turned the possibilities over in his mind. On the surface, the Netsports break-in didn't look like anything more than a routine burglary to him. Julia's instincts were usually good, though, and he went over the details of the case. Since no one had been injured, it wasn't his top priority, and he hadn't been giving the matter much thought.

"The safe." Julia said suddenly, breaking his train of thought. Henry gave her a puzzled look.

"Why steal the safe, Henry? A junkie looking for some quick cash isn't going to haul away something as heavy as a safe. I'm not even sure that one person could have handled it alone."

Henry was about to respond when a fierce gust of wind rattled the living room windows. The lights flickered briefly, but stayed on. Julia stared out the window, lost in her own thoughts as sheets of rain pounded against the pavement outside.

"Only Danny and his VP had the combination to that safe." She spoke aloud, but Henry could tell by the faraway look in her eyes that she wasn't talking to him. She was working something out in her mind, and he stayed quiet, letting her think.

"That could mean a couple of things," Julia continued. "Either whoever stole the safe didn't know the combination and didn't have time to try to break into it, or whoever stole it did have the combo and didn't want anyone to know that."

Henry rubbed his jaw, his fingers tracing the thin line where he had nicked himself shaving that morning. Everything Julia had just said made sense, and it bothered him that he hadn't thought of it himself.

"So you think that Netsports is connected to your attacker?"

"Probably," Julia replied, her eyes still distant. There was something else about that safe nagging at her. According to Daniel Webber, it hadn't contained anything important, so why would anyone go to all the trouble of hauling it out of that office?

Henry recognized the finality in her tone, and he knew he wasn't going to get anything else from her today. He stood, straightening his tie. Glancing out the window, he grimaced at the torrents pouring from the darkened sky. He had left his jacket in the car, and he would be soaked by the time he reached the vehicle. Julia followed his gaze and read the expression on his face.

"You can borrow my umbrella," she told him as she rose and walked him to the door.

She opened the closet in the entryway and removed a small travel umbrella from a hook on the back of the door. Henry took it gratefully. He paused, his hand on the doorknob.

"Would it do me any good to ask you to leave this to the police?" He let out a resigned sigh as Julia simply stared at him. "No, I didn't think so. Just be careful, okay? I don't want anybody bashing in that pretty skull of yours."

That got him a barely noticeable twitch of her lips. He stepped out on the porch, shivering dramatically as the storm blew the chilling rain against his body. He opened the umbrella, fighting against the wind that threatened to turn it inside out.

"I'm always careful, Henry," Julia deadpanned. "I'll see you later."

Henry let out a string of obscenities in English and Chinese as he dashed to his car. Chuckling softly, Julia shut the front door and headed back upstairs. Her bed was still rumpled and unmade, and she ran her hand across the soft flannel. Glancing around surreptitiously to make sure no one was watching but the dust mites, she picked up the pillow Maggie had used and held it to her nose. Closing her eyes, she breathed in deeply, relishing the lingering scent of the reporter's strawberry shampoo.

"Okay, just stop right there," she scolded herself happily. "You're gonna ruin your reputation like that."

Outside, the wind screeched and rain slammed against the side of the house. Thunder rumbled threateningly in the distance, somewhere out over the bay. Julia sighed. It was going to be an ugly day. She hoped Maggie was inside, safe and dry.

****
****

The newsroom was busier than usual when Maggie arrived at work half an hour later than normal. Sipping from her steaming cup of coffee, she headed for her desk. There was a pink post-it note stuck to her monitor, and she instantly recognized Catherine's handwriting. '*You owe me $150 for my shoes.*' Wincing, Maggie crumpled the note and tossed it into the wastebasket beside her desk. She shook her head. She had never in her life owned a pair of $150 shoes.

After leaving Julia's house, Maggie had returned to her apartment to shower and change clothes. Patrick hadn't been there, but she had listened to his message on her answering machine. She wasn't sure what to think. At least he was alive and not in jail, she told herself, but she couldn't help wondering what kind of mess he was in. Patrick had only been in town for a few days. Who on earth could he have met in that short time? Maggie glanced at her phone and made a face. She was dreading telling her parents that Patrick had run off.

"Got in a little late this morning, didn't you?" Jessica appeared at Maggie's elbow.

"Maybe a little," Maggie admitted with a grin. "Hey, what's going on around here, anyway?"

Jessica hopped up onto the corner of Maggie's desk, her feet dangling above the floor.

"What, you haven't heard? Oh, right. I guess you were sort of busy last night, weren't you?" Jessica smirked at her. She turned serious then, leaning forward to tell Maggie the news.

"There was another arson fire on the waterfront. Only this time, a security guard got killed. There's a joint press conference with the mayor's office and the police department scheduled in a couple of hours."

"That's awful. Did the guy have a family?" Maggie felt a pang of sympathy for the security guard. "Are the police any closer to catching anybody?"

Jessica shrugged and pushed her glasses up. "I think that's one of the things they'll talk about at the press conference. But I haven't heard anything to suggest that they have any suspects."

"McKinnon!" Sam Vogelsang, her editor, bellowed from the doorway to his office. "Get in here!"

Maggie and Jessica exchanged a bewildered look. Sam seemed even more agitated than usual. Maggie seated herself in his office, waiting while her editor paced back and forth in front of her.

"I've got another assignment for you," he said finally. "It might turn out to be nothing, but we got an anonymous tip that someone saw a woman leaving the fire last night. I want you to go to the scene and talk to anyone who might have seen anything."

Maggie's eyes widened. This could be a huge break for her.

"What about Catherine? I thought this arson story was hers." The last thing she wanted to do was step on Catherine's toes again.

"It is. She'll be at the press conference." Sam said gruffly. "She's still going to handle the official side of things. But I want you to look into the unofficial stuff. Look, I know the two of you don't get along very well. But I want this story, McKinnon, and I don't have time to soothe your egos. Go get me something good."

Maggie stood. She turned back at the door. "Sam? You've got dozens of reporters out there with more experience. Why me?"

"Because I think you have more potential than all of them combined." Sam never looked up from the papers he was shuffling through. He shoved a note with an address on it towards her. "Now go show me what you can do."

Maggie had been at the paper long enough to know that praise from Sam was virtually unheard of. She had also learned not to press her luck where her volatile editor was concerned, and she quickly slipped out of his office without another word. As she walked back to her desk, Maggie felt as if her feet never touched the floor. Jessica got up as she approached, looking at her expectantly.

"I'm on the arson story," Maggie said, scarcely believing the words that were coming out of her mouth.

Jessica squealed in delight and threw her arms around her dazed friend. "Oh my god! Congratulations, Maggie. This is gonna be so huge!"

Still stunned by her editor's faith in her, Maggie could only nod dumbly as she returned Jessica's friendly hug. She was dimly aware that most of the newsroom was watching them. Most of her co-workers were looking at her with grudging admiration, although a few of them wore expressions tinged with envy.

"Wow, this is turning out to be quite a week for you, isn't it?" Jessica laughed.

"Yeah. It sure is," Maggie answered softly as a slow grin lit up her face. "Thanks, Jess. I guess I'd better get out of here."

She grabbed her damp raincoat, which was draped over the back of her chair. Patting herself down, she checked to make sure she had all of her essential tools: keys, cell phone, notebook and pen. She decided to leave her laptop behind. It would be of little use out in the rain, anyway, she reasoned.

"Okay. Wish me luck," she said, tying the belt to her black raincoat securely around her slim waist.

"Honey, you don't need luck," Jessica replied. "You've got skill."

They looked at each other and burst out laughing. As she exited the newsroom amidst a flurry of muttered congratulations, Maggie could still hear her friend's girlish peals of laughter. She headed down to her car, glancing at the location Sam had given her as she slid behind the wheel. It was just a few blocks away from the site of the previous blaze. Maggie thought back to the night of the previous fire. A chorus of what ifs floated through her mind. What if she hadn't gone to that scene? She probably wouldn't have gotten Sam's attention, and she wouldn't be off on the biggest story of her career. More importantly, she never would have met Julia Cassinelli. Maggie smiled at her reflection in the rearview mirror. Julia's office wasn't far from the scene of the current fire, and she wondered if the private investigator was still at home. It wouldn't hurt to swing by Julia's office on her way back from the warehouse, Maggie decided as she pulled out into the rain-slick street.

It didn't take her long to reach the charred remains of the warehouse. The scene was cordoned off by yellow police tape, but Maggie was surprised to note that there was no one in sight. A single empty squad car sat in front of the building, its presence meant to deter anyone stupid enough to go climbing through the rubble. Maggie parked next to it and sat in her car for a moment, listening to the rain pound against the roof. There had to be an officer to go with the car, and she wondered where he was. Glancing in her rearview mirror, she noticed a small coffee shop half a block away. The officer had probably taken refuge from the storm in there. Maggie smiled at her good fortune. There would be no one to stop her from poking around.

She stepped out of her car and looked up at the sky, wishing that the rain would let up. The black clouds stared back at her implacably. Maggie sighed and briefly thought of the travel umbrella in her car trunk. She decided against it. It would be hard enough for her to take any notes without having one more item to juggle. Pulling her raincoat closer around her body, she resigned herself to the idea of getting soaked. A quick look in both directions told her that nobody was watching her, and she ducked underneath the tape. Black water ran in rivulets from the burned warehouse, and the air smelled like a dozen wet campfires. Splashing through the puddles, Maggie wished she had worn her hiking boots as the water seeped through her thin loafers. She had no idea what she was looking for as she circled around the building.

The city's homeless liked to use these warehouses for shelter whenever they could, and Maggie saw evidence of their presence as she approached a small storage shed near the main warehouse. Trash and tattered bits of clothing littered the ground, and Maggie's nostrils flared as she encountered the unmistakable stench of human waste. The rusted metal door to the shed had been forced open and stood slightly ajar. Nervousness fluttered through her stomach and her hand trembled as Maggie reached out to push it open. Without warning, the door jerked backwards from the other direction. Maggie screamed and staggered back, tripping over her own feet and landing hard on the muddy ground. Crab-like, she skittered backwards as a gaunt, filthy man dressed in mismatched rags loomed in the doorway. He pointed at her with a gloved hand covered in grime.

"Whaddya want? This is mine! Mine!" He shrieked at her. One eye was a deep, impenetrable black. The other had turned milky white.

Slowly, willing herself not to show any fear, Maggie climbed to her feet. She held her hands out, trying to pacify the agitated man.

"I'm very sorry, sir," she said in a soothing tone. "I didn't mean to trespass."

This seemed to mollify him slightly, and he folded his arms across his chest. His bad eye twitched violently and he smacked his dry, chapped lips constantly. Maggie wondered if it would be pointless to question him.

"My name is Maggie and I'm a reporter." She pulled a ten-dollar bill out of her pocket and held it out to him, trying not to flinch when he snatched it from her.

"I was hoping I could ask you a few questions," she continued, encouraged that he seemed to be listening. "Have you been living here long?" Maggie nodded behind him at the rusting, dilapidated shed.

He shrugged indifferently, holding the ten-dollar bill up and examining it closely. He grunted when he found what he was looking for. Maggie watched, fascinated, as he removed his gloves and carefully tore the edge off the bill, removing the thin paper strip inside it. He discarded the thread and stomped on it, grinding it into the mud. The rest of the bill disappeared beneath the rags.

"That's how they track you," he informed Maggie seriously. "Can't let them find you."

"Oh? Okay, I'll remember that." Maggie took a different route with her questions. "Have you ever seen them?"

He regarded her warily with his good eye. Looking around, he put a finger to his lips, warning her to be quiet. He beckoned her closer. Maggie took a step forward, breathing through her mouth to try to avoid the putrid smell emanating from the man.

"One of 'em was here last night," he confided. "I saw what she did."

"She?" '*Sam's sources were right,*' Maggie thought, '*there was a woman here last night.*'

"Yep," the man nodded. "Pretty girl. Just like you."

He took a step closer, hands reaching out for her, a leering grin twisting his mouth. A harsh cackle burst from his lips as Maggie stumbled backwards, nearly losing her balance again. From somewhere behind her, a gunshot ripped through the air. The bullet struck the base of the man's throat, and tore through the back of his neck, sending a fine spray of blood everywhere. Bile rose in Maggie's throat as droplets of the warm, sticky liquid hit her face, and she choked back a scream as the man toppled forward, gurgling helplessly. Another shot whizzed past her ear, close enough that she could hear the whine of the bullet. Her paralysis broke and she ran blindly without looking back.

Ahead of her, there was nothing but the end of the pier, and beyond that, the bay.

She veered left and ducked behind the corner of the burned-out building. Flattening herself against the blackened wall, Maggie squeezed her eyes shut and prayed that someone had heard the shots. Sweat poured down her temples, mixing with the rain, and her breath came in frantic, shallow gasps. Her vision tunneled and brightened around the edges, and she knew she was beginning to hyperventilate. Footsteps sloshed through the mud, and Maggie looked around in a panic. Several yards away, she spotted a door leading down to an underground storage facility. The footsteps were moving closer and there was no time to think. She dashed to the door and tugged on the slippery iron handles. It came open with a whispering groan, and she threw herself down the precariously steep steps. The door shut behind her, plunging her into complete darkness.

****

Chapter Ten

The minty cool flavor still tingled on his tongue as Daniel Webber spit a mouthful of toothpaste into the sink. He turned the faucet on and watched the water and foam swirl down the drain. The phone was ringing. He ignored it. The machine would get it. Hitching up his boxer shorts, he strolled back into his bedroom, pausing in front of the full-length mirror in the corner. His gaze traveled downward, resting on the ugly scar along his left kneecap, a reminder of the injury that had ended his hopes for a professional football career.

"Hi, Danny. It's Julia. Listen, I have a few questions for you, so give me a call when you get a chance."

Lunging forward, Danny snatched the receiver off the nightstand. "Julia? You still there?"

"Danny?" Julia sat down in the rocking chair in her living room. She tucked her long legs up beneath her and picked up the Netsports file she had been compiling.

"Hey, Julia. Sorry about that. I was brushing my teeth," Danny said, sitting on the edge of his bed. "So, what can I do for you?"

Absently cleaning under his fingernails, he listened while Julia explained her concerns about the missing safe. When she was through, he exhaled slowly.

"Well, I guess that rules out me and Allison, then," he joked.

Julia frowned, wondering why Danny didn't seem to be all that concerned about either the break-in, or the missing safe.

"Not quite," she replied slowly. "Maybe the two of you are conspiring to throw me off track."

She had meant it as a joke, but the microsecond of dead silence on the other end of the phone sent a warning signal shooting through her head. Her eyes narrowed thoughtfully. She hadn't suspected Danny of anything. Not Danny, the easygoing former frat boy who had been her chemistry lab partner in college. If she suspected anyone at this point, it was his vice president, Allison Davis, who was rather conveniently out of town. Now, she wasn't so sure. Danny laughed finally, a forced, too-loud laugh that told Julia she had hit a nerve.

"Good one, Julia," Danny said. He raked his fingers through his sandy hair. "Why would we ask you to look into this if we were guilty?"

"To make yourselves look innocent, of course." Julia kept her tone light and friendly. "Relax, Danny. I'm just kidding."

She scribbled a note down on a piece of paper inside her file and underlined it. *Danny and Allison?*

"Besides, I'm sure the police are probably right. It'll turn out to be a couple of junkies," she lied.

Danny laughed again, relieved. He was glad she wasn't planning on pursuing the case any further since he had always liked Julia, and he didn't want to see her get hurt. He exchanged pleasantries with her for a few more minutes before hanging up the phone. Out of the corner of his eye, he could see the blinking icon on his computer, indicating that he had a message. He walked over to the desk and clicked on it.

Julia tossed the handset onto the sofa. Deep in thought, she chewed on the end of her pen. Danny was a terrible liar, and his guilt had practically screamed at her through the phone. Julia searched her mind, but she couldn't come up with a logical motive. According to all the information she had about Netsports, the business was sound, so it couldn't be just about money. She tapped her pen against Allison Davis' name. It was time to find out more about Danny's elusive vice president.

A glance at the clock told her that it was mid-morning. Outside, the storm raged. Her jeep was still parked in front of her office, left behind during her unexpected trip to the hospital, and she hoped she had remembered to roll up the windows all the way. In spite of the weather, Julia decided to go retrieve it and spend a few hours at her office. She dialed the number for a cab company and the dispatcher informed her that she would be picked up in fifteen minutes. Julia sat down to wait. She would get a bit of work done, nothing too strenuous, she promised herself, and then maybe she would see if a certain reporter was free for lunch.

The cab was late, of course, and it was nearly an hour later when Julia unlocked the door to her office. She stepped inside and turned on the overhead lights as she shook the rain out of her hair. Tossing her jacket across one of the leather chairs, she took a look around. Papers were scattered near her file cabinet, where she had struggled with her assailant, and there was a small puddle of dried blood on the floor. Her hand went up to the plastic band-aid covering the stitches in her head. Julia grabbed a handful of damp paper towels out of the bathroom and scrubbed at the stain. Anger coursed through her and she silently vowed to find the man who had attacked her.

Discarding the towels in the trash, Julia sank into her chair behind her desk. She turned on her computer and read the three new messages. Two were unimportant, and she deleted those. The third was from Henry. She read that message again. Another warehouse had burned, and two witnesses claimed to have seen a woman running away from the blaze. The Davis family owned the warehouse.

"Well, *that's* interesting," Julia commented aloud.

The Davis family was wealthy and politically connected in the Bay area, and they had traveled in the same social circles as the Cassinelli's. Allison was the only child of Martin Davis, a city councilman. That was the extent of Julia's knowledge about them. She wasn't even exactly sure what sort of business the Davis' were in, since that type of thing had never interested her. Her father, she recalled, had occasionally played golf with the councilman, but Julia wasn't about to go to him for information.

With a few rapid keystrokes, she surfed into the Chronicle's website and ran a search for articles on the Davis family. Frowning in consternation, Julia stared at the 93 matches found by the paper's search engine. The articles ranged from financial news to appearances at various charity functions. She narrowed down the parameters, typing Allison's name into the little box. This time, only 14 matches came up. The most recent was Maggie's story on the Netsports burglary. She had already read the story. In fact, after Maggie had left, she had clipped the story out of the paper and tucked it into her wallet. Still, she wanted to read it again. Julia clicked on the link and smiled proudly as Maggie's byline appeared on her screen. She skimmed through the article again, but it only mentioned that Allison Davis, vice president, was out of town and unavailable for comment.

The next two links were write-ups of social events that Allison had attended recently. Even before Julia had turned her back on her family, she had always found the society stuff boring, and she scanned those stories without interest. Finally, she found what she was looking for, a short bio that had run in the business section when Allison was hired at Netsports.

Allison had graduated from Stanford with a degree in marketing, two years after Julia and Danny. Julia didn't remember ever meeting her there, but it was a big campus, and she had never been the outgoing type, anyway. She wondered if that was where Allison and Danny had met. After graduation, Allison had gone to work for one of her father's banks. Julia paused there, rereading that sentence. Councilman Davis was in the banking industry. Why would a banker own a warehouse on the pier?

A booming thunderclap rattled the roof of her office, and Julia ducked in reflex. Too much rain was falling in too short a time period, and water was beginning to seep underneath the door. It wasn't enough to cause a panic, and Julia knew that the danger of flooding was pretty minimal. She went into the bathroom and seized a double handful of paper towels. She was about to stuff them under the front door when the lights flickered and went dark.

"Oh, son of a bitch," she muttered irritably.

She made sure her computer was turned off, so that it would not be damaged whenever the power returned. Her hands on her hips, she stood in the dark for a moment as she decided what to do next. A check of her watch told her that it was still too early for lunch. Cursing at herself under her breath, she wished she had jotted down the address of the recently burned warehouse. *Well, it's a burned-out warehouse along the pier. It can't be that hard to find.*

Julia grabbed her jacket and her keys and headed out the door, dodging the minor waterfall cascading down from roof of her building. Pulling her jacket shut with one hand, she trudged to her jeep, ignoring the stinging raindrops pelting her. She slid into the driver's seat. It was like getting into a refrigerator and shutting the door, and she shivered violently for a moment before her body heat began to warm the interior of the vehicle. The cold, damp weather was making her bruised ribs ache, and as she started the jeep's engine, she turned the heater on full blast. The street was clogged with confused drivers since Californians were notorious for their inability to drive in the rain, and Julia ground her teeth impatiently as she waited for an opening in the traffic. Finally, she eased her jeep into the street and headed for the waterfront.

Up ahead, a three-car accident had slowed traffic to an infuriating crawl as rubberneckers gawked at the sight. Julia barely glanced at it as she inched her way past. An unsettling feeling of dread was creeping through her, and she couldn't shake the sensation that something was wrong. On the radio, the disc jockeys were making prank phone calls to local businesses, and their braying laughter was wearing on her nerves. She ran through the preset stations and finally shut the radio off, welcoming the relative quiet. In the distance, a car backfired twice. The light turned green, and Julia started to slowly move her jeep through the intersection. A tiny furrow appeared on her brow as she heard the sounds again in her mind. Two sharp cracks, a minute or so apart.

"That wasn't a car. Those were gunshots!" Intending to notify the police, Julia reached for her cell phone on the passenger seat. As her hand touched it, it started ringing.

"Hello? Hello? I can barely hear you," Julia said into the phone, straining to hear through the crackling static. "Listen, I have to go. I need to make an important call."

As if on cue, the static cleared just enough for her to recognize the panicky, whispered voice on the other end.

"Julia? Oh my god, Julia! I need your help!"

It was Maggie. Julia's stomach tried to crawl up into her throat, and she grimly swallowed it back down. Ignoring the outraged honking of horns, she steered her jeep into the right lane and turned into a nearby parking lot. Julia struggled to stay calm. All she wanted to do was get out of her jeep and run to wherever Maggie was.

"Maggie? I'm right here. What's going on? Where are you?"

"I...I'm underground. It's so dark down here. I'm so scared," Maggie whispered back, her voice sounding very far away.

"Down where, honey? You have to tell me where you are." Julia fought to keep the fear out of her voice. She knew she needed to stay strong for Maggie, but inside, it felt like someone was tying her intestines in knots.

Maggie was huddled in the corner of the underground storage area. Her knees were pulled up tightly against her chest, and she rocked back and forth slowly. There was not a single glimmer of light anywhere, and she had become completely disoriented in the dark. She wasn't even sure where the door was anymore. Maybe there was no door, she thought irrationally.

Something scurried past in the blackness, and Maggie let out a strangled sob. She was eight years old again, and her older brothers had locked her in the basement of the abandoned house on the corner of their street. It was supposed to have been a joke, but they had forgotten about her for hours. Her absence hadn't even been noticed until dinner. After forcing the boys to tell him where she was, her father had rescued her, but not before the rats had come sniffing around.

"Maggie? Come on, Maggie. Tell me where you are so I can come get you." Julia's voice brought her back to reality.

"Julia? Oh god. There was a fire, and I came to ask around. Someone shot..."

A loud thump overhead silenced her. Her heartbeat thundered in her ears, and she was acutely aware of the harsh sound of her own breathing. She wondered if anyone else could hear it, if Julia could hear it through the phone. Julia was saying something to her, but she couldn't hear it. She waited, half-expecting the door to be flung open, and she wondered if the bullets would hurt when they hit her.

"Someone shot at you? Maggie, are you hurt?" Julia paused. No response. "Are you still there?" Still nothing.

Julia screamed in frustration, noticing that the street was still backed up for blocks. There were only a few more piers ahead, and she knew that Maggie had to be at one of those. Turning off her engine, she made a decision.

"Maggie, I'm going to hang up now. Hang in there. I'm coming to get you."

She dialed as she opened her door. Cold air blasted her and rain pelted her immediately, but she was oblivious to all of it. Henry picked up on the second ring.

"Henry, it's me. Send someone out to the warehouse. I'll explain later." Julia hung up without waiting for his inevitable questions. She tucked the phone in her pocket and started to run.

Sitting at his desk, Henry stared at the phone as the dial tone droned loudly in his ear. He had heard the fear in Julia's voice, and that alone was enough to make him very, very worried. A uniformed officer started to walk by and he signaled her over.

"That warehouse that burned last night. Who's supposed to be at the scene?"

"Sanders," the rookie officer replied, her eyes bright with excitement. "He just called in a few minutes ago. Shots fired." "Oh, shit! Julia, what the hell have you gotten yourself into now?" Henry bolted out of his chair and headed for the door.

The rain stung her face, and the wind tore at her hair and clothes. Her breath was visible in large white puffs as she sprinted two and a half blocks. Julia wasn't a runner. She had nothing but disdain for the disgustingly healthy joggers that routinely appeared on her street in their bright Lycra and spandex. Today, though, she wished she ran more often. Her legs burned and her lungs ached as she sucked down huge gulps of cold air. She forced herself to ignore the pain and focus on the only thing that mattered. Maggie.

Less than half a block away, she could see the blackened, hulking remnants of the burned warehouse. Putting her head down, Julia dug deep inside herself and summoned one final burst of speed. She had no idea how long she had been running. Police sirens whined in the distance, but they were undoubtedly slowed by the traffic gridlock that gripped the area.

Drawn forward by some magnetic force, Julia ducked under the police tape surrounding the warehouse and tore around the corner to the rear of the building. She collided with something solid and wool-covered that let out a startled yelp as it went down in a tangle of limbs. Somehow, Julia managed to stay on her feet, and her gaze latched on to a set of metal doors embedded in the ground. She dashed toward them, her shoes squelching in the mud.

"Hey. Hey!" Officer Sanders shouted, scrambling to his feet.

Going full speed, Julia reached the doors and threw them open. Blinking the water out of her eyes, she searched frantically until she spotted what she was looking for. Maggie had pressed herself as far back into the corner as she could, and her eyes were squeezed tightly shut. Julia flew down the steps, nearly losing her balance in her haste.

"Maggie!"

Maggie's heart started beating again at the sound of the familiar voice. She opened her eyes, and let out a sob of relief as the tall, soaking wet, mud-spattered, absolutely beautiful figure stumbled towards her. Tears spilled down her cheeks as she flung herself into Julia's arms.

"Julia," she gasped, burying her face against her lover's shoulder.

They were both trembling violently, and Julia feared her rubbery legs were about to give out. She guided them up the steps, stopping at the top as she was blocked by a muddy, angry police officer.

"Don't move," he commanded, his gun drawn and pointing down at his side.

Julia drew herself up to her full height and fixed him with her most intimidating stare.

"Move. Now," she snarled at him, one arm wrapped protectively around Maggie's shoulders.

Officer Sanders blinked at her uncertainly. A burst of static squawked at him from the radio clipped to his belt. He looked down at it, and Julia used the distraction to brush past him. He stared after them in exasperation as he listened to Inspector Henry Chow's instructions on the radio.

Julia steered Maggie over to the loading dock and sat her down on a crate that had been spared by the fire. In spite of the puddles, Julia knelt in front of her and lifted both of Maggie's hands to her lips. Breathing heavily from her mad sprint, she took a moment to collect herself and suck down some much needed oxygen. She smiled reassuringly at Maggie.

"Are you okay?" she asked tenderly.

Maggie nodded silently, staring at the ground. Julia could tell she was on the verge of breaking down, and she pulled the shaken reporter into a tight embrace. Maggie's shoulders shook as she tried in vain to hold back the tears.

"Ssshh. It's okay. I'm here," Julia soothed her, pressing her lips to Maggie's temple. "I won't let anyone hurt you."

Maggie pulled her head back, searching the depths of those blue eyes.

"Promise?"

Julia leaned in and kissed her lightly.

"I promise."

****

Tom Becker stuffed himself into the passenger seat of the red Camaro. His dripping clothes made a wet, squishing sound against the leather of the seat, and his lips tightened into a thin, harsh smile when the car's tattooed driver cursed in protest. Tom hated this car. The roof pressed down on his head, and riding in it gave him a suffocating, claustrophobic feeling. He felt like he was sitting in a coffin.

He hated the driver too, he thought, glancing sideways as Eddie Machado pulled the sports car into the street with a grating screech. The tires left a trail of rubber in their wake. Cold, hard metal dug into the small of his back, and Tom reached around to pull the gun out of his waistband. He turned it over in his beefy hands and imagined himself pressing the barrel to Eddie's head and pulling the trigger. He let out a short, barking laugh as he returned the gun to the glove compartment.

"Dude, that was too close," Eddie said, turning his head to stare at the big man. His dark eyes flashed with excitement. "That cop ran right past me."

Tom said nothing, and Eddie continued to chatter aimlessly. "That was so fucking awesome. It's about time DC gave me something to do. Shit, yeah!" Eddie slapped his hands against the steering wheel. "So, tell me what happened. Did you blow that guy's brains all over the ground?"

"Shut up and drive, you worthless little punk," Tom snarled, staring straight ahead through the windshield.

Eddie slouched down further in his seat and sulked quietly. He was used to Tom's venom. Tom grabbed the cell phone off the dashboard and hit one of the numbers. While he waited for someone to answer, he pictured the blonde woman who had nearly ruined everything. Even though she hadn't seen him, he had a gut feeling that she would be trouble, and Tom hated loose ends. He would have to find out her name. Finally, someone picked up his call.

"It's me. He's taken care of, but we have another problem. There was some woman asking questions." Tom nodded, listening to the person on the other end. "Do you want me to handle it?"

****
****

The police and the paramedics had arrived, and activity swirled around the burned warehouse. Exhausted, Julia leaned her head back against the backseat of the unmarked police car she was sitting in. Maggie was wrapped in an emergency blanket given to her by the paramedics, and she was pressed against Julia's side, her head nestled against her shoulder.

The police had questioned them both, and at Julia's insistence, Maggie had allowed the EMTs to examine her. Then, Henry had taken charge and ushered them both to his car. Through the front windshield, Julia could see him standing in the steady rain, getting drenched as he watched two men load the homeless man's body into a white coroner's van. Beside her, Maggie shuddered, still shaken by her ordeal, and Julia drew her closer. She brushed her lips across damp blonde hair and tried not to look at the stark white bandage covering the top of Maggie's ear. The second bullet had passed much too close to Maggie, closer than the reporter had even realized. It had grazed the top of her ear, leaving a shallow furrow that she hadn't even noticed until Julia started fussing over it. Maggie had been lucky. It could have been much worse. Closing her eyes, Julia silently thanked whoever was listening for keeping Maggie from being seriously hurt. She refused to even think about the alternatives.

Julia tried to take a deep breath and felt a sharp twinge in her side. So much for her nice, quiet day, she thought sourly as she attempted to hide a grimace. Maggie noticed the sudden tension in the surface beneath her cheek, and she lifted her head to stare accusingly at Julia.

"You hurt yourself, didn't you?" It was the first thing Maggie had said since she had given her statement to the police.

"No, no. I'm fine. Just a little tired." Julia shook her head emphatically.

"Liar," Maggie shot back, the ghost of a grin taking the sting out of the word. Her expression sobered and blonde eyebrows scrunched together in concern, creating a tiny crease in her brow that Julia thought was absolutely adorable.

"Julia, maybe we should have a doctor check you out."

"Uh-uh. I'm fine, I swear," Julia repeated. "I think I just pulled something."

Maggie eyed her skeptically. "Okay. If you say so."

"It's nothing a long, hot bath and a bed won't cure," Julia assured her. A dark eyebrow rose thoughtfully and a mischievous smirk tugged at the corner of her mouth. "Care to join me for that?"

The car door opened before Maggie could answer, and Henry leaned down to look at them. His clothes were plastered to his skin and water dripped from the tip of his nose. He looked completely miserable, but Julia was too exhausted to bother teasing him about it.

"Hey, how are you two doing?" Henry asked, looking from one woman to the other. Julia gave him a slight nod. He rubbed his hands together and blew into them, trying to warm the chilled flesh.

"Okay, listen. I'm having a couple of officers drive you both home," he held up his hand, silencing Julia's sputtered protests.

"I am having someone drive you home," he repeated stubbornly. "Don't worry about your cars. Tow trucks are already taking care of them. Maggie, I didn't know where you lived, so I had them take your car over to Julia's. I hope that's okay." Henry winked at Julia, and she rolled her eyes at his lack of subtlety.

"Henry..." Julia growled at him.

Maggie curled her fingers around Julia's hand and shushed her. She smiled gratefully at the sodden police inspector. "It's fine. Thank you."

He grinned back at her and winked again, ignoring Julia's muffled snort. Straightening, he beckoned to a pair of nearby officers and handed one of them the keys to his car.

"This is Officer Bayley and Officer Clark. They'll make sure you get home safely." Henry stepped back from the car door as the uniformed officers slid into the front seat. "Julia, I'll probably stop by later with some more questions, okay?"

Julia nodded. "Okay. Thanks, Henry."

His eyes widened in mock surprise at the expression of gratitude, and he clutched at his chest theatrically. Julia shook her head at him slowly, rolling her eyes in exasperation. Grinning broadly, Henry shut the door and thumped twice on the roof of the car. He waved as the car pulled away. Once it was gone, the grin vanished and Henry became all business again. First, someone had attacked Julia in her office. Now,

Julia's new girlfriend was getting shot at, and he had the feeling that the two incidents were connected. This case had just become personal, and he vowed to catch the people responsible for attacking his friends.

"Henry!" One of the other inspectors working on the case called out to him. "I just got a call from the coroner's office. The security guard from last night was not killed by the fire."

"No?" Henry asked, curious. "I suppose you're gonna tell me how he did die, right?"

"Gunshot wound to the back of the head, .45 caliber," the officer informed him. "We've got guys searching for the slugs from today's shooting to see if they match."

A long stream of Chinese obscenities tumbled out of Henry's mouth, and a hush fell over the crime scene as his fellow officers eyed him warily. Once he had regained control of his temper, he turned to a young policeman.

"Find me Daniel Webber. He and I need to have a little chat."

Henry stalked away angrily, fumbling in his pockets for a cigarette. Instead, he found a mangled stick of chewing gum, a reminder that he had quit smoking six months before. Glaring at it in disgust, he removed the silver wrapper and popped the gum into his mouth, chewing furiously until the nicotine craving began to subside.

The rain had slowed to a light, annoying drizzle, but the wind was still coming off the water in strong gusts that cut through his soaked clothing. Muttering to himself in a singsong mixture of English and Chinese, Henry headed up the street to the coffee shop on the corner. Halfway there, a woman, walking in the other direction, stopped him.

"Excuse me. Do you know what time it is?"

Henry glanced at his watch and wiped the water from it with the cuff of his shirt. "Uh, yeah. It's almost noon." He gave her an appraising look. She was wearing a long raincoat and the hood was pulled up, obscuring her face, but he caught a glimpse of blonde hair.

"Thank you. Are you a police officer? I heard there was some kind of a shooting up there," she said, gesturing toward the warehouse.

Her voice was light and melodic, and all Henry could see of her face was a pair of full, heart-shaped lips. He smiled and straightened his shoulders, turning on the charm.

"Inspector Henry Chow, SFPD," he introduced himself, extending his hand towards her. She took it, and he noticed that her hands were soft and smooth, and her fingernails were neatly manicured. Her grip was surprisingly strong, and he almost winced at the pressure wrapped around his hand.

"There was some trouble back there, but it's all being taken care of," he said.

"Really? I feel much safer knowing that the police are on top of it," she purred. "So, what happened? Or is that top-secret information?"

Henry laughed. "I'm just a cop, not a spy. There was a shooting, and unfortunately someone got hurt. There was a reporter at the scene, so I'm sure you'll hear all about it on the news tonight."

"A reporter?" she echoed thoughtfully. "How awful. I'm glad she wasn't hurt."

Weighing his options, Henry stared up the street towards the coffee shop. *Oh well*, he decided, *it couldn't hurt to ask.*

"I was about to get a cup of coffee," he pointed towards the street corner. "Would you like to join me?"

The heart-shaped lips curved into a regretful smile. "I would love to, Inspector, but I'm afraid I'm late for an appointment. Maybe some other time."

She resumed walking down the street, and Henry watched her for a moment. Suddenly, he realized that he hadn't bothered to get her name. He swore under his breath and debated calling out after her. *Nah, that would seem too desperate.* It wasn't the first time he'd missed an opportunity with a woman. Shrugging, he headed for the warm, dry sanctuary of the coffee shop.

Julia had fallen into a light doze by the time the car stopped in front of her house. A gentle nudge to her side awakened her, and she opened her eyes groggily. Maggie grinned at her.

"Hey, sleepyhead. You're home," Maggie teased her.

"Hey, yourself," Julia leaned over and kissed her partner, oblivious to the two police officers watching from the front seat.

Now that the adrenaline rush had worn off, the cold weather, her strenuous physical exertion and the long period sitting in the car had all combined to wreak havoc on Julia's muscles. As she tried to get out of the car, she found that she was so stiff that she could barely move. She groaned out loud, her sore legs and back screaming in protest. Maggie turned back, lines of concern etched on her forehead.

"What's wrong?"

Julia gave her a wan smile as she slowly scooted toward the open car door. "Nothing. Just a little stiff." As she stood, pain shot through her lower back and wound around to her side, and she had to bite her lower lip to stifle another groan.

Maggie's sharp eyes didn't miss anything, and she shook her head and sighed. "Just a little stiff, huh?" She turned to one of the waiting officers. "Can one of you please help me get her inside?"

Supported by a policewoman on one side, and Maggie on the other side, Julia made her way carefully towards her front door. Both her jeep and Maggie's car were parked along the curb, and another policeman was waiting on her front porch. He came down the steps to assist them and nearly tripped on a fallen tree branch that was lying across the walkway. Julia tried, unsuccessfully, not to laugh.

"You'll have to forgive my friend. She's really tired," Maggie apologized to the reddened policeman.

Somehow, they all managed to make it up the front steps, and Maggie fished in Julia's pocket for her keys. She turned to the two officers, who were already starting to walk away.

"Thank you for everything," she said sincerely. "We really appreciate it. And please tell Officer Bayley thank you, as well."

The police left and Maggie followed Julia inside. Julia was standing in her living room, staring at the couch and apparently trying to decide if it was worth the effort to sit down. Maggie circled around her until they were face to face. Rising up on her toes, she kissed Julia squarely in the center of her forehead. Julia blinked at her, slightly perplexed.

"What was that for?"

"That was for running to my rescue today," Maggie explained. Tilting her head up, she captured Julia's lips for a longer, deeper kiss. "That was because I love you."

"Oh. Okay." Julia gave her a lopsided grin. Lowering her head, she returned the gesture. "That was because I love you, too."

Maggie beamed at her happily. "Okay. Sit down, if you can manage it." She pushed Julia towards the couch. "I'll go run a hot bath for you. Would you mind if I borrowed some of your clothes? Mine are sort of disgusting, and I would really like to get out of them." She looked down at her damp, muddy, blood-spattered clothing.

"Yeah, go ahead. I'd like to get you out of them, too," Julia cracked, flopping down on the couch with an exaggerated groan.

Maggie cocked an eyebrow at her. "Oh, that's very funny. I'll be right back." She started up the stairs, kicking her shoes off as she went.

"You know, a back rub might be sort of nice, too," Julia called after her playfully.

"Don't push your luck, Cassinelli!"

Julia chuckled, listening to the sound of footsteps moving down the hall upstairs. A moment later, she could hear water splashing, and she sighed, anticipating the hot bath that would help soothe her aching body. Every muscle in her body hurt, and she was so tired she could barely breathe. It was just as well, she mused, since breathing sent tendrils of pain crawling up her side.

Julia shut her eyes and let her thoughts drift. A wondering smile touched her lips at the sound of Maggie moving around above her head. After Kirsten had left, Julia had convinced herself that she enjoyed the solitude, but now, she realized that she had been kidding herself. She had missed the companionship more than she had cared to admit.

A faint scowl darkened her face as she wondered what Maggie had been doing out at the Davis warehouse. She reminded herself to ask the reporter about it. Sleep tugged insistently at her, and she willingly surrendered. Moments later, she was awakened by warm hands brushing against her skin, and a single sleepy blue eye fluttered open, unnoticed by the blonde who was methodically unbuttoning her shirt. Maggie had exchanged her clothing for a pair of Julia's flannel boxers and a t-shirt that was much too large for her smaller frame. She was drowning in faded blue cotton.

"Hey, are you trying to take advantage of me?" Julia teased, her voice scratchy from fatigue.

"Oh, you wish," Maggie laughed, sliding the damp, chilled fabric back from Julia's shoulders. "Come on. There's a bathtub upstairs with your name on it."

Julia slipped her arm around Maggie's shoulders and pushed herself off the couch. She let Maggie help her up the stairs and into her bathroom, where steam rose from a large, gothic bathtub, complete with clawed feet. Thick, peach-scented bubbles trailed over the side, creating a small puddle on the tiled floor.

"Didn't leave much room for me in there, did you?" Julia observed.

Maggie shrugged sheepishly as she unfastened Julia's jeans. "I sort of dropped the bubble bath," she admitted, peeling the denim down the taller woman's hips. Kneeling, she removed Julia's shoes and socks, setting them aside.

"I can probably undress myself," Julia pointed out, though she was thoroughly enjoying the attention.

Maggie looked up, grinning at her impishly as Julia stepped out of her jeans. "I'm sure you could," she replied. "But isn't it more fun this way?"

"Definitely," Julia agreed as Maggie removed the rest of her clothing.

Maggie guided Julia over to the tub and sat on the edge as Julia carefully eased herself into the water. Bubbles spilled over the sides, splashing to the floor. The heat instantly started to unlock Julia's stiff muscles, and a sigh of relief escaped her lips as she slid down until her chin touched the surface of the water. Maggie dipped her hand into the tub, and her fingers left lazy trails through the bubbles. Her throat constricted and tears welled, darkening her eyes.

"Maggie? What's wrong?" Julia interlaced her fingers with Maggie's.

"Nothing. I love you," Maggie's voice cracked as she struggled to hold back the emotion.

Julia blinked uncertainly. "There's something wrong with that?"

"God, no! It's just, I…thank you. I don't know what I would've done without you today."

"You don't have to thank me, Maggie. I wish I could have been there sooner. If anything had happened to you…" she trailed off without finishing the thought.

Julia sat up, letting the water cascade down from her shoulders, and the muscles in her back rippled as she leaned forward. She rested her forearms across Maggie's lap, closing one hand around her knee.

"You don't have any idea who shot at you?"

Maggie shook her head. "I didn't see anything. It was all so fast. One minute, I was standing there, talking to this man. The next minute…there was so much blood. It didn't look like I thought it would. I thought it would be darker, but it was bright red. Like watercolor paint."

Julia stared at her intently, noticing the odd, distant tone of her voice. Maggie's pupils were dilated, her eyes were far too bright, and the skin beneath Julia's hand was cool. Julia sighed and rose from the tub, pulling Maggie up with her as she continued to speak in that faraway voice.

"I ran and hid. I was so sure I was next. Have you ever been shot? Do you think it hurts?"

Julia grabbed a fluffy blue towel from the rack and wrapped it around her body. She took Maggie's hand and led her towards the door. Maggie stopped suddenly, jolted back to the present.

"Wait. Where are we going? What about your bath?"

Julia turned to face her, putting her hands on Maggie's shoulders. "You're still in shock, I think. And I'm tired. So we're gonna go lie down for a while, okay? We can finish the bath later."

A tear rolled down Maggie's cheek, and Julia brushed it away with the back of her hand. Maggie gave her a grateful, trembling smile.

"I don't know what I'd do without you."

"Well, you're in luck. Because you'll never have to find that out," Julia replied as she resumed leading Maggie to the bedroom.

"Although, if you want to repay me, there's always that backrub..."

They crossed into the cool, dark bedroom, and Julia kicked the door shut behind them, blocking out the rest of the world.

****

Chapter Eleven

She was lying on her back in the middle of a field of strawberries. The sun was warm on her skin, and the sky overhead was cloudless and blue. Soft blades of lush green grass tickled her, and she laughed. She was happy and relaxed in spite of the enormous strawberry sitting on her chest. Breathing in deeply, she savored the fruity smell and she longed to have its sweet juice running over her tongue. The strawberry's eyes opened, and they were the clearest, deepest green she had ever seen.

Julia frowned in her sleep. Strawberries didn't have eyes. Slowly, she began to wake up, leaving the dream behind. She stared groggily at her ceiling. There was definitely something heavy on her chest, and whatever it was smelled like strawberries. Looking down, Julia smiled at the top of the blonde head that rose and fell in rhythm with her own breathing. Her arms tightened around Maggie's body. Asleep, she looked soft and vulnerable, and Julia was filled with an overwhelming desire to keep her safe.

"I love you, Maggie McKinnon," she whispered, liking the feel of the words as they rolled off her tongue.

Julia glanced at the window. Twilight had fallen while they slept, and her bedroom was bathed in shadows. She let her eyes drift shut again as she buried her nose in Maggie's hair. The reporter's brush with danger had terrified her more than she cared to admit. Lightly, she ran her fingertips across Maggie's wounded ear and felt an irrational spark of anger growing inside. Someone had tried to kill the woman she loved. Julia stared up at the ceiling again, her eyes turning to chips of blue ice. She would find out who was responsible, and then she was going to rip that someone's throat out.

Maggie whimpered aloud, and her body stiffened. Julia could feel the young woman's pulse racing, and she rubbed Maggie's back

113

soothingly, trying to calm her. After a moment, Maggie relaxed and unconsciously wriggled closer, seizing a fistful of Julia's t-shirt. Julia chuckled softly as she peered at the alarm clock on the nightstand. She never ate at regular hours and only bothered to grab a bite when it occurred to her, but she was painfully aware that she had skipped lunch. Breakfast had consisted of three spoonfuls of vanilla yogurt, and now her stomach was insistently reminding her of its emptiness.

"Well, let's see. We had pizza last night, so that's out. I could order Chinese, I guess. Or maybe we can go out. Technically, we haven't had our first date yet."

"Julia?" A sleepy voice mumbled, cutting through her thoughts. "Whom are you talking to?"

Julia winced, mentally slapping herself in the head for waking Maggie. "Nobody. I didn't mean to wake you. Go back to sleep."

Still using Julia's chest for a pillow, Maggie shook her head, and the friction made Julia's breath catch in her throat. Maggie yawned, grimacing at the audible pop in her jaw. She flopped over onto her back and folded her hands over her stomach.

"I don't want to go back to sleep." Turning her head to the side, she examined the clear blue eyes that were just inches away from her own. "You have the best eyes. Like the ocean on a clear day."

A dark eyebrow lifted and Julia shrugged, unimpressed with her own features. Reaching over, she caressed Maggie's face, running her thumb across the young woman's cheekbone.

"Hmmm. I prefer yours, actually. They're like the Bay. Deep, mysterious, all sorts of life just beneath the surface."

Deep, mysterious green eyes widened in amazement. "Julia Cassinelli, that was almost poetic!" She gave her lover a light poke with her elbow.

Julia snorted and her lips twitched into a sardonic, self-deprecating grin. "Poetic? Me? You must still be in shock."

Maggie rolled over to her stomach and propped herself up on her elbows. She gave Julia her best attempt at an intimidating glare.

"Are you arguing with me?"

Julia bit down on her lower lip to keep from laughing and she shook her head. "Of course not. I wouldn't dare."

"Good," Maggie declared, maintaining her mock-seriousness. She leaned down and planted a kiss on Julia's lips. "Besides, I thought it was beautiful. Just like you." That earned her another kiss and a pair of wandering hands that traveled leisurely up her sides.

Maggie nestled her head against Julia's shoulder and curled one arm gently around her lover's abdomen. She kissed the warm collarbone peeking out from the neck of Julia's t-shirt.

"How are you feeling, anyway? Still sore?"

Julia stretched, testing her arms and legs carefully as she considered the question. She was pleased to discover that she felt much better. There were a few nagging aches, and she wasn't ready for another desperate sprint across two steep city blocks, but perhaps some lighter activity would be acceptable. Her eyes twinkled suggestively at the thought.

"Uh-oh. I think I recognize that look," Maggie teased.

"Oh, really," Julia drawled, sliding one hand down Maggie's hip. "Got me figured out already?"

"Ha! I doubt if I'll ever have you completely figured out."

Julia scooted closer and nuzzled Maggie's throat, paying particular attention to the small hollow at its base.

"Know what I'm thinking right now?"

Maggie tried to ignore the nibbling and sucking going on below her chin, and the sensations that it was causing elsewhere in her body. She pressed her fingers to her temples and squeezed her eyes shut, pretending to be deep in concentration.

"You are thinking, 'I hate to tear myself away from my sexy new girlfriend, but if I don't get something to eat, I just might starve to death.' How's that?"

"What?" Julia sputtered, laughing. The girlfriend reference sent a warm, happy glow radiating through her body, and she was vaguely conscious of the goofy smile plastered on her face. "How did you know that?"

"Your stomach is rumbling." Maggie patted the offending body part affectionately. "Mine is too," she admitted ruefully. "Now, what do you have to eat in this place?"

Julia took a quick inventory of her kitchen and found the results to be rather depressing. She grinned sheepishly.

"I have half a container of vanilla yogurt and some bread that may or may not have green fuzzy things growing on it."

Maggie sighed, struggling to keep a straight face. "Well, I guess we're gonna be eating out a lot." She rolled out of bed, her feet hitting the floor with a solid thump.

"You don't cook either, huh?" Julia watched as Maggie half-skipped across the floor. "What in the world are you doing? Not that I mind watching you hop up and down, of course."

Maggie turned and stuck her tongue out at the comment. "Smartass. Your floors are damned cold. And no, I don't cook. Not unless you want to be poisoned, anyway."

Maggie rummaged through Julia's drawers until she found what she was looking for. She held up a pair of socks triumphantly and bounded back to the bed. Sighing contentedly, she pulled the socks over her cold feet and wiggled her toes. Satisfied, she turned back to Julia, who was watching her with an amused look.

"Okay. Obviously we can't really go out, since I don't have anything clean to wear. And I look like a smurf in your clothes." She held her arms out, letting her borrowed clothes hang from her frame.

"But you're an adorable smurf," Julia interjected, suppressing a snicker.

"Sshhh. Don't interrupt." Maggie swatted her playfully. "I say we pick something up and go back to my place."

"Why don't we just have something delivered here?"

"Because I would like to wear my own clothes. Don't get me wrong, I love wearing your stuff, but I have a favorite pair of pajama pants. They have polar bears on them. And don't you want to see my apartment?"

Julia slid out of bed and willed herself not to shiver as her bare feet touched the icy floor. She loved her polished wood floors, but maybe a rug for the bedroom would be a good idea. Opening her armoire, she pulled out a clean pair of jeans and a thick, cable-knit fisherman's sweater.

"I would love to see your apartment and your polar bears. Just give me a minute to get dressed."

Julia pulled her hair out from under the collar of her sweater and settled the long locks around her shoulders. She ran her fingers through the dark mane a few times to order it. Although her back was still turned, she seemed to sense Maggie's eyes on her, and an embarrassed flush crept up the back of her neck.

"Okay. Ready to go?" Julia smiled awkwardly as she turned around.

"Yep. I'm driving," Maggie replied, holding up her car keys. In her other hand, she carried her still-damp clothes from before.

As Julia followed her down the stairs, a troubling thought entered her mind. Maggie seemed to be rebounding much too quickly from the day's trauma. Julia was still reeling inside, though she was doing her best not to show it, for Maggie's sake. It seemed to her that the reporter ought to be even more shaken, and she wondered if Maggie was really all right or if she was repressing her emotions. Julia made a mental note to try asking her about it later.

They stepped out onto the front porch, and Maggie paused while Julia carefully locked the door. The air smelled fresh and clean, the pollutants washed away by the storm. Branches and leaves, deposited by the gusting winds, were scattered all across the walkway and lawn, and they stepped around the larger ones carefully on their way to Maggie's car.

"So, what do you feel like eating?" Maggie asked as she pulled away from the curb.

Julia settled back in her seat, adjusting the shoulder strap of her seatbelt. She smiled at Maggie, who really did look slightly ridiculous in her clothes.

"I don't care. Surprise me."

They ended up picking up a bucket of spicy fried chicken, complete with biscuits, mashed potatoes with gravy and two large sodas. Julia juggled the food in her hands as they walked up to Maggie's apartment. The reporter hesitated outside the door.

"Just so you know, it's nothing fancy. Not at all like your house."

"Maggie, just open the door. This stuff is getting heavy."

They stepped inside, and Julia quickly set their dinner on the kitchen table before she dropped it all. Maggie's apartment was small, but it was clean and obviously well kept, though Julia could tell she hadn't been in it for long. It didn't have that sense of permanence about it that true homes did. A worn duffel bag peeked out from behind the couch. Patrick's stuff. Julia had a lot of questions about Maggie's younger brother, but they would keep for a different time, she decided.

"Why don't you go change, and I'll get the food set up?" Julia suggested.

"Oh, okay. Plates and stuff are in there." Maggie pointed at the upper cabinet. "And there should be some silverware in that drawer. I'll be right back."

Maggie headed for her bedroom and hurriedly changed into her polar bear pants and her Ohio State t-shirt. The blue pants didn't match the red shirt, but she didn't care and she doubted that Julia would either. She was surprised at how nervous she felt about Julia being in her apartment. Julia Cassinelli was the first rich person she had ever known, except for Billy Bailey, whose father owned the car dealership back in Marion. She wondered what Julia thought about her clear lack of money. *'Oh, stop that, Maggie. She doesn't care about things like that,'* she told herself sternly. She jumped at the soft knock on her bedroom door.

Julia poked her head in cautiously, concern showing in her eyes. "The food is ready. Is everything okay?"

Maggie forced a smile. "Everything's fine. I'm starving. Let's go eat."

They were both even hungrier than they had realized, and the food was consumed quickly. The topic of conversation had stayed fairly light while they ate, and Julia had learned more about Maggie's childhood. She had been quizzed until she could recite the names of the six McKinnon children in chronological order: Steven, Kimberly, Kenneth, Jack, Maggie and Patrick. She also learned that Maggie had graduated from her Catholic high school at the top of her class and that she had attended Ohio State on a partial scholarship. Even as they chatted, Julia could sense a faint undercurrent of tension between them. Up until now, she had always felt at ease with Maggie and the sudden change bothered her.

Julia stood, helping to clear away the plates. Her confusion grew as she noticed that Maggie wasn't meeting her eyes. She took Maggie's arm gently and turned her away from the sink. Reaching behind the reporter, she shut off the faucet.

"Hey. Talk to me. What's going on?"

"Nothing's going on. Why don't you see what's on TV while I finish cleaning up?" Maggie twisted free and resumed rinsing the dishes.

Completely dumbfounded, Julia stared at her back. Suddenly, Maggie was shutting her out, and she didn't like the feeling one bit. Hurt, she backed away and sat down at the kitchen table again. A few minutes later, Maggie had finished with the dishes, and she observed Julia quietly while she dried her hands. Julia was staring at the table, her eyes dark and troubled.

"I thought you were going to turn on the TV," Maggie said, smiling gamely.

Julia didn't look up. Instead, she took a long, deep breath and straightened her shoulders as if bracing herself for an impact.

"Maggie, what's wrong? Did I do something? Is it what happened earlier today? Talk to me. Please." Her plea was met with frozen silence.

"You didn't do anything. How could you think that?" Maggie replied finally. "Oh, shit. The paper. I need to call my editor." She started for the phone.

Julia stood abruptly, nearly knocking over her chair in her haste. Quickly, she stepped in front of Maggie, blocking her path, and she grabbed the blonde's shoulders gently.

"Forget the paper for a second," she began.

Maggie bristled at the remark and jerked herself free from Julia's grasp. Her eyes flashed angrily as all of the day's stress chose that

118

moment to boil over.

"Forget the paper? That paper is my fucking job! I had a huge chance today and I blew it! Besides, I didn't ask you to forget your case after you got bashed in the head!"

"Maggie, that's not what I meant..." Julia tried to explain, stunned by Maggie's outburst.

"Forget the paper," Maggie repeated scornfully. "Sorry, babe. Can't do that. Not all of us are spoiled little rich girls living off Daddy's money while we play private detective."

Maggie regretted the words even before they tumbled from her mouth. She had no idea where her outburst had come from, and she could only assume that it was a delayed reaction to the day's trauma. One look at the shocked expression on Julia's face told her that the words had hit home. Hard.

"Julia, I didn't mean that. Oh my god. I'm so sorry." Maggie took a step toward her, but Julia backed away.

"It's okay. I should go."

"Please don't go. Please," Maggie implored as the back of her throat constricted and salty tears stung her eyes. "I'm so sorry. Please don't leave me."

Julia stopped, her hand on the doorknob. She desperately wanted to stay. Slowly, she turned around and with one look into those pleading, achingly sad green eyes, she melted. Closing her eyes, she swallowed her pride and reached out to Maggie. With a wrenching sob, Maggie stepped into Julia's arms.

"It's okay, Maggie. I won't ever leave you." She guided Maggie over to the couch and sat down with her, never letting go as Maggie cried against her chest.

"When I thought you were in danger.... god, Maggie, I've never been so scared in my life. I can't stand the thought of not having you in my life."

"Someone tried to kill me," Maggie hiccupped through her tears. "Why would someone try to kill me?"

"I don't know, sweetheart." Julia tilted Maggie's chin up and gazed deeply into her red, puffy eyes. Tenderly, she kissed away the tears, tasting the salt on her lips.

"I don't know," she repeated. "But I swear to you, we're going to find out."

Maggie was quiet for a long time. Finally, she lifted her head and smiled sadly.

"I didn't mean those things I said."

"It's fine. Forget about it." Julia kissed the tip of her nose.

"Are you sure you're not mad at me?"

"I'm not mad. You were just upset. I get that."

Silence fell between them for a long moment.

"Julia?"

"Hmm."

"I really do need to call the paper."

Julia let out a resigned laugh and rubbed her eyes with the back of her hand. "Okay. Go call them."

"You'll be here when I get back?"

"I'll always be right here."

Maggie gave Julia a grateful squeeze before she retreated into her bedroom to use the phone. Alone, Julia leaned her head back against the couch as Maggie's angry words chased themselves around in her brain. '*Spoiled little rich girl. Quit it, Julia, she didn't mean it,*' she told herself. The nagging doubts persisted, but she buried them quickly as she heard Maggie's footsteps returning.

"Everything okay at the paper?" Julia smiled at her.

Maggie resumed her seat and rested her head on Julia's shoulder. "Yeah, more or less. It's odd to be the subject of a news story instead of the reporter. I had to answer a few questions."

They sat in a long, awkward silence until Maggie broke the tension.

"Hey, you know what? We just survived our first fight."

"Hmm. I guess we did."

Maggie's hands slid underneath Julia's sweater, and she felt Julia's stomach muscles tense. "I've heard that make-up sex is supposed to be pretty amazing. Wanna try it?"

Julia shook her head doubtfully. "Maggie, I don't know…"

Maggie put a finger against Julia's lips, silencing her. "Julia, I'm fine. I mean, I'm scared, yes. But I feel safer with you than I do anywhere else, and I just really want to feel close to you right now."

Julia thought for a moment as her reservations slipped away. Finally, she smiled and relaxed, allowing herself to enjoy the feel of Maggie's hands against her skin. Maggie rose, pulling Julia down the hall with her, sliding the sweater up over her head as they moved.

"Amazing make-up sex, huh? Yeah, I think I could give that a try."

Maggie laughed, pushing Julia into her bedroom. Julia joined in as the backs of her knees hit the edge of the bed and she tumbled onto the mattress, pulling Maggie down with her.

****

****

Putting his hands against the small of his back, Patrick arched backwards, trying to ease the nagging ache that had settled there. He had spent a full day unloading heavy barrels from a seemingly endless stream of trucks, and it was more physical labor than he had ever done in his life. As he stood at the end of the loading dock, he squinted into the darkness, looking for the driver that would take him back to his new home. The rain had stopped earlier that afternoon, but dark, swollen clouds still loomed overhead, threatening a new downpour. Patrick wanted to be indoors before the next storm struck.

He examined his hands, wincing at the blisters that had popped up on the soft flesh in spite of the heavy leatherwork gloves he had worn. His foreman had laughed and informed him that his hands would toughen up soon enough. Patrick rubbed his jaw, running his fingers across the prickly stubble. The foreman had seemed like a nice man, and so had the rest of the men he had worked with that day. Still, Patrick couldn't shake the bad feeling that had crept over him the night before when he had been locked inside his room.

He had spent most of the night pacing around the room, and it was well after midnight when he had finally stretched out for a few hours of sleep. Rough hands had shaken him awake, and Patrick had rolled over to find Tom Becker towering over him, contempt clearly burning in his eyes. Without a word, Tom had exited from the room, leaving Patrick alone to ready himself for his new job. Fifteen minutes later, another man escorted Patrick to a car and drove him to work.

Patrick jammed his hands deep into his hip pockets, his fingers curling around the wad of money stuffed there. He smiled, enjoying the feel of the crisp bills. His driver was still nowhere in sight, and Patrick considered walking. There was always the possibility of scoring a hit somewhere along the way. He started to turn away from the edge of the dock when he heard a car in the distance. The sound of the engine grew steadily closer, and tires squealed as a red sports car careened around the corner of the building. The car stopped with a screech at the bottom of the loading dock, and the driver poked his head out of the window.

"Come on, dude. Let's go."

Grinning, Patrick jumped off the edge, ignoring the old, battered ladder that was bolted into the concrete. He barely had time to buckle his seatbelt before Eddie threw the car in reverse and zoomed back up the ramp.

"Hey, what's up?" Patrick greeted Eddie enthusiastically. "I was expecting that other guy. The one who dropped me off this morning."

Eddie glanced at him sideways, though Patrick couldn't see his eyes behind the sunglasses. He narrowly missed hitting a bicyclist, and he laughed at the angry curses shouted in his direction. Without divulging too many details, Eddie explained the change in plans to Patrick. His day with Tom had blackened his mood, and Eddie was ready to have a little fun. He wasn't supposed to be the one picking Patrick up, but at the last minute, Eddie had called the real driver and told him that he would be taking the guy's place. DC would be furious once he found out, but Eddie figured that as long as no harm was done, everything would be okay.

"Dude, I think we are both in need of some serious relaxing. I know this club over on Broadway where the honeys will be all over us, you know what I'm sayin'?" Eddie grinned at him and turned up the radio until the bass made the entire car vibrate.

"I'm there, man," Patrick agreed readily.

"Shit, yeah!"

Eddie tore through a red light, and the Camaro was momentarily airborne as he hit one of the city's steep hills. The car came down with a crash that rocked both men in their seats. They looked at each other and started to laugh hysterically.

"Shit, yeah!" Patrick echoed as they sped towards North Beach.

****
****

"What do you mean he told you he was picking Patrick up?" DC screamed at the man standing across from him. "Who the fuck do you work for, huh? You work for me or for Eddie?"

"I work for you, DC."

"Fucking right, you do!" DC's face was flushed dark red with fury and flecks of foam dotted his lips. He loosened the collar of his shirt. He glared at the man before him.

"Get out."

"DC, I'm sorry. Eddie said the orders came from you."

"Do I look like I give a fuck what Eddie said?" DC's voice rose again, and veins pulsed angrily on his forehead. "Get the hell out!"

Once he was alone, DC picked up the exquisite crystal decanter on the desk and hurled it against the wall. It shattered with a satisfyingly loud smash, spraying liquid all over the wall and floor. The door opened and a woman entered, slinking in like a cat. She looked first at DC, fuming behind the desk, then at the broken glass on the floor.

"Problems, baby?"

DC relaxed slightly and stepped around the desk to greet her. He walked with a faint limp, and he favored his left leg. He smiled at her and pulled her into a hug.

"Nothing I can't handle," he assured her.

She looked at him skeptically as she pulled the cascading mass of blonde curls back from her face. She eyed the shards of glass again.

"Hmm. So, you broke my daddy's decanter because there's nothing wrong that you can't handle?"

Sighing heavily, DC released her and leaned back against the edge of the desk. He stared past her, his gaze focused on a spot somewhere behind her head. Telling her the truth meant risking her volatile temper, but lying to her would be even worse. She moved closer, straddling his lap and locking her long fingers behind his neck. He nibbled at her throat, breathing in the light, delicate scent of her perfume. It always intoxicated him.

"Poor baby," she purred, stroking his sandy hair. "Tell Allison all about it."

"Eddie."

Instantly, the room turned to ice. Placing both hands flat against his chest, Allison wrenched herself free from DC's embrace. Dark eyes flashed and the corner of her mouth curled downward in a derisive sneer.

"Eddie. It's always Eddie," she spat. "Explain to me why you put up with that worthless, irritating screw-up? No, wait. Don't bother. I don't want to hear it again. Just tell me what he did this time."

DC shrugged, feigning indifference. "It's probably nothing. Apparently he picked up the McKinnon guy from the warehouse today. Nobody seems to know exactly where they are."

He braced himself for the explosion, but surprisingly, Allison started to laugh softly. After a moment's confusion, he joined in nervously. Smiling, she moved closer to him again. She pressed her body against his, and he responded eagerly. With an almost violent tug, she yanked his zipper down and thrust her hand inside the front of his pants. His ecstatic groan turned to a horrified squeak as Allison seized hold of him and twisted. Leaning close, she whispered into his ear.

"McKinnon was supposed to stay out of sight. If he and Eddie screw this up for us, I will hold you personally responsible. Do you understand? Nod if you understand."

Pained tears brimmed in his eyes, and DC nodded vigorously.

Allison released him and took a step back, examining her fingernails carefully. With a relieved sigh, DC slumped back against the desk. He took several slow, deep breaths as he waited for the nausea to subside.

"Damn. Chipped the polish." Allison pouted, holding up her damaged index finger. "I want this little problem taken care of. Got it?"

Still not trusting himself to speak, DC nodded again. Allison smiled at him and started to turn away.

"Oh, one more thing. There's a reporter poking around where she doesn't belong. A little blonde at the Chronicle. Do something about that too. Okay, Danny?"

A reporter. Danny wondered if it was the same one who had interviewed him about the Netsports break-in. Frowning, he ransacked his brain, trying to remember her name. He shrugged. All he had to do was find a copy of the newspaper. Her name would be on the story. Long fingers snapped impatiently in front of his nose, and he blinked rapidly, jerking his head back out of reach.

"Hey, Danny! Did you hear me?"

Daniel C. Webber smiled at his fiancée. "Don't worry. I'll handle it."

Allison rewarded him with a pat on the cheek. "Good boy."

****

124

Chapter Twelve

Julia awoke to the odd sensation of sunlight hitting her face. Her own bedroom faced away from the sun, and she still had not grown accustomed to waking up in Maggie's apartment. Nearly a week had passed since their night of amazing make-up sex, and they had been together every night since then.

Carefully, she opened one eye, wincing as the bright light pierced her eyeball and drilled into her brain. Groaning, she pulled the pillow over her face, welcoming the darkness. She had spent the previous night showing Maggie the wide variety of bars and clubs in the Castro, and now she was paying for that last margarita.

The shower was running, and Julia could hear Maggie's slightly off-key alto as she sang along with the radio on the bathroom counter. Before she could change her mind, Julia rolled out of bed and padded on bare feet into the warm, steamy bathroom. She paused, admiring Maggie's outline through the frosted glass door to the shower stall. She opened the door and stepped inside, pulling Maggie close for a kiss.

"Well, good morning to you, too," Maggie greeted her breathlessly after they parted.

"Morning," Julia replied, sticking her head under the water and letting the strong jets massage her scalp.

"Headache?" Maggie asked, recalling that Julia had been quite tipsy when they had finally tumbled into bed the night before.

Julia kept her eyes closed and nodded. She sighed happily as Maggie lightly rubbed her temples, easing the painful throbbing in her head. Julia hugged her lover close, enjoying the feel of their bodies pressed together. Reaching behind Maggie, she took the bottle of shower gel from the shelf and squeezed a healthy amount into the palm of her hand. With a devilish grin, she began to spread the gel across Maggie's body, starting with her shoulders.

125

"I already did that," Maggie informed her.

"You can never be too clean," Julia replied, sliding her hands down to Maggie's breasts and working the gel into a thick, slippery lather.

Maggie let her head fall forward against Julia's shoulder and licked droplets of water from the tanned skin. She groaned, biting down on her lower lip as a soapy hand drifted lower.

"Keep that up and I'm never gonna make it to work," Maggie replied.

"And that would be bad?"

"My boss wouldn't like it."

Julia ducked her head, nibbling on a pink earlobe. "Your boss isn't here," she murmured.

"Eww. I hope not." Maggie screwed up her face at the mental image of her editor in the shower. "I definitely wouldn't want to see him naked."

Laughing, Julia relented and pulled Maggie in for a hug. She rested her chin on top of the damp blonde head.

"You crack me up sometimes, Maggie," she chuckled fondly. "Okay, no more shower games."

"Hey, I didn't say that," Maggie protested. "Maybe later, when we have time to play them properly..." Stretching her arm around Julia, she turned the water off. "I really do have to get to work, though."

Stepping out of the shower, they dried and dressed each other, making the task take much longer than it should have. As they headed into the kitchen, Julia inhaled deeply, breathing in the welcome aroma of freshly brewed coffee. She filled two large mugs while Maggie toasted bagels.

"So, what's going on at the paper today?" Julia asked between swallows of the strong black coffee.

"The usual stuff, I suppose. Deadline for my Halloween story is Wednesday, so I'll probably work on that today."

Julia lifted an eyebrow. "That's the day after tomorrow. Have you even started on it yet?"

Maggie shrugged, taking a bite of her whole-wheat bagel. "Technically, no. But I have all the information. I just have to write it all out." She grinned at the reproachful look her lover was giving her. "Besides, I work better under pressure."

Julia sighed, shaking her head in mock-disapproval. "Maggie McKinnon, world-class procrastinator."

"That's me," Maggie agreed solemnly.

She hesitated, debating with herself for a moment before opening one of the kitchen drawers. She extracted a shiny silver key and took a deep breath as she turned to face Julia. Maggie could feel her cheeks growing hot, and she wondered why in the world she was so nervous. She held the key out to Julia.

"Here. I, uh.... I thought you should have this." She continued as Julia blinked at her in surprise. "I mean, it sort of makes sense, doesn't it? You're here half the time anyway."

"This is the key to your apartment?" Julia asked. Her hand trembled as she took the key from Maggie's outstretched hand.

"Well, yeah," Maggie replied, slightly confused by the stunned look on Julia's face. "Oh god. It's too soon, isn't it? I'm sorry. I just thought..." A pair of warm lips pressing against hers silenced her, and she relaxed into the kiss.

"Sshh. It's not too soon," Julia reassured her. "Thank you. Actually, um, I have one for you at home. I've been trying to figure out the best time to give it to you."

Maggie grinned at her as a warm, contented glow spread through her stomach. "Oh. Cool." She glanced at the clock on the microwave and frowned. "Damn. I really have to go."

"Okay. You're meeting me at Mario's for lunch, right?" Julia handed Maggie her briefcase and escorted her to the door.

"Absolutely. I'll see you at noon. Lock up when you leave, okay?"

"Yeah, yeah. Go on. You're gonna be late." Julia shooed her out the door.

Closing the door, Julia tightened her fist around the cool metal key in her hand. She smiled as she went into the bedroom to retrieve her own key ring. Julia stood at the foot of her bed and stared at the rumpled sheets. She loved having Maggie with her at the end of every day. A car backfired in the street outside, and Julia flinched, reminded of the shooting that could have ended Maggie's life. Though she had no solid evidence, Julia suspected that the reporter had been the intended target, and for the past week, she had been obsessed with finding the shooter. She glanced at the alarm clock next to the bed and cursed softly. It was time for her to get to work too.

****

Eddie Machado slouched further down in his seat as he watched Maggie emerge from her unit and get into her car. Neither woman had paid any attention to him, even though his red Camaro was parked directly across the street from the apartment complex. He noted the time on the expensive Swiss watch strapped to his wrist. He waited until Maggie had passed him before pulling his car into the street. Making sure to adhere to Tom's instructions, he stayed two car lengths behind the black Corolla as he followed Maggie to work, mentally mapping out her route. DC had been furious with him for taking Patrick on a tour of the strip clubs on Broadway, and Eddie knew that this was his last chance to redeem himself.

The task he had been given was simple. Follow the reporter for a couple of days and learn her routine. Eddie was sure he couldn't screw this one up. He tailed the Corolla until Maggie pulled into the parking garage. Eddie noted the time again as he circled the block, looking for a place on the street to park. He zoomed into a tight space, nearly hitting a group of tourists. Slumping down in his seat, he adjusted the rearview mirror until he could see the Chronicle building. He lit a cigarette and settled in to wait until Maggie reappeared.

****

Maggie reached the newsroom at the same time as Catherine Richards, and the temperature plummeted immediately. Her relationship with the Hellcat had become even chillier after she had started working on the serial arson story, and the friction between them had started to affect the rest of the staff. As they walked into the room, every pair of eyes instantly found something fascinating to look at on the floor.

Sighing, Maggie sat down at her desk and sifted through the small stack of pink phone messages. The one on the bottom grabbed her attention. Patrick had called the day before. There was no personal message, just the date and time of the call. Maggie stared at the slip of paper and wondered what he had wanted. She still hadn't called her family and told them about her brother's latest disappearance. She made a mental note to call them later that night, when her father would be home from work.

"Halloween piece is due on my desk the day after tomorrow, McKinnon." Maggie's editor tapped the top of her monitor with his pencil as he walked past her desk.

"You'll have it first thing Wednesday morning," she assured him.

"Hey, speaking of Halloween..."

Maggie jumped as Jessica appeared at her elbow. "How do you do that?"

Jessica stared at her through her wire-rimmed glasses. "Do what?"

128

"Appear out of nowhere like that! I'm starting to think you're some kind of mischievous elf, or something."

Jessica nearly doubled over with laughter. "Oh, that's a good one, Maggie. Mischievous elf," she snorted. "Have you been reading Tolkien again?"

"Anyway, like I was trying to say a second ago," Jessica continued. "Luke is having a party on Halloween. You and tall, dark and sexy are welcome to come, but you have to dress up."

Maggie frowned, searching her brain. "Luke?"

"Yeah, you know, the guy I told you about. The biology grad student at Berkeley," Jessica reminded her.

"Oh, him. Okay, I remember now. I'll check with Julia about the party."

"Do that. Luke is gonna dress up as Batman, and I'm gonna be Catwoman. You don't want to miss out on that."

Maggie laughed, trying to picture her diminutive friend in a vinyl jumpsuit. She added whiskers and a whip to her mental picture and nearly fell out of her chair. She wiped the tears from her eyes.

"No, I definitely don't want to miss that," she said. "I'm having lunch with Julia later. I'll ask her then."

Jessica gave her a knowing grin. "Ah, I get it. Hooking up later for a little noontime quickie?"

"Jess!" Maggie hissed, glancing around to see if anyone was listening. She could feel the blood rushing to her face.

"What?" Jessica asked innocently. "I figured the relationship is still young, so the sex is probably still pretty hot. Besides, there's nothing wrong with getting some on your lunch hour. I do it all the time."

"Oh, that's just what I wanted to know, Jessica. Thank you very much for that image," Maggie replied dryly. "And my relationship with Julia is based on more than hot sex."

"Aha! So you admit that the sex is hot, then?"

"I have no complaints." Maggie grinned smugly. "And this conversation is now over."

"Aw, come on, Maggie! We were just getting to the good stuff."

"Excuse me. I don't want to interrupt, but if recess is over, some of us have work to do," Catherine spoke from behind them, her voice dripping with sarcasm.

Jessica glanced sideways at Maggie. "Later," she mouthed before hastily making her exit.

Maggie counted to ten, making sure she had control of her temper, before she swiveled around to face the other reporter. "What do you want, Catherine?"

"Give me your info on the Davis warehouse fire," Catherine demanded. "I'm helping Graphics put together a timeline."

"Here," Maggie handed her a file from her briefcase. "It's not much, so I don't know how much help it will be. The family spokesman wasn't very forthcoming when I interviewed him. I'm meeting with one of their attorneys later this afternoon. I'll let you know if I find out anything interesting."

"Whatever." Catherine snatched the folder out of Maggie's hand. She started to leave. Suddenly she turned around, fixing Maggie with an icy stare. "You are so far out of your league with the Davis family. Try not to embarrass the rest of us when you make a complete idiot of yourself in front of their lawyer."

Catherine leaned down, bringing her mouth close to Maggie's ear. The cloying scent of her perfume was suffocating, and Maggie nearly gagged. She could feel Catherine's hot breath on her earlobe, and it was making her distinctly uncomfortable.

"By the way, I know all about you and your girlfriend. Congratulations. Julia Cassinelli is quite a catch, if you can hold on to her." Catherine's thin lips twisted into a derisive sneer. "Just so you know, it doesn't matter how many of those high-society babes you fuck. You will never be one of them."

Catherine's mocking laughter mingled with the clacking of her heels as she walked away. Maggie's ears burned and she fought to keep tears of rage from spilling from her eyes. The smell of Catherine's perfume lingered around her desk, and Maggie stood abruptly, in need of some fresh air. She could feel the curious eyes on her as she headed for the doors, and she knew that other people had heard Catherine's words and that the whole newsroom would be buzzing about it by the end of the day. Would they all think the same thing Catherine did? That she was only interested in Julia for her money?

Her ire rose as she approached the doors. She had nothing to be ashamed of, and she would be damned if she was going to act like she did. She turned around and waited until a hush settled over the rest of the staff and she had everyone's attention.

"I know several of you heard what Catherine said to me just now," she started. "So let me confirm a couple of things before the rumors get totally out of hand. Yes, I am gay, and yes, I am dating Julia Cassinelli." Fiery green eyes swept across the room, daring anyone to make a comment. No one did.

Whirling, Maggie stomped out the door and through the outer lobby. She was standing outside on the curb for a full minute before she realized that she had forgotten her jacket at her desk and she was freezing.

"Stupid city with its stupid fog every morning," she grumbled, rubbing her arms.

Maggie took several deep breaths until she felt her anger begin to subside. Tentative footsteps approached behind her, and her jacket miraculously floated in the air in front of her. She smiled.

"Thanks, Jess."

"I saw you go flying out of the newsroom without your jacket. Didn't want you to freeze to death out here," Jessica explained, shoving her hands deep inside her coat pockets to keep them warm. "So, I guess Hellcat strikes again, huh?"

"Ugh. You can say that again." Maggie made a disgusted face as she slipped her favorite corduroy jacket on and started walking down the street. "Let's just say that, thanks to Catherine, my relationship with Julia is out in the open now."

"That bitch!" Jessica's dark eyes flashed with sympathetic anger. "Are you okay? Do you want me to beat her up for you?"

Maggie laughed weakly. "I'm fine, Jess. Really. I don't want to talk about it anymore, okay?"

"Are you sure?" Jessica persisted. "Because I really wouldn't mind beating her up for you."

"Yeah, and then who would have to bail you out of jail afterwards? Me."

"Hmm. You're probably right," Jessica agreed, struggling to keep up with Maggie's rapid strides. "Uh, Maggie? Where are we going?"

"I'm just gonna walk around the block or something. You can go back inside if you want."

"No, no," Jessica puffed. "The exercise will be good for me."

Halfway around the long block, Jessica slowed and tugged on Maggie's sleeve. She made a grand show of tying her shoelace, propping her foot up on a cement planter on the curb.

"Don't look, but I think a red car has been following us since we left the paper," she muttered out of the side of her mouth.

"What?" Maggie started to turn around, but Jessica yanked on her sleeve again.

"I said, don't look!" The tiny copy editor hissed as she adjusted her shoelaces.

Out of the corner of her eye, Maggie saw the red sports car as it slowly drove past them. She caught a quick glimpse of the heavily tattooed driver with the dark sunglasses and slicked-back hair. A chill shot up her spine and the fine hairs on the back of her neck stood on end.

"What should we do?" Maggie whispered, her eyes darting around nervously.

"I don't know!" Jessica replied frantically.

Maggie fervently wished that Julia were with her. No, actually, she wished that she were with Julia, far away from the red car with its creepy driver. She glanced back over her shoulder, and suddenly everyone on the street looked threatening. Even the nice old man who sold flowers on the corner seemed to be watching her.

"Okay, calm down. Maybe we're just being paranoid." She chewed on her lower lip as she tried to decide her course of action. "Let's just get back inside."

Jessica nodded, her eyes wide with fear. She hooked her arm through Maggie's as they hurried back down the street towards their building. A few yards from the front doors, they saw the Camaro come around the corner. It parked a few doors down, and they could see the driver through the windshield as his head bobbed along to the loud music blaring from the stereo.

"Shit," they squeaked in unison.

Trying not to draw too much attention to themselves, they dashed inside. The receptionist, Carole, looked at them curiously while she answered the phones. Maggie peeked out the window. The car was still there.

"You should get out of here," Jessica advised. She dug in her coat pocket. "Here. Take my car. I'll get a ride home with someone."

Maggie shook her head. "This is ridiculous. We don't even know for sure that he's following me."

Jessica's eyes widened. "You don't think he's after me, do you?"

"No, of course not! Maybe he's not after either of us. Maybe he was just circling the block until he could find a parking space."

Flattening herself against the wall, Jessica carefully craned her neck around the corner until she could see out the window. The man with the tattoos was still sitting in the car, and now he was talking to someone on a cell phone. She wasn't sure, but she thought he seemed to be watching their building.

"Is he still there?" Maggie asked.

Jessica nodded. "He's on the phone."

"It could be nothing. Maybe he's just waiting for someone," Maggie theorized.

"Maybe," Jessica replied doubtfully. "Maybe you should call Julia."

Maggie shook her head emphatically. "No way. She would just get all upset. It's taken me this long to get her calmed down after what happened last week."

After Maggie's near miss with a bullet the week before, Julia had gone into insanely over-protective mode. She had insisted upon personally installing a new security system for the apartment. Though the reporter couldn't prove it, she also suspected that Julia had called in a few favors from the police department, since Maggie swore she had seen a patrol car cruising her street at regular intervals. Still, she couldn't really complain about all the attention, since it meant that she and Julia had spent every night together for the past week.

Gathering her courage, she peeked out the window again. The car was still there, and this time, the driver seemed to be looking directly at her. Logically, Maggie knew he couldn't see from so far away, especially since she was mostly hidden behind a corner. Her skin prickled anyway, as logic gave way to icy fear. She turned to Jessica.

"I think I'm gonna take you up on your offer."

Jessica pressed her car keys into Maggie's hand. "You know where it's parked, right?"

"Second level, by the elevator."

"Get out of here then. I'll cover for you. As far as I know, you went to meet with a source." Jessica pushed her towards the elevator.

"Thanks. I'll call you later." Maggie stepped inside and punched the number for the parking garage.

"Be careful," Jessica warned her earnestly.

Maggie put on a brave smile. "Don't worry. I'll be fine."

The elevator doors slid shut with a quiet hiss, and Maggie slumped back against the wall. She watched anxiously as each floor lit up with a soft ping as she descended towards the garage. She half expected to find the tattooed man waiting for her when she reached her destination, but the parking level was dim and deserted. The sound of her shoes on the concrete echoed through the cavernous structure as she hurried to Jessica's car. She needed to get to Julia. Then everything would be okay.

She should have turned right upon exiting the garage. Instead, Maggie cut across traffic and turned left, heading towards the red sports car. She held her breath as she passed it, but the driver wasn't looking in her direction. He was too busy flirting with a group of sightseeing women on the street. As she drove by, Maggie noted his license plate number. She would give that to Julia and see what the private investigator could find. Half a block later, when the Camaro was barely visible in the rearview mirror, Maggie exhaled in relief and turned the car towards Julia's office.

****

Julia slammed the phone down in disgust and pushed her chair back from her desk. For the last week, she had been trying to track down more information about Allison Davis and her family. She had called every upper crust college classmate she could find, but the result had been the same. Either they didn't know the Davis family, or they were unwilling to talk about them. A cold, hard knot in Julia's stomach warned her that it was the latter.

Sighing, she flipped through her address book again, hoping that there was a name she had overlooked. Blank pages stared back, silently mocking her. Other than a handful of professional contacts, there were few names in her book. A scrap of paper slipped out from between two pages and fluttered to her desktop. Julia stared at it as a bitter taste filled her mouth. It was the new number that her father had given her eight months before. No, Julia corrected herself; it was the number that her father's secretary had delivered on her voice mail. Joseph Cassinelli had been much too busy to call his daughter himself.

With one finger, Julia pushed the paper back and forth on her desk. Her father and Councilman Davis had been friends at one time. She wasn't sure whether or not they were still close, but she knew that her father would probably know something that would help her. However, the odds of him sharing any information with her were woefully slim.

"Okay, Julia. Remember why you're doing this," she said aloud, convincing herself to make the dreaded call. "This is to keep Maggie safe."

She dragged the phone towards her, steeling herself for the inevitable unpleasantness. As she started to dial, the door to her office opened and Maggie burst in, looking out of breath and wild-eyed. Julia dropped the phone, and leather creaked loudly as she leaped out of her chair.

"What is it? What happened?"

Maggie waved her back and collapsed into the chair on the opposite side of Julia's desk. She smiled gratefully as Julia produced a clean mug and filled it with steaming, black coffee.

134

"So, are you gonna tell me what's wrong?" Julia asked.

"Why does something have to be wrong?" Maggie replied evasively. "We were supposed to meet for lunch, right?"

Julia glanced at her watch skeptically. It was just after 9:30, much too early for anything remotely resembling lunch. Something was clearly wrong. She sat quietly, waiting for Maggie to speak.

"Oh, okay. Here." Maggie handed her a crumpled slip of paper. "Do you think you can find out who that belongs to?"

Julia carefully smoothed the wrinkles out of the paper and read the combination of numbers and letters. Her brow creased. It looked like a license plate number.

"What is this and where did you get it?"

Maggie leaned back in her chair. "I thought you were supposed to be the investigator," she said testily. Exhaling, she reached across the desk and laid her hand on Julia's wrist. "Sorry. I'm a little stressed at the moment."

"So I see," Julia replied, squeezing Maggie's hand reassuringly. "Tell me what happened."

Maggie took a deep breath and launched into the story of the red Camaro and its creepy driver. By the time she was through, she could feel the dark anger pulsating from her fuming lover. The image of a cartoon character with steam pouring out of its ears popped into her head, and she just barely stifled a giggle. The urge to laugh quickly morphed into the urge to cry, and she ended up doing both simultaneously.

Julia hurried around the edge of the desk and knelt next to Maggie's chair. "Hey, it's okay. I'll find out who this bastard is, and I swear, he won't bother you again."

Maggie shoved her chair back so forcefully that she nearly knocked Julia over. As she paced across the small office, her outrage grew with each step. Near the door, she spun around, her green eyes smoldering.

"You know what? This is really starting to piss me off," she said heatedly. She pointed at the computer humming quietly on Julia's desk. "Work your P.I. magic and find out who that car belongs to. Let's get this son of a bitch."

"That's my girl." Julia grinned proudly as she sat down at her desk again. She patted her lap. "C'mere. Help me nail this guy to the wall."

Maggie took a seat, as requested, and watched, fascinated, as her lover's fingers flew across the keyboard. Plastic keys rattled and clicked furiously, and Julia's determined scowl turned into a self-satisfied smirk as the criminal history of Edgar Alejandro Alvarez Machado appeared on her screen.

"This look like him?" Julia asked, flicking the mug shot on her monitor.

"That's him. How did you do that?"

Julia's smirk broadened and her eyes twinkled. "P.I. magic."

She coughed into her fist as Maggie elbowed her in the ribs. "Okay, okay. It's pretty easy actually. Most of this stuff is available on the Internet," she admitted guiltily.

"You are amazing." Maggie planted a kiss on Julia's cheek with a loud, wet smack.

Julia winked at her as she reached for the phone and called Inspector Henry Chow. She told Henry that Maggie had been followed at work, and she gave him the information she had pulled up on Eddie Machado. Henry agreed to have Eddie picked up for questioning, and despite his grumbling, he promised to let Julia observe.

"So, Henry's is going to let you watch while they question this guy?" Maggie asked after Julia hung up the phone.

"Yep. A little thug like that is most likely working for somebody else. I want to know who he takes his orders from." Julia's eyes glinted dangerously. "Henry said he'd call me as soon as they have this guy."

"Well, it's still too early for lunch." Julia changed the subject. "What's your plan for the rest of the day?"

Maggie made a face. "I suppose I should go back to work. I have an interview with one of Councilman Davis's lawyers this afternoon."

Julia's ears perked up. Maybe Maggie would be able to turn up something interesting about Allison. "Oh, yeah? Which one? He has a whole pack of 'em. I've been trying to find out some information about his daughter."

Blonde eyebrows shot skyward, and Julia immediately realized that she could have phrased her last statement much better. Grinning sheepishly, she began to stutter out a clarification. Maggie laughed finally, letting her off the hook.

"Relax. I knew what you meant. I know you think Allison is involved in this whole thing."

Julia's mood sobered. "Yeah, I do. Maybe it isn't such a good idea for you to meet with this guy by yourself."

"It's just a lawyer, Julia. I think I can handle it." Maggie bristled slightly.

"Oh, I'm sure you can," Julia replied hastily. "What time is your meeting? If I'm done at the police station, maybe I can go with you."

"It's at 2:00, and you just want to be my bodyguard," Maggie told her, softening the accusation with a smile.

"Well, hey...someone has to guard that body of yours. I admit I would feel safer if you didn't go alone. But I have a selfish reason, too. I want to know more about Allison, and I'm hoping this lawyer can tell me something."

Maggie sighed. "Okay, then. I guess we'll have to save lunch at Mario's for a different day. Call me when you're done at the police station. I really should get back to work now."

Julia frowned, sensing Maggie's reluctance to return to the paper. She followed her lover to the door.

"Maggie? Did something else happen at work?"

"No. Well, Catherine and I went another round, but it was no big deal." Maggie winced internally at her little deception. That conversation could wait for another time, she decided. "Oh, do you have Halloween plans? Jessica invited us to a party."

Julia stiffened and Maggie could almost see the shadow that fell over her face. "No. No plans. I, uh, I don't usually celebrate Halloween. It's my mother's birthday, and I don't remember it ever being a very happy occasion."

"Oh. Julia, I'm so sorry. I didn't know."

"It's okay. I just never really felt like celebrating it before. But you go ahead and go to the party if you want. It sounds like fun."

"I would rather spend the day with you," Maggie declared. "Unless you would rather be alone, that is."

"I've been alone for thirty years and I think I've had enough of it. I would love to spend the day with you." Julia's face brightened as an idea struck her. "In fact, I know of this place on the coast. Private cabin, outdoor shower, cozy fireplace. Are you interested?"

"Sounds perfect."

"I'll make the arrangement, then."

"You do that. Okay, I'm really going back to work now. I'll see you later." Maggie gave Julia a quick kiss before heading out the door.

She ached for Julia's lost childhood. No Halloween. Birthdays and Christmases were probably lonely affairs, too. She knew that Joseph Cassinelli was a powerful and busy man, but she wondered what kind of father let his children grow up in such an emotionally bleak environment. As Maggie reached the car, she vowed to make this holiday, and every other, special for Julia.

Maggie arrived at the paper just in time to see the police arrest Eddie Machado. She smiled in satisfaction as she watched a uniformed officer unceremoniously shove him into the back of a patrol car. Catherine was nowhere in sight when she entered the newsroom, and the rest of the busy staff barely gave her a second glance. The day was starting to look better and better, she thought as she sat at her desk and began to work on her Halloween story. Julia called her three hours later, sounding disappointed and annoyed.

"The cops didn't get anything out of this Machado guy," Julia reported disgustedly. "Some fancy lawyer showed up and got him released a few minutes ago."

"Damn," Maggie commiserated. "They didn't find out anything at all?"

"No. I got the lawyer's name, though. I was going to see if I could find out who he worked for."

"That sounds like a good idea. Are you still planning on coming with me on my interview?"

"Absolutely. Listen, I thought maybe we could grab some lunch before then. How does that sound?"

Maggie's stomach heard the word 'lunch' and grumbled loudly. "That sounds like an even better idea."

"Good. Because I'm standing outside your newsroom right now," Julia said into her cell phone as she opened the glass doors.

Maggie swiveled around in her chair and beamed as she saw Julia crossing towards her. Julia was like a magnetic force, and all heads turned to watch her as she passed. She ignored them all, her gaze firmly fixed on the small blonde on the other side of the room. She stopped abruptly, startled, as a tiny Asian woman stepped into her path.

"Hi, I'm Jessica. Maggie's friend?" Jessica Sato shook Julia's hand enthusiastically.

"Oh, right. She's told me a lot about you," Julia replied. "Sorry we can't make it to your party."

"I know, you have other plans. That's cool," Jessica said, waving a hand dismissively. "I just wanted to introduce myself and tell you that I have never seen Maggie look so happy. It's a total cliché, but her face lights up every time she speaks your name. It's great. I'm thrilled for both of you. But if you break her heart, I will track you down and kill you. Okay?"

Julia blinked down at the young woman who stood nearly a foot shorter than her. She recognized the fierce protectiveness burning in those dark eyes and had no doubt that Jessica was serious. Julia smiled. They were going to get along just fine.

"I understand completely," Julia said agreeably.

"Good, I'm glad. It was very nice meeting you, Julia." Jessica stepped aside, craning her neck and winking at the woman towering over her. "You know, you really shouldn't keep your girlfriend waiting like this." She waved at Maggie before hurrying away.

"That was Jessica," Maggie said.

"Yes, so she said. She's.... interesting." Julia laughed as they left the newsroom. "Actually, she seemed very nice. I'm glad you have a friend like her."

They had lunch at a small sidewalk café before heading over to a hulking, steel and glass monstrosity in the heart of the city's financial district. Julia grimaced in distaste as she stared up at the top floors of the building.

"I hate these modern buildings. They just look so tacky and out of place next to all the old stone."

She held the door open as they entered the cavernous marble lobby. Her nose wrinkled at the cool, filtered air that chilled the entire room. The security guard at the desk regarded them blandly as they approached.

"Can I help you, ladies?"

"Yes. My name is Maggie McKinnon. I have an appointment to speak with one of the attorneys for Councilman Davis."

The security guard shuffled papers on a clipboard. He looked at them with watery brown eyes and smiled, exposing his tobacco-stained teeth.

"Sorry, ma'am. There's nobody by that name on my list."

Maggie stared at him incredulously. "There has to be a mistake. I set up this interview yesterday. Could you check again, please?"

The guard shrugged and sorted through the pages again, barely glancing at any of the names on them. "Sorry. Nobody named McKinnon on here."

"How would you know? You didn't even look," Julia growled at him. She heard a faint buzz and looked up at one of the six surveillance cameras in the lobby. This one seemed to be focused directly on her, and the red light flashed at her as she stared at it.

"Maybe you could call someone and tell them I'm here?" Maggie suggested.

The guard grinned at her, folding his arms across his narrow chest. "Sorry. They're all in a meeting. Can't be disturbed."

"Every single attorney in this whole goddamn building is in a meeting?" Julia asked, her voice growing colder with each word.

"Yes, ma'am. I'm afraid so. You'll have to come back another time."

Julia leaned forward, intending to grab the smug security guard by the front of his ugly khaki shirt. Shaking him until his puny brain rattled seemed like a good idea. Sensing her lover's deteriorating mood, Maggie smoothly slid between Julia and the desk. She gave Julia a warning look before turning back to the guard, giving him her best small-town smile.

"I really hate to ask this, but maybe you could just let us up there anyway? It's really important and I promise I won't tell anyone you did me this little favor."

"I'm very sorry, ma'am, but I can't do that. If your name isn't on the list, you do not get up to those offices." He couldn't help throwing an arrogant smile in Julia's direction. "Now if you don't leave, I'll have to…"

"You'll have to what? Call security?" Julia scoffed, interrupting him. "Let's go, Maggie. We're wasting our time here."

Julia stomped out the door with Maggie trailing quietly behind her. She stopped on the sidewalk and glowered up at the building.

"Bunch of pompous idiots," she snarled.

"You want to tell me what's going on with you?" Maggie asked as they walked back to Julia's jeep.

Julia sighed. "Nothing. Places like that just get on my nerves."

Maggie absorbed that in silence for a moment. "Because they remind you of your father?" she asked gently.

"Maybe," Julia admitted reluctantly. "So now what? Do you have to go back to work?"

"Hmm. I don't know. Let me call and see if there's anything going on." Maggie made a quick phone call to the paper and found that there was nothing pressing that needed her attention.

"Nothing much going on there," Maggie reported. "Still, I should probably get some work done. I want to find out why this interview fell through. At the very least, I should try to set up a new one."

Privately, Julia suspected that this interview wasn't going to take place; no matter how many times Maggie called to reschedule it. The Davis family had something to hide, and they weren't about to be exposed by a novice reporter. Maggie was talented, but she was inexperienced, and these lawyers would exploit that. Plus, Julia was reluctant to let Maggie out of her sight again. She had been followed to work already, and the punk who had been tailing her was back out on the street. She was determined to do everything she could to keep the reporter safe, and she searched her brain for an excuse to keep Maggie from going back to work.

Julia smiled at her as they reached the jeep. "What do you say we get out of here and have some fun? I've had enough of security guards, lawyers and tattooed punks for one day."

Maggie buckled her seatbelt. "Normally, I would say 'I'm yours, do with me what you will,' but I really do have to get some work done."

"Look, you probably wouldn't be able to get another interview set up for today, anyway. Right?" Julia reasoned. She went on before Maggie could respond. "Probably not. Why not start fresh tomorrow when you have the whole day to talk your way into that building?"

Julia saw Maggie wavering, and she went on for the clincher. She let her lips curl into the quirky, lopsided grin that she knew the blonde absolutely adored. "Besides, technically, we still haven't been out on a date yet."

Maggie realized that Julia was trying to charm her, but she had to admit that everything she was saying made sense. She most likely wouldn't be able to get another interview that day. In fact, given the security guard's attitude, she doubted if she would even be able to get anyone to take her call. *Oh, give it up, Maggie. You can never say no to that cute little grin*, her inner voice prodded her.

"What did you have in mind?" Maggie asked slowly.

"Well, I've never really done anything Halloweenish, and there's this big haunted house thing at this amusement park in Vallejo. Are you up for it?"

"Are you kidding me? My brothers used to run the best haunted house in Marion when we were growing up. We charged a dollar to get in and usually made out like bandits."

"Speaking of making out...." Julia leaned over and kissed her thoroughly. She drew back, grinning. "So, is that a yes?"

Maggie felt a momentary pang of guilt for letting herself be convinced so easily. It was completely unlike her to blow off work in favor of a date. One look into those deep blue eyes melted her resolve, and thoughts of the newspaper vanished from her mind. She pointed to the steering wheel.

"Drive."

Two hours later, they were standing a line for a maze that was guaranteed to give them nightmares, according to the zombie who had directed them there. Many of the park employees were dressed in Halloween costumes, and Maggie and Julia had been forced to dodge out of the way as a trio of clowns chased two teenage girls through the crowd. Artificial fog swirled in the air, lit up by the bright neon lights.

"In another month, they won't need the fake stuff." Julia observed as the line inched closer to the maze entrance.

"In another month, it won't be Halloween, dear." Maggie reminded her.

A loud roar whooshed by and screams pierced the air. Maggie tilted her head back and stared at the rickety, wooden roller coaster. She shuddered.

"Not a big fan of the roller coaster?" Julia asked.

"Ugh. Not really. I'm always afraid we'll go flying right off the track."

Julia wrapped her arms around Maggie's waist. "I would never let you fall."

"Aw. That was really sweet, honey. But I'm still not riding one of those things with you."

Julia laughed. A group of teenage boys in front of them were watching them, contempt evident on their faces. She arched an eyebrow at them silently, daring one of them to make a comment. One, a pasty-faced boy with bad skin and a nose ring, muttered something under his breath. His three companions laughed.

"Julia, maybe we shouldn't do this here," Maggie said, trying to extricate herself from her lover's embrace.

"Just ignore them. We have nothing to be ashamed about," Julia raised her voice a bit; making sure the boys heard her.

The pasty-faced boy rolled his eyes. His buddies laughed again. All four boys turned away, and Maggie breathed a sigh of relief. They reached the entrance to the maze, and the attendant sent the boys through. She stopped Maggie and Julia from following them inside.

"I saw the way those guys were looking at you two. I thought it might be a good idea to let them go through first," she said.

Julia straightened her shoulders. "I'm not afraid of ignorant brats like them."

The attendant looked Julia up and down and grinned at her. "No, I bet you aren't. I was more concerned with their safety, anyway." All three women laughed. "Okay, you can go in now. Have fun."

Julia ducked inside the tent first. It was pitch dark inside. A red light glowed around the corner to her left, and she headed toward it. An open coffin with a decaying corpse inside it rested on a table draped in black cloth.

"Is that the best they can do?" Maggie asked as they neared the coffin.

As they passed in front of it, the corpse popped up and shrieked at them. Maggie jumped backwards, pulling Julia with her. The greenish-black, rotting corpse continued to cackle madly at them as they turned and found themselves face to face with another hideous creature. Looming over them, a pumpkin-headed monster munched on dripping, severed leg. Maggie screamed and darted down another corridor. Laughing helplessly, Julia followed behind her.

"What happened to brave little Miss my-brothers-built-haunted-houses?" Julia panted as they scurried down a long hallway.

"That was a flesh-eating pumpkin monster!" Maggie cried, beginning to laugh with Julia.

They turned another corner and strobing white lights blinded them. The room was filled with fog, and it was impossible to see more than a few inches ahead. Maggie grabbed hold of the back of Julia's leather jacket as they entered the room. Julia crept forward slowly, stretching one hand out in front of her. Her adrenaline was pumping and every muscle was tensed and ready for the next scare. They reached the other side of the room without incident, and Julia glanced over her shoulder at Maggie.

"See? That part wasn't bad at all."

Maggie's eyes widened and she pointed frantically. Julia spun around as a knife-wielding figure with a grinning death's-head charged down the corridor towards them. Its bleached skull gleamed beneath a black hood, and it spouted gibberish at them as it ran.

"Oh shit!"

Julia's composure broke and she ran back into the strobe lights, pushing Maggie ahead of her. It was the wrong move. The swirling fog and pulsing bright lights concealed the creature until it was standing right in front of them. A second skull grinned at them, knife raised and ready to strike.

"Ahhhhhhh!!!!!" They screamed in unison, tripping over each other in their dash out of the room.

Ten minutes later, after laughing and screaming themselves hoarse, they reached the last room in the maze. They could feel the cool night air wafting in from the exit ahead. Maggie and Julia looked at each other, both of them grinning madly. As one, they dashed for the last door. Maggie ducked underneath an arm that reached for her, and she lost her balance, tumbling to her hands and knees. Laughing too hard to get up, she crawled to the door and collapsed on the sweet, scratchy hay outside. Julia sank down beside her, holding her sides.

"Is this what I've been missing out on all these years?" Julia asked.

Maggie sat up, brushing bits of hay out of her hair. She smirked wickedly.

"These are just the tricks. If you're good, when we get home, I just might give you a treat."

Dark eyebrows lifted, and a slow smile tugged at Julia's lips. She scrambled to her feet, pulling Maggie up with her. Unfolding her map of the park, she charted their course.

"Where to?" Maggie asked as they headed towards a giant, swinging pirate ship.

"Carnival of Doom," Julia replied, pointing to another tented area.

They could already hear the terrified screams coming from within.

"Carnival? Oh, I don't know, Julia." Maggie eyed the tent nervously. "That one probably has clowns. Big, scary clowns."

Julia slid her arm around Maggie's shoulders. "It's okay. I'll protect you from the killer clowns."

"Um. Julia?"

Maggie pointed at a pack of extraordinarily fast-moving zombies who were edging towards them. The lead zombie grinned at them, exposing black, rotting teeth.

"Oh, shit." Julia gulped audibly.

Grabbing Maggie's hand, she began to run. The zombies sped in pursuit and chased them screaming into the night.

****

Chapter Thirteen

Droning over the loudspeakers, a weary voice informed them that the park was closing for the evening. Maggie and Julia joined the throng of exhausted thrill-seekers trudging towards the main exit. Blue eyes peeked over a mountainous pile of stuffed animals and souvenirs.

"Are you sure you don't want me to carry some of that?" Maggie asked for the fifth time.

"No, no. I've got it," Julia replied, juggling her prizes to keep the stuffed whale from sliding off the top of the heap.

Much to Maggie's delight, Julia had turned out to be an expert at beating the games on the midway. She had been especially adept at squirting water into the clown's mouth. The first player to blow up a balloon that way won a prize, and Julia had kept trading up until she walked away with the giant killer whale.

Maggie smiled at the park employees as they moved through the main gate. It was a long, uphill hike back to the jeep, and the wind was blowing in from the lagoon. Her new sweatshirt with the cartoon martian on the front blocked most of the chill. Out of the corner of her eye, she noticed that Julia was puffing a bit under her armload of goodies.

"At least let me carry Bert," she said, tugging on the whale's tail.

"Bert?" Julia glanced sideways at her. "You already named the whale, Bert?"

"Yep. That's his friend, Ernie, there," Maggie replied, pointing to the bottle-nosed dolphin peeking out from the crook of Julia's arm.

Rolling her eyes in amusement, Julia held her arms out so Maggie could remove the stuffed whale from its lofty perch. She adjusted her grip on the plastic bag clutched in her right hand and darted a surreptitious glance at her lover. She didn't think Maggie had seen her purchase that particular gift, and it had been easy to hide that bag with all the others. It had caught her eye while she was waiting for

145

Maggie to buy ice cream. Mounted on a piece of polished driftwood, the crystal dolphin had winked and sparkled at her under the lights. She had known immediately that it was perfect. A warm smile touched her lips as Julia imagined the look on her lover's face when she gave it to her.

Tilting her head to study Julia's chiseled profile, Maggie saw the tiny smile twitching the corners of her lover's lips. She nudged Julia lightly in the ribs.

"What's that grin for, huh?"

Julia stared at her innocently as they cut across the mostly empty parking lot. Keeping quiet, she shrugged. Maggie let out a faintly exasperated sigh. She knew that look. That was the look that meant "ask all you want, but I'm not gonna tell you until I'm good and ready." The blonde pursed her lips, trying to figure out what her not-so-innocent girlfriend was up to.

They could see Julia's jeep parked beneath one of the dim yellow lights. A few spaces behind it, four teenage boys passed a paper bag back and forth as they sat in the bed of a battered truck. Maggie's stomach sank as she recognized them. They were the same boys from the haunted house.

Beside her, Julia stiffened as she caught sight of them. Almost unconsciously, she straightened her shoulders and lifted her chin in a defiant challenge as she swaggered towards her jeep. Twin chips of ice bored into the occupants of the truck as her gaze swept from one sullen teen to the next.

Smoothly, she glided around to the passenger's side of the jeep and unlocked the door. Her eyes never left the boys in the truck as she deposited her armload in the back of the vehicle and waited while Maggie buckled herself in. She slammed the door shut and turned to face the dented, rusting truck.

"Something you boys want to say?" Her silky voice dripped with menace.

The pale ringleader with the bad complexion hopped over the side of the truck. His heavy boots landed on the asphalt with a solid thump. Behind him, his buddies snickered as they anticipated a fight.

"People like you make me sick." Leaning back against the side of the truck, he spat on the ground.

"Then we have something in common. People like you make me sick, too."

There wasn't a hint of warmth in the hard smile Julia gave him as she circled around to the driver's side of her jeep. Briefly, her eyes flicked to Maggie's face and she saw the concern in the blonde's expression.

Movement caught her attention as the teen sauntered towards her, his eyes flat and cold in his doughy face. Julia backed away from the jeep, giving herself a wide area to work with. As the boy drew closer, her nose wrinkled. He reeked of stale sweat and cheap beer. Her senses sharpened as he approached. All extraneous noise disappeared and she focused all her energy on the potential opponent in front of her.

"You know what you need? You need a real man," he said when he was nearly toe-to-toe with her.

Julia didn't bother with a response. Her hands dangled loosely at her sides and she flexed them as she waited for him to make a move. She didn't have to wait long. Rubbery lips leered at her as he lunged forward, reaching out for her arm. Julia easily dodged to the side, letting his momentum carry him past her. His friends laughed and hooted, making him even angrier. He whirled around and charged at her, his eyes revealing his intent to do serious damage.

She ducked under a wild swing. As she came up, Julia drove her fist into his solar plexus, and he doubled over as all the air rushed out of his lungs. The blow sent a jolt of pain traveling all the way to her shoulder, and she shook her hand to relieve the stinging. Wheezing painfully, the teen staggered towards her again, and she sighed.

"Haven't you had enough yet?" she asked.

"Fucking bitch," he coughed, lunging for her again.

This time, she brought her knee up into his groin. His eyes bulged and, moaning and croaking like a sick bullfrog, he slumped to the asphalt. Julia carefully stepped around him, her gaze fixed on the rest of his friends.

"Anyone else?"

They stared at her coldly, but no one moved. She got into the jeep and drove away without looking back.

****

Tom Becker watched the entire incident from behind the tinted windows of a black luxury sedan. He grunted in approval when Julia dropped the ignorant young punk to the ground. She was one tough bitch, and he liked that. He had admired her strength since she had fought against him in her office. Tom sighed. If it weren't for her connection to the reporter, Cassinelli might have been a valuable ally.

He had been following them since they left the law offices earlier that afternoon. He hadn't been at all surprised to learn that

147

Eddie had fouled everything up yet again. The idiot had let Maggie McKinnon slip by right under his nose. He would deal with Eddie later.

Tom frowned, speeding up to keep the dark green jeep in sight. Things were becoming too complicated. There were too many loose ends and uncontrolled variables dangling around out there, and he hated that. It was his job to clean them up.

Danny was succumbing to the pressure, and he was slowly unraveling. Tom had expected that. He had always known that Danny was weak and that Allison was the one who was really in charge. Upon learning of Eddie's latest failure, she had walked into Tom's room and calmly given him a set of instructions. Take care of the reporter, then take care of Eddie Machado. She hadn't elaborated, but Tom had known what she meant. Slowly, he increased the pressure on the accelerator, maneuvering his car directly behind the jeep. He reached for the gun sitting on the passenger seat.

****

"Sorry. What were you saying?" Julia asked, shaking the red haze from her mind as she realized that Maggie had been calling her name for some time.

Maggie looked at her critically. She had known that Julia was strong, and that she could be intimidating at times, but she had never expected violence from her. She wasn't sure what disturbed her more, that Julia had clearly enjoyed the scuffle, or that she had enjoyed watching it. She laid her hand on Julia's thigh and could almost feel the crackling energy.

"Are you okay?"

Julia glanced at her briefly before returning her attention to the merging traffic. The thrill of the fight was still sending endorphins flooding through her bloodstream. She darted another glance sideways and saw the hint of uncertainty and fear in Maggie's eyes. Instantly, her adrenaline high began to subside and she shifted gears mentally.

"I'm fine, Maggie." She cleared her throat awkwardly. "I'm so sorry about that. I don't know what got into me."

Maggie relaxed as she saw the odd, hard glitter fade from Julia's eyes. She patted her leg reassuringly.

"It's okay. Those guys were jerks."

"Yeah, but I shouldn't have let them get to me like that," Julia said, flexing her sore right hand. "Unfortunately, there are a lot of jerks in this world. I can't go around beating them all up."

148

"No. Not all of them," Maggie agreed. "Just the ones who try to physically threaten you. Where did you learn to do that, anyway?"

"Self-defense class in college." Julia grinned briefly. "This makes twice in the last month that I've actually had to use those skills."

Before Maggie could reply, the rear windshield shattered inward with a deafening crash, and the dashboard between them splintered. She screamed as Julia swerved wildly across three lanes of traffic.

"Stay down!" Julia shouted, reaching over to push Maggie's head below the level of the windshield.

In her rearview mirror, she caught a glimpse of a dark car with tinted windows. Instinct took over, and she wove in and out of the lanes. Reflexively, she ducked as a two more shots ricocheted off her jeep. One shot ripped her side mirror off. The second hit one of the rear tires, sending the jeep into a sickening spin. Desperately, Julia fought to regain control of the vehicle. The center divide was coming at them much too fast, and she took a deep breath, bracing herself for the impact.

"Hang on!" Julia grabbed for Maggie's hand. Metal shrieked and crunched as the jeep slammed into the concrete barrier.

****

Tom surveyed the wreckage in his rearview mirror as he sped away down the dark stretch of California highway. He cursed at himself in disgust. As he fired the first shot, he had hit an unseen bump in the road, just enough to throw his aim off. The Cassinelli woman was smart. Once she realized what was happening, she had managed to evade his follow-up attempts.

Grinding his teeth in frustration, Tom debated whether or not to go back and finish the job. Twice he had tried to take care of that damn reporter, and twice she had escaped. It wasn't at all like him, and he hated it. He took great pride in his success rate.

Going back was too much of a risk. Even though there weren't many other vehicles on the road that night, some good Samaritan was bound to have stopped by now. He brightened slightly as he considered the possibility that the crash might have succeeded where his bullets had failed. He hoped so. Otherwise, he would have to explain to Allison why the reporter was still alive, and he knew that would not be a pleasant experience.

He shifted his shoulders beneath the merino wool sweater that fit snugly across his thick chest. His entire upper body felt tighter than a giant knot that had been soaked in seawater. Trying to relax, he let out a deep breath as he reached for the CD player and inserted his favorite disc. The soothing strains of Debussy filled the car as he disappeared into the night.

****

"Maggie? Oh my god. Maggie, are you okay?" Julia hastily extricated herself from her seatbelt and leaned over to check on her dazed passenger.

"I'm okay, I think," Maggie replied as she gingerly tested her limbs. "Julia, you're bleeding!"

Frowning, Julia examined the blood trickling from her left elbow. She examined the wound carefully and determined that it was just a small cut, probably inflicted by all the flying glass. Both airbags had inflated, saving them from serious injury, but the entire driver's side of the jeep was a crumpled mess, and Julia knew that she had been extraordinarily lucky. Bright halogen headlights momentarily blinded them as a minivan stopped behind them. A wide-eyed woman got out and hurried over to the passenger side of the jeep.

"Are you two okay?" The woman asked, stepping back as Maggie opened her door. "I called the police. They're on their way."

Maggie smiled at her gratefully as she got out of the jeep. Her arms and legs appeared to be in working order, and except for a bit of soreness in her neck and shoulder from the seatbelt, she was unscathed by the accident.

"Thanks so much for stopping. I think we're okay." She turned back to Julia, who was trying unsuccessfully to open her own door. "Honey, I don't think that's gonna work. Can you climb over the seat and get out this way?"

"Yeah, I guess so," Julia grumbled, wincing as she bumped her tender elbow on the steering wheel.

"I saw the whole thing," the woman was saying. "Why in the world was someone shooting at you?"

"We have no idea why someone would shoot at us," Julia replied before Maggie could answer. "There are a lot of twisted people out there."

They could hear the sirens approaching in the distance as another car slowed to a halt beside them, its tires crunching across the broken glass. A young man with close-cropped, chestnut hair and warm brown eyes poked his head out the window. He squinted at the tall, dark-haired woman bathed in the glow of his headlights.

150

"Jules? Is that you?"

Maggie noticed the way Julia started at the sound of his voice, and she peered closely at the young man. Something about the shape of his face seemed oddly familiar. She caught a glimpse of him in profile and watched the way the shadows played across his high cheekbones and thin, aquiline nose. He almost reminded her of....

"Drew?" Julia took a step towards the car.

Swinging the door open, he got out, towering well over six feet. As Maggie watched, he awkwardly punched Julia in the shoulder, getting a tolerant grin in return. So, this was Drew Cassinelli, Julia's half-brother. She didn't know much about him, other than that he was a law student at Berkeley. Julia rarely mentioned him, and Maggie had always had the impression that family, in general, was a subject she was not comfortable with.

"So what the hell happened here?" Drew asked, nodding at the twisted metal that used to be Julia's jeep.

"Lost control and plowed into the center divide," Julia replied tersely, her eyes searching for Maggie. She beckoned to the small blonde.

"Drew, this is Maggie. She's my, uh..." For some inexplicable reason, the word stuck in her throat.

"Girlfriend?" Drew supplied helpfully.

"Uh, yeah," Julia mumbled, grateful for the dark that covered her burning ears.

She knew Maggie was staring at her, and that if she looked, she would see hurt and confusion on the blonde's face. Good job, Julia, now she probably thinks you're ashamed of her or something. Mentally, she started preparing an explanation, but much to her relief, Drew rescued her again.

"Relax. I'm not him, remember?" Drew told her. He smiled at Maggie with an echo of the same wry grin that Julia frequently charmed her with. "Dad isn't exactly Mr. Supportive when it comes to his children. He saves that for his clients."

Maggie smiled back at him uncertainly. She knew that her lover did not get along with her father, but she had never known the reason. Every time she had tried to bring the subject up, Julia had either artfully dodged it or completely shut down. She had suspected that Julia's sexuality had something to do with the estrangement, but she had never been sure. Drew's offhand comment seemed to suggest that she might be right.

"Not now, Drew." Julia sighed.

"What? It's the truth, isn't it?"

151

The first of two police cars arrived, temporarily ending their discussion. The officers took statements from the two women and the witness to the incident. Maggie noticed that Julia had pretended not to have any idea why they were attacked. She did the same in her statement, though she didn't understand the reason for the deception. The jeep was a complete loss, and the police told them they would have it towed after they were done looking at it. Drew offered to give them a ride back to the city, and Julia reluctantly accepted. She began to transfer their personal belongings to his car, leaving Maggie alone with her half-brother for a moment.

"So, how long have you two know each other?" Drew asked, trying to make conversation.

"Not that long, really," Maggie admitted, wrapping her arms around herself to stay warm. "Just a few weeks."

"Really? I would've thought it was longer than that," he replied, watching as Julia savagely kicked one of her tires as she passed by it. "I bet she doesn't tell you much about me, does she? Most of the time she doesn't even tell people she has a brother."

"She doesn't talk about her family at all, actually," Maggie said quietly. She felt a little guilty having this discussion with him, but she hoped it would help her understand Julia better.

"Our father was having an affair with my mother. She thinks that's why her mother killed herself," Drew revealed bluntly. "We've never been very close."

"I'm sorry. I don't know what to say. I'm sure she doesn't blame you, though."

Drew shrugged. "Hey, it's not your fault. I don't think she blames me either, but I think I remind her that her father is a self-centered bastard."

"He's your father too, isn't he?" Maggie reminded him.

Drew laughed bitterly. "The only thing{ he ever gave me were his name and a nice trust fund." He paused. "That's all he gave Julia, too."

"Looks like Bert and Ernie survived intact." Julia returned, handing the giant stuffed whale to Maggie. She glanced at her brother briefly. "So, what were you two talking about?"

"Aw, we're just getting to know each other a little," Drew replied quickly. "Ready to go?"

They chatted amiably on the way back to the city. Maggie listened while Drew and Julia analyzed the 49ers' Super Bowl chances for the upcoming season. They stared at her in horror when she professed her allegiance to the Cleveland Browns.

152

"I'm just gonna pretend I didn't hear that," Julia teased. "Next, you're probably gonna tell me you're an Indians fan, too."

"Hey! What's wrong with the Indians?" Maggie retorted indignantly.

"You'll have to take her to a Giants game next season, Jules," Drew suggested, glancing over his shoulder at them, snuggled together in the backseat.

"Yeah, I just might do that."

Drew dropped them off at the Chronicle offices so Maggie could retrieve her car. He and Julia exchanged an awkward good-bye, followed by hollow promises to call each other more often. Maggie waited until Drew had driven away.

"He seemed nice," she observed as they headed for her car.

"He's okay," Julia replied absently, her eyes sweeping across the nearly deserted garage. She spotted the silver Mercedes parked in a prominent spot next to the elevator. "Looks like Catherine is still here."

Maggie blinked, a bit surprised that Julia had recognized her rival's car. "She must have gotten something good today." She glanced at her watch, noting that it was nearing midnight. "Catherine never works this late unless she has something good."

"Do you want to go up and see what's going on?" Julia asked as they reached Maggie's car.

The reporter hesitated. Part of her wanted to find out what Catherine was working on, but the rest of her just wanted to go home, crawl into bed and pull the covers up over her head. Plus, the thought of another run-in with Catherine made her vaguely nauseous. She would rather sit and listen to someone dragging fingernails across a chalkboard.

"No," she decided finally, unlocking her car door. "Let's just get out of here."

After a quick stop at Maggie's apartment, they arrived at Julia's house to find a squad car waiting for them. Henry Chow emerged as they parked behind it. There was no trace of humor in his dark eyes as he regarded them soberly.

"What's going on?" Julia asked, getting out of the Corolla.

Henry nodded politely at Maggie. Returning his attention to Julia, he gestured towards the front door. "Let's go inside. There's stuff we need to talk about."

Julia led the way up the narrow front steps. She fumbled in her pocket for her keys, nearly dropping her armload of souvenirs. Henry and Maggie each took a bag out of her hands, and she mumbled a thank you as she unlocked the door and waved them inside. She set the rest of the bags down on the stairs and turned to the grim police inspector.

"Okay. We're inside. Now, what's going on?"

Henry opened his mouth to speak and shot a sideways glance at Maggie. Julia rolled her eyes, quickly losing patience with him.

"There's nothing you can't say in front of her, Henry. Just spit it the hell out."

"Where were you tonight, Julia?"

"Why? What difference does it make?" Julia shot back obstinately.

"Because we found that Machado guy dead a couple of hours ago."

Even Julia looked taken aback by that. Speechless and stunned, she slipped past Henry into the living room and sat down on the sofa. Maggie followed her, sitting down beside her. Henry paced in front of them, his forehead creased with concern.

Acting on an anonymous tip, Henry and two other officers had discovered Eddie Machado's body just after 11:30 that night. He had been shot once in the back of the head and dumped in an alley behind a busy strip club in North Beach. There had been no witnesses that they could find, and so far there was no solid evidence yet either.

"We were in Vallejo," Maggie spoke up. "We just got back, so if you're suggesting that Julia had something to do with this…"

Henry flinched under the onslaught of the twin green daggers piercing his flesh. "Hey, hold on. I didn't say she did. But I had to ask. I know how worried she was about this guy being out on the street, especially since he was stalking you."

He glanced at Julia, who was still silent and staring blankly out the window. "Guys like this end up dead all the time. It'll probably turn out to be a drug deal that went sour, or something like that."

"Someone tried to kill us tonight," Maggie offered, ignoring the warning look Julia gave her. "While we were on our way back to the city, somebody shot at us. Julia's jeep was totaled."

"What?" Henry was becoming more and more agitated. Unconsciously, he searched through his pockets for a cigarette. He glared at Julia. "Why didn't you tell me this immediately?"

Julia sighed, scrubbing her face with both hands. "Because I knew you would get all upset. Like you are now."

"Of course I'm upset!" Henry's voice rose in both volume and pitch. "When someone tries to hurt one of my friends, I get upset! It's a natural human emotion, Jules. You should try it some time!"

Maggie leaped to her feet, her eyes blazing. "That's enough!

Maybe it's just me, but I don't see how yelling at Julia is going to help you find out who's doing this. So back off!"

"Maggie, it's okay," Julia tugged at the sleeve of the reporter's new sweatshirt.

"No. It is not okay." Maggie kept her gaze locked firmly on Henry's face as he turned several shades of red. "You're supposed to be her friend."

Henry shook his head sadly. "I am her friend. I don't want to see either one of you get hurt." His eyes flicked over to Julia. "Which is why I'm telling you to leave this case alone. Let it go, Julia. Let the real cops handle it. In fact, it might not be a bad idea for you both to get out of town for a while."

Julia laughed tiredly. "I can't go anywhere. I don't even have a car anymore."

Maggie eyed her carefully, noticing the weary lines around her eyes and mouth. "Henry, we're both pretty tired. Can we finish this tomorrow?"

Henry's shoulders slumped. "I guess so. I sent a car over to your apartment earlier. You must have just missed them. Are you going to stay here tonight?"

"Yes. I'm spending the night here."

"Okay. I'm gonna have a couple of officers watching the house, just to be safe." He started toward the door, stopping when he reached the entryway. "Julia, I just don't want you to get hurt. Please stay out of this one."

Julia raised her hand to acknowledge him, but she didn't speak. Henry sighed and let himself out. He waved to the two officers sitting in an unmarked vehicle across the street from the house. Julia never backed down from a fight, he knew, but this time, he thought she was outmatched. It was up to him to figure this out before she got in over her head.

He scratched absently at the coarse stubble covering his jaw. This case just didn't make any sense to him. On the surface, he thought he saw a connection between the Netsports break-in, the latest warehouse fire and the attacks on Maggie and Julia. Something about it still didn't ring true, and thinking about it was starting to make his brain hurt. It was almost as if two separate people were working towards the same goal, without telling each other what they were up to.

Henry had spoken to Daniel Webber once already, regarding the security guard killed with his gun. The former athlete had been charming and appropriately bewildered by the situation, sticking to his claim that he had no idea who had broken into his offices. There wasn't a shred of evidence directly linking him to anything, but Henry couldn't shake the feeling that there was something sinister going on there. As he drove away from Julia's house, he checked his notebook for an address. Smiling grimly, he wondered how Daniel Webber would like a late night visit from the police.

****

Chapter Fourteen

Peeking through the heavy curtains, Maggie watched the two police officers across the street. It was an unnerving feeling, knowing that they were there to prevent someone from killing her. She did her best to suppress the shudder that ran through her body. Behind her, Julia slouched wearily on the sofa as she tried to absorb everything that they had been through that day.

"Hey." Maggie crossed the room and sat down beside her again, resting her hand on Julia's knee. "What's going through that head of yours?" She gently smoothed a lock of dark hair back, tucking it behind Julia's ear.

"Nothing, really." Julia covered Maggie's hand with her own. "I'm tired, that's all."

Maggie slid her arms around Julia's waist and hugged her tightly. "Henry had no right to jump all over you like that."

"He's worried." Julia lifted Maggie's chin until they were eye to eye. "Thank you for leaping to my defense, though."

"Somebody has to."

"Yeah, well, the job is yours if you want it."

"I want it."

Maggie leaned in for a tender kiss. In her pocket, her pager began to vibrate and buzz, and she scowled down at it, annoyed by the interruption. Julia laughed quietly as the reporter retrieved the offending device and read the display.

"I knew I was good, but I don't think I've ever set off alarms before," she joked.

"It's my editor," Maggie informed her, turning the pager around so Julia could see the number.

"Ah. I guess you'd better call him, then," Julia sighed, releasing the blonde.

"Be right back."

While Maggie went into the kitchen to use the phone, Julia stretched out on the sofa. Eddie Machado had been picked up for

157

following Maggie, and now he was dead. She was sure that the two were connected, and on some level, she felt responsible for it.

She could hear Maggie's voice growing louder as she argued with her editor. A moment later, muttering under her breath and looking utterly exasperated, Maggie stormed back into the living room.

"I can't believe this," Maggie burst out angrily. "Sam took me off the arson story. He said it was a liability thing. The paper can't have me getting hurt."

"Maggie, I'm so sorry." Julia sat up, reaching for the reporter's hand.

"Oh, it gets even better." Maggie continued bitterly. "I've been placed on leave. Supposedly, it's for my own protection."

"Shit. I'm so sorry, honey," Julia said again. "Maybe he's right, though." She paused, bracing herself for the protestations she was certain would follow.

"What?"

Julia winced, hearing the quiet disbelief in Maggie's voice. She chewed her lower lip as she tried to figure out a way to make the reporter understand. Maggie's job was important, but not as important as her life.

"Maggie, I know you're hurt, but maybe this really is for the best," Julia said softly. "I couldn't stand it if anything happened to you, and if this will help keep you safe, then I'm glad you're off the story."

Maggie's shoulders slumped. Dejected, she stared at her neatly trimmed fingernails. Part of her wanted to be angry with Julia, but she knew that her lover was afraid for her safety, and she couldn't fault her for that. It infuriated her that no one seemed to think she could look out for herself, though. Even worse, Sam had instructed her to turn over all her notes to Catherine, of all people. Maggie could already picture the smug look on her rival's face. Sighing tiredly, she closed her eyes.

"Are you mad at me?" Julia asked, taking the reporter's hand and gently rubbing her thumb across her knuckles.

"No. I'm just exhausted. I think I'm going up to bed now." Maggie stood, groaning a bit at the stiffness in her neck and shoulders. "Are you coming up?"

Julia gave her a small smile. "In a minute. I need to make a quick phone call first. Meet you upstairs?"

Maggie nodded and leaned down for a quick kiss before she headed for the bedroom. Once she was out of sight, Julia reached for the phone. She pulled her leather wallet out of her jacket and dug a small scrap of paper out of one of the pockets. She stared at the string of numbers, written precisely in ink. Taking a deep breath to steady herself, she dialed, her stomach churning anxiously as she listened to the ringing. A deep, masculine voice answered on the fifth ring.

"Hello, Dad. It's me."

"Julia? Couldn't this have waited until morning? It's after midnight," Joseph Cassinelli said in a sleepy baritone.

Julia raked her fingers through her hair as her stomach did flips. Her father always made her nervous, and she felt like a naughty little girl again. She tugged on the hem of her sweater and cleared her throat.

"I know it's late, Dad. I'm sorry." She winced at the aggravated sigh on the other end of the line.

Closing her eyes, Julia could picture her father sitting up in the exact center of his king-size bed. As always, he would be wearing imported silk pajamas. Joseph Cassinelli accepted nothing less than the best. He probably had a court appointment early in the morning. He usually did. Julia chewed her lower lip as she imagined her father's impatient scowl. His pre-trial ritual always included a good night's sleep before presenting his opening argument. He hated interruptions in his routines, especially where his work was concerned.

"All right. What is it?" He asked irritably.

Julia hesitated, sensing her father's foul mood. "Dad, I need to know if you're still friends with Martin Davis."

A long pause followed her question. Finally, the sound of a long, noisy breath filled her ear as her father exhaled slowly. She knew that annoyed sigh all too well.

"You called me at 12:46 in the morning to ask me if Marty Davis and I are still friends? Dammit, I have opening arguments in a very important case first thing tomorrow. There had better be a good reason for this."

She almost hung up the phone. Then the image of Maggie's face filled her mind and strengthened her resolve. She would do whatever it took to keep the woman she loved safe, even if that meant talking to her father. Julia took a deep breath and plunged ahead.

"There is a good reason. I'm...involved with someone." She pretended not to hear her father's groan. Resolutely, she continued. "She's a reporter."

"A reporter? Are you out of your mind?" Her father interrupted her. "Last time, it was a model, now another reporter. You're just looking for a scandal, aren't you? For god's sake, Julia, I had a hard enough time dealing with all the fallout from the last one. What was her name? Christine?"

"Kirsten. And that has nothing to do with this," Julia said, suddenly wishing she hadn't bothered to call. "Maggie's life might be in danger, and I think Martin Davis's daughter has something to do with it. I was hoping you could tell me something useful about her."

Julia heard a sharp click as her father turned on the bedside lamp. Seconds later, she could hear the soft shuffling of papers. A bitter smile tugged at the edge of her lips. Rather than give his daughter his full attention, her father had decided to review his notes for his case. Julia was used to it. She couldn't remember the last time her father had given her his undivided attention.

"Allison? I haven't seen her in years. I heard she was engaged, but I haven't seen a formal announcement yet. I expect her father would have told me if it was true. We still play golf every Friday." Joseph finally answered her, punctuating his response with a mocking laugh. "I'm sure Allison wouldn't be involved in anything as sinister as what you're suggesting."

He went on before Julia could speak. "You know, just because you turned your back on your upbringing doesn't mean that everyone has. Marty Davis's daughter wouldn't go mucking around with the kind of lowlife scum that you seem to enjoy associating with."

Julia let out a harsh, barking laugh. "Oh, that's perfect! Especially coming from a man who spends his life defending rapists, murderers and thieves! Wait, I forgot. You only associate with rich lowlife scum. That makes quite a difference, Dad."

"You ungrateful little brat!" Through the receiver, Julia could hear her father's harsh breathing. "I gave you everything and you just threw it all away. I may not approve of his specialty, but at least Drew is going to law school. You could have been anything you wanted to be, and now look at you."

"I am doing what I want to be doing."

He wasn't even listening to her. "You must really hate me. Well, you can just give the damn trust fund back, then."

Julia stiffened. No matter what they started talking about, the conversation always seemed to come back to money. When she had turned twenty-five, she had inherited a sizeable amount of money, along with the deed to the family vineyard.

"You didn't give me that trust fund. Grandfather did," she said in a dangerously low voice. "He also gave me the vineyard and the house that you have so conveniently forgotten to move out of."

"Is that what this is about? You want the damn house?" Joseph asked.

Julia sighed heavily. She had had enough of this conversation for one night. Out of the corner of her eye, she saw Maggie descend the stairs and take a seat on the bottom step. Tiredly, Julia rubbed the back of her neck, trying to ease the stiffness that had settled into the muscles.

"No, this has nothing to do with the house," she replied after a long pause. "Keep the house, for all I care. I'm happy where I am. Just forget it. I'm sorry I bothered you."

She hit the off button and carefully placed the phone on the coffee table. Her hands shook, and she scowled at them irritably. Talking to her father always had this effect on her. *Dammit, Julia. Don't let him get to you like this*, she told herself. *Oh well, it might not have been a total waste of time. Allison might be engaged, huh? Wonder if Danny Webber is the lucky guy.*

As she turned over the possibilities in her mind, Julia stood and offered a feeble smile to her patiently waiting lover. She didn't want Maggie to know how much the phone call to her father had bothered her. Maggie rose as Julia approached, and without a word, pulled the taller woman into a tight hug. She rubbed Julia's back soothingly.

"You okay?" she asked, her eyes glistening with sympathetic tears.

Julia nodded. "I'm fine. I thought you went to bed."

Maggie tucked her arm around Julia's waist and guided her up the stairs. "I did. But then I heard your voice down here, and I don't know...I had this feeling that you were upset. I caught the end of the conversation. Your father?"

They had reached the bedroom, and Maggie sat on the edge of the bed while Julia changed into her pajamas. She frowned as Julia went into the bathroom to brush her teeth without answering her.

"Let me guess. You don't want to talk about it," she said when Julia returned. Together, they slid under the blankets, and Maggie rested her head on Julia's shoulder.

"There's nothing to talk about, really. I called him because I thought he could help us."

"Help us? With what?"

Reaching over, Julia turned off the lamp on the nightstand. "I thought he could give me something about Allison Davis. I didn't get much, but it turns out she might be secretly engaged to someone. I'm betting on Danny."

"Danny and Allison? Okay. So what does that mean?" Maggie asked curiously.

Julia shrugged. "I don't know yet. Maybe their company is in trouble. Or maybe they're using Netsports as a front for something else." She started throwing out suggestions. "I don't know, but I'm going to find out."

"I'm sure you will," Maggie said, patting Julia's stomach. "I have a feeling you can find out anything you put your mind to. Just promise me you'll be careful."

She wanted to suggest that they take Henry's advice and leave the matter to the police, but she knew that wasn't an option for Julia. Her tall, stubborn private investigator wasn't about to let this go. *Okay, fine. But there's nothing that says you can't watch her back for her. Right, Maggie? Right.* Nodding to herself in the dark, Maggie tried to stifle a yawn.

Julia chuckled faintly and pressed her lips to Maggie's temple. "I'll be fine. Now get some sleep. It's been one hell of a long day."

"Yeah, it has." Maggie agreed, yawning again. "I love you, you know."

"Oh yeah? That's good to know. I love you, too."

Within minutes, the rhythm of Maggie's breathing became slow and steady, and Julia knew that the reporter had fallen asleep. She was glad; Maggie needed the rest. Staring up at the darkened ceiling, Julia planned her strategy. In the morning, she would pay a visit to her old college buddy, Daniel Webber. Then, depending on the information she drew out of him, perhaps she would look up Allison Davis, as well.

Exhaling slowly, Julia closed her eyes, but sleep would not claim her. Her father's voice played over and over again in her mind. In her head, she knew that he was wrong about her, but his words cut deeply just the same. They always had. Nothing she had done had ever been good enough for him. As she stared into the gloom, a long-forgotten memory surfaced. In her senior year of high school, she had been the captain of the varsity volleyball team. They had had the best season in the school's history and had gone to the state championships that year. It was the only time her father had attended one of her tournaments. It had been close, but her team lost. She remembered the disappointment in his eyes as she had come off the court. All of her teammates' parents had been proud of their kids, but not Joseph Cassinelli. In his eyes, it was first place or nothing at all.

Julia shook herself, pushing the memory back into the recesses of her brain. *Whoa. Where did that come from?* She sighed and rested her cheek against the blonde head nestled against her shoulder. Her father didn't matter, she told herself firmly. All that mattered was Maggie. She wrapped her arms more tightly around the reporter's sleeping body and closed her eyes.

Chapter Fifteen

Henry parked his unmarked police vehicle in front of a newly renovated apartment building. He sneered at the fake adobe walls and the brightly colored mural that adorned them. He hated what all these yuppies were doing to the Mission District. This area used to have character, he thought. Now, corporate coffee chains were replacing the family restaurants, and the lovingly hand-painted murals that decorated the old buildings were being painted over. New buildings were springing up overnight, featuring carbon-copied versions of fake adobe and stucco, like Daniel Webber's apartment complex. Even worse, the new places were decorated with stenciled murals spray-painted by huge corporations. Henry's opinion of Daniel Webber dropped another notch.

Shaking his head in disgust, Henry stubbed out his cigarette in his ashtray. It was his second one that evening, and he felt a pang of guilt as he eyed the crumpled pack on the dashboard. He had been clean for months.

"I'll just finish off that pack." Henry muttered, getting out of the car. "Then I'll quit."

He walked up to the iron gate and flashed his badge at the security guard in the booth. After exchanging a few words with the guard, he stepped back as the gate slid aside. Henry double-checked his notepad, making sure he had the apartment number right. He scanned each door until he found 31B. It was a ground floor unit, tucked into a secluded corner. All the lights were off inside, but Henry thought he could hear music playing. He straightened his tie and checked the gun holstered beneath his jacket before knocking sharply on the door. The music stopped, and footsteps approached. Henry tensed slightly as he heard the lock turn.

"Inspector Chow?" Clad only in a pair of blue boxer shorts and a t-shirt, Danny opened the door and stared at the police inspector.

"Mr. Webber." Henry greeted him politely. "I'm sorry. I know it's late, but I have a few follow-up questions to ask you."

Danny hesitated. His heart rate quickened, and he hoped the inspector wouldn't notice the beads of sweat materializing above his upper lip. Grinning broadly to cover his anxiety, he stepped aside and waved Henry in. He turned on the overhead light, revealing a sparsely furnished living room.

"Have a seat, Inspector." Danny indicated the rich suede sofa. "Give me a second to get dressed, and I'll answer whatever questions you have."

Danny retreated into his bedroom and picked up a pair of jeans from the bed. As he dressed, he looked longingly at the phone and wondered if he could risk a phone call. He didn't understand why the police wanted to talk to him again. He hadn't thought they had been suspicious about him at all. Biting his lower lip, he cast a glance over his shoulder towards the door. It was quiet in the living room, and Danny wondered what the inspector was doing. Probably bugging the phones or something, he thought. He couldn't risk calling anyone. Taking a deep breath to calm himself, he went back into the other room.

Inspector Chow was examining the small fishbowl on the counter between the living room and the kitchen. He turned as Danny reentered the room. Danny smiled at him and ran his hand through his tousled sandy hair.

"Can I get you anything? I could make some coffee. I was reading over some reports in bed when you knocked." Danny offered, vaguely aware that he sounded nervous.

"No, thank you," Henry replied brusquely. He went into his no-nonsense cop mode. "I'll be quick, Mr. Webber." He flipped through his notepad. "The gun that was stolen from your office is registered to you. Correct?"

"Uh, yeah. Didn't we go over this already?" Danny frowned. He didn't like where this was going.

"Yes, we did. Bear with me," Henry said. "You've already been informed that your firearm was used in a homicide. Right?"

"Right. A homeless man. I feel really terrible about that."

Henry nodded. "Mmmhmm. I'm sure you do. Do you know a man named Edgar Machado? He usually goes by Eddie."

Danny froze as his guts tightened into knots. There was no way the police could have traced Eddie to him. He was sure of it.

"Never heard of him." He answered confidently. "Why? Is he the punk who broke into my office?"

Henry smiled. He had noticed the moment of hesitation when he had mentioned Eddie's name. "We have no reason to suspect him in the break-in." Henry paused and cocked his head to one side, pretending to be puzzled about something. "Why did you automatically assume that Eddie Machado was a criminal?"

Danny swallowed hard as sweat trickled down his back. "What?"

"You asked if he was the punk who broke into your office. What made you think he was a punk, Mr. Webber?"

"Uh, I...I don't know." Danny stammered. "I couldn't think of any other reason why you'd be asking me about him, I guess."

"Ah. Well, that makes sense." Henry nodded, noting the look of relief that passed over Danny's face. "Actually, Eddie Machado was found shot to death tonight."

The color drained from Danny's face and a loud buzzing filled his ears. He felt like he was going to pass out. Eddie was dead? How could Eddie be dead? He shot a sideways look at the inspector, who still appeared to be engrossed in his fishbowl.

"Really?" He croaked. "And what does that have to do with me?"

"Would it surprise you to hear that Eddie Machado was also killed with your gun? And we have reason to suspect that the same weapon was used earlier in an attack on two motorists west of Vallejo."

Henry was bluffing. The ballistics results on Eddie hadn't come back yet, and as far as he knew, nothing had been recovered from Julia's jeep. He was hoping that Danny wouldn't realize that. He was right.

"I already told you! I have no idea who stole my gun!" Danny burst out loudly.

Henry smiled affably and held his hands up. "Whoa. Easy, Mr. Webber. No one's accusing you of anything."

Danny glared at him. "Well, then why do you keep looking at me like that?"

"Like what, Mr. Webber?"

"Like I'm a fucking suspect! That's what! I didn't know that homeless guy. I didn't know Eddie Machado. Hell, he probably got caught in a bad drug deal or something."

On the outside, Henry remained implacable. Internally, though, he was doing a little happy dance. Daniel Webber knew something. He was sure of it now. He nodded, tucking his notepad back in his pocket.

"You're probably right." He agreed. "I'm very sorry to have bothered you so late."

Henry started moving towards the door. He paused on the threshold. "Oh, one more question. You said your partner, Allison was vacationing in Seattle. Did she fly there or drive?"

"What?" Danny blinked rapidly, flustered by the change of subject. "Uh, she flew, I think." This was getting worse with every minute. First, this cop was asking questions about Eddie. Now, he was digging for information about Allison.

"Hmm. That's odd. I checked with the airlines, and she wasn't listed on any of their flights to the Seattle area." It was another bluff.

"I don't know, then!" Danny was becoming more and more agitated.

"Ah, s☐ you're not that close to her?"

"No, we're just business partners." Danny lied.

Henry nodded again. "Okay. Again, I'm very sorry to have disturbed you. Have a good night, Mr. Webber."

He stepped outside and headed back towards the gate. Once he was out of sight, Henry pulled a strip of photos from one of those coin-operated booths out of his pocket. He smiled at the three pictures of Daniel Webber and Allison Davis. He had them. It was just a question of proving it.

As soon as the police inspector had left, Danny made a frantic phone call. He raked his fingers through his sweat-dampened hair.

"We've got trouble," he said. "That police inspector was just here. I'm pretty sure he suspects something. And why the hell didn't anyone tell me that Eddie was dead?"

"Relax, Danny. Everything's under control," Allison said in a soothing voice. "You just let me take care of it, baby. I have a plan."

Hanging up the phone, Allison turned to the barrel-chested man in the chair across from her. He was nearly a foot taller than she was, and he outweighed her by a hundred pounds, but Tom Becker was terrified in Allison's presence. She was unpredictable, and that made him nervous.

"The police just questioned Danny again," she said.

"They've got nothing on him." Tom shrugged indifferently. He thought Daniel Webber was a spineless weasel, and he didn't much care if Allison's fiancé got caught.

Allison tapped her index finger against her lips and hummed to herself. Without warmth, she smiled at Tom.

"No, they don't. You know Danny, though. He'll crack if they pressure him enough." She circled behind Tom's chair and put her hands on his shoulders. She leaned down until her lips were nearly brushing the top of his ear. "That's why you'll take care of this little problem for me, won't you?"

"Just tell me what you want, Ms. Davis. You want me to take care of the cop?"

Allison's long, slender fingers tightened around his shoulders, and Tom winced as her nails dug into his flesh. He could hear the ice in her voice when she spoke again.

"As tempting as it is, leave the inspector alone. Killing him would bring too much attention. We just need to divert his attention away from Danny. Maybe another fire would throw him off track." Her eyes sparkled at the thought.

Tom nodded. "I can do that."

"You will do no such thing."

Both of them jumped at the authoritative voice. Standing in the open doorway, a man gazed at them coolly. His dark hair was silvered at the temples, and despite the late hour, he was still dressed in an expensive charcoal gray suit. Reaching up, he loosened his tie and undid the top button on his spotless white shirt. Allison beamed at him and clapped her hands together.

"Daddy! You're home."

"Just in time, it seems." Councilman Martin Davis crossed the room and poured himself a drink. He sipped the amber liquid and rolled it around on his tongue before swallowing. "Allison, are you out of your mind?"

Allison's eyes narrowed and her lips tightened to a thin line. The councilman smiled at her indulgently before draining the liquid from his glass and pouring himself another drink. He shot a cursory glance at his daughter's silent cohort.

"Well, Tom, you've made quite a mess of things," he said flatly. "I just got a call from one of my attorneys. It seems someone is asking too many questions about me and about my family."

Allison scowled. "It's that reporter again, isn't it? I'll have her taken care of, Daddy. Don't worry about a thing."

The councilman slammed the heavy crystal glass down on the desk with a booming crack. "You will do nothing without clearing it with me first. Is that understood?" He skewered Tom with a withering look. "If you hadn't gone after that reporter with guns blazing, we wouldn't be in this mess. Didn't it occur to you that you would just draw more attention to us that way?"

Tom kept his eyes on the floor and wisely chose not to answer. He had been working for this family for years, and he was accustomed to their violent mood swings. There was no question in his mind that Allison Davis was her father's daughter.

"Daddy, we had to do something about the reporter. She was asking too many questions. It was only a matter of time before she found out that I was at the fire." Allison explained calmly.

"You don't know that, sweetheart." Her father corrected her. "Even if the witness had told her something, how reliable was he? Besides, that fire never should have happened."

Allison gave her father a puzzled frown. "But you said to get rid of the stuff." "I said to get rid of it, yes. I never told you to set fire to the whole goddamn building. I certainly didn't tell you to murder a security guard, or a homeless man, and I know I didn't tell you to chase Julia Cassinelli down a busy freeway!"

"No, that didn't work out the way I had planned." Allison admitted with a sigh. "But I have something much better in mind this time. It involves Maggie McKinnon's brother. Want to hear about it?"

Martin Davis resumed sipping from his drink. Loosening another button, he sat down in his armchair and waited for Allison to reveal her latest scheme. As he listened to her plan, a pleased smile twitched at the corners of his mouth. This time, he thought, it just might work

****

Chapter Sixteen

Quietly, Maggie padded downstairs, grimacing as her bare feet touched the icy floor. She wished she had remembered to put her socks on. The first pale light of dawn was hitting the kitchen window as she filled the coffeepot with water and carefully sliced a whole-wheat bagel in half. She liked the thickness of the two halves to be as equal as possible

Julia's paperboy had an arm like a cannon, and there was a loud thump as the morning edition slammed against the front door. Maggie held her breath, hoping that the noise hadn't woken Julia. No one stirred upstairs, and she exhaled in relief. Opening the door, she squinted across the street at the two police officers that had been assigned to watch them. She lifted her hand to wave at them as she retrieved the newspaper.

Maggie carried the paper into the living room and tossed it on the coffee table. She turned the television on, hurriedly muting the volume before the noise reached Julia's sleeping ears. An anchorman, wearing an expression of deep concern, was reading the story about their car accident the previous night. She turned the sound up a bit.

".... Julia Cassinelli, daughter of prominent local attorney Joseph Cassinelli, was the apparent victim of a bizarre attack last night. As she and an unidentified friend were driving home on Interstate 80 after a trip to Marine World, a gunman opened fire on their vehicle, causing it to spin out of control and crash into the center divide. Fortunately, no one was injured, and police say they currently have no suspects. Anyone with any information about this incident is urged to call the San Francisco Police Department."

"I hate that picture," Julia mumbled sleepily from the middle of the stairs.

Maggie examined the photo that was still showing on the screen. It was the picture of Julia at the Black and White Ball. After another moment, the anchorman moved on to a story about a fistfight at a local school board meeting.

"What's wrong with that picture? I think you look gorgeous in

169

it," Maggie said.

Julia grunted as she wandered into the kitchen with Maggie trailing after her. She rummaged through the cabinets for a pair of clean coffee mugs while Maggie buttered her bagel.

"That picture makes me look like someone I'm not." She shook her head. "I'm not a part of that world. I never was."

"That's not what Catherine said," Maggie murmured softly, recalling her rival's harsh words the day before.

Julia nearly choked on her coffee. Worried blue eyes darted to Maggie's face as she tried to guess the details of the reporter's conversation with Catherine Richards. She frowned, unable to read Maggie's expression.

"What exactly did she say to you?" Julia asked cautiously.

Maggie shrugged, trying to appear unconcerned. "It was nothing. She just implied that I was using you for your money, or something like that."

Julia swore under her breath, and her knuckles turned white as she gripped her mug so tightly that Maggie was sure it would shatter. Puzzled by her lover's reaction, Maggie crossed the kitchen and took the mug out of Julia's hands. She put her hand on Julia's forearm and felt the taut muscles twitching beneath the skin.

"Hey, it's okay," Maggie said. "She was just trying to get to me. I knew she was full of it."

"No, Maggie. It's not okay. There's something I should have told you."

Julia kept her gaze focused on the wall behind Maggie's head. Preparing for the worst, Maggie let her hand fall to her side. Her stomach tightened as she took a deep breath.

"Tell me," Maggie said, her whisper barely audible in the silent kitchen.

"Catherine and I were lovers." Julia paused, waiting for a response. When none came, she continued. "It was a long time ago, and we were only together for a few months. I ended things after something I said to her in private ended up in a front page story about my father."

"You and Catherine." Maggie repeated the words slowly, not quite believing what she was hearing. Things began to click into place. "That's why she hates me so much. We never really got along, but it got so much worse after I met you."

Stunned by Julia's revelation, Maggie walked out of the kitchen and started to head back upstairs. Julia chased after her, catching up to the reporter in the entryway.

"Maggie, wait!" Julia circled in front of her. "I'm so sorry. I know I should have told you before now."

"Yes, you should have." Maggie shot back, hurt and confused. "Why didn't you?"

"I don't know." Julia let her hands fall limply to her sides. "I didn't think it was that important."

Maggie shut her eyes. Did it really matter to her? She knew she had nothing to be jealous about now. Julia loved her, and she had never shown the slightest bit of interest in anyone else since they had met. In fact, she had displayed nothing but contempt towards Catherine. Still, she hated the idea of Julia and Catherine together, and she didn't understand why Julia had kept it a secret.

"How long ago was it?" Maggie asked, finally.

"Six years."

"Did you love her?"

"No," Julia said simply, and Maggie knew it was the truth.

Sighing, Maggie reopened her eyes and allowed a small, sad smile to touch the corners of her lips. Reaching out, she ran her thumb across the delicate, dark eyelashes across from her, brushing away the tears that had collected there. She laced her fingers together behind Julia's neck and pulled her close.

"It's okay," she said, kissing Julia's cheek.

Julia's chest heaved as she swallowed a sob. "Is it?"

"Yeah. I just wish you had told me a little sooner." Maggie played with a lock of Julia's sleep-tousled hair, weaving it into a thin braid.

"I know. I'm sorry. I'll do whatever it takes to make it up to you."

Maggie's eyebrows arched suggestively and she grinned. "Oh, really?" She drawled, her eyes twinkling "I'm sure I can think of some suitable acts of penance for you to perform."

Julia smiled tentatively at Maggie's bantering tone. "Maybe I should start saying a few 'Hail Mary's'?"

Maggie drew her in for a long, passionate kiss. Once their tongues had become thoroughly reacquainted with each other, she pulled back, dizzy and out of breath. She gasped as warm hands slipped under her shirt and found bare skin. A low, seductive chuckle rumbled in her ear and sent shivers of anticipation running down her spine.

"I think we need to take this upstairs." She panted as lips and teeth nipped at her throat. "And just for the record, 'Mary' is not the name I want to hear you screaming."

Laughing, Julia led the way up the stairs. In the hallway,

Maggie squealed in surprise as Julia bent down and slid an arm behind her knees. She found herself being scooped up and carried into the bedroom as if she weighed little more than a child.

"Julia, put me down before you hurt yourself!"

Strong arms deposited her in the middle of the bed, and the mattress springs creaked faintly as a second body stretched beside the first. Maggie tangled her fingers in Julia's dark, silky hair as hungrily seeking lips found hers again. Sighing happily, she closed her eyes and lost herself in the sensations.

Much later, sunlight streamed through the window as they sprawled together, sweaty and exhausted. Maggie snuggled closer, sliding her lips across Julia's bare shoulder and tasting the tangy saltiness of her skin.

"Hmmm. I think I should take a vacation from work more often," she said, her fingers tracing Julia's jaw.

"Oh, you do, huh?" Julia nibbled lightly on the wandering fingers. "You don't think we'd get bored with each other after a couple of days?"

Maggie propped herself up on an elbow and peered into a pair of amused blue eyes. "Bored? You're kidding, right?"

Grinning, Julia winked at her. "So, what do you want to do today?"

"Besides staying in bed with you all day? Hmmm…. let me think." Maggie made a face. "I suppose I should go down to the paper and turn over my notes. Might as well get that over with. Maybe I'll see if Jessica wants to have lunch. After that, I guess I'm all yours."

"Okay. That'll give me time to take care of a couple of things. I need to call the insurance company about my jeep. Then I think I'll give Danny a call. He and I need to have a little chat."

Maggie frowned. "Be careful with him. If he is involved with these attacks, there's no telling how dangerous he might be."

"I'll be careful." Julia assured her. She glanced at the alarm clock. "What time were you planning to head out?"

"I don't know. Sometime around noon, I guess."

Eyes dancing wickedly, Julia rolled on top of Maggie and grinned at her as her fingers trailed down to the reporter's thigh. "Then we have plenty of time."

****
****

Shortly before noon, Maggie dashed out the door and headed for the newspaper office. Work crews in fluorescent orange vests were digging holes in the middle of the street, and traffic had slowed to a crawl. Maggie hummed along with her car radio as she inched forward through an intersection.

It was well after lunchtime when she finally made her way into the newsroom. A few friendly faces directed smiles her way, but most of her co-workers went about their business without giving her a second glance. Chris Garcia flashed her a toothy grin and waved her over to his desk. He offered Maggie his chair and pushed aside a pile of loose papers and a football-shaped clock, clearing a space for himself on the corner of his desk.

"Hey, Maggie." He greeted her warmly. "It's good to see you. We all heard about your accident. That's some serious craziness."

"Thanks, Chris. It was an adventure," Maggie replied dryly. "So, where's the Hellcat? I would've thought she'd be here to gloat."

Chris rolled his eyes and made a gagging sound. "Don't even get me started. I know how much you must hate turning your part of this story over to her. I think she had a lunch interview, or you know she would be here to rub your nose in it."

Maggie sighed. Chris was right; she hated giving Catherine all her work. It irked her even more, now that she knew about her rival's history with Julia. She stood, pulling a file folder out of her briefcase.

"I'm glad she's not here," she said. "I really didn't want to see her face today. I'll just leave this on her desk and get out of here."

"Hang in there, Maggie. You'll be back to work before you know it. Then you'll be begging for a vacation like the rest of us."

Maggie dumped the file in Catherine's inbox and exchanged pleasantries with Chris for a few minutes longer. As more people started to filter back into the newsroom, she excused herself. She wasn't in the mood to deal with their curious looks and well-meaning questions, and she didn't want to be around when Catherine showed up. In the corridor, on the way to the elevator, a familiar voice called out to her.

"Oh my God, Maggie! Are you okay?" Jessica hurried towards her, her eyes wide with concern. "I tried to call you fifteen zillion times last night, but you're never at your apartment anymore, and you didn't answer your cell phone."

Maggie winced. "I had my phone turned off, and I forgot to check my messages this morning," she admitted sheepishly. "I'm fine, though. Not even a scratch."

"That's a relief. I take it Julia wasn't hurt either?" Jessica asked.

"No, she's fine. I met her brother last night. That was

interesting."

Jessica hooked her arm through Maggie's and pulled her towards the empty elevator. "Oh yeah? C'mon. You can tell me all about it over lunch."

They ended up in a crowded deli, and Maggie told her friend all about Julia's fight in the parking lot, the car chase and Drew. Jessica listened intently, growing more amazed with each part of the story. Swallowing a bite of her sandwich, the tiny copy editor gave Maggie a skeptical frown.

"Don't you think it's odd that Julia's brother just happened to show up at just the right moment? I mean, it seems like a huge coincidence."

Maggie slurped noisily at her diet soda. "I don't know. It was a little strange, I guess, but he seemed pretty harmless. Actually, I liked him."

"That's what they always say," Jessica said, shaking her head. "Then the nice, harmless guy turns out to be an ax murderer."

Maggie laughed, nearly sending a spray of soda across the table. "I seriously doubt that Drew's a killer. You've been watching too many of those late-night TV movies, Jess."

"Uh-huh. We'll see who's laughing when stalker-boy starts sending you bouquets of dead roses." Jessica snatched the check out of Maggie's hand, ignoring her friend's startled protest. "I've got this. I'd better get back to work before someone notices that I've been missing for two hours."

"Next time lunch is on me," Maggie said. "I should probably head over to my apartment and check my messages there. Maybe I should get call-forwarding."

Jessica snorted as they went out the door. "Maybe you should just move in with her and be done with it."

"She hasn't asked me to move in, and I don't want to push her."

"I've seen the way she looks at you, Maggie. It's just a matter of time."

"We'll see," Maggie replied, closing the subject.

She dropped Jessica off in front of the newspaper offices before making the twenty-minute drive to her apartment. A white, windowless van was parked in her space, and she scowled at it in frustration for a moment. Sighing, she drove past it, searching for one of the scarce visitor's spaces in her complex. She ended up parking on the other side of her building, and her irritation grew as she hiked back to her unit.

"Just because I didn't come home last night doesn't mean some idiot can park in my spot," she said to Oscar the cat as she passed him. Oscar stared back at her placidly, undisturbed by her rant.

Maggie stopped at her front door, her key in the lock, as prickles of apprehension raised the fine hairs on the back of her neck. Something didn't feel right. Stepping back, she scrutinized the door and noticed the faint scratches around the lock. Icy bands of fear tightened around her chest, squeezing the air out of her lungs as she realized that someone had been tampering with her lock. Instinctively, her hand went to her pocket in search of the cell phone that she had unthinkingly left in the car. *'Damn, damn, damn.'* Maggie's mind raced. *'Okay, what are the odds that there's someone in there? Whoever was here is probably long gone by now,'* she reasoned. Holding her breath, she cautiously pressed her ear against the door.

"Is something wrong, Maggie?"

With a muffled shriek, Maggie jumped backwards, crashing into the equally startled arms of her neighbor. Her eyes darted towards her apartment, but she heard nothing inside. Embarrassed, she grinned at her confused neighbor.

"Sorry, Spencer. You startled me. Everything's fine."

Spencer, owner of Oscar the cat, blinked at her doubtfully. "Are you sure? I was looking for Oscar, and I saw you over here."

Trying to hide her fear, Maggie gave him a bright, reassuring smile. "I'm sure. It looks like somebody scratched my door, but it was probably just kids or something." She pointed toward the walkway. "Oscar was there a minute ago. He's probably hiding in the bushes."

"Oh, okay then. I haven't seen you around here lately," Spencer said as he headed towards the bushes.

"Yeah. I've, uh, I've been really busy," Maggie replied.

Spencer shot a knowing grin over his shoulder. "Uh-huh. I've seen who you've been busy with." Crouching down, he dragged a growling ball of fur out from under the branches. He cradled the squirming cat in his arms as he walked back to his own apartment.

"See you around, Maggie. Don't be such a stranger."

"I'll try. See ya, Spence." Maggie waved at him as he retreated into his apartment and closed the door.

Alone, Maggie stared at her front door. She would come back later, she decided, and she would drag Julia with her. As she walked back to her car, she shook her head, chastising herself for her lack of courage. *'Oh well,'* she thought, *'better to be safe.'*

Inside her apartment, Tom Becker breathed a sigh of relief as he adjusted his gloves. He hadn't been expecting the reporter to turn up in the middle of the day like that. Working quickly, he pulled two plastic

Baggies out of his pockets. Patrick's forgotten duffel bag was still stashed behind the couch, and Tom bent over it. He unzipped the top and stuffed the two bags inside, burying them deep at the bottom, beneath Patrick's clothes. From another pocket of his coat, he retrieved a thick roll of $100 bills. He buried that inside the duffel bag, as well.

Straightening up with a satisfied grunt, he took a quick look around the apartment. Nothing appeared to be out of place and he nodded to himself as he quietly slipped out the front door. No one was watching him as he got into the white van and drove away.

****

Chapter Seventeen

Like a caged tiger, Julia prowled back and forth across the floor of her home office. She had called the Netsports offices twice, looking for Danny. Both times, the receptionist had politely informed her that Mr. Webber was "in a meeting," and he would return her call as soon as he was available. Julia glanced at the clock again. Her last call had been well over an hour before, and she was starting to get the impression that Danny was avoiding her. Out of patience, she grabbed the phone from her desk and hit re-dial.

"This is Julia Cassinelli. Again," Julia said tersely, cutting off the receptionist's standard greeting. "Tell Mr. Webber that I need to talk to, him now. It's urgent."

She listened in disbelief as the receptionist told her that Danny had already left the office for the day. A long string of curses streamed from her mouth, and she tossed the phone aside in disgust.

"So, the little weasel thinks he can get away from me, huh? We'll just see about that."

Julia stomped downstairs and went into the kitchen to retrieve her keys from the counter. Halfway to the front door, she stopped, suddenly remembering that her jeep had been totaled the night before.

"Son of a bitch!"

Cocking her wrist back, she flung her car keys across the living room. She watched in dismay as they ricocheted off the wall and slid behind one of her tall bookcases. 'Shit,' she swore internally. Julia squeezed her eyes shut and slowly counted to ten, letting her irritation fade. Once she felt the urge to snap something in two subside, she crossed the living room and began trying to fish her keys out of their hiding place.

Easing her arm into the narrow space between the bookcase and the wall, she stretched her fingers as far as she could. Ten minutes later, her forehead was damp with sweat, and she was out of breath. She had fished out a quarter, a chess piece and a dust bunny the size of

177

her fist, but no keys. With a resigned sigh, Julia rose and brushed herself off. Briefly, she thought pulling the broom out of the hallway closet and using that to drag her stubborn keys out, but that seemed dangerously close to housework.

"That's it. Time to get the spare." Temporarily giving up the fight, she went into the kitchen and dug her spare house key out of a drawer. Tucking that into her pocket, she flipped through the phone book until she found the listings for cab companies. Randomly, she chose one and returned to the living room to wait for her ride.

Precisely twenty minutes later, a car horn blared outside, and she raised an eyebrow, impressed by the cab driver's punctuality. Putting on her jacket on the way out the door, she hurried down the front steps to the waiting vehicle and nodded politely to the driver. She had written Danny's home address on a post-it note, and she double-checked that before giving the cab driver a destination.

She stared blankly out the window during the drive to Danny's apartment. The cab driver had the radio on, and she could just barely hear the local news report in between bursts of static. Julia strained her ears to listen as the disc jockey read from the morning's headlines. The top story was Eddie Machado's murder and his possible link to both the Netsports burglary and the arson fires. An unnamed police source had leaked the fact that Eddie and the warehouse security guard were shot with a gun registered to Daniel Webber. Julia smirked mercilessly as she imagined the panicked look on Danny's face. He had to be sweating buckets by now. As the cab pulled up to the gate of Danny's apartment complex, Julia found she was looking forward to grilling her old college buddy.

She leaned forward to exchange a few words with the indifferent security guard. He gave her a bored nod and pushed a button on the panel in front of him. Slowly, the gate slid aside. The cab driver stopped in front of Danny's unit and waited as Julia exited the vehicle. She glanced around, taking note of her surroundings. Danny's complex was home to hundreds of young, upwardly mobile, professionals like him. As a result, there were few residents around on a Thursday afternoon.

"Hang on a minute. Let me see if he's home," she said, handing the driver a crisp twenty.

The driver shrugged and slouched down in his seat as Julia made her way to the door. Frowning in concentration, she listened carefully, but there didn't seem to be any sounds coming from within the apartment. The morning newspaper still waited on his front step. *'Hmmm, either he left for work awfully early, or he was never home at all last night*,' Julia thought to herself. She knocked sharply on the front door, the sound echoing through the stillness. No one stirred inside, and Julia sighed in frustration as the silence confirmed her suspicion that Danny wasn't there.

Impulsively, she checked the doorknob and was stunned when it turned easily in her hand. Glancing over her shoulder, she held up five fingers toward the waiting cab driver, indicating that he should give her a few more minutes. Julia turned back to the door and gnawed on her lower lip as she considered her options. If she were caught inside Danny's apartment, she would have a lot to explain. On the other hand, if she passed up this opportunity, there was no telling what kind of evidence she might miss. Steel blue eyes narrowed thoughtfully. Images flashed through her mind --- images of the fear in Maggie's eyes after her attack at the burned warehouse, images of her own attack in her office, and images of her crumpled jeep after the previous night's car chase.

"God help you if you're the one behind this, Danny," she whispered harshly.

The decision made, she cautiously pushed the door open and stepped inside. The apartment looked like it had been in the center of a violent windstorm. Papers and clothing were strewn about on the floor; the cushion had been thrown off the sofa and a dining room chair rested on its side. Julia carefully picked her way through the mess as she headed for Danny's bedroom. She found it in the same state. Drawers and the closet had been emptied, and Julia had the impression that someone had packed and left in a hurry.

Nothing in Danny's bedroom looked useful, so she returned to the living room and began sifting through the papers on the floor. They were mostly copies of receipts and bills, and Julia noted with interest that Danny had reached or exceeded his limit on three separate credit cards. At the sound of a car driving away, she scrambled for the door, reaching it just in time to see the taillights of her cab turning the corner.

"Son of a bitch."

Taking her phone from her pocket, she dialed one of the pre-programmed numbers and hoped that Maggie would answer. She wasn't disappointed, and a warm glow spread through her body at the sound of the reporter's voice.

"Hi, honey. Listen, I need you to do me a favor and pick me up." Julia paused, listening to Maggie's question. "I'm at Danny Webber's apartment." She answered. "No, he's not here. I'll explain later. Can you just come get me before I get caught?"

She gave Maggie directions to the apartment and settled down to wait. A flash went through her mind, and she recalled seeing a computer in Danny's bedroom. She hurried towards it, nearly tripping over an empty briefcase in her haste. Sitting down at the desk, she booted up, wincing as the electronic hum seemed unusually loud in the silence. Within minutes, Julia was browsing through the contents of Danny's hard drive. Most of what she found appeared to be standard, business-related files and her initial excitement was turning to frustration and disappointment. She glanced at her watch. Maggie would arrive soon, and she hadn't found anything significant yet.

Scowling, Julia opened an untitled document and through it. It was a list of names and figures. Towards the bottom of the page, three familiar names jumped out at her --- Eddie Machado, Patrick McKinnon, and her own. Her scowl deepened as she tried in vain to make a connection between the names and the numbers on the list. She printed the document and stuffed it into her pocket, just as a car door slammed outside. Quickly, she shut down the computer and moved away from the desk.

"Julia? Are you in here?" Maggie's voice, lowered to a whisper, drifted through the open doorway.

"Hey." Julia met the reporter in the living room.

"Hey, yourself. What are you doing here?"

"C'mon. Let's go before someone sees us. I'll explain in the car."

Julia slipped her arm around Maggie's shoulders and propelled her towards the door. Once they were pulling away from the complex, she let out a tense breath. Patrick's name on that list disturbed her, and she searched for the best way to tell Maggie what she had found. Glancing sideways at Maggie's profile, she wondered if it would be better to stay quiet until she had more information.

"So, are you going to tell me what's going on?" Maggie asked.

Julia shrugged. "I wanted to talk to Danny, and his receptionist kept putting me off. Then she told me that he had already left the office, so I called a cab and went to his apartment."

"And you broke in." Maggie finished the story.

Julia grinned briefly. "Technically, no. Not exactly, anyway. The door was unlocked."

"And, of course, you just had to go inside."

"Of course," Julia said innocently. "What kind of friend would I be if I didn't make sure everything was okay?"

"I hope Danny realizes what a devoted friend he has." Maggie returned wryly.

Julia's grin disappeared and her eyes turned dark and cold. "Oh, he will. When I'm through with him, he will."

A chill ran down Maggie's spine at the almost-savage quality to Julia's voice. She knew she never wanted to be on Julia's bad side.

"Well, did you find anything interesting while you were there?"

Julia thought about the printout in her pocket. "A couple of things. First, Danny's pretty heavily in debt. He's maxed out three credit cards, all of them gold or platinum level. I took a quick look at his statements, and it appeared that most of the significant charges came from cash advances."

Maggie's brow creased as she considered the implications. "What would he need with so much cash?"

"That's an excellent question. I'm not sure I have the answer to that yet." Julia hesitated for a moment before continuing. "I also found a list of names and figures. They looked like dollar amounts, but I'll have to do a little checking to be sure. Eddie Machado's name was on that list."

Maggie steered the car into the crowded parking lot of their favorite Chinese take-out restaurant. She had checked Julia's refrigerator that morning, and she knew that it was virtually empty. They exited the car and headed for the door, joining the long line of people seeking a quick meal.

"Eddie Machado was working for Danny?" Maggie asked. "Did you recognize any of the other names?"

Julia fidgeted uncomfortably as she scanned the menu. "Uh, sort of. My name was on it," she admitted.

Maggie stared at her, eyes wide in surprise. "Your name? Why?"

"Well, he did hire me to look into the break-in. Maybe that list was a payroll of some kind." She had decided to tell Maggie about the presence of her brother's name, but a crowded public restaurant didn't seem like the proper place to do it.

"I guess that makes sense." Maggie conceded as they edged toward the front of the line.

Julia was a regular at the restaurant, and she smiled at the wizened, frail-looking man behind the counter. Speaking in flawless Cantonese, she ordered steamed rice, kung pao chicken and vegetable egg rolls. Maggie gaped at her in amazement, and she grinned modestly as they waited for their food. Julia had learned at an early age that she had an ear for other languages. She also spoke passable Spanish and a tiny bit of Japanese.

"When I was growing up, we had a Chinese gardener. He taught me a few words," she explained. "Henry taught me a few, too, but they're not the kind you repeat in polite company."

"Oh yeah? Well, you're gonna have to give me a few private lessons." Maggie teased.

Julia's eyebrows shot up into her hairline and she grinned wickedly. "I think I can arrange that."

Thanking the elderly man behind the counter, she took the food and led the way back to the car.

"Let's go home. I'm starved."

Julia was quiet during the short drive back to her house, and Maggie could feel the tension coming off her in waves. Out of the corner of her eye, Maggie examined her lover's face, noting the worried creases around her eyes and mouth. She began to suspect that Julia had found something else in Danny Webber's apartment. Something that she wasn't prepared to share yet.

"You're awfully quiet. Is everything okay?" Maggie asked casually as she parked in front of the house.

"Sure. Everything's fine," Julia said with a weary smile. "I'm just hungry."

With difficulty, Maggie swallowed her reply, not wanting to push Julia on the issue. Whatever it was, she trusted that Julia would tell her in time. She took the take-out cartons while Julia fumbled in her pocket for her key. A sudden jolt of apprehension ran through her as Maggie remembered the odd scratches on her apartment door. Julia, noticing the tension in the reporter's frame, looked at her questioningly.

"I stopped by my apartment after I left the office." Maggie began slowly, preparing herself for the inevitable reaction. "I was about to unlock the door and I noticed all these marks around the lock. It's probably nothing, but it sort of freaked me out at the time."

Julia's chest tightened, and she took a long, slow breath to calm herself. She opened the front door and ushered Maggie inside, taking care to turn the deadbolt behind them. Maggie started for the kitchen, but Julia grabbed her elbow and held her in the entryway. She turned the blonde around so that they were eye to eye.

"What kind of marks?" Julia's voice had a hard, dangerous edge. Any thoughts of Maggie's brother and the mysterious list were instantly forgotten.

Maggie shrugged, trying to appear unconcerned. "Scratches. It's really no big deal."

"You didn't go inside?"

Maggie shook her head, starting to feel embarrassed about the whole thing. "No. I sort of, well, I..."

To her surprise, Julia pulled her into a tight hug, nearly crushing their dinner. Maggie felt soft lips brushing the top of her head.

"You did the right thing, Maggie. Even if it does turn out to be nothing, it's always better to be safe." Julia said, looking deeply into the reporter's eyes. "I can't be sure until I see for myself, but it sounds like someone might have been trying to break in."

"Why?" Maggie whispered.

They both knew the answer. Someone obviously believed that Maggie knew too much. Neither woman wanted to think about what might have happened if Maggie had entered her apartment.

"Maybe we should call the police," Maggie said. "Or Henry. We could call Henry and have him check it out."

Julia shook her head. "No. No police. Not even Henry. I can find things out faster on my own."

"It's too dangerous." Maggie protested, putting herself between Julia and the door. "I really think we should at least call Henry on this."

"Maggie, this is what I do. Remember?" Julia smiled at her reassuringly. "Besides, if there was anyone in your apartment, I'm sure he's long gone by now. I just want to take a look."

Maggie let out a resigned sigh. She could tell that Julia could not be talked out of this. Switching tactics, she held up one of the take-out containers and swung it under Julia's nose. The spicy smell of Kung pao chicken wafted out.

"Okay, but like you said, if anyone was there, he's gone now. So there's no reason why we can't have dinner first, right?" Maggie swung the container again. "Kung pao chicken. Your favorite."

Much to her chagrin, Julia felt her stomach rumble insistently. Her resolve slipped a notch. Maggie was probably right, she thought. It couldn't hurt to grab a bite to eat first. Giving in, Julia followed the blonde into the kitchen and watched while Maggie spooned the food onto a pair of plates.

"Fine," Julia said gruffly. "Dinner first, then I'm going to check out your apartment."

"Sounds like a plan." Maggie handed her a steaming plate. "You do realize that I'm going with you. Right?"

Blue eyes narrowed as Julia regarded her thoughtfully. "I don't suppose I could talk you out of it, could I?" She asked around a forkful of rice.

"Nope."

Julia sighed. "Didn't think so. Okay, we'll both go. There are a couple of things I want to talk to you about anyway."

Chapter Eighteen

Catherine tugged on the heavy glass door and shivered as a blast of chilled, recycled air hit her in the face. The cavernous lobby was empty, except for a single security guard, and Catherine approached him imperiously, her heels echoing on the polished marble floor. Earlier that day, while sifting through Maggie's notes, she had noticed her rival's mysteriously canceled interview with one of the Davis attorneys. Using Maggie's name, Catherine had called the law firm and rescheduled the appointment. Much to her surprise, the clerk had given her a meeting with Joseph Cassinelli at 5:30 that afternoon. This would be the interview of her career, she gloated. Of course, he would recognize her immediately, but it wouldn't matter. Once she was in his office, Catherine knew that the prominent attorney would be forced to talk to her.

Her eyes flicked briefly to her watch as a smug smile touched her thin lips. It was precisely 5:25. She impatiently tapped her index finger on the desk to get the guard's attention and peered down her nose at him with a haughty glare.

"I'm Maggie McKinnon, with the Chronicle," she said in a frosty tone. "Mr. Cassinelli should be expecting me."

The guard's watery eyes roamed across her curves, and he grinned at her appreciatively. She ignored him as she examined her manicure. Realizing that the reporter was not going to succumb to his charm, the guard frowned in disappointment as he checked a list of names on a clipboard. He nodded once.

"McKinnon, right." He pointed to the twin elevators at the rear of the lobby. "Mr. Cassinelli is on the 15th floor."

Without a word, Catherine strode towards the elevators. She paused, checking her reflection in the shiny brass doors. She had heard that Joseph Cassinelli had an eye for beautiful women. '*Must be where his daughter got hers from,*' she mused with a harsh laugh. Catherine tucked her auburn waves behind her ears and smoothed a few faint

185

wrinkles out of her tailored jacket. Satisfied with her appearance, she pressed the call button and waited for the elevator car to arrive.

Out of earshot, the security guard picked up the phone, his gaze never leaving the tall, willowy reporter. He whispered a few words into the receiver and watched as Catherine stepped into the elevator.

On the 4th floor, Tom Becker prepared himself, flexing his fingers, encased in leather gloves. He stuffed his phone back into his pocket and shifted his shoulders beneath his form-fitting black turtleneck. He glanced sideways at his nervous companion. Beads of sweat clung to Patrick McKinnon's temples and he fidgeted uncomfortably, drumming his fingers against his thighs. Patrick had no idea what was going on. He had been working out on the loading dock when Tom had driven up and told him to get in the car. Eddie was dead, and Patrick suspected that Tom had something to do with it. He wondered if he was next.

Tom had offered no explanation on the way to the law offices. In fact, he hadn't said a single word to Patrick during the entire drive. They had arrived nearly 30 minutes earlier, and they had been waiting on the deserted 4th floor since then.

"Calm down," Tom said, his gravelly voice rumbling through the silence.

He removed a handgun from his waistband, and Patrick stared at it fearfully. This was it. Tom had brought him here to kill him, just like Eddie. Sweat poured down Patrick's back, and he irrationally wondered if he could outrun a bullet. Tom noted the panic-stricken look in his companion's eyes with a mixture of contempt and pleasure. Gripping the gun by the barrel, he thrust the weapon toward Patrick.

"Here. Hold this for a second, wouldja?" He laughed at the young man's hesitation. "Relax. It isn't loaded. I carry it for show. Just in case I need to put the fear of God into someone."

Patrick slowly took the gun as Tom bent to fiddle with his shoelace. The cold metal warmed quickly to his bare hand, and he hefted the weapon in his palm, feeling the weight of it. Straightening, Tom took the gun back and tucked it away beneath his coat. He smiled, and Patrick felt an icy shiver run down his spine. He had never seen Tom smile before, and the sight unnerved him. The urge to flee was overwhelming.

The elevator pinged softly, and both men turned toward the sound. The doors slid open noiselessly, revealing a tall, pale woman with a mane of auburn waves. She barely glanced at them as they stepped inside the car. The doors shut again, and Tom gestured towards the panel in front of the woman.

"Could you hit 12, please?"

The woman complied and the three rode in silence, watching the lights change as the elevator continued its ascent. Tom surveyed the auburn-haired woman thoughtfully. He didn't know who she was, but she was not Maggie McKinnon. He wondered why she was using the reporter's name.

"So, are you a lawyer?" It was the best conversation-starter he could come up with.

Catherine glanced at him and gave him a condescending smile. "No. I'm a reporter. I have a meeting with Joseph Cassinelli."

"Hey, I've heard of him. He's supposed to be some rich big shot, isn't he?"

"He's a very important man, yes. He's also one of Councilman Martin Davis's personal attorneys."

Tom nodded soberly. "I see."

So, she was a reporter after all, Tom thought. They were nearing the 12th floor, and he had to make a decision quickly. Once this new reporter reached her destination, she would discover that there was no meeting scheduled. That could not happen. Tom let out a resigned sigh as he reached under his coat. He had no choice; Allison would understand that.

Patrick watched in horrified disbelief as Tom took action. Moving with deceptive speed, the big man crossed the elevator and punched the stop button, halting the car with a sudden, rumbling jolt. Catherine glared at them, annoyance clearly stamped on her features. Before she had time to speak, Tom smoothly pulled his gun from his waistband and fired, striking the reporter in the chest.

The impact slammed her back against the wall, and her eyes widened in shock. A choking, gurgling cough bubbled forth from her lips as she slowly crumpled. The acrid smell of gunpowder mixed with the sharp, metallic scent of blood, and Patrick fell to his knees, retching violently in the corner. Warm wetness trickled down his leg as his bladder emptied.

Tom gazed at him in disgust. Calmly, he pressed another button on the control panel, and the elevator resumed its journey. They reached the 12th floor, and the doors opened. Tom had chosen this floor because it was being renovated and would be deserted. With one hand, he hauled Patrick to his feet and shoved him into the corridor. The doors shut behind them, and the elevator continued to climb. They had to hurry now, before the body was discovered. Pushing Patrick in front of him, Tom moved towards the stairwell. He paused momentarily outside the door, discarding the gun in a trash bin. Patrick was already starting to descend the dimly lit steps, and Tom grabbed the collar of his shirt, yanking him back.

"Hang on a sec," he said.

As Patrick turned toward him, Tom swung his massive fist, connecting squarely with the young man's jaw. He left Patrick sprawled, unconscious, on the landing and hurried down the stairs, whistling softly to himself. The lobby was quiet when he emerged. He exchanged a quick glance with the guard at the desk as he exited the building and unhurriedly strolled down the street.

The guard watched him leave and double-checked to make sure the security cameras had not recorded anything. Within seconds, a red light began to flash frantically on his phone. He answered and managed to sound appropriately shocked as a secretary on the 15th floor informed him that a woman had been shot in the elevator. Slowly, he counted to ten, letting Tom get a bit further away before he called the police.

Groaning, Patrick opened his eyes. His head throbbed and his jaw ached where Tom had hit him. The memories came flooding back in a rush, and Patrick's stomach heaved again. He rolled to his knees, and once the nausea had subsided, he gripped the rail and pulled himself to his feet. Tom was gone, and Patrick realized that he had been set up. He had no idea how long he had been out, but he knew that the woman's body had probably been discovered. Patrick shuddered, remembering the blood and the look in the woman's eyes as she fell. He was sure she was dead. She had looked dead. He scrubbed at his eyes with the heel of his hand, trying to collect his thoughts. He had to get out. Quickly. Before the cops showed up.

Fighting through the dizziness, Patrick ran down the stairs. The lobby was completely empty when he stumbled through the door, wild-eyed and sweating profusely. He dashed out the exit into the cool evening air, drawing curious stares from the people passing by. Sirens screamed in the distance, rapidly approaching. Dodging the traffic, he sprinted across the street and blended into a tour group, just as the first squad car turned the corner and screeched to a halt in front of the law offices. Keeping his head down, Patrick followed the tour group down the street. One thought kept racing through his mind. Maggie. He had to get to Maggie. She would know what to do.

****

"So, what did the insurance company say?"

"Hmm?" Julia asked, stirred out of her thoughts by Maggie's question.

"You called the insurance company about your jeep, didn't you?" Maggie prompted her.

"Oh that. I filed a claim and the agent said she'd have a check for me in a few weeks."

"That's good news," Maggie said, trying to keep the conversation going. Julia had been quiet and distracted since leaving Danny Webber's apartment earlier.

"Do you know what kind of car you want? Another jeep, or something different this time?"

Julia shrugged and resumed her thoughtful gaze out the window of Maggie's car. "I don't know. Haven't really thought about it yet."

A thick wall of fog had rolled in from the Bay as soon as the sun had set. As they passed the park, the mist hugged the ground, making visibility even worse. Maggie slowed the car to a crawl, unable to see the intersections until she was right on top of them. She nearly missed her street and made a sharp turn, throwing Julia off balance.

"Sorry," she said, as Julia braced herself against the dashboard.

"Well, I guess that's one way to get my attention."

Maggie grinned at the joke. "You just seem a little out there tonight. Is something wrong? Earlier, you said we needed to talk."

Julia squirmed. She had been dreading this conversation. So far, she hadn't been able to come up with an easy way to tell Maggie that her brother was most likely involved with criminals. Patrick was infuriating, but she knew that Maggie still loved him.

"Yeah, about that --- when I was at Danny's, I found something else." She began slowly. A startled exclamation from Maggie interrupted her.

"What on earth?"

Perplexed, Julia followed Maggie's gaze. They had turned into the apartment complex, and three squad cars were parked in front of Maggie's building. Maggie stopped the car abruptly and got out, running towards her apartment. Cursing, Julia unbuckled her seatbelt and chased after her, catching up to the blonde just as a police officer materialized before them.

"Sorry, but you need to stay back. There's an investigation going on here," he said, blocking their path.

"But that's my apartment," Maggie protested, pointing at her open door. Inside, they could see several officers searching the living room.

Julia loomed over the younger policeman, a fierce scowl on her face." What's this all about?" She demanded with a menacing growl.

An authoritative voice drifted towards them, and the young officer breathed a sigh of relief at the sight of his superior standing in the doorway. He took a step back, away from the tall, intimidating woman in front of him.

"Henry, what the hell is going on?" Julia asked, moving towards the stocky inspector.

Henry put his hands up, grabbing her by the shoulders and preventing her from entering the apartment. His eyes darted behind her to Maggie's ashen face. He smiled at her gently before returning his attention to his bristling friend.

"Calm down, Jules. Let me explain," he said.

Julia folded her arms across her chest and glared at him, waiting for him to continue. Henry steadied himself, doing his best to ignore her steely blue stare. He stepped out onto the doorstep, forcing Julia back a few feet.

"We have a situation," he said. "Catherine Richards was shot."

"What?" Julia's voice hissed between her clenched teeth.

"What?" Maggie echoed weakly, scarcely believing what she was hearing.

Henry put a sympathetic hand on each woman's arm and steered her into an alcove. After a quick glance to make sure no one was listening to them, he continued his explanation.

"She was in an office building downtown. We're not entirely sure what she was doing in there. The guard on duty claims he never spoke to her, and the security tapes don't show us anything. My best guess is that she was meeting with a lawyer. A receptionist for one of the lawyers on the 15th floor found her when the elevator opened." "Oh my god." Maggie whispered, stunned. Her knees buckled and she would have fallen if Julia hadn't been supporting her. She looked up at Henry as tears started in her eyes.

"Is she dead?"

Henry shook his head. "No. She's in surgery now, but it doesn't look good." He hesitated and cleared his throat softly. "Maggie, did you know Catherine? Do you have any idea why she might have been meeting a lawyer?"

Maggie stifled a sob, and the sound tugged at Julia's heart. She glared at Henry, her face grim.

"Not now, Henry. Don't you think she's upset enough, already?"

Henry sighed and rubbed the flat of his hand across his jaw. He always hated this part of his job, especially when it involved someone he knew. There was more to the story, too, and he knew that Julia would become even more defensive once her father's name was mentioned. To his surprise, Maggie came to his rescue.

"It's okay, honey," she said, squeezing Julia's forearm lightly. She directed a faint grin up at the concerned inspector. "You have to ask these questions. I understand."

Henry returned the grin with a relieved smile of his own. Out of the corner of his eye, he saw Julia relax slightly and take a half step back, giving them room to talk.

"To answer your question, yes, I know Catherine," Maggie said, taking a deep breath. "We're co-workers, but not friends, exactly. I had an interview with one of Councilman Davis's attorneys, but it got canceled. Maybe Catherine rescheduled it."

Henry scribbled furiously in his notebook. He looked up with a puzzled frown. "Why would Catherine reschedule one of your interviews?"

"I'm on leave from work. She took over my story." Maggie answered simply. She stole a quick glance at Julia's stony expression.

"None of this explains what you're doing here, Henry." Julia spoke up. "Do you have any leads? Any idea who did this?" A question was gnawing at her, but she wasn't sure she wanted to know the answer.

"We have a preliminary suspect." Henry confirmed. "And I'll explain what we're doing here in a minute. Just between us, though, something doesn't feel right."

"So, you don't know who Catherine was going to meet?" Julia asked, dreading the answer.

Henry coughed into his fist. "Not specifically." He took a deep breath and plunged ahead. "Jules, you know your father has an office on that floor."

Julia nodded slowly. She had been expecting this. "You think Catherine was going to see my father." It wasn't a question. She continued, her voice flat and unemotional. "He and Martin Davis are friends, but I honestly couldn't tell you if they have a working relationship."

Before Henry could respond, one of his uniformed officers summoned him. He excused himself and stepped back inside Maggie's apartment. They could see him in a hushed conference with two of his men, who were gesturing excitedly behind the couch. After a moment, the inspector returned with a troubled frown.

"Maggie, I need you to come take a look at something. You too, Jules." He led them both inside the small apartment. "Try not to touch anything. We still need to dust for fingerprints."

191

Henry stopped in front of the couch and pulled a pair of white latex gloves out of his pocket. He put the gloves on, the rubber snapping against his skin, and dismissed the other officers with a curt nod. Dropping to one knee, he dragged a half-unzipped duffel bag out from behind Maggie's couch.

"Do either of you recognize this bag?" He looked at them, his eyes moving from one face to the other.

"Yes." Maggie's whisper was almost inaudible. Her stomach plummeted further when Henry reached inside the bag and extracted a plastic baggie filled with a white, powdery substance. Her heart sank and she closed her eyes.

"That little shit!" Julia burst out angrily.

Henry waited for one of them to say something else. When neither did, he spoke again. "Okay, one of you needs to tell me who this bag belongs to."

"Why? You already know the answer to that, don't you?" Julia asked pointedly. "That's why you're in Maggie's apartment, right?"

Sighing, Henry loosened his tie and unbuttoned his collar. Julia always had to be difficult. Carefully, he placed the plastic bag back inside the duffel bag and stood. He turned to Maggie, wishing he didn't have to ask her these questions.

"Fine." He muttered in Julia's direction. "Maggie, does this bag belong to your brother, Patrick Robert McKinnon?"

Maggie blinked at him in confusion. She was certain that she had never discussed her brother with the police inspector. That meant that either Julia had mentioned him, or.... The alternative hit her squarely in the chest and knocked the air out of her lungs. Her mouth opened in disbelief and she stared at Henry with widened eyes.

"Patrick? You think my brother had something to do with this?" Her voice rose as a surge of protective anger began to burn in her veins. "That's ridiculous! Patrick could not possibly be involved in anything so, so..."

"Maggie, I'm sorry. I hate being the one to tell you this." Henry interrupted her indignant protestations. "We found a gun at the crime scene. We're still waiting for a complete ballistics report, but we're pretty confident that it's the right weapon. We pulled a partial thumb print off it, and it matched the prints your brother has on file in Ohio."

"Your brother has a police record?" Julia asked, staring at Maggie incredulously. She had known that he was an addict, but Maggie had never mentioned anything about a criminal record.

"He was arrested a few years back for vandalism, assault and possession of a controlled substance." Henry said, his voice trailing off as he realized that Julia had not known about Patrick's background.

"Most of those charges were dropped." Maggie defended her brother.

Julia was stunned, and she wondered what else she didn't know about Maggie's brother. Suddenly, she remembered the sheet of paper in her back pocket. She pulled the page out, unfolded it and handed it to Henry. He read it and looked at her, puzzled.

"You didn't get this tip from me." She warned him. "I pulled that out of Daniel Webber's home computer today. I think it's some kind of payroll or something. As you can see, it has Patrick McKinnon's name on it."

"What? You didn't tell me that earlier!" Maggie spun to face her lover.

Julia flinched at the intensity of the fire burning in the reporter's green eyes. "I was going to tell you."

"But you thought you'd accuse him of attempted murder first?" Maggie shot back angrily.

"Hey, hold on! I didn't accuse him of anything!" Julia objected heatedly. "But I don't think it's a coincidence that his prints are on the gun used to shoot Catherine. Your brother is in this up to his beady little eyeballs. My god, Maggie! What if you had been the one to show up at that office?"

"Okay, first of all, you don't even know what my brother looks like. And second, he would never hurt me."

Henry edged away, giving them room to continue their discussion. In the kitchen, he took his cell phone from his pocket and dialed the police station.

"This is Chow," he said tersely. "I need a search warrant for Daniel Webber's residence and office, and I need it now." He listened for a moment. "I don't care how! Just get it! And while you're at it, issue an arrest warrant for Patrick Robert McKinnon. The charge is attempted murder."

Reading from his notepad, Henry provided a detailed physical description of his suspect. He hoped Maggie was right and her brother was not the shooter. Either way, though, Henry was determined to solve this case in a hurry. Two people had been shot in the last 24 hours, and he had an uneasy feeling that, unless he moved quickly, they wouldn't be the last.

In the living room, Julia and Maggie were still arguing. They were facing each other, eyes flashing dangerously. Henry had seen that look in Maggie's eyes before, when he had yelled at Julia. He knew that she was fiercely protective of the people she loved. And Julia was the most bullheaded, obstinate woman he had ever known. So, this is what happens when an irresistible force meets an immovable object, he thought wryly.

"Maggie, open your eyes! There's all this evidence that points straight at your brother. If he didn't shoot Catherine, then he sure as hell knows something about who did!" Julia insisted vehemently

"Patrick did not do this." Maggie retorted, just as forcefully. "Somebody is obviously setting him up, and you don't even seem to care! Do you want to see an innocent man go to jail?"

"Maybe jail would do the little punk some good." Julia suggested sarcastically, instantly regretting the comment.

Green eyes narrowed into slits, and Maggie's jaw trembled from the strain of gritting her teeth. "You know what? I'm out of here." She glanced at Henry, and he blinked under the force of her stare. "I'll be at my friend Jessica's if you need to reach me. Julia can get you the number."

"Maggie, wait a minute. Don't be silly." Julia called after her. "Come on, you have the car. How am I supposed to get home?"

Maggie never stopped moving. "I'm sure one of your police buddies can give you a ride." She left the apartment, and a few moments later, a car door slammed and an engine revved.

Julia blinked in disbelief. Maggie had really left her there. Her mind whirled as she tried to figure out how their argument had spun out of control s☐ quickly. Maggie clearly had a blind spot where her brother was concerned, and all she had tried to do was show the reporter what was right in front of her. Julia's irritation rose again.

"Fine." She muttered under her breath. Still seething, she glared at the empty doorway. "Just fine!" She shot a frustrated look at her mutely waiting friend. "Henry, I think I'm gonna need a ride home."

****

Chapter Nineteen

Maggie shifted uncomfortably on the lumpy couch as she flipped through the worn pages of an old magazine. The evening news was playing on a muted television in the corner of the hospital waiting room. Maggie glanced up at the clock. Two days had passed since Catherine was shot, and she had finally regained consciousness earlier that afternoon. There was a policeman talking to her, and Maggie hoped that she would remember something that would clear Patrick.

"Here." Jessica appeared at her elbow and handed her a steaming cup of coffee. "It's disgusting, but at least it's caffeinated."

Maggie gave her a wry, tired smile. "Thanks."

She scooted over so Jessica could sit beside her. They had been at the hospital almost constantly since Catherine had come out of surgery. Though she had a long, painful road ahead of her, the doctors believed that she would make a full recovery. Maggie had heaved a sigh of relief at that. Despite Jessica's insistence to the contrary, she felt somewhat responsible for Catherine's condition. Especially since the bullet had most likely been meant for her.

"Your mother called again. Twice."

Jessica's voice broke through her thoughts, and Maggie turned to face her friend. She looked down at the small silver phone in Jessica's hand. As soon as the news about Patrick had reached Ohio, her phone had been ringing incessantly. After one conversation with her hysterical mother, she had given her phone to Jessica and was letting her screen the calls.

"I can't deal with my mother right now, Jess," Maggie said, rubbing her weary, red-rimmed eyes. She peeked hopefully through her fingers. "Did anyone else call?"

"Just one of your brothers. Jack."

Maggie groaned. "Great. He probably wants to yell at me too."

Jessica nodded in sympathy. Every family had members who didn't get along, and in the McKinnon clan, it was Maggie and Jack.

"Do you want to call him back?" Jessica asked.

Grimacing, Maggie shook her head and sipped from her coffee.

"Not a chance. He'll just lecture me about how I should have called them as soon as Patrick disappeared." She paused. "Okay, maybe I should've. But it's not like there was anything they could have done. And I thought he'd be back in a few days. He always comes back."

"Take it easy, Maggie. You don't have to convince me of anything," Jessica said. "Oh, I almost forgot. You got a few calls from unlisted numbers, and when I answered them, nobody said anything."

Maggie tossed the magazine aside and snatched the phone from Jessica's hand. Rapidly, she searched through the phone numbers. After a moment, her shoulders slumped and the back of her throat tightened as tears threatened. None of the numbers looked familiar.

"I'm sorry," Jessica said awkwardly. "I know you were hoping she would call."

Maggie nodded faintly but said nothing. She hadn't heard from Julia since their fight, and she was beginning to wonder if she ever would. '*Of course you haven't heard from her. Why should she call you? You walked out on her, remember?*' It was true. At her apartment, she had walked out on Julia and driven away without looking back. It hadn't hit her until she was halfway done the street, and by then it had seemed too late to go back. She had circled around the block twice before finally deciding to go stay with Jessica for a few days.

'*Still, I thought for sure she would have called,*' Maggie thought. She shook herself angrily. '*Wait a minute. I have every right to be mad at her. She practically turned Patrick over to the police and she didn't even discuss it with me first,*' Maggie reminded herself. '*So, if I have every reason to be upset, then why do I feel so horrible?*' She closed her eyes, remembering the look on Julia's face just before she had walked out. She had seen the shock and confusion in those deep blue eyes. '*What if she never forgives me,*' Maggie wondered desolately. '*Am I really prepared to lose her over this?*'

Suddenly, Jessica grabbed her wrist and pointed at the television. "Maggie, look!"

Maggie followed her gaze and sucked in a sharp breath as a live shot of Councilman Martin Davis entering police headquarters. She shot out of her seat and rushed across the room to turn the volume up. Stunned, she listened as an earnest young reporter informed her that the councilman had decided to voluntarily answer questions about his connection to Catherine's attack and the arson blaze at one of his warehouses.

As she watched, another car pulled up in front of the building, and a man with impeccably groomed silver hair exited the vehicle. For just a moment, he faced the camera and Maggie found herself staring into an achingly familiar pair of intense blue eyes. Joseph Cassinelli had arrived to serve as the councilman's attorney during this interview.

Jessica eyed her friend shrewdly, noting the trembling lower lip as Maggie tried to hold back her tears. Although she hadn't said much, Jessica knew that she was deeply troubled by Julia's silence, and she was desperately trying not to show it.

"Maggie, just call her." Jessica advised, placing a comforting hand on her friend's shoulder.

Biting her lip, Maggie shook her head sadly. "I can't. What if she doesn't want to talk to me?"

Jessica sighed and turned Maggie to face her. She gazed sternly into her friend's glistening eyes.

"You can't think like that. She loves you. I saw it in her face the first time I met her and I see it in yours every time I look at you. She's probably sitting at home right now, hoping that you'll call."

Maggie started to speak, but Jessica cut her off with a sharp wave of her hand.

"She loves you, Maggie," Jessica repeated. "Do you have any idea how rare that is? Don't you dare let that slip through your fingers just because of a silly little fight."

"I don't know, Jess," Maggie whispered doubtfully.

Exasperated, Jessica let her hands fall to her sides. "Do you love her?" She asked simply.

"Yes." Maggie answered her without hesitation.

"Then quit being so boneheaded and call her. Tell her that."

An orderly who told them that the policeman had finished talking to Catherine interrupted them. They were allowed to visit her, but only for a few minutes. As they started down the sterile white corridor, Maggie took a sip from her cup and made a face. The coffee had grown cold and she tossed it into the nearest trashcan. A few yards from Catherine's door, a man heading in the opposite direction inadvertently bumped into her.

"Sorry about that. Didn't see you there." He muttered before continuing.

Something about his deep, scratchy voice made Maggie's skin crawl. As she entered Catherine's room, she shot a curious look over her shoulder, but the man had already turned the corner and disappeared. Maggie shrugged and directed a guarded smile towards the woman in the hospital bed. Catherine's eyebrows arched as they approached. She waited until her visitors were seated and Jessica had handed her a card.

"It's from a bunch of people at work." The tiny copy editor told her.

Catherine responded with a tight, frosty smile. "I'm surprised you got anyone to sign it. I know what you all call me behind my back."

She ripped open the envelope and opened the oversized card. Her icy demeanor slipped a bit as she realized that almost everyone in the newsroom had signed it. Maggie's name was not among them, and Catherine directed a questioning gaze at her rival reporter. Smiling faintly, Maggie took another envelope from her purse and handed it to the auburn-haired woman.

"This one is just from me."

Catherine set it aside to be read later. "Thanks." Her eyes narrowed and she regarded Maggie appraisingly. "Why are you really here, McKinnon?"

"First of all, I wanted to make sure you were really okay," Maggie said, a bit defensively. "We may not like each other very much, but that doesn't mean I want anything bad to happen to you." She paused, her lips twitching in a grin. "Well, okay. Maybe once or twice I might have wished for you to be hit by a runaway cable car, but that doesn't count. I wasn't serious about it. And what are the odds of that happening, anyway?"

She heard Jessica's soft snort as she tried to stifle a laugh, and much to her surprise, even Catherine smiled briefly. The injured reporter struggled to sit up and gasped as her efforts sent pain shooting through her. She clutched at her chest and coughed weakly. Instantly, Maggie jumped out of her chair and sat on the edge of the bed. She slid her arm behind Catherine's shoulders for support and carefully helped her into a more comfortable position. She gave Jessica a grateful look as her friend handed her a cup of water and a straw. Maggie held the straw to Catherine's lips and waited while she sipped from it.

"Thank you," Catherine said, pushing the cup away. She tried to take a deep breath and winced as another bolt of pain ripped through her.

"You're welcome," Maggie replied. "Take it easy. I don't want you hurting yourself any further."

"Quit being so nice to me, McKinnon. It's creepy," Catherine said, eyeing her suspiciously. "Now, why don't you tell me why you're really here?"

Maggie hesitated. "I, uh, I wanted to know if you remembered anything about what happened. About who did this to, I mean."

Catherine closed her eyes and her mouth tightened into a hard, thin line. "So that's what this is about. You just want the scoop on the story. I should've known." She opened her eyes and gave Maggie a piercing stare. "Let me ask you something first. Where's your girlfriend? Or doesn't she give a damn if I live or die?"

Jessica started to leap to her friend's defense, but Maggie silenced her with a look. She gazed placidly at her rival, determined not to let Catherine know that she and Julia were apart.

"Julia couldn't make it, but I'm sure she doesn't want you to die." It was the truth, sort of. Maggie continued. "And I'm not after any story, either. I'm still on leave from the paper, so I couldn't write it even if I wanted to. In case you forgot, someone tried to kill me not too long ago, so I was just curious. That's all." She held her breath, hoping Catherine didn't know about her brother.

Catherine softened slightly. "I already told the police everything I remember, which isn't much." Her gaze became distant as she recalled the events of that day. "I had an appointment to meet with Julia's father." She glanced at Maggie. "I used your name to get the interview. If I had used my own, there's no way Joe Cassinelli would have agreed to see me. He likes me about as much as his daughter does."

"Anyway, I went up in the elevator. Somewhere before my floor, two men got in, but I didn't really look at them. They didn't interest me." Catherine frowned, struggling to remember. "I don't even remember the gun. There was a loud noise and it felt like something just shoved me backwards. It didn't even hurt."

"Two men? Are you sure there were two?" Maggie interrupted her.

Catherine stared at her, puzzled. "Yeah. I couldn't tell you what they looked like, but I'm sure there were two of them. You know, the cop that was just here asked me that same question, even though I already told this story to the two cops that were here when I woke up. Why is that?"

Maggie froze. Something was setting off alarm bells in her head, and her mind worked frantically to process what Catherine had just said. *'Two sets of cops? No, wait. One pair of cops, then another policeman, apparently working alone. Why would they ask the same questions, though? Unless...'*

Jessica made the connection first. "Catherine, the cop that just left. What did he look like?"

Catherine shrugged. "He was big. Kind of heavy-set, like a boxer or a wrestler. I didn't pay that much attention to his face." She shuddered weakly. "His voice creeped me out, though. It was all low and gravely. It was like the voice the killer uses when he calls you from inside your house."

The description clicked in Maggie's mind. 'Sorry about that. Didn't see you there.' The words of the man she had run into in the hall echoed through her head. Quickly, she described him to Catherine, and the other reporter nodded.

"Yeah, that sounds like him," Catherine said.

Maggie leaned forward excitedly. "Did he give you his name?"

Catherine thought for a moment. "Beck. Officer Beck. He told me they didn't have any suspects yet. I was probably just in the wrong place at the wrong time. He asked a couple of questions about you, though. Probably because I used your name when I set up the interview." She paused, observing as Maggie and Jessica exchanged glances. "Will somebody tell me what the hell is going on here?"

Maggie stood hurriedly, nearly knocking the water pitcher off the small table beside the bed. Fumbling through her purse, she pulled out a plain white business card and used the hospital phone to dial the number on it.

"Henry? I can barely hear you." She listened while he explained that he was crossing the lower deck of the Bay Bridge. "Never mind that. I need to ask you something. Do you know an Officer Beck?"

As she expected, Henry answered negatively. Maggie raked her fingers through her hair as she paced back and forth.

"Okay, I need you to do me a favor. Send someone to Catherine's hospital room. There was a man here a little while ago, posing as a police officer. He asked her a bunch of questions about the shooting and about me." She held the receiver away from her ear as Henry squawked at her in alarm. "I know. I'll be careful. Just send someone over here."

Henry agreed, and she hung up the phone. Maggie turned to Jessica.

"Can you stay here until the real police show up?"

Nodding, Jessica shooed her towards the door. "Of course. Go do whatever you need to do. We'll be fine here."

Catherine waved her hand at them to get their attention. "Excuse me. Somebody needs to start explaining right now."

The two friends glanced at her briefly.

"Get out of here. Just promise me you'll be careful." Jessica practically pushed Maggie out into the hall. "And tell Julia I said hi."

Maggie tossed a faint grin over her shoulder as she hurried down the corridor. She exited the hospital and paused for a moment on the curb, letting her eyes adjust to the darkness. The lights in the parking lot were dim, and she frowned as she tried to spot her car. As she walked towards her row, she felt exposed and vulnerable. She picked up her pace, glancing around nervously. Suddenly, leaving the nice, crowded hospital didn't seem like such a good idea. Footsteps approached behind her and she tensed, clutching her keys in her hand like a weapon. A young woman passed by her without a glance, and Maggie breathed a sigh of relief.

She reached her car without incident and dialed Julia's home as she drove out of the parking lot. There was no answer. Even the answering machine failed to pick up. Frowning, Maggie called the private investigator's office, but there was no answer there either. This time, though, she was directed to Julia's voice mail, and she listened to the outgoing message.

"Out of town? Where the hell did she go?"

The traffic light turned red, and she slowed to a stop. Impatiently, she tapped her fingernails on the steering wheel. Where would Julia go? Maggie drifted back to a conversation from a few days before. Julia had mentioned something about a cabin on the beach. It was very secluded, she had said, and Maggie had gotten the impression that it was someplace she went when she needed time alone.

"I guess it's worth a shot," Maggie told herself. "Now, if I could just remember what beach she was talking about."

The light changed to green, and Maggie made a left turn. Her eyes darted briefly to her purse where her cell phone waited. She would call Henry again at the next light. If anyone knew exactly where Julia had gone, it would be the police inspector. And if he didn't know, then she would search every damn beach along the California coast. With new determination, she turned her car towards the Golden Gate Bridge and the coastal highway that stretched beyond.

At the last moment, Maggie decided to stop at her apartment and check her messages before heading out of town. She was sure that there would be more frantic phone calls from her mother, but she hoped there might also be something from Julia. Recklessly, she spun the steering wheel and swung her car into her parking spot, narrowly missing the rusty iron pole that separated the spaces. As she headed for her front door, she took a chance and dialed Julia's cell phone. There was still no answer from the missing private investigator.

Maggie's stomach churned as worry and doubt gnawed at her insides. She still had to check with Henry, but it seemed like Julia had vanished without a word. Maggie refused to believe that Julia would simply abandon her. It was more likely that her stubborn, moody lover had needed some time alone. An insistent whisper sounded in Maggie's mind, but she tried to ignore it. *'What if Julia didn't leave voluntarily? What if something happened to her?'*

"No. Don't think like that." Maggie told herself firmly as she unlocked her door. "She's fine. Maybe she got a lead on a case or something. Yeah, that's probably it."

Maggie stepped inside her apartment and closed the door, making sure to lock it behind her. The police had searched her place thoroughly and hadn't found any fingerprints other than hers; Julia's and Patrick's, but being there alone still made her nervous. Splotches of bluish-gray dust, left behind by the crime scene unit, dotted everything in her apartment, and Maggie absently ran her index finger through the powder. Her gaze automatically drifted to the empty spot behind the couch where Patrick's duffel bag had been. The police had taken anything that belonged to her brother. She shook her head stubbornly. Patrick wasn't a saint, but he wasn't a killer, either, and she was determined not to let anyone pin a crime on him that he hadn't committed.

The red light on her answering machine was blinking furiously at her, begging for her attention, and Maggie crossed into the kitchen to stare apprehensively at the little black box. The machine was completely full of messages, and she dreaded listening to them. With a resigned sigh, she hit the playback button and her mother's shrill voice immediately filled the room. Grimacing, Maggie skipped to the next message. That one was from her mother, as well. She kept scanning, ignoring the urgent voices of various family members. Sam, her editor, had called once, and she made a mental note to call him back. She was nearing the end of the messages, and her disappointment was growing steadily. Finally, her heart soared hopefully as a welcome voice filled her ears.

"Hi Maggie. It's, uh, it's me." An awkward pause as Julia cleared her throat. "I know you're not there right now, but just in case you checked your messages, I wanted you to know that I'm heading out of town for a few days. I just didn't want you to worry or anything."

Relief flooded over the reporter as she listened to the message, which had been left early that morning. She still didn't know where Julia had gone, but at least she knew that nothing sinister had happened to her. Maggie replayed the message, letting the warm tones of her lover's voice wash over her. Julia still cared enough to let her know that she was all right. That was something, at least.

Glancing at the clock, Maggie realized that it was getting late, and she debated waiting until morning to start her search. No, she decided, she didn't want to spend one more minute without Julia and she was eager to tell the private investigator about Catherine's mysterious visitor. She was confident that Julia would be able to make sense of it. Her mind made up, Maggie cleared her answering machine and reset it before heading for the door. In a hurry, she yanked it open and crashed headfirst into a warm, solid body. She let out a startled yelp and backpedaled fearfully, adrenaline pumping through her veins.

"Maggie? God, I'm sorry. I didn't mean to scare you or anything."

With one hand, Maggie steadied herself against the kitchen counter and forced herself to breathe normally. Drew Cassinelli was standing on her doorstep, peering at her anxiously. She gave him an embarrassed half-grin.

"It's okay. I guess I'm a little jumpy these days."

Drew returned the smile warmly. "Understandable, considering everything you've been through lately." He glanced at the keys in her hand. "Were you on your way out?"

As Maggie started to respond, Jessica's warning flashed through her mind. Was Drew really who he seemed to be? It seemed strange that he was at her apartment, especially since she didn't recall ever telling him where she lived. Maggie's heart thundered in her ears and her smile was frozen to her face. She was sure he could see the uncertainty behind it.

"Actually, I was about to go run a few errands." She lied, hoping he wouldn't notice the flush she could feel creeping up her neck. "If you're looking for your sister, she's not here right now."

"Oh, I know." Drew replied hastily. He shifted his weight from one foot to the other and jammed his hands in his pockets. "I was sort of hoping that you and I could talk. Maybe we could go grab a cup of coffee or something?"

Maggie desperately searched for a way out. "I don't know, Drew. I'm awfully busy tonight."

"I don't want to keep you," Drew began. "It's important, though."

Maggie regarded him warily, trying to gauge his intentions. Despite Jessica's cautionary words, she wasn't getting the impression that Drew was dangerous. She did suspect that there was something he was holding back, though, and she wondered if it had anything to do with Julia. She checked her watch.

"It's about Julia." Drew blurted the words out, and that sealed Maggie's decision.

She nodded briskly. "Okay. Let's go get some coffee and then we can talk." She held up her car keys. "I'll drive, if you don't mind."

Drew stepped back so she could exit her apartment. "Sure. Whatever you want."

They headed down the walkway towards Maggie's car, and she made sure to keep Julia's half-brother in her line of vision at all times. She felt she could trust Drew, but it was still better to be safe. They were both quiet during the short drive to the coffee shop where Maggie stopped every morning. Drew seemed uneasy and his nervousness was contagious. By the time they sat down at a small corner table, Maggie was ready to jump out of her skin.

"Okay, Drew. Whatever it is, spit it out," Maggie said bluntly, folding her hands on the table.

Drew fidgeted uncomfortably. "Uh. Well, you see…" His voice trailed off and he stared at his feet, as if he expected the answers to be written on his shoelaces.

Maggie was losing patience quickly. "What's going on? Did you want to talk to me about something or not?"

Drew looked so crestfallen that Maggie would have laughed if she hadn't been so irritated. She glared at him, exasperated, and waited for him to start explaining.

"She told me not to tell you anything," he muttered.

"Who did? Julia?"

Drew nodded sullenly. He looked just like his sister when he pouted. They wore the same scrunched up eyebrows and jutting bottom lip. Maggie tried unsuccessfully to suppress a smile. Fortunately, he didn't notice her amusement.

"Jules called me early this morning and asked me to keep an eye on you while she went out of town." He admitted, keeping his eyes on the floor. "It took me all day to track you down. Finally, I ended up just waiting outside your apartment and hoping you'd show up there eventually. I'm surprised your neighbors didn't call the cops on me."

Maggie blinked at him incredulously. Julia had sent her brother to watch over her. The more she thought about it, the more it seemed like something she would do. Maggie couldn't decide whether she was touched or irritated by it.

"Julia asked you to watch out for me." Maggie echoed, still trying to figure out what it meant. "She didn't tell you where she was going, did she?"

Drew shrugged. "She said something about following up on a lead, but she didn't give any details and I didn't ask. I learned a long time ago that Julia only tells you what she wants you to know."

Maggie leaned across the table and took Drew's hand, noticing that he tensed slightly at her touch. She tried not to grin as she realized that he was blushing furiously. *'Oh, please don't tell me Julia's brother has a crush on me,'* she chuckled silently. She banished the thought from her mind on focused on the matter at hand.

"This is really important, Drew. I need to find her and she isn't answering her phone. Are you sure she didn't give you any idea where she was headed?"

Drew's forehead creased as he thought for a moment, trying to recall the details of his conversation with his closemouthed sister. He looked up at Maggie doubtfully.

"She really didn't say much." His face brightened as he remembered something. "Hey, I don't know if this helps, but I could hear waves in the background when she called. So I guess she was somewhere near the ocean."

Maggie sighed. "Well, that gives me someplace to start, at least," she said, more to herself than to the young man sitting across from her.

Drew stared at her. "What are you planning on doing? Driving up and down the coast until you find her?"

Determined green eyes gazed back at him. "If I have to. But I think I'll stop by her house first. Maybe I'll find something there that will tell me where to look."

She pushed her chair back and stood, turning towards the door. Drew rose, as well, and cleared his throat to get her attention. She looked at him expectantly.

"Want some company?" He went on before she had a chance to decline. "Look, I promised her I'd look out for you, and you know what she'll do to me if I break that, right?"

Smiling, Maggie nodded and Drew gave her a familiar, lopsided grin.

"Then it's settled. I'm going with you." His expression sobered. "Besides, I want to make sure she's okay, too."

To his surprise, Maggie pulled him into a friendly hug. He sputtered and squirmed, trying to free himself from her embrace. When she released him, Maggie noticed that his blush had extended all the way to his scalp.

"Thank you," she said simply, unable to find the words to fully express her gratitude.

Drew ducked his head and shrugged sheepishly. He pulled a wad of money from his pocket and dropped a few crumpled bills on the table to pay for their coffee. His eyes met Maggie's, and although they were brown instead of blue, they still held the trademark Cassinelli twinkle.

"C'mon," he said. "Let's go track down my bullheaded sister."

Maggie and Drew left the bustling coffee shop and headed for the reporter's car, parked at the far end of the lot. The Corolla was engulfed in shadows and neither of them noticed the figure crouched behind the vehicle. As they approached, he straightened slightly, his head just barely visible over the hood of the car. Drew saw him first and stopped in his tracks. He seized Maggie's arm, pulling her back behind him.

"Drew? What the…"

The words died in her throat as she followed his gaze to the person standing beside her car. The outline seemed vaguely familiar, and she strained her eyes to see him better as Drew took a step forward.

"Who's there?" The young man demanded in a threatening, belligerent tone that Maggie had never heard from him before.

The figure flinched, as if planning to flee, and Drew tensed, preparing to give chase if necessary. Maggie stepped around her well-meaning protector, still trying to get a better look. The fog was not as dense as usual that night, and she could make out the lowered chin and the slightly hunched set of the man's shoulders. It was not the stance of an attacker. It was the stance of someone who was trying to hide. She took another, faltering step forward as realization began to dawn on her.

"Maggie, stay back." Drew warned her, trying to catch her arm again.

She shook free from his grasp. "No, I think it's okay." Squinting into the darkness, she took yet another step towards the shadowy man. "Patrick?"

"Maggie, I need help." Patrick McKinnon whispered back, his voice cracking from fear and desperation.

Uttering a soft cry, Maggie rushed forward and enveloped her brother in a tight embrace. He was cold and shivering, and he reeked of dirt, stale sweat and god knew what else, but at least he was alive and safe. Taking his face between both hands, Maggie peered into his eyes, noting the dark circles beneath them and the purplish-black bruise that covered his jaw and most of his left cheek. He looked tired and scared, but sober, and she took that as a good sign.

"Patrick, are you okay? Where have you been? What happened?" Maggie asked, her voice filled with urgency.

"Uh, guys?" Drew scanned the parking lot and adjacent sidewalk nervously. "I hate to interrupt, but maybe we should take this someplace less public."

Maggie nodded. "Right. Good idea." She unlocked the car doors and ushered both men inside. "Let's go. We can talk when we get there."

Ducking his head, Patrick slipped into the backseat and immediately slouched down, out of sight. Drew sat up front, next to Maggie, and they exchanged a nervous glance. Maggie started the car and slowly pulled out of the parking lot, observing every traffic law. The last thing she wanted to do was attract attention with her fugitive brother hiding in the backseat.

"Where are we going?" Patrick asked.

Maggie glanced at him in the rearview mirror. "Julia's house."

"Oh. Okay." He paused, frowning. "Who's Julia?"

Maggie coughed into her fist as Drew hid a grin behind his hand. She had forgotten that Patrick did not know about Julia. She had a feeling that this was going to be a night for all sorts of revelations.

"I'll explain when we get there." She answered her brother tersely.

He shrugged, unconcerned for the moment. "Whatever."

Maggie returned her attention to the road, and after a few minutes of silence, Drew leaned toward her.

"Do you think it's safe there?" He asked, keeping his voice low.

Maggie exhaled slowly. Suddenly, everyone was looking to her to take charge, and she wasn't sure she had any answers. Julia would know what to do, she was sure of that. But Julia wasn't there.

"I don't know," she said finally. "I think it's probably safer than my apartment. No one would expect Patrick to show up at Julia's house. At least, I hope they wouldn't."

"I hope you're right," Drew said.

'Me too,' Maggie thought as she turned the car toward Julia's neighborhood.

****

-

Chapter Twenty

Allison Davis paced impatiently across the balcony of her father's retreat. Nestled amongst the evergreens, the house sat high on a sheer cliff, overlooking the Pacific Ocean. Waves crashed rhythmically against the rocks below, invisible in the inky darkness. Behind her, Allison could hear her fiancé clicking away on his laptop.

"Danny, stop that. It's giving me a headache," she said without turning.

Pausing, Daniel Webber looked up at her, silhouetted in the sliding glass doorway that led from the master bedroom to the balcony. Allison had always been excitable, even in college, but tonight she appeared even more agitated than normal. She was full of nervous energy and her dark, unreadable eyes were far too bright.

Allison had been edgy since her father had ordered them out of town early that morning. For the past few days, Danny had been hiding at the Davis estate while the police searched his home and his business. The cops had found nothing. The councilman had made sure of that, but Danny was drawing too much attention and people were beginning to ask questions about Allison and her father, as well. His solution had been to send his daughter and his future son-in-law to his coastal retreat. Few people knew he owned the beach house, and no one would look for them there.

Gradually, Danny became aware that Allison had turned around. She was staring at him expectantly, waiting for a response to her directive.

"Stop what?" He asked cautiously, trying not to trigger her explosive temper.

She snarled, glaring at him, and he shrank back on the bed. In a few long strides, she closed the distance between them and swept the laptop off the black satin sheets, knocking it to the floor with a clatter.

"That incessant click, click, click," she said, pretending to type on an imaginary keyboard. "I can't think clearly with all that damn noise!"

Danny reached out to her, but she pushed him away savagely, nearly throwing him off the edge of the bed. He watched her as she resumed pacing, her hands gesturing spasmodically as she carried on a private conversation with herself. Slowly, he rose and moved toward the open bathroom door. As he expected, a small paper envelope had been discarded on the floor in front of the sink. Kneeling, Danny checked the contents and discovered that it was empty, except for a few granules of powdery residue. He licked his finger and his tongue immediately went numb.

"Allison, I thought we agreed you would lay off this stuff for a while." Danny stood, holding up the envelope for her to see.

She giggled and covered her mouth with her hand. "That was supposed to be a secret."

Danny sighed and tossed the empty envelope into the wastebasket. Allison pouted, poking her lower lip out as she glided towards him on bare feet. Throwing her arms around his neck, she nibbled his ear.

"It was just a little bit," she murmured. "I was so tired earlier. I needed a little something to keep me going. That's all."

Her mood changed again and she pushed him away. "Daddy said he would call as soon as he was done with the police. Why hasn't he called yet?"

Danny followed her back out to the balcony, where she was leaning precariously over the rail. Gently, he put his hands around her waist and pulled her back.

"I don't know, baby. Maybe the cops are still talking to him. I'm sure he'll call soon and everything will be just fine."

"Hmmm. Maybe you're right." Allison's face brightened and she moved past him, back into the bedroom.

"I think I'll go down to the pool." She gave him a sly glance. "Join me?"

Danny smiled at her indulgently. "Sure. Go on down. I'll grab the towels and the wine and meet you in a few minutes."

"Bring the phone with you. Can't miss Daddy's call." She gave him a hard, steely grin and he thought he detected a threat lurking behind her impossibly dark eyes.

"Oh, and Danny? Don't keep me waiting."

She brushed past him and left the room, humming airily as she descended the stairs. A spacious living room stretched out below her on the first floor. The entire rear wall consisted of plate glass and a sliding door that opened onto a wide redwood deck. A few steps down, a swimming pool and a connecting hot tub waited.

As Allison strolled through the living room, a soft thump alerted her. She stopped, cocking her head to the side, listening. It had sounded like it had come from the front steps, and her eyes narrowed as she padded towards the door. She pressed her ear against it but heard nothing further.

"Fuck this," she muttered under her breath, yanking the front door wide open.

There was no one there and not a car in sight as far as she could see in either direction. Allison stepped out onto the front patio, shivering a bit in the cool night air. A brisk sea breeze rustled through the dense evergreen branches, but other than that, everything was still and quiet. As she turned to reenter the house, her bare foot brushed against something hard and prickly. She looked down at the small pinecone that rested near the door.

"Damn squirrels."

She kicked the offending object into the darkness, grunting in satisfaction as something skittered away into the night. Her high was wearing off and she could feel the headache building behind her right eye. The pain would be blinding soon, unless she did something about it. Heading back into the house, she paused at the foot of the stairs.

"Danny? Be a dear and bring me one of my migraine pills too." She shut the door behind her and continued out to the pool.

Once the footsteps had receded from earshot, a tall figure materialized out of the dark recesses to the side of the house. Julia heaved a sigh of relief. While checking the lock on the front door, her small flashlight had slipped out of her hand. There had been just enough time to grab it and duck out of sight before Allison ripped the door open. Moving carefully to avoid making any more noise, Julia crossed the front patio. She tested the knob again, hoping that Allison had forgotten to lock up. It would not turn.

"Damn."

Deep in thought, Julia chewed on her thumbnail as she planned her next move. For two days she had skulked outside the Davis estate, trying to figure out a way to get past the guards and get inside. Martin Davis had more security than she had expected, and there had been several close calls as she eluded them. Finally, just after dawn that morning, her luck had turned. The gates had opened and Danny's shiny red sports car had emerged. It had sped away, but not before Julia had caught a glimpse of his passenger. Her suspicions had been confirmed. There was something going on between Danny Webber and Allison Davis.

In her brand-new Toyota 4-Runner, Julia had followed, taking care to stay several car lengths behind them as they fled San Francisco. They had led her to the councilman's secluded coastal retreat. She had driven past the house at first, and then doubled back once she was sure that Danny and Allison were inside. After leaving her vehicle out of sight around a sharp curve, Julia had hiked back to the house, taking cover amidst the dense thicket of trees that surrounded it. When night had fallen, she had begun trying to devise a way to get inside.

Scowling in frustration, Julia took a step back and stared up at the house. '*Okay, Julia. Think this through*, she reasoned with herself. *You get into the house and then what? Walk up to them and say 'tell me what's going on, or else'?*' A heavier set of footsteps descended the stairs, and she prepared to hide again. Danny's footsteps, she surmised, listening as they moved away from the front door. There was a splash, followed by a pair of low voices.

'*The pool*,' Julia thought. This was the perfect opportunity to get into the house and have a look around. She was positive that there would be something inside to connect Danny and Allison to the attacks on Maggie. Perhaps she would even find evidence to help clear her lover's good-for-nothing brother, though Julia wasn't as convinced of that. She still believed that Patrick was, at least, peripherally involved in whatever game Danny and Allison were running. Julia didn't understand her lover's loyalty to her brother, but she had decided to do what she could to help him. For Maggie's sake.

Their argument had bothered her more than she cared to admit. When Maggie had walked out of the apartment that night, Julia had been positive that they were over. Everyone she had ever remotely cared about walked out on her eventually. Kirsten. Her mother. Why should Maggie be any different? Besides, Julia knew that she made a mistake by blurting out the information about Patrick without discussing it with Maggie first. She had known it the second the words had tumbled out of her mouth. It was a realization that came too late, and she couldn't blame the reporter for being angry. She would not be surprised if Maggie never forgave her.

Henry had driven her home and stayed the night on the couch, watching over her while she drank herself into a stupor. He had tried several times to talk to her, but she had been beyond listening. She had destroyed the best thing in her life. Maggie was gone. Nothing else mattered. When she woke up the next morning, alone, she made a decision. Even if Maggie didn't want her anymore, Julia vowed to solve the case and make sure that the reporter stayed safe. It was the least she could do.

There was another loud splash, and laughter cut through the night, reminding Julia of her purpose. *'Come on, Julia. Focus,'* she chastised herself mentally. There was a good chance that the answers to her questions were in that house, and she was determined to do whatever it took to find them.

Flattening herself against the side of the house, she edged around to the back. Carefully, she poked her head around the corner until she could see Danny and Allison lounging in the hot tub and sipping from wineglasses. They had their backs to her, and more importantly, they had their backs to the house. Sizing up her chances, Julia calculated the distance between herself and the half-open sliding glass door. She would have to move quickly and silently, but she thought she could cover the ground and slip inside the house without being seen. It was risky, but it was worth a shot.

"What the hell," she whispered. "What have I got to lose?"

She clenched her fists, her fingernails leaving deep crescents embedded into her palms. She would only have one shot at this. One chance to get inside the secluded beach house without being seen by the couple relaxing in the hot tub just yards away. Julia could feel her heart rate quickening and she forced herself to take slow, deep breaths. Bouncing lightly on the balls of her feet, like a boxer sizing up his opponent, she gauged the distance between her hiding place and the back door. Ten seconds. Maybe fifteen. That was all she would need.

On noiseless feet, she moved, staying in the shadows, keeping her back pressed flat against the side of the house. She placed each step with the utmost care, knowing that the crack of a twig underfoot could be her undoing. All the while, her eyes never left the man and woman in the steaming hot tub. As she inched toward the redwood deck, the theme to Mission: Impossible resounded through her head in an endless loop, and she almost laughed at the absurdity of her situation. Then she remembered the sound of gunfire ripping through metal mingling with Maggie's screams, and all traces of humor vanished. This was no game.

Julia paused at the edge of the deck. This was the tricky part. Once she stepped up onto the deck, she would be completely exposed until she was inside the house. It would only take a few seconds, but if Danny turned his head a fraction of an inch to the left, he would see her.

With exaggerated slowness, she placed her boot on the edge of the deck. The wood creaked beneath her weight, and she tensed, expecting to hear shouts of alarm. When none came, she continued, covering the space in four long strides. Turning sideways, she slid

213

through the partially open door, the frame brushing against her soft leather jacket.

Quickly, Julia ducked behind the curtains and risked a glance outside. Allison still had her back turned, but Danny's position appeared to have changed. Julia's stomach tightened and she wiped her damp palms on her jeans as she tried to recall exactly which way he had been facing.

"Be reasonable," she said under her breath. "If he had seen you, he would have said something and it would be all over."

Dismissing the roiling in her gut as mere paranoia, she turned to survey the living room. The sparse, precisely arranged furniture made her feel like she was standing in the pages of a magazine. Her instincts told her that the information she sought was elsewhere and she headed for the stairs, taking care not to disturb anything. Danny wouldn't notice if the throw rug had moved a quarter of an inch, but Allison might.

The polished banister was slick and cool beneath her hand as she climbed to the second floor. Every nerve ending in her body stood at attention and she started at every tiny sound. Her own breathing sounded too loud in her ears. She had to admit that in all her years as a private investigator, she had never been this nervous. The stakes had never been this high. Julia wondered again if leaving Maggie behind had been the best idea. It had been one of the most difficult decisions she had ever made, and she hoped that her brother was keeping a close eye on the reporter, as he had promised.

With a little luck, the whole ugly mess would be over soon, she told herself as she entered the master bedroom. Various articles of clothing spilled out of two open suitcases resting on the floor, and she started toward them. At the last moment, she swerved over to the bed as something more interesting caught her eye. Cocking her head to one side, she examined the closed laptop balanced at the foot of the bed. She opened it and cursed in frustration when it prompted her for a password. Typing in words at random got her nowhere, and Julia searched her mind for a clue that would point her towards the right password. *Face it,*' her inner pessimist mocked her, *'you don't even know who this thing belongs to. You could sit here all night and still not come up with the right word.'*

Though she hated to admit it, the voice was right. Julia put the computer back on the bed and stood; smoothing away the wrinkles she left on the satin sheets. She returned her attention to the open suitcases and began to sift through the contents. Danny's contained nothing of interest. As she dug beneath Allison's hastily folded clothes, Julia's hopes were fading.

"There has to be something here," she said, her desperation growing.

She searched the walk-in closet and rifled through the dresser drawers, finding nothing out of the ordinary. She was running out of time and she knew it. Her gaze was drawn to the thin sliver of light shining through the crack at the bottom of the bathroom door. Julia moved toward it hopefully. She nudged the door open and stepped inside the glossy black tiled room. There was nothing on the counter or in the sink. A quick glance inside the sunken bathtub revealed nothing there either. Julia spun in a slow circle, searching for something, anything that would help her crack this case. Downstairs, the sliding door opened.

"Oh, shit." She breathed, heading for the bathroom door.

Her instincts screamed at her. *'Get out or find a place to hide.'* At the edge of her vision, she caught sight of a scrap of paper poking out from behind the wastebasket. Julia snatched the small white envelope between her thumb and index finger and shoved it into her pocket. She would examine it more closely later. If she managed to escape without being detected.

Returning to the bedroom, Julia paused, listening. Every muscle in her body tensed, waiting for a confrontation. She expected to hear footsteps on the stairs at any moment. Instead, the faint clinking of dishes told her that someone was in the kitchen. Keeping her guard up, she eased out into the hallway.

"Allison, where's the bottle opener?" Danny's voice floated up to her.

There was a short pause, then a muffled reply. Julia listened as Danny opened drawers and rummaged through their contents. He emerged from the kitchen with two beer bottles in one hand and a bottle opener in the other. Julia stepped away from the railing, back into the shadows. She sighed in relief, allowing herself to relax when he returned to the swimming pool without looking in her direction. It was time for her to get the hell out of the house.

Patience had never been one of her virtues, but Julia forced herself to wait. After counting to twenty, she started down the stairs, keeping an eye on the back door with every step. As she reached the bottom, the phone rang. She froze, panic rising. She was completely vulnerable. There was nowhere to hide if Danny or Allison came back into the house. On the second ring, Allison answered the call outside, her voice drifting through the half-open door.

"Daddy! It's about time. I was getting worried."

Julia knew she should get out while Allison was occupied, but the opportunity to eavesdrop on this conversation was one she could not pass up. She crept into the living room and ducked down behind the corner of the sofa. She strained her ears, trying to hear more of the phone call.

Judging by Allison's reactions, Julia surmised that the councilman was giving her a list of instructions. Allison objected vehemently, but she was overruled. She and Danny were to stay at the house, out of sight, until further notice. Julia could almost picture Allison's sullen, child-like pout. A long stretch of silence followed, and Julia's anxiety rose. Her heart nearly stopped at the sudden mention of Maggie's name.

"What about those reporters, Richards and McKinnon?" Allison asked. "What are you going to do about them?"

A delighted squeal turned Julia's blood to ice. Ignoring the risk, she edged closer, needing to hear more of the details. Peeking through the curtains, she watched as Allison finished the exchange with her father and replaced the cordless phone on the deck.

"Well, well." Allison turned to Danny gleefully. "It seems Maggie McKinnon lost her great protector. Daddy says no one has seen your friend Julia in days. He's sending people to take care of both of our reporter problems."

A red haze filled Julia's mind and a steady stream of profanity swirled endlessly in her head. Struggling to control her blinding rage, she suppressed the urge to storm outside and throttle the gloating socialite. She clenched her fists reflexively, imagining the feel of Allison's throat beneath her fingers. This wasn't the time, she told herself. First, she had to make sure that Maggie, and Catherine, stayed safe. Swift, silent and resolute, she exited the house. As soon as she was out of earshot, she broke into a run, dashing down the road to the spot where she had left her truck.

Back in the hot tub, Danny smiled vacantly while Allison filled him in on the plan. In her excitement, she failed to notice that he wasn't looking at her. Instead, Danny's eyes were focused on the house. He wondered if Julia had found anything useful. If she had, it would not take her long to act on the information. He had to make a decision. Soon.

****

Chapter Twenty-One

Maggie parked across the street from Julia's Victorian and left the engine idling while she surveyed the neighborhood. Everything looked normal. There were no unfamiliar vehicles on the curb or sinister figures lurking in the shadows. During the drive over, she had checked frequently to ensure they were not followed. Even so, she could not shake the almost palpable feeling of dread that had settled over her since finding Patrick outside the coffee shop. She had a whole slate of questions for him, but she had been too tense during the drive to ask them. Maggie exchanged a glance with Drew, and she could see the same concerns written in the deep creases on his brow. A voice from the backseat made them both jump.

"What are we waiting for?" Patrick wondered.

"Nothing. Let's get inside." Maggie shut off the engine and led the way toward Julia's house.

She kept her eyes moving, flicking from side to side as they headed up the walkway. There would be no surprises. Behind her, Patrick stepped on a dry twig, and the snap seemed to echo up and down the quiet street. Both Maggie and Drew turned, fixing him with a reproachful glare.

"Sorry." He muttered, shoving his hands deep in his pockets.

Maggie was familiar with both the attitude and the gesture. She had seen and heard Patrick's halfhearted apologies hundreds of times before. She sighed, relenting.

"It's okay. We're all a little on edge, I think."

"Hey, do you have a key to this place? Because I don't," Drew said as they reached the door. "How are we gonna get inside? Is there a spare hidden under the doormat?"

Maggie gave him a thin smile as an answer. She knelt in front of the door and probed the edges of the porch floorboards with her fingertips. A splinter jabbed the fleshy pad of her thumb, and she let out a pained yelp. The injured part went directly to her mouth, a childhood habit she had never been able to break. She continued her search with her other hand until she found the loose board. As Drew and Patrick looked on, Maggie pried one end of the board up and retrieved the spare key taped to its underside. She stood, holding up her prize triumphantly.

"You know, you'd think a private investigator would think of a better place to hide a key." Drew commented as Maggie unlocked the door.

"Your friend is a private investigator?" Patrick asked, following his sister into the house.

Maggie nodded and directed the others into the living room. She locked the front door behind them, testing the knob twice to make sure it was secure. Drew had taken a seat on Julia's sofa, while Patrick stood in front of the fireplace, examining the photograph on the mantle. Maggie crossed the room and pulled the drapes shut. Once she was sure that no one could spy on them, she turned her attention to the two waiting men.

"Is this your friend?" Patrick removed the framed picture and held it out towards his sister.

"No. That's Julia's mother," Maggie said.

"Huh. She's hot."

Maggie's frayed nerves snapped. "Patrick, put that back and get serious for once! You're wanted for murder. People keep trying to kill me. I want to know why!"

Patrick shrank back against the fireplace, startled by Maggie's outburst. He replaced the picture on the mantle and scratched at the three-day growth that covered his jaw. With a helpless shrug, he jammed his hands into his pockets again.

"What do you want me to say, Mags?" He asked.

Maggie stared at him incredulously. "What do I want you to say? How about telling me why the police think you shot one of my co-workers? Let's start there!"

The blood drained from Patrick's face and his eyes grew wide. "I didn't shoot anybody! I swear, Maggie! I didn't shoot that woman!"

His eyes darted around the room, like he was looking for someplace to hide. Maggie had never seen him look so afraid. She moved towards him and placed her hands on his shoulders, trying to calm him.

"It's okay, Patrick. I believe you," she said, soothing him. "But I need you to tell me everything so we can clear you. Do you understand?"

Patrick nodded. He took a deep, hitching breath and wiped the back of his hand across his nose. Maggie glanced over to Drew.

"Drew, could you get us some water or something?" She asked.

"Uh, yeah. Sure." Drew agreed, sensing that Maggie needed a private moment with her brother. "I'll be right back."

Once the siblings were left alone, Maggie guided Patrick over to the sofa. Gently, she sat him down, seating herself on the edge of the coffee table across from him. She took both of his shaking hands between hers.

"Tell me everything."

In a faltering monotone, Patrick revealed everything he knew. He told her about D.C., the drugs, Eddie, Tom, everything. Maggie seemed particularly interested in the warehouse that he had been working at. Patrick wondered about that. To him, it seemed like the least significant part of his story. He was about to explain what had' happened with Catherine when Maggie interrupted him.

"Wait. About this warehouse that D.C. had you working at. Do you remember where it was?"

Patrick shrugged. "Not really. Eddie or Tom drove me back and forth. I didn't really pay that much attention to where we were going. What difference does it make?"

"I'm not quite sure yet." Maggie frowned, thinking. "What did you do there?"

Drew returned, carrying a glass of water in each hand. He gave one to Maggie and offered the other to Patrick. Sensing the tension in the room, he excused himself and headed upstairs. Maybe while Maggie and her brother were talking, he would be able to figure out where Julia had disappeared.

Patrick was growing tired of the questioning. "I dunno. I did warehouse stuff, I guess. Loading and unloading trucks."

The pieces were starting to fit together. The warehouse. The drugs. A dealer named D.C. with a hired thug named Tom. There had to be a connection. She just had to figure out what it was. Maggie gasped as a memory flashed through her mind. The man she had bumped into at the hospital early that day fit the description that Patrick had just given her. Could that have been Tom? Was he there to finish the job on Catherine? And what about the man who had attacked Julia just after they met? Was that him too? Maggie jumped up and practically ran into the kitchen.

"I have to make a call. Don't move." She shouted over her shoulder.

Julia's address book was on the counter beside the phone, and Maggie pawed through it frantically. The pages mocked her, sticking together until she was ready to scream in frustration. Finally, she found what she was looking for. She dialed Henry Chow's cell number and waited, heart pounding, for him to answer it.

"Chow." The terse growl boomed through the receiver.

"Henry, it's me. Maggie."

"Maggie? What the hell is going on?"

Maggie could hear a muted public address system in the background, along with a steady hum of activity. She nearly sobbed in relief. Henry was already at the emergency room. She gave him Patrick's description of Tom, without telling him that she had found her brother. Henry was a friend, but he was still a cop. If he knew where Patrick was, he would feel compelled to make the arrest.

"I can't explain right now, but I think Catherine's life is in danger. Please, Henry. I need you to keep an eye on her. My friend Jessica, too, if she's still there."

She could hear the confusion and exasperation in Henry's voice. "Yeah, she's still here. She won't go away. Said something about a promise she made to you. Come on, Maggie. Let me help you. Don't be like your stubborn-as-hell girlfriend. Tell me what's going on."

"I can't. I'm sorry. Just keep them safe, okay?" Maggie pleaded.

"You know I will. Where are you? Let me send a car to get you or something."

"I'm sorry, Henry." Maggie repeated before hanging up on the perplexed police inspector.

She felt horrible for keeping Henry in the dark. Right now, though, she had to protect her brother. That had to be her top priority. Maggie returned to the living room and found Patrick where she had left him, sitting on the sofa with his head buried in his hands. She sat beside him and slid an arm around his thin shoulders.

"It'll be okay, Patrick. I promise. I'll take care of everything."

It was such a familiar refrain. She had been taking care of Patrick forever. Since they were kids, every time he got into trouble, she had been there to bail him out. When the rest of the family had been on the verge of giving up on him, she had been his staunchest defender. Even after the incident in college, she hadn't turned her back on him. She had made sure that no charges were filed against him, even though his behavior had begun to frighten her. When he had gone into rehab the last time, Maggie had left for California, hoping to build her own life. She wondered now if she would ever truly be free from Patrick and his problems.

"I didn't shoot that woman. It was Tom." Patrick told her,

220

repeating his earlier claim. "I thought for sure he was going to kill me too."

Maggie shook her head. "They set you up. They thought I was going to be in that elevator, and they wanted it to look like you had killed me."

Patrick's head shot up and he stared at her, horrified. His lips moved, but no sounds came out. With a calmness she didn't really feel, Maggie held the glass of water to his mouth and steadied it while he took a sip. Patrick wiped his lips with his sleeve and tried again.

"Tom was trying to kill you? Why?" Patrick stood, agitated, and began to pace around the room. "Maggie, if I had known he was after you..."

Maggie shushed him with a wave of her hand. "I know. It's a long story. They seem to think I know something, but I don't. Not really. I mean, I'm starting to put things together now, but there are still a lot of pieces missing."

"Does somebody want to tell me who "they" are?" Drew stood at the bottom of the stairs, eyeing them both curiously.

"Did you find anything upstairs?" Maggie ignored his question, hoping he wouldn't notice.

Drew shook his head. He had checked Julia's bedroom and her office, but he hadn't found anything to point to her whereabouts. He was about to suggest searching downstairs when they were interrupted by Maggie's cell phone.

Maggie dug the phone out of her coat pocket and checked the display. Her heart leapt into her throat. It was Julia. She struggled to keep her voice even.

"Julia?"

"Maggie? What's wrong? Is everything okay? Did something happen?"

Tears filled Maggie's eyes at the sound of the rapid-fire questions. She could hear traffic in the background, through the occasional crackle of static. Julia was on the road somewhere, but at least she was all right.

"No, nothing's wrong. I'm just so happy to hear your voice. Where are you?"

"I'm out near the coast. I followed Danny and Allison here." Julia told her. "Is Drew with you? Put him on the phone if he's there."

Maggie was surprised and a little disappointed that Julia wanted to talk to her brother instead. Mutely, she held the phone out to Drew.

"Jules? What's up?" Drew asked, his brow furrowing as he listened to his sister's reply.

221

He nodded a few times, then glanced at Maggie and pantomimed writing. She took the hint and got him a piece of paper and a pen. Still listening, he tucked the phone between his shoulder and his ear and began to scrawl a series of directions on the sheet.

"Okay. I got it." He paused, a smile spreading across his face. "Don't worry. I'll take care of her. Hang on."

Turning back to Maggie, he winked and handed the phone to her again. "She wants to talk to you again."

Maggie smiled at him gratefully. "Julia? I'm here."

An awkward silence met her. She was starting to wonder if she had lost the connection when Julia finally spoke.

"Listen, I'm sorry I didn't get the chance to tell you what I was doing. It all happened sort of fast, and I wasn't really sure you wanted to hear from me, anyway. After what I said, I get why you left me."

Maggie closed her eyes as a wave of sadness passed over her. She could almost picture the dejected look on Julia's face.

"How could you think I wouldn't want to talk to you? Because we had a fight? Julia, couples fight. It happens. It doesn't mean that I don't still love you."

"You still love me?" The whispered question was almost lost in a burst of static.

"Of course I do, you great, big goof. You're not getting rid of me that easily."

Another loud burst of static squawked in Maggie's ear, and she had to hold the phone away for a moment. She realized that she hadn't told Julia about Patrick yet.

"Julia? Are you still there? I have to tell you something."

She received no answer. She waited for a few seconds to see if the interference would clear. When it didn't, she hung up and let out a frustrated sigh. She glanced a Drew and made a face.

"Lost the connection." She explained.

"Damn cell phones," Drew replied with a wry grin.

They both turned at a noise behind them. Patrick was gaping at his sister, his eyes nearly popping out of his head. Maggie almost laughed. Instead, she led him back into the living room and sat him down on the sofa again.

"Okay, I guess there are a couple of things I need to tell you," she said.

****

Martin Davis leaned back in the leather chair and surveyed the view from the office window. He watched the tour boats carrying gawking sightseers beneath the Golden Gate Bridge. He should have had an office like this one. He had been destined to be a much more powerful man. He knew that. He should have been a senator, at least. Sighing, he fiddled with the crystal paperweight on the polished cherry desk. The fates had conspired against him, saddling him with a mentally unbalanced daughter. If word of Allison's problems ever leaked out, it would ruin the family name. He couldn't let that happen. No matter what the cost.

A knock at the door drew his attention away from the window, and he swiveled around in the chair. His attorney, Joseph Cassinelli, stood in the doorway. It had been a long day for both of them. The police had grilled him for hours, though Joe had smoothly deflected most of the more distressing questions. The councilman reminded himself to give his attorney a sizable bonus this year.

"Is everything okay, Martin?"

Joe glanced meaningfully at the telephone. He had left his friend alone in his office for a few minutes, letting Martin speak to his daughter in private. He didn't want to know the details of the conversation. In his profession, the truth tended to complicate things.

Martin stood, vacating his friend's chair. "Everything's fine. Just fine."

"Good." Joe rubbed his hands together. "Well, unless there's something else I can do for you tonight, I think I'll head home. I have some briefs to look through before morning."

Martin nodded slowly. He started to leave his attorney's office, but stopped in the doorway. Without turning, he spoke.

"Do you love your children, Joe?"

He could feel the other man's eyes burning into the back of his head. An uncomfortable silence hung between them. Martin exhaled, letting the tension seep from his body. This mood wasn't helping anything. He had to snap out of it. There was too much work to be done. Without waiting for answer to his question, he left.

From the hallway, Joseph Cassinelli watched the councilman march down the corridor. A soft ping announced the arrival of the elevator, and the brass door slid open. Martin Davis straightened his tie as he stepped into the newly cleaned car where a woman had been shot just days before. As the doors closed, he lifted his chin and gazed directly at his friend and confidant. An icy finger touched the watching attorney's heart. The councilman's eyes held a bleak coldness that he had never seen before.

Once the elevator had gone, Joe returned to his office. He sat behind his desk and stared out at the same scene the councilman had been surveying earlier. His friend's odd question nagged at him. Did he love his children? Of course he did. Hadn't he given them both the best that money could buy? He shrugged. Martin had been behaving strangely for weeks. The councilman was clearly under too much stress, and Allison wasn't helping the matter any.

Joe recalled his recent conversation with his own daughter. Even then, Julia had suspected that Allison was involved in something illegal. For a moment, he wondered if she had been right. No. He shook his head firmly. He could not allow himself to think like that. A lawyer maintains his client's innocence until the end. Even if it required him to lie to himself. Pushing his questions from his mind, he gathered his papers and left the office.

Standing on the curb outside the tall building, Martin Davis watched his friend and attorney drive away. He hoped that Joe had understood his warning and would tell his nosy daughter to stay out of this case. Fathers should protect their children at all costs. The councilman did not want to hurt Julia Cassinelli, but he would do whatever he had to, in order to keep his own daughter out of trouble.

He sighed and pulled his overcoat tighter around his body. The wind had picked up and it stung his cheeks. He signaled to a parked car across the street and waited while the driver made a hasty u-turn and pulled up next to him. Without a word, Martin slid into the soft leather seat and slammed the door shut. He gave a slight nod to the driver. Leaning his head back, he lost himself in contemplation as Tom Becker merged into the busy city traffic. There was still so much he had to do. The reporter at the hospital was his most pressing concern. Once that mess was cleaned up, he would turn his attention to the troublesome McKinnon's.

****

Maggie shifted uncomfortably in the strained silence that filled the car. She wanted to turn around and check on her brother in the back seat, but she was afraid she would see the revulsion in his eyes again. Patrick had barely said two words to her since finding out about her relationship with Julia. Maggie had expected his reaction, though she had been hoping to avoid the inevitable for a bit longer. It would only get worse when the rest of her family learned the truth.

She sighed and slumped down further in the passenger seat. Before they left Julia's house, Drew had convinced her to let him drive. After a half-hearted protest, she had conceded, acknowledging that he knew the area better than she did. Maggie checked the handwritten directions again, though she knew that they were still miles away from their exit. Julia had checked into a small inn, and Drew seemed to know where it was. They were on their way to meet the private investigator.

"Why don't you try to take a quick nap?" Drew suggested.

His voice made Maggie jump. She shrugged listlessly. Patrick's obvious discomfort bothered her even more than she had thought it would. Out of all her siblings, she had believed that he would be most likely to understand.

"Come on, Maggie. You look exhausted. A nap might do you some good." Drew tried again.

"I'm not sleepy," Maggie said insistently.

She turned the radio on and fiddled with the stations until she found a song she liked. It was one of the few that she and Julia agreed upon. They were so different in so many ways, yet in others, they complemented each other perfectly. Maggie turned the radio volume up, drowning out the quiet. She closed her eyes and pictured a warm sapphire twinkle and a lazy, lopsided grin. She imagined Julia's arms wrapped around her, holding her tight. Within minutes, Maggie was asleep.

"It doesn't bother you? Knowing what your sister is?" Patrick spoke up.

"You're an idiot," Drew said quietly, darting a sideways glance at Maggie to make sure she was still sleeping.

Her breathing was slow and even. He returned his attention to Patrick.

"Maggie loves my sister, and Julia loves her back just as much. That's all I need to know."

Patrick leaned forward suddenly, putting his hand on the corner of the driver's seat. He refused to look at his sister and kept his gaze focused on the windshield in front of him. He completely missed the hard, warning look that Drew shot at him.

"It's unnatural." Patrick declared, pounding his fist against the seat for emphasis.

"Sit back and shut up." Drew tightened his grip on the steering wheel until his knuckles turned white. "Because if you wake her up, I will pull this car over and beat the shit out of you on the side of the road."

After a moment's hesitation, Patrick leaned back, away from the young man behind the wheel. He stared moodily out the window, though he could not see much through the inky darkness. The moon was hidden from view, and Patrick could barely make out the shapes of the trees along the side of the road as they sped by.

"I should have never come to California," he muttered, his voice muffled by his hand.

Patrick plucked at the clean sweatpants and t-shirt that had replaced his own filthy clothes. His new garments belonged to Julia, and he hated wearing them. He had never met the private investigator, though according to his sister, she virtually walked on water. He snorted in disdain and cast a quick glance at Drew to make sure he hadn't been heard. Another chill swept over him and his hands began to tremble. He started to shiver uncontrollably as withdrawal made its ugly presence known again. He had been suffering through the pain and cravings for two days, and it was only getting worse. Patrick wrapped his arms around his body and pressed himself as far back into the corner of the seat as he could. Closing his eyes, he tried to think of something other than the drugs he so desperately needed. Exhaustion settled over him, and soon, Patrick's light snoring mingled with his sister's.

Twenty minutes later, a gentle tap on her knee awakened Maggie. She blinked, momentarily disoriented until she remembered that she was in her car. Rubbing her stiff neck, she turned to Drew.

"Are we there?" She asked, peering through the windshield.

Drew shook his head, and she saw the tense, fearful look in his eyes as he checked the rearview mirror. She twisted around to look out the back window. A pair of bright headlights dazzled her eyes. A dark car was following behind them, about two car lengths back. Maggie's insides tightened into knots as she recalled the last time a car had been following her. An image of Julia's crumpled jeep flashed through her mind.

"It's been back there since we left the city limits." Drew told her. "I can't tell if it's following us or if it's just heading in the same direction we are."

Maggie nodded. She expected to hear gunfire ripping through her car at any moment. Julia would know how to react in this situation, but Julia was still miles away. Drew kept looking at her, waiting for instructions, and Maggie knew that it was up to her. She shut her eyes and tried to imagine Julia's comforting presence beside her, telling her what to do.

"Slow down a little. See what he does," Maggie said.

Drew eased his foot off the accelerator, slowing the car down. Two sets of eyes were fastened on the mirrors as they waited to see what the other driver would do. After a long, agonizing moment, the other car moved into the next lane and passed them. They watched until the night swallowed the vehicle, then both Maggie and Drew heaved a sigh of relief.

"Sorry about that." Drew gave her an embarrassed grin. "I guess I'm a little paranoid."

"Don't worry about it," Maggie said, returning the smile. "I think we're all a little jumpy these days."

A flash of green caught her attention as they sped past. Maggie craned her neck around, trying to read the sign before it was lost from view. She double-checked the paper clutched in her hand and turned back to Drew. Her face lit up with anticipation.

"We need to take the next exit and turn left at the light."

"I know the way." Drew reassured her. "And I'm sure she'll be happy to see you too."

For a split second, Drew took his eyes off the freeway ahead and grinned at her. Neither of them saw the dark sedan waiting patiently on the side of the road. After the Corolla went by, the engine sprang to life and the driver carefully eased the car out into the empty lane. He hung as far back as could, keeping Maggie McKinnon's vehicle in his sight. He would not be spotted again. Too much was at stake.

The next ten minutes dragged on with excruciating slowness. Maggie's heartbeat quickened as each passing second brought her closer to a reunion with Julia. Each red traffic light was an obstacle standing between her and her stubborn private investigator. As they passed through a well-lit intersection, Patrick stirred. Maggie heard the loud yawn, indicating that he was awake. She tensed, waiting for him to say something, but he remained silent. Though she wanted to straighten things out with her brother, Maggie was grateful for the quiet. She was not in the mood for another altercation with him. That would come soon enough, when he came face to face with Julia. She grimaced at the thought of the inevitable confrontation between her brother and her volatile lover. It would not be a pretty situation.

An eternity passed before Drew turned the car into the parking lot of the secluded inn. The small cluster of buildings was nestled back amongst the evergreen trees, and under other circumstances, Maggie would have found it incredibly romantic. She hopped out of the car almost before it had stopped moving, and she began to peer anxiously at the private cabins. The cold sea air bit at her exposed skin, but she was oblivious to the chill. Footsteps approached behind her as Drew and Patrick hurried to catch up. She didn't give them a second glance as she moved from building to building. Maggie'{ heart fluttered in her throat as she found the right door.

Before she could knock, the door flew open. A tall figure filled the entryway, bathed in the light from the room. With a soft cry, Maggie flung herself into the waiting arms. In spite of everything, a warm feeling of peace and happiness flooded her as she clung to Julia's embrace. She buried her face against a soft, flannel-covered shoulder and smiled as achingly familiar lips brushed the top of her head. She tightened her grip on Julia's midsection.

"I missed you so much," she mumbled into Julia's thick flannel shirt.

"I missed you too. More than I could stand."

A strong finger lifted Maggie's chin, tilting her head up until she was staring into a welcome pair of sparkling blue eyes. Julia smiled at her tenderly and brushed a teardrop from the reporter's lower lashes. Maggie leaned closer, anticipating the kiss. Behind her, Patrick cleared his throat loudly, interrupting the moment. Julia's gaze flicked to the gaunt young man with the haunted eyes, and Maggie reminded herself to strangle her brother later. For the moment, she simply met Julia's questioning look and shrugged.

"Julia, meet my brother, Patrick."

Julia disentangled herself from the reporter's embrace and took a step forward. She recognized the clothes that the young man was wearing and a dark eyebrow twitched in amusement. Patrick exuded a strange mixture of hostility and fear, shrinking away from her as she drew near. In actuality, she was less than an inch taller than he was, but she appeared to tower over him. She could tell she intimidated him, and a hard-edged smile played across her lips as she decided to use that to her advantage. Like twin daggers of ice, her eyes cut into him.

"So you're the one that has been causing us all this trouble," she said coolly. Her eyes darted to the second young man, and she nodded at him briefly. "Hello, Drew."

"Hey, Jules."

Fascinated, Drew watched the interaction between his sister and Maggie's brother. He had never seen Julia at work before. The cold glitter in her eyes sent a chill down his spine. Suddenly, he understood where her reputation came from and why so many were frightened by her. He hoped Patrick had enough sense not to antagonize her.

Julia saw the slight quiver of Patrick's shoulders as he flinched away from her. Inwardly she smiled, though her face remained an expressionless mask. She knew men like Patrick would back down as soon as they were challenged. Anxiety radiated from the reporter at her side, and Julia knew that she had been dreading this moment. Julia relaxed her stance slightly, relenting for Maggie's sake. Casually, she slipped her arm around the reporter's shoulders and jerked her dark head toward the open door.

"Let's get inside. We have a lot to talk about."

Without waiting, she turned and guided Maggie into the room, confidant that their brothers would follow. Drew, the last one inside, shut and locked the door behind them.

Less than a minute later, a dark sedan turned into the small parking lot. The driver switched off the headlights and rolled to a stop two spaces away from Maggie's car. With a faint electric hum, the window lowered just enough to let a thin stream of cigarette smoke escape from the interior. Unseen by the group inside, a pair of dark eyes watched the building, waiting.

****

Chapter Twenty-Two

Silent images flitted by on the muted television in the corner of the room. Patrick sat slumped in an overstuffed armchair that had been moved clear of the window. A precaution, Julia had said. The dimmer switch on the lights was turned down low to minimize the shadows they would cast on the curtains. Anyone stalking them would have a hard time finding a clear target. Julia sat on the edge of the bed with Maggie by her side. Drew had closed his eyes and stretched out on the floor, his back against the far wall.

Julia had listened attentively while Maggie filled her in about the drug dealer and the warehouse that Patrick had been working at. Tom's description jogged her memory and she agreed that he might have been the man who attacked her in her office. In turn, Julia told them about what she had found at the beach house. The envelope she'd retrieved from the bathroom had contained traces of heroin. If Danny and Allison were dealing drugs, then one of them was sampling the merchandise. Julia's money was on Allison. They were still trying to figure out where Patrick had fit into their plans.

Maggie watched her brother helplessly as he tried to stop the violent trembling that wracked his thin frame. She wanted to put her arms around him and tell him that everything would be all right, like she did when they were children. As soon as she tried to get up, Julia put a hand on her knee and gave her an almost imperceptible shake of her head. Maggie hesitated.

"He's going through withdrawal, Maggie," Julia said quietly. "You can't help him right now."

"There has to be something we can do for him."

Julia couldn't resist the imploring look in those clear green eyes. With a resigned sigh, she yanked a blanket off the bed and threw it at him. He jerked in surprise, but caught it with one hand.

"Try to keep warm," she advised.

Patrick did not respond, but he wrapped the blanket around

231

himself. Julia rolled her eyes in exasperation. She did not have time to deal with Patrick's disapproval of her relationship with his sister. A gentle pressure on her shoulder caught her attention, and she rested her cheek against the top of a blonde head.

"Tired?" She asked the reporter leaning against her.

Maggie nodded. "A little. I haven't been sleeping very well."

Julia gave her a rueful grin. "Me neither," she admitted. "Why don't you lie down and get some rest?"

"Later," Maggie said. "We need to figure this stuff out first."

"Get some sleep, Maggie. I just need to think this through. I know the answers are here somewhere."

"Then we'll both find them," Maggie said, squeezing Julia's hand. "We're in this together, right?"

Julia smiled at her. The gaping hole in her heart had closed as soon as she had held Maggie in her arms. The love and trust shining from the reporter's eyes sealed her fate. Everything was going to be just fine. She would make damn sure of that.

"Together, huh? I think I like the sound of that."

"Me too," Maggie agreed, snuggling closer.

Julia stole a quick glance toward the huddled figure in the armchair. A wicked gleam entered her eyes, and she chuckled deep in her throat. Maggie lifted her head and examined her suspiciously.

"What was that evil little laugh for?"

Julia gave her a playfully ferocious grin. "What do you suppose he'd do if I kissed you right now?"

Maggie blinked and glanced at her brother. Though he was trying to hide it, she could tell Patrick was watching them out of the corner of his eye. She felt a grin tugging at her lips. Slowly, her hand slid up and rested at the base of Julia's neck. She leaned closer, their faces mere inches apart.

"I think he would probably swallow his tongue." Maggie informed the grinning woman.

"Good thing I know CPR, then," Julia murmured.

Unable to restrain herself any longer, she reclaimed Maggie's lips. Soft, gentle pressure gave way to a deeper urgency as Maggie drew her closer, just as hungry for the contact as she was. Julia hands moved down the reporter's body, stopping at the small of her back. A fire had ignited inside, and it took all the self-control she had not to throw Maggie down on the bed and rip her clothes off. Although she could feel the need and desire pouring from the smaller woman, she doubted that either of them really wanted to make love with an audience.

"I should have rented a second room," Julia said wryly, breaking the kiss.

Maggie laughed softly, stroking Julia's cheek. "Yeah, maybe you should have."

She stood and stretched her arms up towards the ceiling. It had been a long day and she felt decidedly grungy. Maggie shot a longing glance at the bathroom door. Before leaving Julia's house, she had packed a change of clothes, but in her haste to find Julia's room, she had left the bag in her car. She debated going outside to retrieve it.

"What are you thinking about?" Julia asked her, brushing her lips across the palm of Maggie's hand.

Maggie shivered at the welcome sensation. "I was thinking about grabbing a shower, actually. Care to join me?" She teased. She continued without waiting for a response.

"I left my bag in the car. Do you think it's safe enough to go out and get it?"

Julia held out her hand. "Give me the keys. I'll get it."

Maggie swatted her hand away and scooted back out of reach. She gave Julia a reproachful look.

"I am perfectly capable of getting my own bag out of my own car."

"Yes, you are," Julia agreed, stalking her prey around the room. "But you should give me the keys anyway and let me do it for you."

Drew chose that moment to unfold his long legs, nearly tripping his taller sister. She glared at him as he rose, yawning. He searched his pockets and dug out a set of keys attached to a Scooby-Doo key chain.

"Oh, shut up, both of you. I'll get the damn bag. I'm the guy with the keys, remember?" He dangled the key chain in front of Julia's nose, jerking it out of reach when she lunged for it.

"I thought you were asleep," Julia said, making another grab for the keys that Drew had concealed behind his back.

He smirked at her, his eyes twinkling. "Who can sleep after the floor show that you two put on a minute ago?"

Julia and Maggie turned complementary shades of red. Mumbling something about heating the water, Maggie excused herself to the bathroom. The door slammed shut behind her, cutting off Drew's laughter.

"Aw, come on, Jules. Relax. I was only joking." Drew backed away, recognizing the threat in Julia's expression.

She relaxed and gave him a wry grin. "I guess we did get a little carried away. Fine. Go out to the car, if you insist. Just be careful."

"I'm always careful," Drew replied, heading out the door.

The faucet was running in the bathroom, and judging by the splashing sounds, Julia guessed that Maggie was washing her face. She stretched out on the bed, crossing her legs at the ankles. The television remote was on the nightstand, and she reached for it, raising the volume so she could hear the late night news. She could feel Patrick's eyes on her. Turning her head a fraction of an inch, she glanced at him expectantly. *'Might as well get this over with,'* she thought. She gathered up all the self-righteous indignation she could manage. *'Who the hell does he think he is? He has no right to judge us, considering the mess he's made of his own life.'* Letting her anger grow, Julia prepared for battle.

"Well?" The low drawl dripped with implied menace.

Patrick leaned forward, resting his elbows on his knees. Julia was close enough to him to smell the stale, fearful sweat that emanated from his body. She didn't flinch and her gaze never wavered. Instead of the earlier anger, she now saw mostly curiosity mingled with suspicion in his bloodshot eyes.

"Do you love my sister?"

It wasn't the question that she had been expecting. Julia blinked, tilting her head towards the young man, sizing him up. She had been prepared to detest him. Truthfully, part of her did. If not for Patrick, none of them would be in this ridiculous situation. For Maggie's sake though, she had promised herself that she would give him a chance. Sitting there, huddled underneath a blanket, he looked more like a frightened teenager than a violent drug addict. With a sigh, Julia was forced to admit that he might not be as dangerous as she had originally thought.

"Yes. I love her very much." Julia answered his question.

She braced herself for the outburst. Families were forever accusing her of seducing their loved ones. Most of the time, they had been right. This time, though, it was the other way around. Maggie had stolen her heart. It took Julia a few moments to realize that Patrick was merely watching her thoughtfully. Julia said nothing. Patrick's shoulders slumped and he buried his face in his hands. When he raised his head again, tears streaked his face. She almost felt sorry for him.

"I didn't mean for any of this to happen," he whispered, more to himself than to Julia.

Julia shrugged. She had nothing to say. She suspected he wanted her to tell him that it wasn't his fault, to absolve him of any responsibility. Julia was not about to do that. Whether he had meant to or not, Patrick's actions had brought them all here. His regrets, if sincere, meant very little.

"Why did you come here, Patrick?" Julia asked him, keeping one ear tuned to the running water in the bathroom. "Why can't you just let her live her own life?"

Patrick scratched at the back of his hand, leaving long red streaks on the skin. Julia had to reach out and stop him before he drew his own blood. He looked at her, and the misery in his eyes melted her resolve, just a little. Tears welled in his eyes again.

"I don't know," he said, his voice hoarse. "Mags always took care of me. When she left, I didn't know what to do."

"You're a grown man. Take responsibility for yourself for a change."

The door flew open, interrupting them, and Drew dashed in, wild-eyed and out of breath. He dropped Maggie's shoulder bag on the floor, and quickly crossed to the window. Julia jumped off the bed and joined him, peering through the curtains. A noise to her left alerted her and she glanced at Patrick. He had slid from the chair and pressed himself into the corner. She returned her attention to her breathless brother.

"What are we looking at?" She asked, keeping her voice barely above a whisper.

Catching his breath, he pointed. "There's someone in that car. I think he's watching us."

Julia's eyes narrowed. She couldn't see through the car's tinted windows, but she thought she could make out a trail of smoke emerging from the driver's side window. While they watched, a shower of sparks scattered across the ground as someone flicked a cigarette butt out the window. Julia's mind raced as she formulated a plan.

"Can you follow directions?" She asked Drew.

He nodded. "Of course. Just tell me what to do."

Julia grunted in satisfaction. She crossed to the other side of the room and tapped on the closed bathroom door. After a moment, the water stopped and Maggie cracked open the door. Julia gave the reporter the most reassuring smile she could muster. She handed Maggie's shoulder bag through the crack.

"Sorry to interrupt. I need you to get dressed and come back out here."

Maggie caught the edge to Julia's voice and realized that something was wrong. She nodded and ducked back inside the bathroom. She dressed hurriedly and reemerged, her hair still dripping water down her back. Drew and Julia were standing near the window, and she joined them.

"What's going on?" Maggie rested her hand on Julia's upper arm, feeling the tension there.

Placing both hands on Maggie's shoulders, Julia moved her back, away from the window. She glanced back to the other side of the room and beckoned to Patrick. Keeping his head below the level of the windowsill, he crawled around the edge of the bed and joined them.

"There might be someone out there," Julia said, trying to keep her tone as light as possible. "Drew and I are going to check it out. I need the two of you to stay here. Keep your heads down and don't leave this room unless you absolutely have to."

She took Maggie's hand, pressing the reporter's car keys into it. Maggie started to protest, but Julia placed a silencing finger against her lips.

"Ssshh. It'll be okay." She paused, searching for the right words. "Look, if something happens, just take Patrick and get the hell out of here. Don't wait for me."

Maggie shook her head and refused to let go of Julia's hand. "No. Not a chance. I won't leave you behind."

There was no sense in arguing with her. Instead, Julia leaned forward and placed a gentle kiss on her forehead. She stood, giving Maggie a quirky half-grin.

"Then I'll make sure you don't have to."

Julia resumed her position at the window and pointed to the building at the far end of the parking lot.

"See that building? That's the office." She glanced at Drew, making sure he was listening carefully.

"I'm going to head in that direction. Count to ten, very slowly; then follow me out the door. Circle around behind this building. Stay low and come up on the car from this side. By that time I should be on the other side of it. We'll trap whoever it is between us. Once you get into position, don't do anything unless I give you a signal. Got it?"

Drew nodded and blew out a few hard breaths, psyching himself up for the task.

"What if they have guns?" He asked.

Julia gave him a grim smile. "Then I hope you can dodge bullets."

Together, they moved toward the door. Julia opened it and stood silhouetted in the doorway. She gave her brother a jaunty thumbs-up.

"Count slow." She reminded him.

As the door began to close behind her, Maggie called out.

"Be careful, Julia. I love you."

Julia cast a quick glance over her shoulder, catching a glimpse of the reporter's face just before the door closed. She tried not to think about the fear she had seen in Maggie's eyes.

"I love you too, Maggie," she whispered.

Taking a deep breath, she tried not to look suspicious as she headed toward the mysterious car. She kept her gaze focused on the office at the other end of the lot, taking care to keep her movements easy and natural. The last thing she wanted to do was call closer attention to herself. She counted silently. Passing behind the car, she resisted the urge to look. Instead, she played with the button on her sleeve and kept walking, as if she had no idea that there was someone inside.

On the count of eight, the door to her room opened. Her lips twitched into a faint grin. She had been expecting Drew to be impatient. It didn't matter; she was already on the other side of the vehicle. Her truck was parked across from the mysterious car, and she turned towards it, pretending to dig in her pockets for the keys. A flicker of motion caught the corner of her eye, and she saw Drew creeping through the shadows toward the passenger side. Snapping her fingers, she turned back towards her room.

"Damn. Forgot the keys," she said aloud, keeping up the charade.

Her eyes met her brother's, and an unspoken agreement passed between them. Moving with an easy speed and grace, Julia closed the distance between herself and the car, as Drew did the same from his angle. Before anyone had time to react, she yanked the door open and hauled the startled driver out of the vehicle. Holding him by his shirt collar, she slammed him against the side of the car.

"Hello, Julia." He choked the words out.

Gasping in surprise, Julia released him and took a step back.

"Dad?"

Joseph Cassinelli straightened his shirt collar and took a few wheezing breaths. With the palms of his hands, he smoothed the sides of his precisely trimmed silver hair. Turning his head, he nodded at his son, who had joined Julia on that side of the car.

"Andrew. It's been a while."

Drew stared at him, speechless. Agitated by this latest turn of events, Julia began to pace. Gravel crunched beneath her boots. At last, she whirled to face her father, her eyes blazing with an accusation. For all she knew, Councilman Davis had sent his attorney to spy on them.

"Why are you here, Dad? Doing your friend's dirty work?"

Her father sighed and held his hands out to placate her. "Calm down, Julia. Don't be so melodramatic." He ignored his daughter's sputtered protestations. "Let's get inside before someone really does see you."

He reached inside the car and retrieved his briefcase from the front seat. Locking the door by remote, he hurried past his children and headed for Julia's room. After a stunned moment, Julia and Drew trailed after him, catching up as he reached the door. Julia slid around him and folded her arms across her chest. He was not going inside the room until she was satisfied that he could be trusted. She gestured toward the briefcase.

"Drew, grab that."

Her father rolled his eyes in irritation, but he acquiesced without a struggle. Calmly, he handed his briefcase to his son and watched while Drew searched its contents. He gave his children a hard, mocking smile.

"Well, if you two are done playing cops and robbers, I would like to go inside," he said, his tone condescending.

He held his arms out to his sides. "Are you sure you don't want to frisk me?"

"What? You expected me to trust you?" Julia shot back, opening the door for her father.

"Oh, of course not. I know better than that," he returned glibly, striding past her into the darkened room.

Julia stormed in after him, a dangerous glint in her eyes. Protectively, she positioned herself between her father and Maggie. Glaring at him, both eyebrows raised, she waited for him to explain his sudden appearance. She pretended not to see the charming smile that he directed towards Maggie.

"Why are you here, Dad?" Julia asked again.

He unbuttoned his shirt collar, taking his time before answering. Julia knew he did it simply to infuriate her. She exhaled slowly, determined not to let him see her growing irritation and impatience. Patrick was running for his life, and she and Maggie were caught in the crossfire. She didn't have time to play her father's games.

"Aren't you going to introduce me to your friends?" He asked.

Julia ground her teeth in frustration. "I'm pretty sure you already know who they are," she countered.

Maggie could sense the tension rolling off Julia in waves. With the knuckles of one hand, she kneaded the Julia's lower back, trying to relax the muscles. Ducking beneath Julia's arm, she smiled politely at her lover's father.

"Hello, Mr. Cassinelli. I'm Maggie McKinnon." She kept her voice neutral, attempting to defuse the impending explosion.

"My daughter was right. I know who you are Ms. McKinnon," he said, his demeanor suddenly grave. He glanced at Patrick behind her. "I know who your brother is, as well. And I know why he's running from the authorities. I would like to help you, if I can."

Her father's false concern was more than Julia could stand. Her lips twisted into a disbelieving sneer, and she applauded slowly, mocking him with every clap of her hands.

"Bravo, Dad. That was quite a little performance. Don't buy it for a second, Maggie. One thing about my father, he always has his own agenda."

"Jules, maybe we should at least hear what he has to say." Drew flinched under the sudden intense gaze from his sister.

"Please tell me you aren't defending him. When has he ever done anything for either of us?" Julia snarled through clenched teeth.

"Never," Drew said. "We both know he's a son of a bitch, but I think we should at least hear him out. He might actually be able to help us."

Maggie reminded herself to give Drew a big thank you hug later. His words of reason seemed to penetrate the angry haze clouding Julia's judgment. Her hand was still resting on Julia's lower back, and she felt the tension ease slightly. She let her hand drift a bit lower and gave the taller woman an encouraging pat, and the muscles beneath her palm twitched as Julia suppressed a chuckle.

Julia sighed and nodded at her father. "Fine. Spill it, then."

"I believe your lives are in danger," he said bluntly.

Julia began to laugh, emitting a sound somewhere between hilarity and hysteria. With one hand, she wiped the moisture from her eyes and sniffed, catching her breath. She knew the others were looking at her as if she had lost her mind. She shrugged, letting her hands fall to her sides.

"You tracked us here to tell us that?" She asked incredulously. "News flash, Dad. Our lives have been in danger for a while now."

Joseph Cassinelli waved a dismissive hand at his scoffing daughter. "I'm aware of your recent problems. But I have reason to believe that another attempt on your lives is imminent."

He looked at Julia, grudging regret on his face. "You told me you thought Allison was involved in something criminal, and I dismissed your suspicions. Lately, I've come to believe that you were right."

Julia bit back the sarcastic retort that popped into her mind. Instead, she willed herself to stay calm and reasonable.

"That's all very nice, but it doesn't really help us. I need something solid."

She watched curiously as he took his briefcase from Drew's hand and extracted a thick manila folder. He selected a black and white photograph and tossed it on the bed. Behind her, Maggie and Patrick both gasped in surprise.

"Do you recognize this man?" He pointed at Eddie Machado's mug shot.

Julia remained silent, her face betraying nothing. She glanced down at the photo, then back up at her father, waiting for him to get to the point.

"That is a low-level drug dealer named Eddie Machado. Or, perhaps I should say was. He's dead now. Murdered." He paused. "Do you want to know how I know that?"

"It was all over the news," Julia said dryly, not giving him an inch.

He sighed. "Yes. Of course. But I know things that the reporters couldn't tell you. I know that Eddie made several large cash deposits into a special account located at one of Martin Davis's banks. At the same time, Allison was making withdrawals for similar amounts. The amounts were never exactly equal. That would have been too obvious. And I know that Allison's account was much larger than her Netsports salary or her trust fund would allow."

He tossed a copy of a bank statement on the bed next to the picture. Julia picked it up and examined it, letting out a low whistle at the seven-figure balance. Things were beginning to fall into place. Allison and Danny were running drugs through at least one of the Davis warehouses and using the Internet Company as a front. Julia figured it was a safe bet that they had also been working out of the one that burned down, though she wasn't sure why the fire had been necessary. Now, Julia mused wryly, all she had to do was prove it. She regarded her father skeptically.

"Why bring this to me? Why not go to the police?"

Her father dropped the rest of the file on the bed. "Nothing in that file can conclusively prove anything. But it can certainly tell someone where to look. I'm giving this to you in exchange for a favor. When this all goes to hell, and it will, I want my name kept out of it."

"I can't promise you that," Julia said quietly.

He gave her a small, cynical smile. "I know. But you'll do your best. You have your mother's sense of honor." He faltered as the mention of her mother turned Julia's face to stone again.

"Look, take what you can from that file. And watch out for Martin. He's on the edge. He'll do whatever it takes to keep Allison out of trouble."

She nodded once, the only indication that she'd heard his warning. Julia let her finger brush against the exterior of the thick file folder. Part of her wanted to believe in her father's sincerity, even though she knew he was really just covering his own backside. Still, the little girl in her wanted to think that he cared the way a father should. *'Okay, Julia. No time for sentimental nonsense. Thank him for the information and send him on his self-serving way,'* she told herself firmly.

"Go back to the city, Dad. Keep a low profile. Well, low for you anyway." Julia amended, giving him the faintest glimmer of a smile. "If any of this stuff you brought pans out, I'll do what I can to keep you clear of it."

Julia hesitated, biting her lower lip thoughtfully. "Wait, I have one more request. Take Drew back with you."

Sputtering in surprise, Drew started to argue with her. She silenced him with a look. Reaching out, she pulled him into a stiff, awkward hug. Despite their recent strides, Julia was still unaccustomed to this level of closeness with a half-brother who had been little more than a stranger for most of their lives. Feeling him relaxing in defeat, she patted his back and whispered into his ear.

"I want you to stay out of this from now on. Stay safe."

Startling both of them, she planted a quick kiss on his cheek. "Thank you for keeping an eye on Maggie. I owe you one, little brother."

The tips of his ears were glowing when he managed to extricate himself from her embrace. Embarrassed, he scrubbed at his cheek with the heel of his hand. His blush deepened as Maggie stepped forward and kissed the other side of his face with a resounding smack. She gave him a warm, grateful smile.

"Thanks, Drew. You're a good friend."

"Yeah, well, you guys take care of each other. Give me a call when this is all over." He pointed at Patrick. "And you behave yourself, or I really will beat the crap out of you."

Drew glanced at his father and tilted his head towards the door. Both men left without looking back. A few minutes later, a car engine sprang to life and gravel crunched beneath tires as the two Cassinelli men pulled out of the parking lot.

"So what next?" Maggie asked from her perch at the end of the bed.

Julia took a deep breath, steeling herself for the dispute that was sure to follow. Reaching into the small closet, she removed a tight roll of bills from her jacket. In her peripheral vision, she saw the startled, vaguely hungry look in Patrick's eyes when she handed the money to Maggie. To an addict, cash meant only one thing --- the next fix. Julia gave him a hard, warning look before turning her attention to the dumbfounded reporter.

"I want you to take that money. Take your brother and get as far away from here as you can."

Maggie just stared at her, incredulous and unable to believe what she was hearing. She and Julia had already been apart for three of the longest days of her life. They were finally together again, and now Julia wanted to send her away. The indignation boiled up from the pit of her stomach, and exasperated fire flashed in her eyes.

"You've got to be kidding," she said flatly.

Julia tugged at her earlobe and shifted her weight from one foot to the other. She had known that Maggie would not be easily convinced. Quickly, she ran through her argument in her mind. Maggie and her brother would be safer if they got further away from San Francisco, at least for a while. She was certain of that. She opened her mouth to speak, but Maggie cut her off before a single word crossed her lips.

"Don't even say it." Maggie warned her. "Don't you dare tell me that I'll be safer somewhere else. I won't leave you here, in danger, just so I can run away and hide. Besides, haven't I told you that only feel safe when I'm with you?"

Julia clamped her jaw shut. How could she argue with that? Mutely, she looked past Maggie to Patrick, appealing to him for help. Surely he could see that they would be better off elsewhere. Plus, Julia figured he would jump at the chance to get his sister away from a bad influence like her. To her surprise, he merely gave her a tiny shrug and dropped his gaze to the floor. It would be up to her to talk some sense into the reporter.

"Maggie," she began awkwardly. "It's not that I want you to go. I just don't want you to get hurt. Don't you know that's my worst nightmare?"

Maggie nearly lost her resolve in the pleading look in Julia's eyes. She took Julia's hand and pulled her down to sit beside her. Gently, she kissed their interlocked fingers.

"I know. The thought of you getting hurt is my greatest fear too." She paused, gazing deeply into a pair of troubled blue eyes. "But I honestly believe that we're better together than apart. We can watch out for each other."

A kiss stopped Julia's protest. "Julia Cassinelli, you are my lover and my friend, but you do not have to be my bodyguard. We are in this together and we will finish this together." A smile lit up the reporter's eyes. "Now, do you really want to waste time arguing about this?"

"Can I say something?"

Patrick spoke from the corner. Both women turned toward him expectantly. After a brief glance at his sister, he addressed his comments to Julia.

"Part of me, well, most of me, wants to take that money and get the hell away from here." He paused, clearly uncomfortable under Julia's steady gaze. "I'm still not sure I like you, but when my sister looks at you, she's happy. So I think you should let her stay."

He fell silent again and resumed his position, slouched in the armchair. Julia sighed, realizing that she had just lost the argument. Closing her eyes, she gave Maggie a slight nod and felt the gentle squeeze of her hand in return.

"Well, let's see what else is in this file."

Julia turned towards the other side of the bed. She picked up the folder and began thumbing through the neatly ordered papers inside. There were bank records, short bios, newspaper clippings and criminal histories on Eddie Machado and Tom Becker. Julia examined the information on Tom with particular interest. She held up the attached photo, showing it to Patrick.

"Is this the guy who set you up?"

Patrick nodded, a shudder running down his spine at the sight of Tom's cold, hard eyes. Julia could see the fear in the young man's face.

"Yeah. That's him."

"Okay. I'm gonna call Henry and give him a little tip. See if I can put him on this guy's trail."

Maggie looked up from the newspaper stories she was sifting through. "Check on Catherine and Jessica when you talk to him, okay?"

Julia mumbled an affirmative reply as she searched for her phone. The activity gave her time to think of a plausible story for Henry. He would want to know exactly how she had received the information and who had given it to her. Although she trusted her oldest friend, Julia also knew that he would not be able to deny his training. If Henry honored her request and didn't haul her father in for questioning, the guilt would tear him apart. She couldn't put him through that, so she had to come up with something else to tell him. When she finally spoke to him, he was predictably agitated. Julia ended up giving him a vague tale about a confidential informant, though she was sure that he didn't believe a word of it. Thankfully, he didn't press the issue like she had thought he would. His stakeout at the hospital had been quiet so far. No one had been to visit Catherine except Jessica and assorted medical personnel, and the officers stationed outside her room were carefully checking everyone's credentials. Henry was confident that all the proper security measures had been taken, but he promised to get an arrest warrant issued for Tom Becker.

After thanking Henry, Julia ended the call. She stood and arched backward until her spine gave a satisfying pop. Maggie was scrutinizing her intensely, but she pretended not to notice as she moved toward the open bathroom door.

"I could use a shower." She glanced toward Patrick. "Will you two be okay alone for a few minutes?"

Patrick shrugged but said nothing, and Julia took that as an affirmative response. She grabbed a change of clothes from her scuffed leather backpack on the floor. Two steps from the doorway, Maggie slid around her and blocked her path. Julia stared down at her, eyebrow raised in question.

"You never really answered my question before." Maggie reminded her, folding her arms and refusing to budge. "So, what do we do now? Hide out here?"

The shower was tantalizingly close and Julia gazed at it longingly. A few more seconds and everything would have been fine. If nothing else, it would have given her time to think of something to tell Maggie. She cocked her head to one side and grinned at Maggie, hoping to disarm the young woman.

"What do you think we should do next?" She countered.

Always answer a question with a question. It was one of her private investigator rules. The technique kept people from learning what she was thinking, and more often than not, they left believing that she had given them a response. Unfortunately, Maggie knew her a bit better than most people. Julia flinched under the reporter's steady gaze.

"What?"

Maggie gave her an exasperated sigh. "You know what." She laid her hand on Julia's forearm. "Come on, Julia. There's something you aren't telling me and I want to know what it is. Or was my speech about togetherness all for nothing?"

"No." Julia mumbled.

She knew Maggie well enough to realize that she would not be deterred. Julia relented and decided to tell her everything.

"Before you got here, Danny called me." She shook her head at Maggie's startled exclamation. "It's okay. He doesn't know where we are, exactly."

"What do you mean not exactly?" Maggie asked, her eyes wide.

Julia shrugged. "He knows I'm in the area. Apparently he saw me break into the house earlier. He wants to meet with me tomorrow morning."

"You're not going to do it, are you?" Patrick interjected from the other side of the room.

"Yes. I am." Julia replied simply.

"Then you're either crazy or stupid. Or both."

Julia ignored him and glanced apologetically at Maggie. Hurt, anger and confusion shone from the reporter's eyes.

"Let me explain."

Maggie cut her off. "You weren't even going to tell me." It was more of a statement than a question.

"I was planning to sneak out before you woke up." Julia admitted. "But I was going to tell you everything afterwards."

"Yeah, if Danny didn't kill you first!"

"Maggie, I don't think he intends to hurt me." Julia paused, searching for the words to explain. "If he had wanted to, he could have sold me out or worse when he saw me break in. He didn't. Instead, he called me and set up a meeting. I think maybe he wants to help."

Maggie snorted in disbelief, but Julia pressed on. "I think Danny got in way over his head, and now he wants out. That's the only plausible explanation that I can come up with."

"I have another one for you," Maggie said bitterly. "He and Allison are setting a trap for you and you're walking right into it."

"I don't think so."

"Then when you go to meet him tomorrow, I'm going with you." Maggie decided, leaving little room for discussion. She continued before Julia could disagree with her. "If it's as safe as you think it is, then there shouldn't be a problem. Right?"

No matter how hard she tried, Julia couldn't come up with a logical excuse to say no. Maggie's argument made sense. If meeting Danny wasn't going to be dangerous, then there was no reason that the reporter could not accompany her. Then why do I have such a bad feeling about this, she wondered. *'Because you're not as sure of Danny as you keep pretending to be,'* her inner voice told her. Julia ignored it, pushing the voice to the back of her mind.

"Okay." Julia looked at Maggie, her face resolute. "You two can come, but you do exactly as I say. No questions. Got it?"

Maggie nodded. "Understood. We'll follow your lead."

Julia glanced at Patrick, who was trying to find a comfortable position in the armchair.

"Are you okay with that too?"

"Whatever," Patrick returned sullenly. "Not like I have much of a choice, is it?"

"No. You really don't." Julia agreed. She turned back to Maggie and gave her a tentative smile. "I think I'm going to take that shower now. Why don't you lie down and get some rest?"

Maggie grabbed her arm as she started to turn away. "Promise me something. Promise me you won't leave here without us tomorrow."

"I promise."

"Okay. Thank you." Maggie stood on her toes and gave her a brief, almost chaste kiss. "Go take your shower."

Fifteen minutes later, when Julia emerged from the bathroom, Maggie was already asleep. Patrick was watching her through half-closed eyes, and Julia glared at him. Without lifting his head, he spoke, warning her.

"If you let her down, I'll kill you myself."

Fuming, Julia choked on a sharp retort. She didn't want to wake Maggie by strangling her brother. Instead, she pinned Patrick with her coldest stare and gave him a feral grin. She almost laughed as he shrank back further into his chair.

"Don't worry about me," she said. "But if you let her down again, I will make you wish you had never even heard of California."

Though Patrick didn't move, Julia knew he had heard her. Chuckling silently, she pulled back the covers and slid into bed. On cue, Maggie rolled over in her sleep and curled up against her. Julia wrapped one arm around the reporter's shoulders as she turned off the bedside lamp. She stared up at the darkened ceiling. With any luck, tomorrow it would all be over.

Patrick broke through her reverie as he threw his blanket and the chair cushion to the floor. Through the darkness, Julia heard him stretch out beside the bed. Careful not to wake Maggie, she leaned over and checked the alarm clock on the nightstand. They could not afford to oversleep. Satisfied, Julia closed her eyes and allowed herself to drift into a light, restless sleep.

****

They had risen before dawn. Maggie could sense the nervous energy flowing from Julia as they exited the small motel room. The parking lot was silent and dark. Broken glass littered the ground beneath the streetlamps, and they ground it to dust beneath their feet as they hurried towards the car. Maggie was in the middle, with Julia's arm snaked protectively around her waist. Patrick walked beside her, and Maggie could hear his ragged, anxious breathing. She wanted to tell him to calm down, but Julia had warned them both about the need' for silence. Without a word, they walked on.

Something fluttered at the edge of Maggie's vision and she stopped abruptly. Patrick halted a few steps ahead and turned back towards her. Julia stared down at her, frowning in confusion. Ignoring them, Maggie turned in a slow circle. She knew she had seen something. The back of her neck tingled. She started to speak. Then the first shots shattered the stillness.

Maggie watched, horrified, as Patrick's head snapped back. He stumbled backwards, hands clawing at his throat, trying to stop the bright red arterial blood that squirted between his fingers. He fell against the hood of a car and slid slowly to the ground. Maggie tried to go to him, but her feet disobeyed her. She turned to Julia and the shots rang out again.

"Maggie! Get down!" The frantic words resounded through her mind.

There was no time to think. Oxygen exploded painfully out of Maggie's lungs as Julia hurled her to the ground. Gravel dug into her palms. She tried to get up, but a tall, strong body fell on top of her. Sheltering her. Bullets screamed around them, ripping through the parked cars. Maggie felt Julia's upper body jerk. As quickly as it had begun, the gunfire ended.

"Julia? It's over. You can get off me now." Maggie whispered as she struggled to her knees. "I have to check on Patrick. I think he needs a doctor."

Julia did not answer. Maggie's hands were wet, and she looked down at them. They were covered in blood. Slowly, she turned her head and saw Julia lying on her back, her eyes closed. A dark stain spread rapidly across the front of her t-shirt.

"Oh god. No." Maggie fell to her knees beside her motionless lover.

Footsteps pounded behind her and a hand clamped down on her shoulder. She screamed.

****

Julia pulled the struggling, thrashing reporter into her arms and held her tight. She stroked Maggie's hair and whispered meaningless words of reassurance until the shaking blonde began to calm down.

"Julia?" Maggie sobbed, reaching out to touch Julia's cheek. Julia kissed her palm. "Shhh. It's okay. I'm right here."

The terror of the nightmare receded and Maggie realized that she was not in the cold, dark parking lot. She was warm in bed, in Julia's motel room, with strong, comforting arms wrapped around her. Awakened by her screams, Patrick stood beside the bed. He blinked at her dazedly and she gave him a weak smile.

"Sorry." She mumbled. "It seemed so real."

"I know, sweetheart. But it was just a bad dream. I won't let anyone hurt either of you."

Julia's soothing whisper tickled Maggie's ear. Fear eased its death grip on her heart and she started to relax. Her eyelids grew heavy as she drifted back to sleep, secure in Julia's embrace. She smiled, feeling the vibrations as Julia hummed an old Irish lullaby.

"Where did you learn that?" She asked sleepily.

Julia chuckled deep in her throat. "I have my sources."

Maggie sighed and burrowed closer, letting sleep claim her once more. Julia waited until the reporter's breathing became deep and regular. She nodded at Patrick and he stretched out on the floor and went back to sleep, as well.

"Sleep now, Maggie." Julia murmured into the smaller woman's fair hair.

"I have the feeling you're gonna need it.

Chapter Twenty-Three

Danny shivered as the cool night air blew in through the open balcony doors. Goosebumps prickled his skin, though he wasn't sure if they were caused by the chill or by his own fear. He checked his watch again, squinting to read the numbers in the moonlight. Beside him, Allison stirred in her sleep and her hand fell across his bare chest. He froze. His heart thumped wildly and he wondered if she could feel it.

A fraction of an inch at a time, he lifted her arm and slid out of bed. She did not wake, and Danny breathed a quiet sigh of relief. He grabbed his clothes from the floor and crept out of the bedroom, buttoning his shirt as he descended the stairs. He was supposed to meet Julia at dawn. Allison usually slept late and Danny hoped to be back before she woke. A pang of guilt tugged at him as he made his way through the living room.

'I'm sorry, Allison,' he whispered mentally as he reached for the car keys on the coffee table. *'There's just no other way, and I'm not letting you drag me down with you.'*

Over the past few weeks, Allison's drug use had escalated dramatically and her behavior had become even more erratic. Danny was worried. The police were too close. Julia was even closer. He knew it was only a matter of time before everything fell apart. Anger rising, he wiped a bead of nervous sweat away. None of this was his fault. Not really. True, running drugs had been his idea. It had seemed like an easy way to pay off his huge gambling debts. Allison had been eager to go along, offering to let him use her family's warehouses. No one was ever supposed to get hurt. Then Allison's father had discovered their activities and everything had started going straight to Hell.

Still bemoaning his situation, Danny padded quietly towards the front door. Above him, the floorboards creaked. He stopped in his tracks, scarcely daring to breathe. He imagined Allison up there, watching him, plotting against him just as he was plotting against her. Another droplet of sweat rolled down his temple as he waited. The house stayed silent, and he relaxed. It was a false alarm. Taking his shoes in his hand, he slipped out the door. As he headed for the driveway, he risked a glance up at the second story bedroom window. There was no one there. He smiled to himself; Allison was still asleep. She never had to know that he had betrayed her.

****

They rose well before dawn, awakened by the insistent beep of the alarm clock. Maggie sat on the edge of the bed and watched while Julia laced her boots. After her nightmare, she had managed to fall asleep again, but her body protested as if it had been deprived of sleep for days. Her back and shoulders ached, and her eyes felt like she had rubbed them with sand.

Julia probably felt even worse, she realized. Maggie doubted that she had been able to close her eyes again after being awakened by her screams. Outwardly, Julia appeared composed, but a tiny twitch of her shoulder blades betrayed her. Though she was doing her best not to show it, Maggie could tell that she was just as anxious as the rest of them.

"I'm going to walk over to the office and drop off the room key." Julia rose and pulled on her jacket.

"Is that such a good idea?" Maggie asked.

Julia gave her a casual shrug. "Why not? It gives me a chance to take a look around before we leave. Make sure there's no one lurking out there."

"And if there is? What are you gonna do? Glare them to death?" Patrick asked, his voice dripping with sarcasm.

Maggie grimaced, bracing herself for Julia's scathing reply. She had been hoping that Julia and Patrick would get along better in the morning. Evidently, that would not be the case. She sighed. She would have to work on both of them, and it wasn't a task that she was looking forward to. To her surprise, the corner of Julia's lips lifted into a wry grin.

"Are you worried about me, Patrick? I'm touched. I can take care of myself, though. Thanks."

Patrick rolled his eyes. "I'm gonna go wash up."

The bathroom door slammed shut, leaving Julia and Maggie alone for a moment. They regarded each other in the quiet of the room. Maggie stood and slipped her arms around Julia's waist, pulling her close. The memory of her nightmare was still far too vivid, and she hated the idea of Julia going outside alone. A finger under her chin tilted her head back, and Maggie smiled up into a pair of dazzling blue eyes.

"I'll be fine," Julia said, reading her mind.

"I know you will," Maggie replied, leaning in for a quick kiss. "Be careful."

Julia nodded and took a step backwards, disentangling herself from the embrace. Smiling, she gave Maggie a saucy wink before heading out the door.

Maggie tried to ignore the churning in her gut that started the second Julia left her sight. She turned on the television to keep her mind occupied. Pulling the armchair in front of the small set, she sat down and flipped channels until she found the early morning news. She heard Patrick shut the water off, and she looked up as he came out of the bathroom. His hair was limp and dull. Dark purple shadows beneath his eyes stood out in stark contrast to his pale skin. His uncontrollable trembling seemed to have abated for the moment, and Maggie hoped that was a good sign.

He met her eyes for a moment, and she thought she saw regret there. There were so many things that she wanted to talk to Patrick about, but it didn't seem like the right time. Instead, she smiled at him.

"It's supposed to rain later," he said, thrusting his chin towards the television.

Maggie turned back to the screen. According to the weather report, a storm front was moving in. She shuddered as a dark sense of foreboding washed over her. Patrick sprawled out on the floor beside her, resting his back against the edge of the bed. Together, they watched the rest of the news in silence. During the night, police had pulled a man's body out of the Bay. So far, he was still unidentified.

"Poor guy," Maggie murmured.

Patrick eyed her curiously. "Why?"

Maggie twisted her upper body so she could face him directly. "He died all alone. He probably has a family out there, somewhere. Somebody has to be missing him or worrying about him."

She hoped Patrick would get the hint. A fleeting shadow of guilt flickered across his face, and he dropped his gaze. He shrugged.

"You care too much, Maggie." He fiddled with the frayed end of his shoelace. "Maybe that guy isn't worth your concern. Maybe he's just some punk that got drunk or wasted and fell in."

"Maybe." Maggie acknowledged the possibility. "But even punks have loved ones."

A light tap on the door interrupted their conversation. Maggie hastily turned off the television and swallowed her fear. She motioned to Patrick to stay down. Careful to minimize her sounds, she moved towards the door. Her eyes swept the small room, looking for something to use as a weapon. Swiftly, she grabbed the small lamp on the nightstand and yanked the cord out of the wall. She hefted it in her hand, testing its weight.

"Maggie, open the door. It's just me."

Maggie let out the breath she had been holding. She opened the door and stood aside to let Julia in. Julia glanced at the lamp in Maggie's hand, and a dark eyebrow lifted. She shook her head as Maggie grinned at her sheepishly and set the lamp on the dresser.

"Okay. Everything looks pretty quiet out there. Are we ready to go?" Julia asked.

Maggie glanced back at her brother and he nodded. She gave Julia a resolute smile. Taking a deep breath to settle her fluttering stomach, Maggie started towards the door. She let out a small, startled yelp as Julia seized the tail of her shirt and hauled her back.

"Hey! Hold on a minute, Hotshot. Nobody's going anywhere until we get a couple of things clear."

"First, when we get outside, stay quiet and stick close to me. Like I said, it doesn't look like anyone found us, but it's better to be safe." Julia gave them instructions in a clipped, no-nonsense tone. "Second, when we get where we're going, the two of you stay in the truck. No matter what happens, don't get out."

Maggie nodded briskly, rubbing her hands together. She wondered if she looked as nervous as she felt.

"Where are we going, anyway?" Patrick asked.

Maggie frowned. She wondered why it had not occurred to her to ask that question. Silently, she scolded herself for her inattention. She stiffened her resolve. If Julia was going to insist upon taking the risks, then Maggie was going to do whatever she could to watch her back. Her reporter skills would come in handy. She would be Julia's eyes and ears, observing the little things that the private investigator might miss.

Gradually, Maggie became aware that Julia and Patrick were staring at her with odd expressions on their faces. She blinked at them.

"What?"

"Were you talking to yourself just now?" Julia asked, a faintly amused twinkle in her eyes.

Maggie felt the flush start just beneath her collar. "Why?"

"Because your lips were moving." Patrick supplied.

Maggie's blush deepened. She glared at them both. "Whatever. Are we getting out of here or not?"

252

"Yes, we are." Julia confirmed, opening the door.

Summoning her courage, Maggie stepped through first. She turned back to watch as Julia carefully shut the door behind them.

"So where ARE we going, anyway?" Maggie echoed her brother's earlier question.

She winced as her whisper seemed to reverberate through the dark, desolate parking lot. Julia shot her a warning look and pointed to a new SUV parked a few spaces from Maggie's car. Maggie barely heard the quiet reply.

"We're supposed to meet Danny near the Golden Gate Bridge."

Maggie digested that tidbit of information. A pedestrian walkway ran alongside the bridge, separated from vehicular traffic, so sightseers and photographers could enjoy the view of the Bay. Julia wasn't offering any more details, so Maggie assumed that was where the rendezvous would take place. Before dawn, traffic on the bridge would most likely be light. The lanes wouldn't be clogged with commuters for another hour or two.

Was that good or bad? Maggie wondered. At such an early hour, they would be less likely to be seen. On the other hand, there would be fewer potential witnesses if Danny or Allison decided to murder them and pitch their lifeless bodies into the Bay. Maggie made a face as she pictured the scene.

The soft chirp of a car alarm brought her back to reality, and she blinked. They had stopped at Julia's new truck. Maggie stood back, nudging Patrick out of the way as Julia opened the door.

"Patrick, get in the back. When we get close to the bridge, keep your head down. I don't want Danny to know that you're there," Julia said as she tossed her backpack on the seat.

Patrick grunted in acknowledgment and climbed in. Maggie handed her shoulder bag to him before pulling herself into the front seat. She inhaled deeply, breathing in the new car smell. Julia slid in beside her and flashed her a tense grin.

"Ready?"

Maggie nodded, trying to dismiss the uneasiness gnawing at her, insides. Random images from her nightmare flew through her mind, adding to her discomfort with this plan. She pushed the negative thoughts away. Swallowing hard, she gave Julia a trembling smile.

"Let's do this."

****

The sky was just beginning to turn a pale shade of pink when the southern end of the Golden Gate Bridge appeared before them. Low-lying fog clung to its underside, obscuring the view of the Bay. Julia eased her foot off the accelerator as she scanned the bridge. Traffic was light, but steady, even at this early hour. The constant stream of vehicles eased her anxiety a bit.

She spotted Danny's bright red sports car in a parking lot that led to one of the pedestrian walkways on the bridge. He appeared to be alone. A quick glance in the rearview mirror revealed nothing. As far as Julia could tell, no one had followed them from the inn. She made sure that Patrick had his head down like she had instructed. Reaching over, she found Maggie's hand and squeezed it.

"Here we go," she said.

The tension was thick inside Julia's truck as she smoothly parked next to Danny's car. As they had agreed, he got out of his vehicle when she pulled up. He held his hands out to show that he was unarmed, and Julia thought he looked as nervous as she felt. So far, everything was going according to plan. She shook off the uneasiness that had been plaguing her since the previous night. Maggie's nightmare had unnerved her more than she wanted to admit. Before getting out of the truck, Julia turned to Maggie to give her some last-minute directions.

"This shouldn't take too long," she said as she shut off the engine and left the key in the ignition.

"Remember. Stay inside the truck."

Their eyes locked, and Julia saw the fear on Maggie's face. She wanted to take the terrified blonde into her arms and reassure her, but there was no time. Instead, she took a deep breath to steady her nerves. Reaching for the door handle, she hesitated.

"When I get out, slide over. If something goes wrong, get the Hell out of here. Go to Henry. He'll know what to do. Understand?"

Julia could read the conflicting emotions flickering across Maggie's face. For a moment, she was certain that Maggie was going to refuse. If their positions were reversed, Julia knew that nothing would make her leave the woman she loved behind. Finally, Maggie gave her a tiny nod.

"I love you." Maggie's whisper barely reached her ears as Julia opened the door and stepped out.

"I love you, too. It'll be okay."

Julia smiled at her and winked as she slammed the door shut. She waited until Maggie locked it. Before turning away, she kissed her fingertips and pressed them to the window where Maggie was watching anxiously.

Danny had walked out onto the bridge. He was standing on the sidewalk, near the railing and staring out at the mist. Every nerve ending in her body was on alert as Julia headed towards him. With each step, her back straightened and her scowl deepened. She thought of the fear she had seen in Maggie's eyes and let her anger build. By the time she reached Danny's side, she was in full intimidation mode. Julia folded her arms across her chest and stared at him, waiting for him to speak first. Danny continued to gaze out at the fog, as if the sluggishly moving mist had hypnotized him.

"Do you know who Tom Becker is?" He asked, breaking the silence.

Icy blue eyes narrowed as Julia considered the odd question. This was not how she had envisioned the beginning of their conversation. With slow and deliberate movements, Danny turned his head to look at her. She held his gaze calmly. Though her face remained expressionless, Julia was taken aback by the despair and resignation haunting his dark gray eyes.

"He's dead." Danny continued without waiting for her answer. He let out a short, barking laugh and resumed his contemplation of the fog.

"They found him floating in the Bay last night. I heard it on the radio this morning."

Julia studied him carefully, noting the defeated slump of his shoulders. Daniel Webber was a man who believed he had nothing left to lose. Julia wasn't sure if that made him an ally or an even more dangerous opponent. If Danny was telling her the truth, and Tom Becker was dead, then someone was growing desperate.

Danny laughed again, a hollow, broken sound. "Allison's father killed him. I know he did. And guess what, Jules? I'm gonna be next."

"What makes you think that?"

He shrugged. "It's obvious. They're cleaning up after themselves. First Eddie, now Tom. It's only a matter of time before they find you and Maggie. Patrick. Even that other reporter. And me."

"Listen to me, Danny. They can't get all of us. Not if we work together. If you help me out, maybe I'll be able to do something for you."

"Work together?" Danny echoed in a faraway voice.

Julia grabbed his upper arm and shook him, trying to focus his attention. She needed to snap him out of this daze. A car slowed as it passed them, and she tensed. The vehicle went by without incident; its driver gave them little more than a cursory glance. Julia exhaled slowly.

"Danny, I need you to give me something I can work with.

Something that I can use to bring Allison and her father down."

Danny leaned out so far over the rail that Julia feared he might jump. Keeping a firm hold on his arm, she gently eased him away from the edge. More cars were crossing over the bridge now as early commuters made their way into the city. With each passing vehicle, Julia's anxiety grew. Sooner or later, Allison was going to realize that Danny was gone, and Julia did not want to be trapped on the bridge when that happened. She took a deep breath and put on her most intimidating scowl, determined to scare the truth out of Danny if necessary. Grabbing his shoulders, she spun him around to face her. Sparks crackled in her eyes, and he flinched.

"I'm so sorry," he whispered. She could barely hear him over the rush of traffic. "I never meant for anyone to get hurt."

"I don't have time for your regrets!" Julia snapped at him. Her irritation and impatience were rising quickly. "People I love are in danger because of you. Now, did you come here to help me, or not?"

Danny closed his eyes and brushed away a lone tear that trickled down his cheek. He sniffed quietly and rubbed his sleeve across his face. He looked so lost and dejected that Julia felt a momentary twinge of sympathy for him. Glancing over her shoulder, she saw Maggie watching her from the truck. Though Julia could not see her face clearly, she could still sense Maggie's fear. Her resolve hardened. She had seen fear in those eyes far too often, and Danny was partially responsible for that. Any shred of compassion she had felt for him vanished.

"Now, Danny. Or I'm out of here." She threatened him.

Opening his eyes, he looked at her, and a chill crawled down her spine. An image flew through her mind, and she remembered the first time she had seen a corpse. She had been participating in a drug raid and a shoot-out with the police had ensued. In the aftermath, she remembered looking down at the body of a young drug dealer. His blank, lifeless eyes had stared up at her, chilling her to the core. Julia suppressed a shudder. Looking into Danny's eyes was like looking into the eyes of a dead man.

"The drug-trafficking was my idea." Danny began his confession. "I had racked up some pretty hefty gambling debts, and this guy in San Diego offered me a lot of money. All I had to do was receive the shipments, store them for a while, then transport them further up the coast. He let me keep a certain amount each month."

"Allison got one of her father's old warehouses for us to use. She was the one who first suggested that we should sell some of the stuff ourselves." He paused, clearing his throat.

"Go on." Julia prompted him to continue.

"Allison's father found out what we were doing. He went nuts and ordered us to get out of it and destroy all the evidence. He said it would ruin him if anyone ever found out. Allison came up with the plan to burn down the warehouse. We figured the police would think it was that arsonist guy." He shrugged. "It seemed like a good plan at the time."

Julia snorted in cold disdain. "Was murdering the security guard part of your great plan? How about trying to kill Maggie and me? Did that seem like a good idea at the time, too?"

Danny sighed. "Of course not. Nobody was supposed to get hurt. Things just got so out of control. When Allison and Tom went to set the fire, some homeless guy saw her running away. We weren't that worried about it. He was a lunatic. Even if he told his story to the cops, they probably wouldn't listen to him."

"No, but a hungry, young reporter might." Julia filled in the blanks.

"Right. When they realized that the press was sniffing around, Tom and Eddie went back to the warehouse to take care of the guy. Tom saw him talking to Maggie, and he overreacted, I guess."

"You guess?" Julia shouted at him, her anger spilling over. "Your hired thug gunned a man down in front of her. He damn near killed her too! More than once. She didn't know anything, Danny! Nothing!"

"I'm sorry, Jules. It wasn't supposed to happen like this." He reiterated, backing away from her.

Julia raked her fingers through her hair and glowered at him. She couldn't afford to yell at him too much. She still needed more information from him. She ground her teeth and gestured for him to continue.

"Getting rid of Maggie was Allison's obsession, I swear," Danny said. "Allison fixated on her. Especially after we discovered that Patrick was her brother. Allison and her father thought it was too dangerous to let Maggie go. They were worried that Patrick would contact her and spill everything he knew. Which wasn't much, but it was probably enough to get people asking questions about us."

"Where does Patrick fit into all this? Why him?"

Danny shrugged. "He was an easy target. Eddie found him in the park one night, looking to score drugs. He brought Patrick to me. I flashed a wad of money in front of him and offered him a job. Simple." He shrugged again. "Patrick was our insurance policy. If we had to, we could pin the fire and the shooting on him. Once the cops and the media hear the word 'junkie,' they don't look too hard for another motive."

"Can you prove any of this?"

He nodded and pointed to his car. "My laptop is in the trunk. There are copies of e-mail messages between Allison and me. She mentions the fire in one of them, and says something about 'taking care of the reporter'. That should be enough to take to the cops."

"I tried to get into your laptop at the house yesterday," Julia said. "I couldn't get past your password."

Danny gave her a sad smile. "You didn't think about it hard enough then. It's 'cardinal'."

Julia shook her head, unable to believe she had not thought of that. It made perfect sense. The Stanford graduate, whose athletic dreams were dashed by a bad knee, had chosen the university mascot as his password. Julia wanted to slap herself in the head for not figuring it out sooner.

"I'll get the laptop," Danny said.

He started to walk away, and Julia followed him back into the parking lot. The sun had risen, and she squinted into the glare, momentarily blinded by the light. She wanted to ask him why he had decided to help her. So far, he hadn't asked for anything in return, and that bothered her. As Julia opened her mouth to speak, a blur of motion caught her eye. Fear crawled down her throat and settled in the pit of her stomach as she spotted a car that was bearing down on them much too fast. She watched, paralyzed, unable to make a sound. At the last second, she realized that the driver intended to run them both down.

"Oh, shit!" She cried out.

She threw Danny to her left and dove in the opposite direction. She landed on the asphalt with a bone-rattling crash and rolled towards the sidewalk. The car screeched to a halt a few feet away. Ignoring the hot, coppery taste of blood that filled her mouth, Julia scrambled to her knees. The palms of her hands were scraped raw, and she winced in pain. She couldn't see Danny from her current angle, and she wondered if he was all right. It hadn't sounded like the car had hit anything. Julia heard Maggie calling her name and realized that she had ignored directions and left the truck. From her position, she couldn't see Maggie either. The car stood between them.

Four car doors flew open simultaneously. As she struggled to rise, Julia heard Maggie's strangled cry. The next sound she heard was an ominous click as someone cocked back the hammer of a gun. Three-inch heels stopped in front of her, and she looked up to find Allison Davis standing over her. Allison smiled and pressed the barrel of her gun against Julia's forehead.

"Get up." She commanded.

Julia stood slowly. A brief wave of dizziness engulfed her, but she clenched her teeth and fought through it. She could see her truck over the roof of Allison's car. Her heart sank. As she had suspected, Maggie was not in the driver's seat. Instead, she was standing halfway between the truck and the car. One of Allison's beefy goons had his arm around her throat.

"Julia?" Maggie called out, struggling against her captor.

"It's okay, Maggie. I'm fine." Julia replied, trying to stay calm.

Allison laughed. "Oh, that is just so sweet!"

With difficulty, Julia tore her gaze away from Maggie and glared at her own tormentor. Allison's eyes were glassy and bright. She seemed oblivious to the electric blue daggers shooting from her captive's eyes. Julia let a low growl escape from her throat.

"Stop that." Allison wagged a finger at her. "You don't scare me, Julia. As long as poor, little Maggie is in danger, you're going to do exactly as I say."

Allison was right. Julia fumed as she tried to come up with a plan. A pained groan to her left grabbed her attention, and she focused her gaze on a scene over Allison's shoulder. Two other men were roughly hauling Danny to his feet and dragging him towards the car. Danny was bruised and bleeding from a gash on his cheek, but he did not appear seriously injured. The men threw him to the ground beside Julia, and she heard a sharp crack as his wrist snapped. He whimpered, cradling his hand against his chest. Allison pushed Julia back a step and leveled her gun at both of them.

"You've been a naughty boy. Haven't you, Danny?" She gave him a cold smile.

Julia's hands twitched, and Allison's gaze instantly flicked toward her. "I wouldn't try it, if I were you." She confided, speaking in a conspiratorial whisper. "You'll be dead before you take a step."

"What do you want, Allison?" Julia demanded, trying to buy some time.

"Don't be dense, Julia." Allison shook her head. "You know what I want."

Cars slowed as they drove past the parking lot entrance, and drivers peered at them curiously. Julia wondered if any of them had a clear view of what was going on. She hoped at least one of them had the sense to call the police. So far, Patrick had not been discovered in the back of her truck, and she wondered if she could use that to her advantage somehow. She prayed he wasn't stupid enough to try something on his own.

Allison snapped her fingers in front of Julia's nose. Irritated, she flung a lock of long, blonde hair away from her face.

"Hey! Pay attention!" Allison smiled when she realized she had Julia's attention again. "That's better. Now, where were we?"

"Oh, yeah." The smile disappeared. "Rumor has it that someone gave you a file filled with all sorts of nasty lies about me. I want it."

"I don't know what you're talking about." In a heartbeat, Allison closed the distance between them. She seized a handful of Julia's hair and yanked her head back. She shoved the gun beneath Julia's chin. Her eyes flashed dangerously.

"Don't play games with me, Julia." Allison warned her. "Give me what I want. Or my friend will rip your girlfriend's pretty blonde head off. And we wouldn't want that, now would we?"

"No. We wouldn't." Julia answered through clenched teeth.

Allison released her hair and patted the top of her head. "Good girl."

"Julia, don't give her anything." Danny spat, his voice laced with pain. One of Allison's men kicked him in the ribs, and he groaned.

"She's going to kill us all, anyway. Don't give it to her." He repeated.

A mad giggle leaked out from between Allison's parted lips. She shrugged at Julia and grinned.

"He's right, you know. You're all going to die. But if you don't give me that file, I will make sure that Maggie has a slow, painful death. And you'll get a front row seat."

Julia's muscles twitched as a surge of adrenaline rushed through her. She had to make a move soon, or she would lose the chance. Could she overpower Allison before she had time to fire the gun? Julia considered the odds. It was a huge gamble, but she didn't see another option. Allison's thugs would jump in to help her. Maggie was smart and stronger than she looked, and there was a chance that Maggie could get away from her captor in the chaos. All she had to do was break free long enough to make a dash for the truck. Briefly, Julia's eyes darted to the two men looming over Danny. Neither of them appeared to be armed, and judging from their considerable bulk, she was fairly certain that she could outrun them, if things got that far.

It wasn't a good plan. Julia knew that. It was a plan that would almost certainly end in her death. However, it was the only plan she had. Looking past Allison, she caught Maggie's eye. Instead of the expected fear, she saw anger and fierce determination there. Julia smiled, filled with quiet pride. Maggie was tough. She would survive.

The green eyes widened, and Julia sensed that Maggie knew what she was planning. She gave her lover a miniscule shrug and a quirky, lopsided grin. Love poured from her eyes as she mouthed a silent "I love you." Maggie shook her head and struggled to free herself.

When Julia returned her attention to Allison, the loving grin had been replaced by a cocky, ferocious smirk. Allison's eyes narrowed. Julia was poised for the attack. She envisioned her muscles coiling up, ready to spring into action. A deep, humorless chuckle bubbled up from her throat.

"What the fuck are you laughing at?" Allison demanded.

Julia grinned at her, baring her teeth. "You," she replied.

She kept her vision focused on the gun. Get the gun. Keep Allison and her goons occupied long enough to give Maggie a chance. Those were her goals. She exhaled, letting the nervousness seep from her body. She started to move.

The wind had picked up, blowing a thick blanket of clouds across the sun. A low rumble of thunder rolled in from the Pacific. Fat raindrops darkened the concrete, sporadically at first, then steadily as the downpour intensified. The stiff breeze thinned the fog and sent wispy tendrils swirling around the legs of the people standing near the Golden Gate Bridge.

Julia had been about to pounce on her captor when an unexpected noise stopped her. Horrified, she watched as Patrick McKinnon barreled around the back of her truck. A rabid yell tore loose from his throat as he flung himself at the man holding his sister hostage. Julia tried to call out a warning, but the words got stuck. A feeling of helplessness washed over her as Allison whirled around, gun in hand, and took aim.

In the mere seconds that Allison's back was turned, Julia realized that this was the opportunity she had been waiting for. Her vision tunneled until all she could see was the murderous socialite in front of her. Gathering her resolve, Julia lunged forward and seized Allison's arm. The gun fired. The two women tumbled to the ground in a tangle of arms and legs. Julia's hand was clamped around Allison's slim wrist, and she viciously slammed the other woman's hand against the asphalt. Shouts of alarm mingled with Maggie's scream, though Julia scarcely heard any of it. Everything sounded as if it were being filtered through a thick layer of cotton.

Allison's thugs regained their senses and reacted to their employer's plight. Julia heard an angry snarl, and she kicked out instinctively as rough hands grabbed at her. Her assailant crumpled

261

with a groan after she landed a hard blow to his midsection. She had no time to wonder where her other attackers were. Allison's long fingernails were digging into her back, and the blonde's shrill, piercing shrieks assaulted her ears.

"You are so fucking dead!" Allison screamed as she tried to free herself. "All of you are so fucking dead!"

The sound of a nearby struggle captured Julia's attention, and grunts and groans told her that Danny was fighting with a second goon. A thousand thoughts competed for dominance in her mind. She wanted to help Danny, but she already had her hands full with the writhing, squirming woman pinned beneath her. Julia's hand was growing slick with sweat and rain, and the muscles in her arms and shoulders trembled from the strain. Her concentration was starting to slip. Then, Maggie's voice cut through the haze. She was yelling wildly, though she sounded more enraged than frightened. That was all Julia needed to regain her focus.

A primal growl started deep in her chest. With a full-throated roar, Julia hammered the heel of her free hand against Allison's nose. She grunted in satisfaction at the wet crunch. Allison howled in pain, and her grip on the gun loosened. Crying out in triumph, Julia ripped the weapon free and rolled out of reach. Keeping the gun trained on Allison, she bounded to her feet.

"Maggie?" She called out anxiously, fearing the worst.

Her eyes widened in shock. Several yards away, Maggie had somehow managed to overpower her captor, and she was pummeling him like a woman possessed. Fire blazed from her eyes as blow after blow rained down upon the semi-conscious man. Nearby, Patrick was lying in a slowly growing pool of blood.

"Oh my God." Julia took a tentative step towards them.

"Maggie? You can stop now. It's over. He's now going anywhere."

Maggie's head turned at the sound of Julia's voice. She met Julia with a blank, uncomprehending stare. She looked down at the man at her feet and blinked slowly, as if she didn't understand what was happening. A few feet away, Patrick twitched. Maggie's gaze flew to her fallen brother, and the color drained from her face as comprehension overwhelmed her.

"Patrick's hurt," she said in a small voice. She took a faltering step towards her brother.

Julia was torn by indecision. Maggie needed her, but she knew that she could not turn her back on Allison. The blonde was still writhing on the ground and clutching at her broken nose.

"Julia, give me the gun. I'll keep an eye on them."

A soft voice to her left startled her. Despite his fractured arm, Danny had been able to subdue their other assailant. He stood off to the side, his wide eyes fixed on Patrick's still form. Without looking at Julia, he held his hand out.

Blue eyes narrowed into thin slits as Julia debated whether or not to trust him. A flicker of motion drew her gaze away. Maggie had stumbled to her brother's side and dropped to her knees next to him. She cradled his head in her lap and desperately searched for the source of the blood. Julia made her decision. She handed the gun to Danny.

"Don't even think about trying anything." She wasn't sure if her growled warning was for him or for Allison.

Danny adjusted his grip on the gun and shifted to a better position. He kept Allison and her two employees in front of him, and his finger twitched nervously on the trigger. Julia hesitated just long enough to make sure that he had the situation under control. Danny gave her a grim smile and nodded.

Satisfied, Julia dashed around them and stumbled to a halt at Maggie's side. Her throat constricted painfully at the sight of Maggie's tear-streaked face. Swallowing her own tears, Julia crouched and took Patrick's wrist in her hand. She closed her eyes and sighed in relief. His pulse still throbbed weakly beneath her fingertips.

"I can't stop the bleeding," Maggie said, her voice hollow.

Gently, Julia pried her hands away. She shuddered as she tried not to look at the blood that stained them. Maggie made a tiny, mewling sound of protest, but Julia shushed her quietly as she examined the Patrick's wound. The bullet had struck him just below his left shoulder, and he was bleeding profusely. She turned him over carefully and checked his back. She found the exit wound and nodded to herself. She was fairly sure that was good. Patrick's eyes fluttered open.

"Ouch." He struggled to rise, but Julia held him down firmly.

"Keep still. You're gonna be fine."

Dazed, he blinked at her. "Maggie?"

"It's okay, Patrick. I'm right here. Everything is okay." Maggie soothed him.

Leaning down, she kissed the top of his head. The simple, heartfelt gesture made Julia's heart ache. Though she didn't much care for her lover's younger brother, she knew that Maggie loved him deeply. In spite of everything he had put them through, forgiveness and worry shone from green eyes that sparkled with tears. Maggie smoothed his damp hair back with the palm of her hand, leaving reddish-brown streaks behind.

"What did you think you were doing, anyway?" She asked him. He shrugged. "I couldn't let them hurt you. I couldn't forgive myself if anything happened to you, Mags." He wheezed, his breath coming in short gasps.

Maggie shook her head at him as tears rolled down her cheeks. "Hush. We'll talk later. Just rest for now."

His eyes rolled back in his head, and he fell unconscious again.

Sirens wailed in the distance, their screams growing nearer by the second, and Julia hoped that the police were on the way. She was dimly aware of the traffic slowing near the bridge as drivers slowed to gawk at them. She cast a quick glance over her shoulder to check on Danny. She frowned, and dark eyebrows knit together in concern.

Allison had regained her feet and she seemed to be whispering to Danny. Julia was too far away to hear the words, but she could tell that they were agitating him. As she watched, his angry scowl deepened. He swung the gun back and forth in a wide arc, covering all three of his charges. Allison threw her head back and laughed. The harsh, grating sound chilled Julia's blood, and the hairs on the back of her neck prickled. Her stomach churned and tightened. She stood slowly.

"Julia? What's wrong?" Maggie asked, looking up at her quizzically.

Julia cast a troubled glance at her. "I'm not sure. I'm getting a very bad feeling about this."

Chaos broke loose as soon as the words left her mouth. Julia felt like she was watching a movie unfold in extreme slow motion. She shouted a warning, but it was too late. Acting in unison, both of Allison's thugs lunged at Danny. He stumbled backwards, and his finger jerked reflexively on the trigger. The gun fired harmlessly into the air. The two hulking men fell on him, and he lost his grip on the weapon. It tumbled from his hand and skittered across the pavement, finally coming to rest against the front tire of Allison's car. Allison's gaze followed its path, and her eyes glowed brightly.

Julia cursed under her breath and sprinted towards the scene. She flew around the front of the car and tackled Allison as she reached for the gun. This time, Allison was ready for her. She stumbled but did not fall. Julia sucked in a sharp breath. Allison looked nothing like the haughty socialite that she remembered. Dried blood encrusted her upper lip, and her nose was purple and swollen. Another dark bruise marred her pale cheek. Her sunken, glassy eyes were evidence of her drug abuse. Allison's gaze darted back and forth from Julia to the gun at her feet. The sirens were drawing ever closer, and Julia could see the

Golden Gate

first set of flashing lights in the distance.

Behind Allison, the two thugs were beating Danny into a bloody pulp. Julia winced in sympathy as one landed a savage blow to her old friend's kidneys. She couldn't help him at the moment. She kept her attention focused on the twitching blonde in front of her. Allison seemed to have realized that the police were quickly closing in. Her head whipped around wildly as she searched for an escape route. For a moment, Julia thought she was going to try to run. She shook her dark head. There was nowhere for Allison to go.

"Forget it, Allison. It's over. You lost," she said.

The sirens were deafening now. Two squad cars screeched to a halt on the bridge, while three others sped into the parking lot from the other direction. Car doors flew open, and uniformed officers crouched behind them with their guns drawn.

"Nobody move! Everyone get your hands up!" An officer shouted through a bullhorn.

Julia complied, lifting her hands to shoulder-height to prove that she was unarmed. The two goons that were pounding Danny stopped, as well. They backed away, leaving him unconscious on the ground. Julia darted a quick glance over her shoulder. Maggie still had Patrick cradled in her lap, and she seemed oblivious to the police officers that surrounded them.

A soft laugh from Allison recaptured her attention. She met the blonde woman's eyes and noted the hunted look in them. Julia frowned at her, wondering what was going through Allison's head.

"Daddy's going to be very angry with me." Allison confided in her. She giggled quietly and pressed her finger to her lips.

"Shhh. Don't tell him. I've been a bad girl."

"Allison," Julia began. She was cut off before she could finish.

Ignoring the shouted warnings from the police, Allison took a step towards Julia. She leaned in closer and lowered her voice to a mere whisper. Julia could see the madness that glinted in her eyes, and she felt a momentary pang of sympathy.

"I have to hide so he won't find me."

Before anyone could stop her, Allison turned and bolted for the bridge. Cursing, Julia gave chase and hoped that the police wouldn't shoot. Allison was fast, and Julia felt the burn in her legs as she tried to catch up. She grabbed for the fleeing woman's arm. Her fingertips brushed the edge of Allison's sleeve, but she could not maintain her grip. Sickened, she watched as Allison dashed towards the edge. A warning shot rang out, but the blonde ignored it as she picked up speed. Two police officers were pursuing them now, but she had too much of

265

a head start. As she neared the rail, she shouted over her shoulder. The wind carried her voice back to Julia.

"You're wrong, Julia! I win!"

She was still laughing as she threw herself over the side. For a brief instant, she hung, suspended in mid-air. Her arms and legs flailed, and her long blonde hair swirled around her face. Then she was gone, plummeting into the Bay below.

Julia squeezed her eyes shut. This was not how she had wanted things to end. She wondered if she had done the right thing by coming out here without back up. If she had called Henry and told him everything, it might have turned out differently. She knew she would never forget the look in Allison Davis's eyes just before her mad dash towards her death. Nor would she ever forget the sight of blood covering Maggie's hands. Bloodshed that might have been avoided if she hadn't been so stubborn, she realized bitterly.

"Ma'am?"

Fingers snapped abruptly in front of her face. Julia's eyes flew open, and she found herself staring at a concerned young officer. He scanned her carefully, looking for signs of injury.

"Are you all right, ma'am?" He asked again.

Julia nodded slowly. "I'm fine."

An ambulance had arrived on the scene, and two paramedics were tending to Patrick. He slipped in and out of consciousness as they loaded him into the vehicle. Maggie hesitated, looking back at Julia. 'Go.' Julia mouthed to her. She would follow Maggie to the hospital as soon as she could. Maggie gave her a sad, grateful smile as she climbed into the back of the ambulance. A police officer shut the rear doors, and the vehicle sped away.

The young officer was talking to her again, and Julia blinked. She tried to listen to what he was saying. He mentioned Henry's name, and that got her attention. She shook her head.

"Wait. What was that?" She asked.

The officer sighed impatiently. "Inspector Chow got an anonymous tip. Someone called to warn him about a threat against your life. When we got the call about an incident on the bridge, somehow he knew it was you."

"Oh." It was all she could think to say. She wondered if her father had called with the tip.

"We need to ask you a few questions about what happened here," the officer said.

A scowl darkened Julia's face. The shock was fading and she was beginning to feel like herself again. Maggie would need her, and she didn't feel like wasting her time answering a bunch of pointless questions. Behind her, Danny moaned. She turned in time to witness a pair of officers gingerly tending to his wounds. A third policeman stood over them and read Danny his Miranda rights.

"Is he going to be okay?" She called out.

One of the officers looked up at her. "We think so," he answered. "Another ambulance is on its way for him."

"Good. I have a few things to settle with him, too."

"Ma'am?"

Slowly and deliberately, Julia turned her head and pinned the young officer with a piercing stare. She gave him a fierce grin and chuckled silently at his hard, nervous swallow.

"Don't call me that," she said.

"I need to meet my friend at the hospital. Once we get there, you can ask all the questions you want."

Since Maggie still had the keys to her truck, Julia took a few steps towards one of the parked patrol cars. Backpedaling furiously, the officer stayed in front of her. He held his hands out.

"Wait! You can't just..."

His protests died in his throat as she fixed him with an even harder glare. She arched an eyebrow, waiting for him to continue his argument. Nothing was going to stop her from meeting up with Maggie.

"Never mind," he muttered.

He waved at one of his fellow officers and pointed to Julia's back. "I'm going to escort her to the hospital."

Erin Jennifer Mar

Chapter Twenty-Four

They arrived at the emergency room in record time, and Julia jumped out of the car before it had stopped moving. Breathlessly, she dashed through the doors and searched the crowded waiting room for a familiar face. Relief flooded over her as she spotted two. In the far corner, Henry and Maggie were sitting together. Henry saw her first. He nudged the exhausted woman beside him and pointed. Maggie's eyes lit up and she met Julia halfway across the room.

Oblivious to the crowd around them, they embraced. A lump rose in Julia's throat as she pressed her cheek against the top of Maggie's head. She wrapped her arms around the trembling blonde and held her tightly. Maggie choked back a sob, and Julia felt hot tears stinging her own eyes.

"Are you okay?" She asked.

Maggie nodded. "I'm fine."

"God, Maggie. When I heard that shot, I thought…"

"Don't Julia. Not right now. Please."

Julia sighed. They would have plenty of time to talk later. Right now, she realized, Maggie was desperately worried about her brother.

"How is he?" Julia asked.

"They're working on him now. I don't know." Maggie buried her face into Julia's shoulder.

Julia guided her back over to the corner, and Henry scooted over to make room on the worn couch. She sank down on it. The events of the morning had drained her physically, mentally and emotionally. She caught the stern look in Henry's eyes and shook her head at him. The lecture could wait until later. He nodded and unwrapped a stick of gum.

Maggie was leaning against her heavily, and Julia kept her arm securely around her shoulders. She was glad to see that Maggie had washed the worst of the blood from her hands, though rust-colored stains still streaked her clothing. They sat together in silence. Both Julia and Maggie were too tired and emotional to speak, and Henry had

269

enough sense not to pester them. Twenty minutes passed before a doctor came out to speak with them. Patrick was on his way to surgery, but the prognosis looked good.

"See? I told you everything would be all right," Henry said after the doctor had left.

"I guess I should have listened you." Maggie smiled at him through tears of relief. She stood. "I need to go wash my face. I must look awful."

Julia rose as well. "Do you want me to go with you?"

Maggie caught the almost imperceptible shake of Henry's head. She smiled at Julia and patted her arm.

"Thanks, but I think I can manage. I'll be back in a few minutes."

Julia watched as Maggie disappeared down the corridor. She turned to Henry and waited expectantly.

"Well?"

"Well what?" Henry echoed her.

She glared at him. She was at the edges of her patience and she had no desire to play games with him. Henry seemed to sense her growing irritation and he relented. He stood and pointed to a door that led out to a small balcony.

"Let's go outside. We need to talk, and I'm dying for a cigarette."

Wordlessly, Julia followed him outside and waited while he fumbled through his pockets. They kept their backs pressed to the wall, careful to stay beneath the overhang. Silently, they watched the rain continue to pour from the sky. Henry took a long drag on his cigarette.

"I thought you quit smoking," Julia said, breaking the silence.

"I did." Henry returned. He rubbed his palm across his bristling scalp.

"Councilman Davis is gone."

Julia blinked, letting the words penetrate her brain. A dozen different emotions, ranging from rage to relief, washed over her. She raked her fingers through her damp, tangled hair.

"We sent a car to his house and to his office," Henry continued. "Both came up empty. He's probably halfway to Mexico by now."

He paused and cleared his throat delicately. "Jules, I don't exactly know how to say this. I think that someone tipped him off and he ran."

"And you think it was my father." Julia finished for him.

"Yeah, I do. What do you want me to do, Julia? Should I bring him in for questioning?"

270

Julia thought for a moment, remembering her promise to her father. She doubted that he had warned the councilman. When they had last spoken, he had seemed eager to get as far away from this situation as he could. It was more likely that Martin Davis had seen the signs, and he had simply disappeared before he could be held accountable. Shrugging her shoulders, she glanced sideways at her waiting friend.

"Leave my dad alone. He isn't involved in this."

Both of Henry's eyebrows shot up in surprise. He dropped his cigarette and crushed it out beneath his shoe. Finally, he nodded.

"Okay. If that's what you want. I'll probably still have to ask him a few basic questions, but I'll keep the gloves on." He hesitated, searching Julia's face. "I hope you know what you're doing. Martin Davis could still be a dangerous man."

Julia had no response. Henry was right; the councilman was still a threat. A light tap on the door rescued her and she turned. Maggie had returned from the bathroom. Julia smiled at her through the glass and reached for the door handle.

"Hey, Jules." Henry stopped her. He grinned at her and nodded towards Maggie. "Hang on to this one. She's good for you."

Julia laughed softly. "Thanks. I intend to."

She went back into the waiting room and smiled as Maggie took her hand. They resumed their seat on the worn, faded couch. While they waited for Patrick to come out of the operating room, Henry took their official statements. When he was done, he excused himself and went to the nurse's station to use the phone.

Maggie squeezed Julia's hand gently. "It's hard to believe that it's all finally over."

Uncertainty gnawed at Julia. She didn't want to keep secrets from Maggie, but she didn't want to give her anything else to worry about, either. With Patrick wounded, she had enough to worry about. Her discomfort must have showed on her face, because Maggie's eyes narrowed. Julia knew that she realized something was wrong. She decided to tell her everything.

"Maggie, I have bad news. Martin Davis is missing."

Maggie was quiet for a moment as she absorbed the information. "Do you think he'll come after us?"

Julia sighed. "Ordinarily, I would say no. If he's smart, he'll just get out of the country."

"But?" Maggie prompted her.

"But I'm not sure we're dealing with a rational man. Henry will have every cop in the city keeping his eyes open for him, but he could

271

still be a threat."

Maggie nodded and snuggled closer. "Okay. Then we'll be careful for a little while longer. We're going to get through this, and then we're going to live a normal life together."

Julia smiled faintly. "We are, huh?"

"Yep. I'm tired of all the intrigue and excitement. I just want to have a nice, normal, uneventful life with you."

The words tugged at Julia's heart. She realized that she never wanted to be alone again. Taking a deep breath, she plunged forward and hoped that she wasn't moving too fast. She twisted around so she was looking directly into Maggie's eyes, and she took both of the other woman's hands into her own.

"I never thought I would say this again, but I want that too. I want to spend the rest of my life getting to know you better. Move in with me."

A slow smile lit up Maggie's eyes. "Really?"

Julia smiled back at her. "Really. That way I can keep you out of trouble."

Maggie snorted softly and backhanded Julia in the stomach. "Very funny, Cassinelli. You get into plenty of trouble all by yourself. I should be the one keeping you in line."

"Is that a yes?" Julia asked, hope coloring her voice.

"Yes. Of course. Absolutely. How soon can we start moving my stuff in?"

Julia laughed and pulled her closer. Leaning down, she stole a leisurely kiss. Their bodies melded together, and she nearly forgot they were in the middle of a crowded hospital waiting room.

"Is tomorrow soon enough?" She was dizzy from the combination of euphoria and exhaustion.

"I think I'm free tomorrow," Maggie said.

Her voice sounded drowsy, and Julia noticed that she was struggling to keep her eyes open. She slid her arm around Maggie's shoulders and settled back against the couch. Although it was only mid-morning, it had already been a long day. They were both running on sheer stubbornness and willpower.

"Get some rest, okay?"

"You'll wake me when the doctor comes back, right?"

"Of course I will."

Maggie sighed and fell asleep to the sound of Julia's faint humming. Henry was still leaning against the desk at the nurse's station, and Julia met his gaze. She was more concerned about Martin Davis's whereabouts than she had let on. She had a sinking feeling that they weren't through with this game yet. Maggie murmured something in her sleep, and Julia tightened her arms around her protectively. *'Take your best shot, Davis,'* she whispered silently. *'I'm ready for you this time.'*

****

Golden Gate

Chapter Twenty-Five

"Maggie, wake up. We're home." Julia reached across the front seat to shake her dozing passenger.

Home. Julia rolled the word around on her tongue. It had been a long time since she had thought of her dark, empty house as a home. For years, her house had simply been a place for her to sleep and change her clothes occasionally. Maggie's presence would change all of that, and finally bring some much-needed light into her gloomy residence. Julia allowed herself a tiny, hopeful grin as she parked her truck alongside the curb. She nudged Maggie again.

"C'mon, Maggie. Wake up."

Maggie swatted her hand away and let out a sleepy sigh. "I'm awake already. Quit poking me."

They were both exhausted. All Julia wanted to do was take a long, hot bath and crawl into bed for at least a week. She made a face as she climbed out of her truck. She would be lucky if she managed to sleep for more than a few hours. Maggie would want to be back at the hospital first thing in the morning.

They had spent most of the morning waiting for Patrick to come out of surgery. Maggie had been frantic with worry, and Julia had provided moral support while she called her family and broke the news about Patrick's situation. That had been interesting. After ten minutes of listening to Eileen McKinnon's shrill, accusatory shrieks, Julia had begun to understand why Maggie was reluctant to call her parents.

A few hours later, the doctor had come to inform them that the operation had been successful. Maggie had sobbed with relief. She had insisted upon waiting with Patrick in recovery until he regained consciousness. Finally, late that evening, Julia managed to convince her to leave for a little while. The lure of a hot shower and a soft bed had been more than Maggie could resist. They had promised Patrick that they would return in the morning. To ensure Patrick's safety, Henry had posted two guards outside his room and vowed to stay the night there himself. Julia doubted that Martin Davis would be foolish

275

enough to show up at the hospital, and even if he did, she was confident that Patrick was secure under Henry's watchful eye. The drive to Julia's house had been uneventful, and Maggie had fallen into a light doze almost as soon as the truck started moving.

As she led Maggie up the steps to her front door, Julia glanced over her shoulder at the police escort that had accompanied them home. Despite her half-hearted objections, Henry had insisted upon it. One of the officers waved at her, and Julia lifted a hand to acknowledge him. She was forced to admit that she felt safer knowing that two armed police officers were parked across the street. Fumbling with her keys, she turned back to the door.

"I've got first dibs on the shower." Maggie yawned as she entered the darkened house.

Julia chuckled as she turned on the lamp in the living room. "Fine. Go take your shower. I'm hungry. I think I'll order a pizza."

"Don't forget the extra mushrooms," Maggie called over her shoulder.

"Yeah, yeah. Extra mushrooms," Julia muttered under her breath.

She reached for the phone and called in an order to her favorite pizza place. Upstairs, she could hear the water running, and she considered joining Maggie in the shower. Shaking her head, she dismissed the idea. She needed to listen in case Henry or the hospital called.

Bathed in the warm, muted glow of the lamp, her sofa looked particularly soft and inviting. With a weary groan, Julia collapsed on the buttery leather and threw her arm over her eyes. In the darkness of her mind, she saw Allison, laughing at her. Julia squeezed her eyes shut tighter, but she could not rid herself of the images that played over and over in her head. In excruciating slow motion, she saw Allison running for the edge of the bridge. Her throat constricted as she recalled the soundless way that Allison had plunged to her death. Hot tears burned the backs of her eyelids. Determined not to cry, she clenched her teeth until her jaw trembled. Again, she saw herself reaching for Allison's arm and felt the fabric as it slipped through her outstretched fingers.

Self-doubt seized her and Julia wondered if she had tried hard enough to save her. She rubbed her eyes angrily. 'Stop that,' she told herself. 'Allison Davis was a lunatic. She tried to kill Maggie, and you didn't owe her anything.' The doubts persisted; so Julia turned the television on to silence them. It was time for the evening news, and every channel she flipped through seemed to be showing her picture or

Allison's. Groaning, she hit the mute button.

Outside, the wind was picking up again. Julia went to the window and peered out, scowling at the darkness. She could barely make out the silhouettes of the two figures across the street. Martin Davis wasn't foolish enough to show up at her house, she reminded herself. The police surveillance was just a precaution.

Julia watched as a flurry of dried leaves blew across her walkway. A tree branch scraped against the kitchen window, and she flinched at the unexpected sound. *'Paranoid, much?'* She let out a soft, self-disgusted laugh. She tilted her head up towards the second floor and listened. The shower had stopped, and she smiled, anticipating her turn. Before Maggie returned downstairs, Julia wanted to be certain that the house was secure. She checked the locks on the front door. Both were solid. The back door was bolted, as well, and all of the windows on the first floor were tightly shut. She nodded in satisfaction.

"So, are we all locked in?" Maggie's voice behind her made her jump.

Maggie grinned and reached out to steady her. "Sorry. I didn't mean to startle you like that."

Julia swallowed hard as her pulse thundered in her ears. She didn't want Maggie to sense her nervousness. Taking a deep breath to calm herself, Julia arched and eyebrow and plastered a cocky half-grin across her lips. She gave Maggie a casual shrug.

"You didn't scare me," she insisted. "I just didn't hear you come in. That's all."

"Sorry," Maggie repeated, softly stroking Julia's arm.

Julia gave her a saucy wink. "Don't worry about it. I'll just put a bell around your neck next time." She ducked her head and lightly planted a kiss on the bridge of Maggie's nose. "My turn in the shower."

Maggie accompanied her to the foot of the stairs, and Julia turned, her face serious. She glanced at the door, visually inspecting the locks again. A nagging feeling of uneasiness gnawed at her, and she didn't like leaving Maggie by herself.

"I'll be quick," Julia promised. "I ordered a pizza, but I should be out of the shower before it gets here."

Maggie gave her an understanding smile and gently pushed her towards the stairs. "I'll be fine. Don't worry."

Julia nodded. "I know." She hesitated. "I checked all the locks downstairs. Nobody can get in. Still, if you see or hear anything weird..."

"I'll call the police and come get you," Maggie interrupted.

"Right. Okay." Julia smiled at her. Maggie's calm outer

demeanor was helping to soothe her own fears.

Maggie squeezed her hand reassuringly before wandering into the living room. Julia stood in the entryway, watching her for a moment as Maggie began flipping through the television channels. Maggie seemed to sense the attention, and she looked up quizzically. At a loss for words, Julia struggled to find something to say. The memory of Patrick in a pool of blood popped into her mind. It easily could have been Maggie lying there, she realized. She suppressed a shudder. Maggie had enough to worry about without dealing with her trauma on top of it, Julia thought.

"I love you," she said.

"I love you too, Julia." Maggie stopped and peered at her more closely. Her forehead wrinkled in concern. "Is everything okay? Did something happen while I was upstairs?"

Julia shook her head and gave her a weak smile. "No. Everything's fine. I'm just tired, I guess."

Maggie frowned and took a step forward. "Are you sure?"

Julia waved her off and started climbing the stairs. "Positive. I'll be back in a few minutes."

Pretending not to notice the deep concern in Maggie's eyes, Julia continued up the stairs and into her bedroom. She paused in the darkness, gathering herself while she kicked off her shoes. She was not going to have a nervous breakdown. Not now, when Maggie still needed her to be strong. Resolutely, Julia pushed her own doubts and fears aside. She would deal with all of that later, she promised herself. She crossed the bedroom to her half-open armoire and began pulling out a fresh set of clothes. As she rummaged through a drawer and searched for a pair of matching socks, a cold breeze hit the back of her neck. She straightened, her shoulders stiffening.

Julia whirled around. Her bedroom window was open, and the curtains were fluttering in the wind. Her stomach tightened and every nerve ending stood at attention as she approached the open window. She knew that she hadn't left it ajar, and she wondered if Maggie had opened it while she was upstairs. Carefully, Julia parted the curtains and poked her head outside. She scanned the ground below, paying particular interest to the thick hedges that separated her house from her neighbor's. A man could easily hide in the dense growth unnoticed. She saw nothing. She was just being overly paranoid, she told herself. She glanced at the tall oak outside her window. It was a difficult tree to climb, but not impossible. A thick, sturdy branch stretched along the side of the house --- just close enough to possibly provide access to her window.

The back of her neck prickled, and she was sure that a pair of malevolent eyes was boring into her. Slowly, she turned. The empty bedroom mocked her, and she frowned. She moved out to the hallway and started towards the door to her office. It was closed, which was odd. Julia rarely kept her office door closed unless she had company. She glanced over the rail and saw Maggie, sitting on the sofa, absorbed in a television show. Maggie didn't see her, and Julia didn't want to draw her attention yet. She thought about the police across the street and wondered how quickly they could respond, if needed.

On bare feet, Julia silently crept towards her office. She turned the knob slowly and pushed the door open a tiny crack. She waited for several long heartbeats, half-expecting someone to yank the door open from the other side. She was met by silence. Steeling herself, she widened the crack until she could peek inside the room. Inky blackness enveloped her as she took a step inside the office. Her fingers scrabbled along the wall as she felt for the light switch, and she wondered what had possessed her to adorn every window in her house with such heavy drapes. Finally, she felt the cool plastic switch beneath her fingertips, and she flipped it up with a flick of her wrist. The room stayed dark. The soft creak of leather alerted her that someone had just risen from her chair.

"Oh, shit," Julia breathed.

She half-turned, intending to warn Maggie. In the darkness, she heard her chair rolling across the floor. Unseen, someone was rushing at her, and she had little time to react before Councilman Martin Davis charged into view. His face was twisted into a hateful mask, and Julia braced herself for the impact as he slammed into her. She tumbled backwards to the hardwood floor with a loud crash. The jarring blow forced the air from her lungs and lights exploded in front of her eyes. Julia blinked rapidly to focus her vision. She had to tell Maggie to get out of the house.

The snarling councilman threw himself upon her. Seizing her collar, he lifted her head and slammed her back down against the floor. Julia pushed the heel of her hand beneath his chin and tried to shove him away, but he was too heavy. He straddled her, pinning her down, and wrapped his massive hands around her throat. Leaning down, he whispered into her ear, his voice dripping with venom.

"You murdered my daughter, you little bitch! Did you really think I would let you get away with that?"

He pounded her against the floor again, and Julia saw the madness dancing in his eyes. "I won't let you ruin me! I'll kill you! You and your little whore!"

Julia felt like her head was a balloon that was about to pop, and her chest burned from lack of oxygen. Desperate, she raked her fingernails across the councilman's cheek. He hissed in pain as she drew blood, but his grip on her did not loosen. Julia turned her head to the side as her vision began to dim. Her eyes widened. Maggie was standing halfway up the stairs, staring at them in horror. Julia tried to call out to her and tell her to run, but she couldn't utter a sound through the councilman's stranglehold.

Maggie seemed to snap out of her trance, and she raced up the stairs toward them. Fury shone in her eyes, and Julia recognized the look. Maggie had that on the bridge, after Patrick was shot. The same animal intensity had burned in her eyes when she attacked the thug who had been holding her hostage.

"Get your hands off her, you son of a bitch!" Maggie screamed.

Martin looked up at the sound of her cry. His lips twisted into a vicious sneer and a chilling laugh burst forth from his throat. Hatred and anger seemed to flow from every pore as he stared at her. He trembled with rage, and Julia could see the vein pulsating in his forehead. She focused on it and willed herself to stay conscious.

"You." Martin growled at Maggie through clenched teeth. "I'll make you wish you had never laid eyes on my Allison."

His crushing grip on Julia's throat slackened slightly. It was enough. Julia felt a fresh surge of adrenaline rush through her bloodstream. She kicked out with her legs, throwing the councilman off balance. She closed her hand into a tight fist and jabbed hard, aiming for the base of his throat. Choking and gagging, he fell away. Julia scrambled out from beneath him and stood, using the wall to support her. Her head spun, but she shook the dizziness away.

Maggie was hesitating on the landing. Julia saw the look in Martin's eyes, and she knew that he was going after Maggie next. With a roar, he lunged for the paralyzed blonde. Julia caught him around his waist and pushed him sideways, ignoring the painful wrench in her shoulder. Martin grabbed hold of her wrist and dragged her with him as he stumbled toward the railing. Surprise and sudden comprehension dawned on his face as he tumbled backwards over the top of the rail. His fingers were still clamped around Julia's wrist, and she felt like her arm was about to be ripped off. She braced her other arm against the rail and felt the wood pressing into her ribs as she was pulled forward. She was losing her balance. Grimly, she dug her nails into Martin's hand, forcing him to let go. With an agonized cry, he fell. He hit the floor below with a loud thud.

Julia was dimly aware of the strong arms around her waist,

anchoring her. Gasping for air, she slumped to the floor. Her vision flickered and she blinked dazedly as Maggie hovered over her. She felt a gentle hand tilt her chin up, and then worried green eyes were peering into hers.

"Julia? Are you okay?" Maggie asked. Her voice sounded very far away.

"I thought I was going over, too," Julia croaked.

"I wasn't going to let you fall," Maggie said.

Hot tears splashed on her face, and she realized that Maggie was crying. She reached up to caress Maggie's cheek.

"I'm okay," she said. She gave Maggie a weak grin. "Think we should go tell the cops we took care of everything?"

Maggie smiled back at her. "Probably."

Julia started to rise, but Maggie pushed her back down. "Shhh. Stay there. I'll get the police."

Julia cast a doubtful glance over her shoulder. Martin Davis had landed on his back and his leg was bent at an unnatural angle. He appeared to be unconscious, and Julia couldn't tell if he had survived the fall. She narrowed her eyes until she could see the faint rise and fall of his chest.

"He's still alive." Julia jerked her head toward him.

Maggie glanced at him. "He's not going anywhere. Don't move. I'll go yell for the cops."

Maggie kissed her lightly before hurrying down the stairs. Julia heard her open the door, and she tried not to laugh at the indignation in Maggie's voice as she summoned the officers across the street. Julia leaned her head back against the rail and shut her eyes. She was strangely light-headed --- almost giddy with relief. Allison was dead. Martin was lying unconscious at the bottom of the stairs. It was all finally over.

Maggie was scolding the inattentive police officers as they hurried over to the house, and Julia smiled. When she had answered Danny's call about a break-in at his business, she'd had no idea that her life was about to change forever. Julia opened her eyes again as Maggie dashed back up the stairs to her side.

"An ambulance is on the way. I'm going to call Henry and have him get you a room in between Catherine and Patrick," Maggie joked lightly.

"I wouldn't change a thing," Julia mumbled.

Maggie tilted her head in confusion. "What?"

"If we had the chance to go back and do this all again, I wouldn't change a thing."

"Oh." Maggie sat down next to her. She slipped her arm around Julia's shoulders and pulled the dark head towards her. "I wouldn't change anything either."

"Really?" Julia asked in wonder.

Maggie paused. "Well, maybe I would change a few things. But definitely not the part when I met you."

Julia was silent. She heard the police moving about downstairs, and an unfamiliar voice asked her if she was all right. She mumbled an incoherent answer. She was too tired to think. She didn't know how many minutes passed before she heard the ambulance wailing in the distance. It was a sound she'd heard too many times in the last few weeks, and one she never wanted to hear again. Suddenly, Julia realized that the siren's scream had been replaced by another slightly off-key sound.

"Maggie?"

"Hmm?"

"My head hurts. Please don't sing."

Maggie laughed, and Julia felt the vibration beneath her cheek. She smiled. The rest of the world fell away as Julia listened to the sound of Maggie's heart beating beneath her ear. A last thought drifted through her exhausted mind before she fell asleep. Maggie loved her, and everything was going to be just fine.

****

Epilogue

Two weeks later, Julia stood on her front porch and watched while Maggie and Henry loaded two sets of duffel bags into the back of her truck. Indolently, she leaned against the doorframe and stuck her tongue out at Henry as he shot her a dirty look. He rolled his eyes in her direction.

"It's been two weeks, Jules." Henry reminded her. "I think you're perfectly capable of loading your own luggage. How long are you planning on milking this concussion thing?"

Julia shrugged and grinned at him. She refused to admit it out loud, but she was enjoying being pampered. Maggie came around the back of the truck and backhanded Henry in the stomach.

"Leave her alone. She's still recovering," Maggie said. She winked at him as she headed up the walkway to join Julia on the porch.

Henry rolled his eyes again and shook his head. "Whatever."

He settled the small ice chest in the back of the truck and slammed the hatch shut. Turning, he leaned against the rear bumper and watched the two women in front of the house. Julia had her back against the doorframe and her arms wrapped around the waist of the smaller blonde. They both looked more relaxed than he had ever seen them. He let out an envious sigh. Henry was happy for them, and he had to admit that they deserved a long weekend away after everything they had been through.

Both Catherine and Patrick had been released from the hospital. They were expected to make full physical recoveries. Patrick was temporarily living with Henry until Councilman Davis's trial was over. The district attorney still hadn't decided whether or not to file charges against Maggie's younger brother. Henry suspected that Patrick would be allowed to return home to Ohio, as long as he promised to complete a rehabilitation program. To his credit, Patrick seemed to be serious about putting his life back together, and Henry hoped that would hold true, for Maggie's sake.

Martin Davis was still in the hospital, recuperating from his injuries. His attorney's were trying to claim that the councilman had been driven temporarily insane after his daughter's death. Though she suspected it was simply a ploy, Julia couldn't argue with the tactic. She had seen the madness in Martin's eyes.

Danny Webber was cooperating with the D.A.'s office, and he had cut himself a deal to reduce his jail time. With his testimony, plus the physical evidence, Henry was certain that the councilman would be going away for a very long time. He had already volunteered to drive Martin up to the state prison in Sacramento himself.

"I don't think this is fair," Henry declared. "I still have to go to work while the two of you head off for a beach vacation."

"It's one of the benefits of being your own boss." Julia told him.

"Whatever," he repeated. "Maybe I should become a private investigator. How about it, Jules? Are you looking for a partner?"

Without looking at him, Julia shook her head. She was lost in the jade green depths in front of her. "Nah. I've already got a partner."

Maggie turned around and giggled at him. "Besides, it's not like you're going to be working every second. Jessica told me that you guys hit it off. She said something about a date, too. That's tonight, isn't it?"

Henry flushed, turning beet-red to the roots of his crew cut. "Maybe."

Chuckling deep in her chest, Julia shut the front door and locked it. She took Maggie's hand and led the way down to the curb. Smirking wickedly, she playfully punched her oldest friend in the shoulder.

"Behave yourself tonight," she advised him.

Henry's blush deepened, and he cleared his throat awkwardly. "I'll try to remember that. Get out of here, would ya? Have a good time."

"We will." Julia's smirk broadened. She sobered and handed him a piece of paper with a phone number written on it. "That's where you can reach us. If anything goes wrong with Davis or Patrick, or anything..."

"I'll call you." Henry assured her. "But I doubt that I'll have to. Everything is gonna be fine. Don't worry about us."

Julia nodded. "Okay, then."

She moved around to the driver's side of the truck while Maggie climbed into her seat. Henry stepped back from the curb as they pulled away. He lifted his hand to wave as Maggie rolled down her window and poked her head out.

"See ya in a few days, Henry. Say hi to Jess for me."

Henry waited until they had turned the corner and driven out of sight. He checked his watch. His lunch hour was over, and he sighed as he headed to his car and went back to work.

****

As it traveled along a winding, treacherous stretch of Highway 101, the metallic blue SUV hugged the tight curve. In some areas, tall eucalyptus trees lined the road. In others, there was nothing but a sheer cliff between the vehicle and the rocky coast far below.

The warm November sun shone in a bright blue sky, and a cool autumn breeze drifted through the open windows and sunroof, ruffling the hair of the vehicle's two occupants. The driver navigated a blind turn, moving with the easy confidence of someone who had traveled this road many times before. The passenger reached over and cranked up the volume on the radio.

"I love this song." She sighed happily, resting her forearm on the doorframe. She began to sing at the top of her lungs. "All the leaves are brown. And the sky is gray..."

"You love this song?" Julia interrupted, a faint note of surprise in her voice.

"Mmhmm." Maggie replied, alternating between humming and singing. "Come on, sing it with me. California girl like you must know the words."

Laughing, Julia shook her head. "Oh, no. I couldn't carry a tune if it had a handle."

Maggie looked at her skeptically. "What do you mean? I've heard you hum."

"Humming and singing are two entirely separate skills. Besides, we wouldn't want to scare the local wildlife."

Maggie whipped her head around and peered curiously into the dense forest. "What kind of wildlife?"

A grazing doe stepped out from behind a tree and gazed at them placidly with her big brown eyes as they drove past.

"Hey! Deer!" Maggie exclaimed.

"Yes, honey?" Julia returned absently, concentrating on the highway ahead.

"Not you, silly. There was a deer in the forest." Maggie swatted Julia's denim-clad thigh with the back of her hand.

"Oh. That kind of deer." Julia grinned sheepishly at her mistake as she checked her rearview mirror. Nothing behind them. No oncoming traffic in sight either, at least as far as she could see. Quickly, she leaned over and planted a kiss on her startled partner.

"Hey, take it easy, Speed Racer. Keep those blue eyes on the road," Maggie scolded her playfully.

She licked her lips, tasting the cherry slurpee that Julia had picked up at the gas station earlier. The truck still had that distinctive new car smell, and Maggie inhaled it deeply as she leaned back in her plush seat. Her eyes wandered, drinking in the sight of the breathtaking woman beside her.

Cut-off denim shorts covered Julia to mid-thigh, leaving the rest of her long, bronzed legs bare. A snug black t-shirt teased the reporter with a deep v-neck that revealed a healthy glimpse of cleavage. Glossy black hair was pulled back in a ponytail, much like it had been the first time they met. A few wispy tendrils had come loose, and Maggie resisted the urge to tuck them behind her lover's ear. Even in profile, she saw the dark eyebrow arch in amusement.

"You're staring at me," Julia said matter-of-factly.

"Yep. I sure am."

"Why?"

"Because you're beautiful and sexy, and I'm having a hard time keeping my hands off of you."

Julia chuckled deep in her throat, and the sound sent a warm, sensual jolt through Maggie's entire body.

"I can pull over and let you have your way with me, if you want," Julia suggested, grinning wickedly.

"Don't tempt me. I just might take you up on that," Maggie replied, returning the grin. "How much longer until we reach this beach of yours?"

Julia glanced at the odometer. "Just a few more miles."

Ten minutes later, Julia deftly turned into a parking lot and backed the truck into a space at the foot of a narrow trail. Since it was a weekday, there were very few other cars in the lot. Julia glanced at the new waterproof sports watch strapped to her wrist. It was almost noon. They would have to hurry if they were going to make it to her favorite spot before the tide came in. She hopped out and moved around to open the back hatch.

Maggie was already standing at the foot of the trail, eagerly sucking in a lungful of the crisp, salt-laden air. She bent down and picked up a handful of sand, letting the fine grains sift between her fingers. It was cool in the shade, and she shivered slightly.

She had spent hours that morning deciding what to wear for their trip to the beach. Finally, she had settled on khaki shorts, a tight-fitting white tank top and a white button-down shirt. While she waited for Julia, she ran her fingers through her hair, fluffing it out from under her collar. Without turning around, she sensed Julia's presence behind her, and she smiled as long fingers brushed her hair out of the way and warm lips nibbled the back of her neck.

"Think anyone would notice if I dragged you into the bushes?" Julia whispered huskily, biting down lightly on Maggie's earlobe.

Maggie laughed as a surge of desire rushed through her. "I think the birds might," she answered, listening to the chirping and rustling coming from deep within the lush, green foliage that lined both sides of the trail.

Julia let out an over exaggerated sigh. "Oh, all right then. Wouldn't want to disturb the poor birds."

She handed Maggie a purple nylon backpack and helped her slip it over her narrow shoulders. Her own pack, the heavier of the two, was already resting securely against her back. She took Maggie's hand, interlacing their fingers.

"Ready?"

"Absolutely. I want to see the ocean," Maggie replied.

Side by side, they walked up the trail, emerging at the top of a gentle slope. Maggie stopped in her tracks, awestruck. Pale sand stretched out before them, darkening as it met the foam-tipped waves that crashed against the beach. Miles of impossibly blue water reached as far as she could see. A light layer of fog still hung over the ocean, and the sun colored the mist a faint, burnt orange.

"Wow."

"Just wait. It gets better," Julia assured her.

Maggie hurriedly kicked off her shoes. She squealed in delight at the feel of the soft, sun-warmed sand between her toes. Picking up her shoes in one hand, she cast a mischievous look in Julia's direction.

"Race you to the water?"

Julia grinned as she removed her own shoes. "You're on."

"Ready, set..." Maggie took off as fast as she could. "Go!" She shouted over her shoulder.

"You little brat!"

Running on the beach was much harder than she had anticipated, and Maggie quickly felt the burn in her calves. Footsteps pounded behind her, and she knew Julia was catching up. Putting her head down, she pumped her arms furiously as she sprinted to the water's edge. Julia shortened her strides, letting Maggie stay a few steps in front of her. They were both puffing and giggling madly. Maggie shrieked as the first wave crashed over her feet and foam swirled around her ankles.

"Argh! Why didn't you tell me the water was so cold?"

"You didn't ask," Julia replied, smirking at her flushed, out of breath lover.

Green eyes narrowed, and Julia started to back away as another wave hit them. Swiftly, Maggie bent down and flipped a double handful of water at the backpedaling woman, soaking the front of her t-shirt.

"Hey!" Julia sputtered, licking the tangy saltwater from her lips. "You're getting me all wet!"

"Huh. You don't usually complain about that. In fact, I thought you kind of liked it."

Julia stared at her with a puzzled look. "Liked what?"

Maggie twitched an eyebrow at her saucily. "When I get you all wet."

"Oh." Julia blinked. "Oh! Yeah, I do. I like it a lot." She pulled Maggie into a hug, wrapping her arms tightly around the smaller woman's waist.

"Here. Let me return the favor." An almost predatory gleam shone in her eyes as she began tugging Maggie deeper into the surf.

"Oh, no! Julia, don't you dare!" Maggie struggled frantically to break free from Julia's firm grasp.

Julia stopped when they were knee-deep. "Relax. I wouldn't throw you in. I don't want to share you with the sharks."

In a flash, Maggie was back up on the beach, well out of reach from the waves. She eyed Julia and the ocean suspiciously.

"Are there really sharks out there?"

Julia waded out of the surf. She shrugged casually. "Sure. That's why there aren't many swimmers around here. Although the surfers at the other end of the beach don't seem to care about the warnings."

Taking Maggie's hand again, Julia led the way down the beach. They stopped in front of a large cluster of jagged rocks, and she sat down on one.

"Put your shoes back on. We have to do a little rock-climbing now, and I don't want you cutting your feet," she directed.

"Where exactly are you taking me?"

Julia nodded at the rocks. "There's another strip of beach a little ways beyond these rocks."

Maggie stared up at the towering wall. She glanced back over her shoulder at the perfectly good sand behind them. "What's wrong with the beach we're on?"

"Nothing. But you'll like this one even better. It's very secluded. Romantic, even." Julia gave her a seductive grin.

290

"Oh yeah? How secluded?" Maggie asked as she tied her shoes.

Julia chuckled. "Let's just say that we won't have to worry about anyone seeing us."

Maggie's grin broadened. She grabbed a firm handhold and boosted herself up onto the rocks. Placing her hands on her hips, she stared down at Julia.

"What are we waiting for, then? Let's go find your beach."

Twenty minutes later, they were standing at the top of the rock face. Maggie's shoulders and thighs ached a bit from the strain of climbing up the wall. She wasn't accustomed to this kind of exercise. Julia, she noted enviously, had hardly broken a sweat. Maggie looked down at the steep, slippery pile of rocks below them.

"This part is a little tricky. You have to sit down and basically slide." Julia pointed to a narrow chute. "I'll go first so I can catch you."

Julia sat down, bracing herself. Carefully, she eased herself down the chute, gripping the sides with her hands to slow her momentum. She reached the bottom and stood.

"Okay. Your turn," she called up. "Try to go slow. Once you start to slip, it's really hard to stop."

"Great," Maggie muttered as she got herself into position.

She tried to emulate Julia's example, pressing the palms of her hands flat against the sides of the chute. Her arms trembled from the strain as she cautiously eased her way down. She was more than halfway down when one of her hands slipped and she started to slide out of control. Rock walls whipped by much too fast, and she squeezed her eyes shut, expecting a painful crash. Instead, she collided with a warm, strong body. Julia pulled her to her feet, and Maggie felt gently probing hands checking her over for cuts and bruises.

"Are you okay?" Julia tilted Maggie's chin up and peered worriedly into her eyes.

Maggie grinned weakly as she waited for her heart to stop pounding. "Perfect. Piece of cake."

Julia kissed the top of her head. "Okay. This next part is all timing. See that clump of rocks there?" She indicated a massive rock formation that jutted out into the surf. "In between waves, we just have to dash around that. Don't worry. It's not very far."

Maggie nodded and followed Julia down to the base of the rocks. She waited while Julia watched the waves carefully, memorizing their pattern. Julia's hand gripped hers tightly.

"Ready?" Julia asked. Maggie nodded back. The waves started to pull back. "Now!"

They ran through the ankle-deep water, and Maggie could feel the hungry wave trying to pull her out to sea with it. Her feet sank in the wet sand, but she plunged forward. They rounded the bend and found themselves in a small cove, nestled back amongst the rocks. Julia led Maggie up onto the beach, grinning at her proudly.

"See? Isn't this great?"

Maggie turned in a slow circle. It was absolutely perfect. Rocks surrounded them on three sides. Before them, an endless expanse of blue stretched out for miles. Two large, flat rocks partially blocked their view from the ocean.

"In another half an hour, it will be high tide. No one will be able to come in the way we did until it goes back down," Julia informed her.

Maggie nodded slowly as she tugged two brightly colored beach towels out of her backpack. She spread them out side by side on the warm sand.

"So, we're all alone out here?"

"All alone," Julia confirmed, sliding her backpack off her shoulders and dropping it to the sand.

Maggie sat down on the towels and crooked a finger at her smirking lover. Julia knelt beside her, and goose bumps covered her arms as she stared into a pair of green eyes darkened with desire. She shivered in anticipation.

"This is good," Maggie said, grabbing a handful of Julia's t-shirt and pulling her closer. "I've been wanting to get you alone all day."

Without breaking eye contact, Maggie found the hem of Julia's shirt and lifted. She pulled Julia's head down and captured her lips eagerly, darting her tongue into her lover's open mouth. Julia let her take the lead, and Maggie gently pushed her to her back. Her hand drifted down to the waistband of Julia's shorts, and she fumbled with the metal buttons. In a few moments, their ecstatic moans were lost amid the crashing waves.

Maggie waited until the last shudder had traveled through Julia's body. Placing one last tender kiss, she crawled up and stretched out beside Julia, resting her head on a sweat-dampened shoulder.

"You were right. I love this beach," she grinned, idly tracing patterns on Julia's bare stomach as they both caught their breath.

Julia rolled over onto her side, propping herself up on an elbow. She gazed seriously down at Maggie as she gently stroked her lover's cheek.

"I love you, Maggie. More than I thought I was capable of. All of my life, I felt like I was nothing. When you look at me, you make me feel like I'm worth something."

Tears glistened in Maggie's eyes as she wrapped her fingers around Julia's arm. "You are worth something. You're worth far more than you will ever know. My god, Julia. You showed me what love is. No one has ever made me feel as safe or as wanted as you do. I don't know what I did to deserve you, but I will thank every god in the universe for sending you to me. I love you so much."

Julia grinned at her crookedly as a single tear slid down her cheek. "I love you too." She lowered her head to gently brush her lips against Maggie's. "Now it's my turn to show you how much."

Maggie shivered as Julia's lips trailed down her shoulder. "How much time do we have until the tide goes back out?"

Julia chuckled as she kissed her way across the top of a firm breast. "Oh, don't worry. We have plenty of time," she drawled. "We have all the time in the world."

The End

About the Author:

Erin Jennifer Mar is a life-long Sacramento area resident. She currently resides in Citrus Heights where she works at an assistant point-of-sale manager at a grocery store. Erin is in a committed relationship with her partner, Isabelle, and she is working on half a dozen second novels, including a follow-up to Golden Gate.

Order These Great Books Directly From Limitless, Dare 2 Dream Publishing

The Amazon Queen by L M Townsend	15.00	
Define Destiny by J M Dragon	15.00	The one that started it all…
Desert Hawk, revised by Katherine E. Standelll	16.00	Many new scenes
Golden Gate by Erin Jennifer Mar	16.00	
The Brass Ring by Mavis Applewater	16.00	HOT
Haunting Shadows by J M Dragon	17.00	
Spirit Harvest by Trish Shields	12.00	
PWP: Plot? What Plot? by Mavis Applewater	18.00	HOT
Journeys by Anne Azel	18.00	NEW
Memories Kill by S. B. Zarben	16.00	
Up The River, revised by Sam Ruskin	16.00	New scenes & more
	Total	

South Carolina residents add 5% sales tax.
Domestic shipping is $3.50 per book

Visit our website at: http://limitlessd2d.net

Please mail orders with credit card info, check or money order to:

Limitless, Dare 2 Dream Publishing
100 Pin Oak Ct.
Lexington, SC 29073-7911

Please make checks or money orders payable to **Limitless**.

I

Order More Great Books Directly From Limitless, Dare 2 Dream Publishing

Daughters of Artemis by L M Townsend	16.00	
Connecting Hearts by Val Brown and MJ Walker	16.00	
Mysti: Mistress of Dreams by Sam Ruskin	16.00	HOT
Family Connections by Val Brown & MJ Walker	16.00	Sequel to Connecting Hearts
A Thousand Shades of Feeling by Carolyn McBride	15.00	
The Amazon Nation by C. Osborne	15.00	Great for research
Poetry from the Featherbed by pinfeather	16.00	If you think you hate poetry, you haven't read this.
None So Blind, 3rd Edition by LJ Maas	16.00	NEW
A Saving Solace by DS Bauden	17.00	NEW
Return of the Warrior by Katherine E. Standell	16.00	Sequel to Desert Hawk
Journey's End by LJ Maas	16.00	NEW
	Total	

South Carolina residents add 5% sales tax.
Domestic shipping is $3.50 per book
Please mail orders with credit card info, check or money order to:

Limitless, Dare 2 Dream Publishing
100 Pin Oak Ct.
Lexington, SC 29073-7911

Please make checks or money orders payable to **Limitless**.

Order These Great Books Directly From Limitless, Dare 2 Dream Publishing

Queen's Lane **by I. Christie**	17.00	HOT
The Fifth Stage **by Margaret A. Helms**	15.00	
Caution: Under **Construction** **by T J Vertigo**	18.00	HOT-NEW
A Sacrifice for Friendship **Revised Edition** **by DS Bauden**	17.00	NEW
My Sister's Keeper by Mavis Applewater	17.00	HOT-NEW
In Pursuit of Dreams by J M Dragon	17.00	Destiny Book 3-NEW
The Fellowship **by K Darblyne**	17.00	
PWP: Plot? What Plot? **Book II** by Mavis Applewater	18.00	HOT-NEW
Encounters, Book I by Anne Azel	15.00	
Encounters, Book II by Anne Azel	15.00	
Hunter's Pursuit **by Kim Baldwin**	16.00	NEW
	Total	

South Carolina residents add 5% sales tax.
Domestic shipping is $3.50 per book

Visit our website at: http://limitlessd2d.net

Please mail orders with credit card info, check or money order to:

Limitless, Dare 2 Dream Publishing
100 Pin Oak Ct.
Lexington, SC 29073-7911

Please make checks or money orders payable to **Limitless**.

I

Order More Great Books Directly From Limitless, Dare 2 Dream Publishing		
Shattering Rainbows by L. Ocean	15.00	
Black's Magic by Val Brown and MJ Walker	17.00	
Spitfire by g. glass	16.00	NEW
Undeniable by K M	17.00	NEW
A Thousand Shades of Feeling by Carolyn McBride	15.00	
Omega's Folly by C. Osborne	12.00	
Considerable Appeal by K M	17.00	sequel to Undeniable-NEW
Nurturing Souls by DS Bauden	16.00	NEW
Superstition Shadows by KC West and Victoria Welsh	17.00	NEW
Encounters, Revised by Anne Azel	21.95	OneHuge Volume - NEW
For the Love of a Woman by S. Anne Gardner	16.00	NEW
	Total	

South Carolina residents add 5% sales tax.
Domestic shipping is $3.50 per book
Please mail orders with credit card info, check or money order to:

Limitless, Dare 2 Dream Publishing
100 Pin Oak Ct.
Lexington, SC 29073-7911

Please make checks or money orders payable to **<u>Limitless</u>**.

Printed in the United Kingdom
by Lightning Source UK Ltd.
117443UKS00001B/473